STOLEN PREY

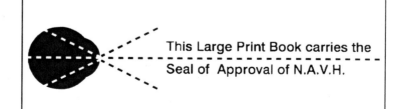

This Large Print Book carries the
Seal of Approval of N.A.V.H.

STOLEN PREY

JOHN SANDFORD

LARGE PRINT PRESS

A part of Gale, Cengage Learning

GALE
CENGAGE Learning·

Detroit • New York • San Francisco • New Haven, Conn • Waterville, Maine • London

GALE
CENGAGE Learning®

LIBRARY OF CONGRESS CATALOGING-IN-PUBLICATION DATA

Sandford, John, 1944 Feb. 23–
    Stolen prey / by John Sandford.
        pages ; cm. — (Thorndike Press large print basic)
    ISBN 978-1-4104-4722-7 (hardcover) — ISBN 1-4104-4722-7 (hardcover)
    1. Davenport, Lucas (Fictitious character)—Fiction. 2. Private investigators—Minnesota—Minneapolis—Fiction. 3. Families—Crimes against—Fiction. 4. Large type books. I. Title.
PS3569.A516S75 2012b
813'.54—dc23   2012011001

ISBN 13: 978-1-59413-611-5 (pbk. : alk. paper)
ISBN 10: 1-59413-611-4 (pbk. : alk. paper)

Published in 2013 by arrangement with G. P. Putnam's Sons, a member of Penguin Group (USA) Inc.

Printed in the United States of America
    1 2 3 4 5   17 16 15 14 13

For Gabriel

1

That was the summer of the cast and the cell phones. Cell phones everywhere. He sometimes felt as though he were caught like a fly in an electronic spiderweb, and anytime anyone, anywhere, had an urge to waste his time, they could reach out and ring his bell.

When it began, though, at that one specific moment, he had no phone. . . .

Lucas Davenport ran through the night, a fine mist cool on his face, the tarmac smooth and reliable under his Nike training shoes. They'd been through a rough winter. Most years, the last of the parking lot snow piles would be gone by early April. Now, as April ended, with the temperatures ballooning into the seventies, there were still mounds of ice at the edges of the larger lots, and they'd still be there on May Day.

But not on the streets — the streets were

finally clear.

As he ran, he thought about everything and anything, about the life he'd led, the children, the snatches of time frozen in his mind: a moment when he'd gotten shot in an alley, and the flash of the man who'd shot him; the first sight of a newborn daughter; his mother's face, crabby with an early morning slice of toast in her hand, her image as clear in his mind as it had been twenty-five years earlier, on the day she died. . . .

They all came up like portraits and landscapes hanging on the wall of his memory, flashes of color in the black-and-white night. With all the trouble and struggle and violence he'd seen, the deaths of parents and friends . . . it'd been pretty good, he thought. Not much to regret. Not yet.

He was getting older, with almost as much gray hair as black at his temples, with the beginnings of what would someday be slashing lines beside his mouth, but right now, on this spring day, he could run five miles in a bit less than thirty minutes, even on wet city streets; and at home, there were four people who loved him.

As much as he could have hoped for.

Running through the mist in a faded Bass

Pro Shops sweatshirt with cut-off sleeves and gray sweat shorts, he turned up the hill off Mount Curve and eventually slowed and looked through the windows on the Ford Parkway Wells Fargo ATM. The booth was empty, which was good. He was panting and smelled like he'd just run a hard five miles, which is not necessarily what somebody else wants to see from a stranger inside an ATM booth.

He went inside. He had nothing with him but the ATM card, his driver's license, and fifteen dollars, in a Dunhill money clip. No phone: for this rare half hour, no cell phone. He stuck the card in the ATM slot, punched in his four-digit code, hit the video square that said his most frequent withdrawal was five hundred dollars, and in the next few seconds, collected his card, his five hundred in twenties, and the receipt. He pushed the card and his ID back in the money clip and slipped the money clip back in his pocket, and was looking at the receipt, which showed he had $19,250 in his checking account, as he pushed through the door.

The tweeker was right there, with a piece-of-shit chromed revolver shaking like a leaf, three feet from Lucas's eyes. The hole of the muzzle large as the moon, and the man was saying, "Gimme the money gimme the money gimme the money . . ."

The gunman's eyes were pale blue, almost as though they'd been bleached. He had spiky reddish hair, hanging raggedy over his ears, as though it had been cut with pinking shears. He was missing several teeth, his face was touched with a patchy rash, and the muscles of his gaunt forearms twitched like pencils under the skin.

Lucas thought, *I could die.* It'd be a weird way to go, killed in a street robbery with this clown, after chasing down dozens of heavy hitters in his life, serious killers with functioning brains.

Lucas became aware of a woman, looming two or three feet behind him. He glanced at her, quickly: she was big, rawboned, and empty-handed, with the same gaunt meth-addled eyes as the man. Across the street, another woman was walking toward the bookstore at the top of the hill, under a black umbrella, a dachshund on a leash beside her, the dog's legs churning like a caterpillar's as it tried to keep up. There were cars passing by, their tires hissing on the wet streets, and he could smell the fleshy stink of run-over worms, and the tweeker was almost screaming, spit rolling down his chin, "Gimme gimme gimme," and Lucas handed over the five hundred dollars.

He'd lost track of the woman, as he concentrated on the muzzle of the gun and the man's fingers on the butt and trigger. If they turned white, if he started to squeeze, Lucas would have to go for it.

But as soon as her partner had taken the money, the woman hit him between the shoulder blades with both hands, and simultaneously hooked his ankles with her foot. With his feet pinned, he went down hard, full-length, broke the fall with his hands but still smacked his knees and chin on the concrete sidewalk, and rolled, and saw the two of them hoofing it down the block. The woman was large with broad shoulders and wide hips, but bony for all of that; the man was thin, jagged-looking.

Lucas got to his feet, his first thought to give chase, but the man turned as he ran and waggled the gun at him. Lucas had nothing on him: nothing but the money clip, two cards, and fifteen dollars in cash. No gun, no phone.

And he hurt. His back hurt from the impact, his hands and knees were skinned, his wrists sprained. He touched his lower lip, came away with a bloody finger, and realized that he'd cut his lip on his upper teeth. His teeth felt okay; nothing wiggled.

He took a few steps after the robbers, then stopped as they turned the corner. A few seconds later, a car screeched away, out of sight. Lucas looked around: nobody there on a wet Sunday night, nobody but the woman across the street, and her umbrella and her dog, rapidly headed away, up the hill, unaware that anything had happened.

He said, "Shit," and limped toward home. Reviewed what had happened, walked through it in his mind. He had, he decided, done the right thing. The piece-of-shit revolver was probably a .38. Not the most powerful weapon, but one that could have sprayed his brains all over the street. And he thought, *They've done it before.* The woman had taken him down like a pro, smooth, efficient, practiced.

Lip hurt. Knees hurt. Hands hurt. Five hundred dollars gone.

But they'd made a large mistake.

Sooner or later, he'd see them again.

Weather, his wife, a surgeon who had spent part of her internship in an emergency room, tried to be the calm one, talking tough while she fluttered around him. She said his lip was nothing, he just had to suck it up like a man, instead of whining about it. His knee required a Band-Aid and some antiseptic, and he might have a couple of small pulled muscles in his back, but he hadn't lost any function and his spine wasn't involved.

"You've got muscles in your neck, which is good. Helps prevent whiplash," she said. She was kneading his shoulder as he sat in a kitchen chair, eating an Oreo, tasting a little blood with the creme filling.

She was most worried about his left wrist.

His teenaged adoptive daughter, Letty, asked, "What are you going to do about this?"

"Put them in jail," Lucas said. "If it's the last thing I do."

Letty, her arms crossed over her chest, grunted, "At least."

He called the St. Paul cops, and a couple of uniforms rolled around and took a report and suggested he come to the station and look at the meth files. When they were done, Weather drove him over to Hennepin County Medical Center and told the doc on duty that she wanted Lucas's wrists x-rayed. Because of her status in the place, Lucas got instant service.

The doc came back in five minutes, took them around to a computer screen, tapped on some keys. The X-rays came up on the high-def screen, and he said, "You busted your left scaphoid."

"Ah, God," Weather said. She peered at the digital image. "Yeah, it's clear." She pointed at a line on a wrist bone.

The line looked like somebody had dropped a white hair on the screen. Lucas said, "It can't be too bad. The bone's about the size of —"

"Never mind what it's the size of," Weather said. Lucas tended to compare the size of almost anything, either large or small, to his dick. "You'll need a cast."

"A cast?" He flexed his wrist. It hurt, but not all that bad. He looked at the doc, who nodded, and then at Weather. "You've got to be kidding."

"With luck, we can take it off in three months," the doc said. "A lot of people go six."

"What? For that?" He couldn't believe it. A little crack, barely visible in the X-ray.

Weather explained in big words. He didn't know all of the words, but understood that the carpal bones, of which the scaphoid was one, and which was once called the navicular because it supposedly looked like a boat, allowed the wrist to turn and the hand to work. If the bone was cracked, and didn't heal, it might die, and rot. Then his hand wouldn't work right.

That didn't sound good.

Forty-five minutes after they walked in, they walked back out of the emergency room, Lucas with a fiberglass cast from his elbow to knuckles, and a bottle of hydro-codone in his pocket.

"One good thing," Weather said, "it's your left hand."

"This cast is like a fuckin' rock," Lucas said. "If I catch that fuckin' tweeker, I'm gonna use it to fuckin' beat him to death."

"That's your daily quota on the f-word," Weather said. "And don't worry about that guy. If he's as far gone as you say, he's a dead man anyway."

"He's a dead man if I catch him," Lucas said.

When they got home, Letty said, "Whoa, that cast's the size of —"

"Never mind," Weather said.

The cast was a constant annoyance. Lucas was a touch-typist and, unable to spread his fingers, had to learn to use the keyboard us-ing only one finger on his left hand. And he had, over the years, gotten used to carrying an old-fashioned Colt .45 ACP, which really required two functioning hands. He switched to a double-action nine-millimeter,

15

but never really liked it. He couldn't hang on to a steering wheel, though he hardly ever held on tight with his left hand anyway.

The biggest frustration came one day when he was fishing off the dock at his cabin and hooked into a small bluegill, only to watch the bluegill get chased down, right at the surface, by what he estimated to be a two-foot-long large-mouth bass. He got the bass back close to the dock, but he couldn't just lift it out of the water: he wasn't even sure it was hooked. He needed to hold the rod in one hand, and use a net with the other . . . and stood helplessly looking down at the fish as it ran crazily back and forth, finally did a heavy-bodied leap, and came off.

He was pretty sure, as the fish swam away, that it gave him the finger.

The cast was cut off, momentarily, at three months, and his wrist was x-rayed again, and the doc said it needed another month. A scum of dead skin covered his arm, and the muscles looked too thin — withered, Lucas thought. His arm reminded him of the tweeker's too-thin forearm. The doc let him scrub the dead skin off before he put the new cast on. Under his arm hair, the new skin was as pink and soft as a baby's butt. "Come back in a month," the doc said. "In a month, you're good. And lucky. Some people go six."

"That's what the last guy said. But he said if I was lucky, I'd get out in three."

"That's really lucky," the doc said. "You're only a little lucky."

The summer of the cast and cell phones, though meteorologically excellent, was professionally slow. Lucas's job at the BCA was mostly self-invented, and included politically sensitive cases, or cases that might attract a lot of media attention. That summer, the politicians stayed away from ostentatious felonies, as far as anyone knew — something could always pop up at a later date. ("I didn't know she was fourteen. Honest to God, she said she was thirty-two.")

So Lucas focused on a self-invented, long-term, statewide intelligence project that involved finding, working, and filing police sources in Minnesota's criminal under-world. The project was kept secret for fear that it would encounter media ridicule. Most people didn't believe that there actually *was* a Minnesota criminal underworld, and those who did — the cops — often didn't want to give up sources.

Just as in any other state, Minnesota had plenty of crooks. Ten thousand people sat in prison, from a population a little short of six million, with a constant coming and going. Of those, quite a few were one-timers, or criminals of a kind that didn't interest him: repeat drunk drivers, people convicted of manslaughter or negligent homicide, or white-collar crime. Those kinds of people were singletons, who generally acted alone, out of stupidity and greed, and, aside from the drunk drivers, were not given to repeated mayhem.

He was interested in the repeaters, the professionals, the people who lived and worked in a criminal culture — bikers, gang members, burglars, robbers, pederasts, drug dealers. Lucas had a theory that every county, and every town, would have a "node" that pulled in criminals of that area — a bar, a bowling alley, a roadhouse.

Furthermore, he thought that criminals in one area would know most of the nodes for the surrounding areas, no matter how urban or rural the countryside might be, and would be attracted to those nodes when away from home.

He wanted a thousand names of sources who'd talk to the cops, across that whole web of nodes; at least one or two sources for each.

They would all know him by name, and there would be certain implicit guarantees in their transactions. Like no police comebacks.

To set up his system, he first had to learn about spreadsheets, and then a bit about computer secrecy: he had no interest in building a general criminal database, and needed a way to keep the work away from prying cop eyes. It wasn't that he didn't want to help other cops, it was just that as soon as more than one person began operating the database, it would stop functioning. Tipsters wanted a relationship: they didn't want their names in a cop newspaper, and if they thought that was what was happening, they'd shut up or disappear.

So Lucas had spent the summer talking on the phone, taking long rides out into the countryside to meet unusual men and women at sandwich shops and parks, filling out the database.

He realized, at some point, what the computer had done for him. He'd been tempted, at one time or another, to move to a bigger police agency — one of the federal agencies, or to a really large city, like New York

19

or Los Angeles. He'd not done that because he'd realized that the Minneapolis–St. Paul area was the largest size he could comprehend.

In Los Angeles, a cop was caught in a blizzard of shit, and there was never any way to tell where the shit was coming from. You get three murdered in Venice, and the killer was almost as likely to come from Portland or St. Louis as from LA; was likely to be unknown to the local cops. Serial killers had operated for decades in the LA area, without the cops even knowing about it. Chaos ruled.

That wouldn't happen in the Twin Cities. There were three million people outside his St. Paul door, but he could just about understand who was out there, and where the shit was coming from.

There were another two million in the state of Minnesota, and with the help of a computer and a spreadsheet, he was beginning to hope that he might also come to comprehend the state's criminal base.

The rise of the cell phone added another aspect to it: with the cell phone, an office was anywhere you wanted it to be. At one time, you might drive out to a crime scene, however many minutes or even hours from the office, and then drive back to get started on the case. With cell phones, you could constantly be hooked into a developing web of contacts, sources, and records.

The downside, of course, was that you were constantly hooked into a web of contacts, sources, and records, and didn't often have the time needed to simply *think*.

A side benefit to the construction of the intel network was that he had time to look for the robbers who'd taken his five hundred dollars and broken his wrist. He quickly found out that he'd been right about one thing: they'd done it before.

They'd done it four times on the south side of the Twin Cities and its suburbs, and a half dozen more times trailing down I-35 to the south, which made Lucas think they lived down that way.

As he pulled together his intelligence nodes south of town, he asked about them — thin shaky guy, big rough woman, up to their eyebrows in meth.

He hadn't yet found them when, in August, the peace and quiet ended.

The BCA superintendent, who didn't particularly like Lucas, but found him to be a valuable foil when it came to dealing with political issues, called him at home as Lucas was working his way through the *Times* and a bowl of steel-cut oatmeal, which his wife and daughter said was good for something — it was organic and saved the whales, or lowered his cholesterol, one of those things. He yearned for a simple glazed doughnut, but not if it doomed Mother Earth.

His cell phone began ringing, and simultaneously rattling like a snake, on the table next to his hand.

"Really big trouble," the superintendent said. "There's gonna be a lot of media. Shaffer and his crew are on the way. You'd better get out there, too, so you're up to speed. I'm trying to find Rose Marie to tell her about it."

Murder, he said. An entire family slaughtered.

Lucas backed the Porsche out of his garage and found a gray sky and a cool day going cold; rain coming, disturbing the summer, hinting at what all Minnesotans knew in their bones: winter always comes.

The death house sat down a leafy black-topped lane, a stone, brick, and white-board lakeside palace where the Great Gatsby might have lived, made for summer soirees with mimosas and mint juleps. The deep-green summer trees grew in close and dense, so thick that even nearby noises seemed muffled and distant, and a perfect lawn dropped down a gentle slope to Lake Minnetonka. A floating dock stuck into the lake like a finger; a fast fiberglass cruiser was tied to one side of the dock, an over-sized pontoon boat to the other, ready to party.

The scene was dead quiet, except for the moaning wind in the trees. The incoming clouds were so gray and low, the house so touched with a cool decorator chic, a tight-ness, a foreboding, that a Hollywood camera corkscrewing down the lane to the front door would have automatically hinted at horrors to be found behind the well-scrubbed window glass. A crazy housewife with poison, a husband with a meat cleaver in his hand, a couple of robotic kids with a long-barreled revolver and blank gray eyes . . .

None of which would have done justice to the real horror behind the door.

Lucas got to the house at a little after eleven o'clock in the morning, and walked back out on the front porch five minutes later, looking for a breath of fresh air and maybe a place to spit, to get the taste of death out of his mouth.

He was a tall, hard, very rich man with broad shoulders and a hawkish nose, wearing a two-hundred-dollar white shirt and a dark blue Purple Label suit with a red Hermès necktie, the necktie twisted and pulled loose behind the knot. His face was tanned, and the thin white line of a scar dropped across one eyebrow onto his cheek; another white scar showed in the pit of his neck, where a young girl, barely into her teens, had shot him with a street pistol that he hadn't seen coming.

He rubbed his face with the fingers of his left hand, which protruded from a slightly dirty-looking cast. Del Capslock followed him out onto the porch. Del looked back over his shoulder and said, "I don't think I've ever been to a crime scene this quiet."

"Whatta you gonna say?" Lucas asked. He sniffed at the cast. Nasty. He needed to wash it again.

"You know what freaked me out?" Del asked. "It wasn't the kids. It was the dogs. The dogs couldn't tell us anything. They weren't witnesses. They weren't attack dogs. Two miniature poodles and a golden retriever? They killed them anyway. Hunted them down. They were killing everything, because they liked it."

"I don't know. There's a lot going on in there," Lucas said. "Maybe they killed the dogs first, to extort information. Went around and shot them just to prove that they'd do it. Then the boy, then the wife and daughter, then the guy. They wanted something from the guy."

"We don't know they did it that way," Del said. Del was too thin — grizzled, some would say — unshaven, dressed in jeans and a T-shirt and Nike cross-trainers. The T-shirt said *Menard's,* which was a local building supply chain. His comment reflected an ingrained skepticism about any unsupported assertion: he wanted facts.

"I feel like they did," Lucas said. He was more comfortable with assumption and speculation than Del. He looked up and down the street, past the cluster of official cars and vans. He could see pieces of two houses, one in each direction. There were more along the way, but out of sight. "The thing is, they shot the dogs, that's three shots. They shot the boy three or four times. That's a lot of gunshots. Even in a neighborhood like this, with the doors closed and the air conditioners going, and boats . . . that's a lot of shots. Makes me think they had silencers, makes me think they were pros, here for a reason. Then the guy, they go to work with a knife. They started out terrorizing him, ended up torturing him."

"Drugs?"

"Gotta be. Gotta be, here in the Twin Cities. Too calculated for anything else. Shaffer says the guy ran a software place that peddles Spanish-language software down in Mexico. It looks custom-made as a money laundry," Lucas said. He looked back into the house, though he couldn't see anything from the porch.

Del said, "Here's something."

Lucas turned back to see a lone patrolman jogging back down the street. He was overweight, and his stomach jiggled as he ran. The patrolman cut across the lawn.

"The neighbors," he said to Lucas. He was red-faced and seemed to run out of words, tried to catch his breath.

"Yeah?"

"The neighbors, the Merriams, they're three houses down." The cop pointed down the street. "The husband, Dave, saw a van parked in the driveway yesterday afternoon. He saw it three times, coming home, going out, and coming back from town. There for a couple hours, at least. He says it was a blue van, a Chevy, and he says the first three letters of the plate were S-K-Y. He thinks it stuck with him because of sky-blue. Sky on

26

the plate and blue on the van."

Lucas nodded. "Okay, that's good stuff." He turned and yelled back into the house, "Shaffer? Shaffer?" He said to the cop, "Go tell that to Shaffer. We need to run that right now."

The cop went inside and Del asked, "What are we going to do?"

Lucas shrugged: "Call everybody. Look for blue vans. Push the DNA on the wife and daughter . . . I wouldn't bet on semen. If they were professionals, they were probably wearing rubbers. We might pick up some blood or something, maybe one of them scratched or bit somebody."

Del nodded. "You look around the house, around the neighborhood, and it's screaming *rich*. Could have been a couple of crazy dopers thinking they kept a lot of money in the house."

Lucas said, "Nah."

Del scratched an ear and then said, "All right."

"They were looking for something," Lucas said. "It *looks* like drugs. It looks like that stuff in Mexico. So harsh. So cruel."

"Maybe they'll pop right up in the DNA bank," Del said.

"Fat chance."

"Yeah." Del looked up in the sky. "It's

27

gonna rain."

"We need it," Lucas said. "Been hot for a long time. First cool day in a while."

"Fall's coming," Del said.

They went back inside, where an agent named Bob Shaffer was talking to the patrolman. When he saw Lucas, he said, "Maybe a break."

Lucas nodded, once. "Anything more?"

"Romeo's worked out a sequence. I think it's probably right."

Romeo was a lab tech, a short man with a swarthy complexion, a fleshy nose, and a neat little soul patch that actually looked good. Lucas and Del found him in the living room, looking at the dead adult male, a notebook in his hand. He might have been taking inventory in a dime store. But the living room didn't smell like a dime store; it smelled like the back room at a meat locker.

The dead man, who was almost certainly named Patrick Brooks, forty-five, blond, once good-looking with big white Chiclet teeth, lay on his back, on the living room carpet, in a drying circle of blood. His arms, down to his elbows, were taped to his sides with ordinary duct tape. There were no fingers on his hands: they'd been cut off, one knuckle-length at a time, and lay around the room like so many cocktail wieners. He had no eyes — they were over by the television. His pants had been pulled down to his knees; he'd been castrated. They'd cut off his ears, but left his tongue, probably so he could talk. He had apparently died while the killers were cutting open his abdomen, because they hadn't finished the job.

"Shaffer said you have a sequence," Lucas said.

"I think so," Romeo said. He ticked his yellow pencil at the dead man. "He went last. I think they came in with guns, to keep everybody under control. Rounded them up, taped them up, put them on the floor. They started out shooting the dogs. The golden got it right here, the poodles ran into the kitchen. Shot them there. Did the wife next: Candace. Raped her, beat her, whatever, then cut her throat. Then the kid, uh, Jackson, started screaming or struggling or something, and they shot him: some of the blood splatter and brain tissue from the head shot landed on his mother's leg, which was already naked, and didn't move after the blood landed on it."

"So she was dead first," Del said.

"Right. Then they did the daughter, Amelia. She's pretty messed up, so I'm

29

thinking . . . they did a lot of stuff to her. The ME'll have to give you that. Then they cut her throat. She bled out, and you can see, there are a couple finger joints on her blood. It looks like they rolled across her blood and picked some of it up."

"Unless it's his blood," Del said.

"No, it looks like they rolled across wet blood. I think it'll turn out to be hers."

"Like we were talking about," Lucas said to Del. "They wanted something from him, or they were sending a message."

"Did they bring the knives, or use the kitchen knives?" Del asked.

"Brought them. The knife block is full. Looks like razors, or scalpels, and for some of it, it was probably pliers, side cutters. You get that kind of crushing cut with side cutters. They knew what they were going to do," Romeo said.

"Then they wrote on the wall," Lucas said. They all turned and looked at the wall, where a bloody message said: "Were coming." No apostrophe.

"Yeah . . . they took a couple of the finger joints and used them like markers. The joints are the ones on the couch. They've got wall paint on them, like chalk. We're hoping we might get some DNA, but I'll

30

bet you anything that they were wearing gloves."

"Didn't gag them — had the tape, but didn't tape their mouths," Del said.

"I think they wanted them to talk back and forth. I think they wanted them to hear each other dying," Lucas said.

"That would be the gloomy interpretation," Romeo said.

"You got another one?" Lucas asked.

"No, I don't," Romeo said. "You're probably right. One thing: we've got precision, rather than frenzy. Del was talking before, about maybe some crazy guys. I don't think so. I think it was cold. It feels that way to me. Three or four guys."

Lucas looked at the bodies, at the mess. "What about DNA? Any chance?"

"Oh, yeah. We'll get some DNA," Romeo said. "We'll get sweat or skin cells off the woman's or the girl's thighs, if no place else."

Del said, "If they're professionals, they'll know that sooner or later they'll do time, and if they pop up in a DNA bank, they'll go down for this. So I'm thinking, they're not too worried about DNA banks."

"Because they're stupid?" Romeo suggested.

"No," Del said, surveying the shambles.

31

"It'd be because they're not from here. They're from someplace else. Mexico, Central America. Could be Russia."

"Good thought," Lucas said.

Shaffer called from the next room: "Hey, Lucas, Rose Marie's here."

"Got it," Lucas said.

Rose Marie Roux, the commissioner of public safety, once state senator, once Minneapolis chief of police, once — for a short time — a street cop, was coming up the sidewalk. She was a stocky woman in a blue dress who looked a lot like somebody's beloved silver-haired mother, except for the cigarette that dangled from her lower lip. She was a quick study, and a longtime winner in the backroom battles at the Capitol.

She shook her head at Lucas: "I'm not going in there. I don't want to see it," she said. "I do need something to tell the media."

"They're all four dead," Lucas said. "Patrick Brooks, his wife, son, and daughter. Tortured, the females raped. I wouldn't give them any detail — just, brutally murdered."

"Is there anything . . . promising?" Roux asked.

"No, not that I've seen," Lucas said. "It looks professional. Brutal, impersonal.

32

Meant to send a message. We might never find them, truth to tell."

"I don't want to tell three million people that we're not going to catch them," Roux said.

"So, say that we're looking at some leads, that we have some definite areas of interest that we can't talk about, and that we'll be doing DNA analysis," Lucas said.

"Do we actually have any possibilities? Or am I tap-dancing?"

"One," Lucas said. "They wrote on the wall, 'Were coming,' no apostrophe in the *were.* But that suggests . . . suggests . . . that they may be looking for somebody else. The way they did this, looks like there may have been an interrogation. Like they were questioning Brooks, trying to get something out of him, and he didn't have it."

She mulled that over for a few seconds, then said, "Excuse me, but did you just tell me that they might do this again? To somebody else?"

"Can't rule it out," Lucas said.

"That's bad. That's really bad," she said.

"Gives us another shot at them," Lucas said, looking on the bright side.

"Ah, jeez . . . Who's got the detail?"

"Shaffer."

"Okay." She mulled that over for a minute,

then said, "He's competent. But keep talking to him. Keep talking to him, Lucas."

"What are you doing out here?" Lucas asked. "Is there some kind of . . . involvement?" He meant political involvement.

"Yeah, some marginal engagement," she said. "Candace Brooks was going to run for something, sooner or later. Probably the state senate, next year, if Hoffman retires. The Brookses maxed out contributions for the major offices last few elections, and they're strong out here in the local party . . . but, it's not any big political thing."

"So it won't make any difference if we find out that they were running a drug-money laundry, and giving cash to the local Democrats?"

She shrugged, a political sophisticate: "It'd hurt for about four minutes. Then, not. But, you know, they were our people." She meant Democrats.

Del asked, "So what are you going to tell the media?"

She looked him up and down, raised her eyebrows, and said, "Jesus, Del, you look like you just fell out of a boxcar."

"Professional dress," Del said. "Around home, I wear Ralph Lauren chinos and Tiger Woods golf shirts."

She made a rude noise and turned to look

down toward the end of the street, where the media was stacked up, out of sight. "I'll tell them the truth, just not all of it — four brutal murders, motive unknown. That we've got lots of leads and expect to make an arrest fairly quickly."

"That'd scare the shit out of me, that promise, if anybody had an attention span longer than two seconds," Lucas said.

"That's what we're working with," Roux said. "Though I have to say as the state's chief law enforcement official, I do expect you to catch them." She poked Lucas in the chest. *"You."*

Lucas walked halfway down the block and watched from a distance as Rose Marie spoke to the media. She gave them the basics, and nothing more. She stood in a neighbor's lush green yard, a mansion in the background, with the media in the street. She used the word *brutal,* and refused to enlarge upon that.

That was accurate but, in the eyes of the reporters, inadequate.

One of them knew a cop who was working the roadblock, and Channel Eleven headlined his comments: rape, torture, murder. Finger joints, eyeballs, castration, throats cut with razors. The message on the wall. "We're coming" — the producer supplied the missing apostrophe on the phonied-up blue-screened graphic behind the anchorwoman.

The Channel Eleven report set off a media firestorm, which intensified when another station "confirmed rumors from earlier today. . . ."

The media was large in the Twin Cities. A juicy murder would go viral in seconds.

Rumors of the massacre at the Brookses' house swept through Sunnie Software minutes after the bodies were discovered. Patrick Brooks had been scheduled to meet with marketing and development and hadn't shown up. Neither he nor anyone else answered the home phone, and his cell phone rang and was never picked up.

The vice president for sales, named Bell, had had a bad feeling about it. A lawyer friend of Bell's lived near the Brooks home, and Bell had asked the lawyer to call his wife, who ran over and found the front door cracked open.

Nobody answered her call, so she'd pushed the door open with a fingernail and peeked inside. . . .

Started screaming.

As she ran back down the street, she called

911, and then her husband, who called back to Sunnie with a garbled story of blood and murder.

The cops came, and then the BCA.

Then the media, ambushing employees in the street.

"This is really fucked," said one of the account managers, a young man with hair to the middle of his back. "Who are they going to suspect, huh? The guy with the hair . . ."

"Rob, stop thinking about yourself," one of the women said. "They're all dead."

"But who are they gonna think did it?" Rob cried.

Several of them told him to shut up, and guiltily gave thanks for their neatly coiffed hair.

The murder story caught Ivan Turicek and Kristina Sanderson at work in the systems security area at Hennepin National Bank. Sanderson was getting ready to go home: she worked the six-to-two shift, while Turicek came in at noon and took it until eight. They were alone, with a bank of computers. Turicek had seen a fragment of a story on a television in the Skyway, and now had one of the computers set to catch the Web broadcast from Channel Eleven.

Channel Eleven was the one with the source: rape, torture, murder, eyeballs, castration . . . "We're coming" with an apostrophe.

"Oh my God, what have we done?" Sanderson blurted, staring at the screen. A thin schizophrenic with blond, frizzy hair and a fine white smile, when she used it, she was pale as a sheet of printer paper, one hand to her mouth.

Turicek shook his head: "Not us."

"Ivan, I don't want to be bullshitted," Sanderson said, as she looked down at the flat panel. "This was us and you know it."

They were alone in the security area, but cameras peered down at them from the end of the work bay. They supposedly didn't record sound, but Turicek was an immigrant from Russia, and never believed anything anybody said about limits of surveillance. In his experience, somebody was *always* listening.

He said, "Shh." Then, after a moment, "We need to call Jacob. Or you should go see him. He's probably still asleep, doesn't know about this."

She looked at her watch: two o'clock. Nodded. Jacob Kline normally worked an eight-to-four shift, but was out, sick, again. "Yes. I should probably go see him."

"And it wasn't us," Turicek said again. He turned to her, worried. Sanderson suffered from a range of mild psychological disorders, and he considered her fragile. She didn't use meds, and the bank put up with her occasional acting-out because she was also obsessive-compulsive when it came to the neatness of numbers. If a number was out of place, Sanderson could sense it and push it back where it belonged.

That made her an excellent programmer and an asset for a bank. But still, she was a head case, and, at times, delicate. "One thing I learned in Russia is, if you didn't do it, you didn't do it," Turicek said, pressing the case. "You're not responsible for what other people do. You can't be. If you are, there's no end to the chain of responsibility, so then nobody winds up being responsible."

"I don't need a philosophical disquisition. I was a philosophy major for three semesters," Sanderson snapped.

"We need to be calm," Turicek said. "We keep working, we keep our heads down. We know nothing. *We know nothing.*"

"What about the 'We're coming'? If they get to us? Eyeballs gouged out and cut throats? No thank you. *No thank you!*"

Turicek dropped his voice. "Twenty million," he said. "Twenty million dollars."

That stopped her. Her eyes narrowed, and she said, "More like twenty-two, now. We need to call Edie: it's time to get out."

"How much more is in the system?" Turicek asked.

"Two million. Not enough to risk moving. Time to finish the harvest," she said.

"I agree. You go see Jacob, I'll call Edie."

Edie Albitis freaked when she heard. She was standing on the Vegas strip, outside Treasure Island; it was 105 degrees and an obscenely fat woman was rolling down the sidewalk toward her, carrying a small dog and wearing what looked like a tutu. "I'm the one who's dangling in the wind out here," she said into her cell phone, one eye on the fat woman. She didn't want to get run down. "The banks have about a million pictures of me."

"But they don't know it," Turicek said in his most comforting tone. "In every one, you look like the Sultaness of Istanbul."

Albitis was wearing a *hijab,* a traditional Arabic woman's robe, and, though even most conservative Arab states allowed an uncovered face, she also wore a *niqab,* or veil. These were somewhat culturally uncomfortable for a woman who'd danced

40

both topless and bottomless, sometimes simultaneously, in both Moscow and New York; whose parents were Jews now living in Tel Aviv, which was where she picked up her Arabic; and who was blond, to boot. But, if you were doing major money laundering through America's finest banks, it was best to show as little skin as possible when you were setting up the accounts.

She did speak Arabic well enough to fake her way past North African Arabs, or Iranians, who got most of their Arabic from the Koran, but if she ran into a Jordanian, or a Lebanese, or an Iraqi, she could be in trouble. Of course, most Arabs working in American banks seemed to be Jordanians, Lebanese, or Iraqis. That was just the way of the world, she thought: set up to fuck with you. "Who the hell did it? This killing?"

"The police don't know. They're investigating," Turicek said.

"Ah, God. It'll take me a week to clear out the accounts."

"No, no. We're going to leave it," Turicek said. "Kristina is correct: there's not enough for the risk involved. What if we just buy what we've already got online, and collect what we've already paid for?"

Albitis thought about it for a moment,

41

then said, "If I run, I can do it in three or four working days."

"Then do that. Are we still solid with the dealers?"

"Yes. They won't ask any questions as long as the wires keep coming," Albitis said. "But they won't ship the gold until they clear the transfers. That's a full day, sometimes. They know that when the gold is gone, it's gone."

"I can't leave here right now," Turicek said. "Not with these murders. We need to be really quiet. I doubt they'll even talk to us, but if they do show up, we all need to be here."

"Shit. Why'd this have to happen right now? Another week . . ." Albitis pulled at her lip, through the veil. "All right, listen: let me think about this. I don't know if I can widen out the number of dealers, so I'm going to have to make up some bullshit story and sell it to the ones we've got. Some reason to jack up the purchases. There are not that many goddamn Arab women running out the door with a quarter million in gold. You know what I'm saying?"

"I know what you're saying, but what *I'm* saying is, we might not have a choice," Turicek said.

Getting the gold was the touchy part. There were gold dealers all over the place, and they sold a lot of gold — but they might start to wonder if the amounts got too big. They might wonder about drugs, or spies, or terrorists, or something. . . . She didn't need to walk into a dealer's office and find the FBI waiting for her. "Just routine, ma'am," they'd say, and then discover a blonde with a shaky passport.

"So we're getting out," Turicek said. "Jacob will go along."

"You've got to watch Jacob," Albitis said.

"I know. We will. Kristina has him under control."

"They're both nuts."

"And I'm watching both of them."

"Okay. Do that, Ivan. I'll start right now. I was going to set up four more accounts this afternoon, but I'll quit and get out of here. Get down to LA, make some pickups, put in some more orders," Albitis said. "Make up my story."

"Be careful," Turicek said. "If you feel anybody is looking at you, quit. Better to take what we've got now, than spend the next twenty years in prison. Or have these crazy people come down on us."

"I thought it was a hedge fund," Albitis said. "This isn't something a hedge fund would do."

"No, it's more like the fuckin' *Vory*," Tu-

43

ricek said, and he shuddered as he said it. If they'd stolen from the Russian mob, the mob would want both the money and their heads; or, if forced to choose, just their heads.

"Jesus," said Albitis. She glanced nervously up and down the street: the fat woman was receding in the distance. Albitis worried about her epithets. Being disguised as an observant Muslim woman was fine for handling bank cameras, but as a natural-born wiseass, she'd never been that good at controlling her language.

Did conservative Arab women walk around blurting out, "Jesus Christ," or "Holy shit"? She suspected they did not. "All right," she said. "I'm running."

While all that was going on, three Mexican males were checking out of the Wee Blue Inn in West St. Paul, fifteen or twenty minutes apart.

The Wee Blue Inn catered to hasty romances and to men who arrived on foot, who really needed a shower and a few hours' sleep, a sink to wash their clothes in, and who had no credit card to pay with. Didn't bother the owner: cash was as good as credit, but you had to have the cash.

The Mexicans had checked in two days

before, a half hour apart, small young men — two of them were still teenagers — but with muscles in their arms and faces, no bellies at all; and with hard eyes that reminded the owner of the obsidian-black marbles of his childhood, the ones called peeries.

They checked in a half hour apart, and got separate rooms, but they were together. The owner didn't ask them any questions. That didn't seem prudent. An illegal Latino was cleaning up around the place, saw them check in, and told the owner he was going to take the next day or two off.

"I didn't hire you to take no days off," the owner said.

"I take them anyway," the illegal said. "You wanna fire me, so fire me. I'm going."

He went.

It occurred to the owner that the temporary departure of his wage slave might have something to do with the small men.

Once again, it didn't seem prudent to ask.

In certain businesses, prudence is mandatory.

<hr>

2

Patrick Brooks had run Sunnie Software out of an office suite in a rehabbed brick warehouse north of Minneapolis's downtown. Lucas decided to swing by on his way back to the BCA offices to sniff around and get a feel for the Brooks operation.

He left the car on the street and climbed the internal stairs to the third floor; the office was glass and gray carpet, with potted palms sitting around on redbrick room dividers. The place smelled like feminine underarm deodorant and carpet cleaner. A dozen employees were sitting in a low-walled cube farm, each with his or her own computer, but nobody was working. Instead, they'd pulled their chairs into groups of three and four, and were talking about the killings.

A BCA agent named Jones was keeping an eye on them. He spotted Lucas at the door, and as the employees turned to watch, came over and said, "We're talking to them one at a time. Not seeing much yet."

Lucas said, "Shaffer says they do Spanish-language software."

"Yeah. We already talked to the office manager. She said some of the sales are down in the Southwest, but most of them are south of the border — Mexico and Central America. They do some down in South America, Colombia and Venezuela."

"All drug countries," Lucas said. "You think they're running a money laundry?"

"Can't tell yet," Jones said. "If it is, it's not that big. They only did about two million in sales last year. Brooks took out about two hundred thousand, himself. They got a million-dollar payroll on top of that, they're paying some stiff rent, they contract for the software, there're taxes. . . . There's not really much left over."

"Is there any way to verify the sales?" Lucas asked.

"Not really, not if somebody wanted to tinker with the books. It's all delivered on-line, there aren't any physical deliveries." Jones nodded at the office, and added, "We've got all of these people sitting here, they all say they get paid, we know they pay rent on the office space . . . It'd be a hell of a conspiracy."

"We've got a killing that looks like it's dope-related, we've got people peddling untraceable software in Mexico. It's gotta be here somewhere," Lucas said.

Jones shrugged. "You're welcome to look. I'll tell you one thing. If it's a laundry, and they were stealing money, it wasn't worth it." Jones had been to the murder house and had seen the damage.

"No, it wasn't," Lucas agreed.

"So . . . Dick and Andi are in the back, doing the interviews," Jones said. "You want to sit in?"

"Maybe . . . but you're done with the office manager?"

"For the time being."

"Let me talk to her," Lucas said.

Barbara Phillips was a heavyset blonde in her late forties or early fifties, with an elaborate hairdo, low-cut silky tan blouse, and seven-inch cleavage. She'd been crying, and had mascara running down her face, with wipe lines trailing off toward her ears. She'd been sitting in her office with two other employees when Jones stuck his head in: "We have another agent who'd like to chat with you," he said to Phillips.

She nodded and said, "You guys be careful," to the other employees, and they all shook their heads and trooped out of the room. When Lucas stepped in, Phillips asked, "You think the killers are looking for us?"

Lucas took a chair and said, "I doubt it . . . unless there's some reason you think they might be."

"Mr. Chang, Agent Chang, said they thought maybe a Mexican drug gang did it. What does that have to do with us?"

Lucas shrugged. "I don't know. Can you think of anything at all?"

Tears started running down her face, and she sniffed and wiped the tears away, and said, "Our business is with Mexicans. We *like* Mexicans. Half the people working here are Mexicans, or Panamanians."

"Liking Mexicans doesn't mean much to these people, if they're actually a drug gang," Lucas said. "Most of the people they murder are Mexicans."

"Well, I don't know," she said, her voice rising almost to a wail.

Lucas sat and watched her for a moment, and she gathered herself together and said, "Those poor kids. God, those poor kids. I just hope they didn't suffer."

Lucas didn't know how to respond to that, given the truth of the matter, so he said,

"Tell me one thing that would let this business . . ." He paused, then continued, "What am I asking here?" He scratched his chin. "Tell me one thing that would allow a drug gang to use this business for their own purposes. I'm not asking if they did, just make something up. One possibility."

She peered at him for a moment, confused, and then sat up, looked at a wall calendar as if it might explain something to her, then looked back and said, "There isn't any. Not that I can think of. We don't buy or sell any physical product, so you can't use us to smuggle anything. There aren't any trucks, nobody crosses any border. We don't make that much in profit . . . and all of our income is recorded because it's all done with credit cards. So, I don't know."

"Is there any way they could use your computer systems for communications of some kind?" Lucas asked. "Or anything like that?"

"Why would they?" she asked.

"I don't know. I'm just trying to think of anything that might help," Lucas said.

Phillips said, "Listen, if they want to communicate, they can buy an encryption package, for a few dollars, that the CIA couldn't break, and just send e-mails. Why would they go through us?"

Lucas turned his palms up. "Don't know. Maybe they didn't. But somewhere, there's a reason they were killed. Possibly in this company. Did Mr. Brooks speak Spanish?"

"Oh, yes. He was fluent. So was his wife," Phillips said. "They lived in Argentina for five years, and that's where Pat got the idea for the company. Everybody's got computers down there, but it's hard to get good software in Spanish. His idea was, get some of these really good, inexpensive, second-level software packages — business software, games, whatever — and translate them into Spanish. That's what we did. We'd buy the rights, get a contractor to recode in Spanish, and put it online."

"Then the customers would download it and that'd be the end of it," Lucas said.

"That's it," she said.

"But couldn't a drug gang be somehow using the . . ." He faltered, then said, "But why do it that way, when they could do it with an encrypted e-mail?"

"I can't think of why," she said.

"Who does the books?"

"Merit-Champlain, they're an accounting company over in North St. Paul."

"I know them," Lucas said. He'd used the same outfit when he was running his computer company in the mid-nineties. As far

51

as he knew, they were straight. "Did Brooks finance the company himself?" he asked.

"As far as I know, yes. He used to work for 3M, he made very good money," Phillips said. "He had savings, and he borrowed money from his 401K. I think his brother chipped in. When we started, there were only three of us, full-time, Pat and me and Bob Farmer, who was the computer expert. Candy would come in after the kids were at school, and she'd stay until it was time to pick them up. Everything else, we'd farm out. Contract work."

"Pretty much a success right from the start?"

"Not hardly," Phillips said, shaking her head. "It was two years before Pat took his first paycheck. After that it came on pretty good, and we're still growing. Well, we were still growing . . . I don't know what'll happen now."

"Are Brooks's parents still alive?" Lucas asked.

"Yes. Nice folks. They live out in Stillwater. Agent Chang —"

"Dick," Lucas said.

"Yes, Dick said they were being contacted."

"They'd probably inherit," Lucas said.

"Unless it's his brother," Phillips said. "I

really don't know. Nobody thought . . . this could happen. That they'd all be gone. Never in a million years."

Lucas worked her a bit more, got the name and address of Brooks's brother, but had the feeling he was pushing on a string. He thanked her and left her in the office. Chang was standing in the hallway with a water-machine paper cup in his hand, and Lucas nodded and asked, "Anything?"

Chang shook his head. "Lot of Mexicans here, but I'm not seeing anything. They're all confused as hell. The confusion feels real."

"I wish they were making more money," Lucas said. "I'm not seeing how they could be running a laundry. Maybe the accountants will have something."

"Maybe," Chang said. There was doubt in his voice. "You want to talk to anyone else?"

"Should I?"

Chang shrugged. "Well . . . no. If there's some kind of secret deal going on, I don't think they're all in on it. Probably only one of them . . . and he'll lie about it. Just talking to them won't help much."

Lucas headed back to his office, a nice quiet space where he could brood. In a complicated investigation, he found it useful to take whatever pieces he had and concoct a story around them. Even if the story was far-fetched, it gave him a starting place, and angles to work.

On the drive from Wayzata to downtown Minneapolis, his lead story had been "Money Laundry": that the Brookses had been killed by a drug gang, after doing something fancy with the gang's money. Chipping off an extra piece.

Other kinds of organized crime, where you might see the same level of violence, didn't need the same level of money laundering, because they didn't operate with huge numbers of small bills. Their violence was usually aimed at eliminating competition.

Sunnie would have been perfect for a drug gang, with small payments coming in from all over Latin America, consolidated, and moved to a bank. Except, if Phillips and the books were telling the truth, the money wasn't large enough.

That one little fact was hard to get around. If it was a laundry, where was the money?

The other problem, and it could probably be checked, was that the business had been shaky at the start. If it had been set up as a laundry, it shouldn't have been. Perhaps, he thought, it had been set up as a legitimate business, and had only later been spotted by the gang as a potential laundry.

His other story — but it was far back, number ten on his list of two — was Del's suggestion, that the murders had been the result of a home invasion by a couple of crazy killers, who'd picked a random house in a rich neighborhood. A couple of stupid, crazy guys who looked at the house and thought that there must be big money inside, not being all that familiar with checking accounts and American Express. When they got inside and found that there wasn't much in the way of money, they amused themselves with rape, torture, and murder. That happened, a few times a year, most often in California or on the East Coast; not in Minnesota, though.

Another problem with that scenario was that the crime-scene people in Wayzata were positing at least three killers, and maybe four. House invasions of the crazy, murderous kind usually involved one or two people: three or four crazy people would be unusual.

Of course, there was always Charlie Manson to worry about. . . .

Yet he didn't like the Manson scenario, even with the bloody "were coming" written on the wall. The murders didn't seem crazy enough for crazy people. They'd taken too long, there was that apparent progression, and there wasn't the level of frenzy that you'd expect.

He was halfway back to the office when a phone call came in. The identifying tag said "City of Northfield." He answered and a man asked, "Is this Lucas Davenport?"

"It is."

"This is Chuck Waites at Northfield PD. I'm calling about your flyer. You said you'd be interested in ATM robberies, man and a woman, knocking down the victim."

"Yeah, I sure am," Lucas said. "You bust them?"

"No, no. They picked out one of our college kids taking cash out of a street ATM, robbed him with a gun, knocked him down, and ran off. This happened last night. Kid's got a broken arm and he's out eighty bucks."

"Man and a woman?"

"Yeah, it's like that flyer said: skinny guy, big woman," Waites said. "Have no idea who they are, but we've got a *clue* for you."

"I don't like the way you said 'clue,' " Lucas said.

The other cop laughed. "Well, it might be an identifier."

"What is it?"

"The kid said they smelled like horse shit. Horse shit, specifically. We asked him if he was sure it wasn't cow shit or sheep shit, but he said, 'No, sir, it's horse shit.' He grew up on a dairy farm, and they ran a couple of riding horses and a few other animals. Sheep, chickens," Waites said. "He said anybody who grew up on that kind of a place could tell the difference between cow shit, horse shit, sheep shit, and chicken shit. He said they had all those animals, and the people who robbed him smelled like horse shit. Like they'd been shoveling out a stable."

"You know any meth addicts who run a riding stable?"

"Not me personally, but there're a lot of meth cookers out in the countryside," Waites said. "If these people are far gone on meth, like your flyer says, I don't think they could be running a commercial stable. That's pretty heavy work and takes some ability to concentrate. . . . If it really was horse shit on them, I'd have to believe that they're farmhands somewhere."

"Huh. That's interesting," Lucas said. "It's weird, but it narrows it down, and shoveling shit is about what I'd expect of those two. You know of any kind of organization that would have a list of stables?"

"Somebody in the state would, probably — they got a list of everything else," Waites said. "If I were you, I'd just call the county agents. They'd know all the farms in their county, and maybe who works on them."

"Thanks. If this works out, you'll get the reward," Lucas said.

"Really? What is it?"

"I go around and tell people that Chuck Waites is alert."

Waites laughed and said, "And America needs more lerts."

Lucas spent the rest of the day at his office, making phone calls and scratching his left arm, under the cast, with the end of a coat hanger. He'd been told not to do that — scratch with a coat hanger — and he'd thought there was some good medical reason for the advice until Weather told him that it was to keep him from cutting himself and infecting the wounds.

That, Lucas thought, was advice for children. He wasn't going to cut himself with the coat hanger, and besides, he'd rather cut himself than itch to death.

So he sat scratching and calling, making trips to the candy machine, interspersed with spasms of note-taking on yellow legal pads.

■ ■ ■ ■

Most of it involved the tweekers. The horse shit, he told himself, was actually a pretty interesting clue. Most people — he thought, but didn't know — would clean up immediately if they'd come in contact with horse shit. But people who were in contact with it all the time might not even know that they smelled. He believed the kid, and his identification of the odor. He himself could tell the difference between the odor of fish slime from a northern pike and fish slime from a crappie.

A smaller percentage of his time was spent on the murders: he was not the primary investigator there, and the investigation seemed likely to turn into a long, slow grind. If you were intent on locating and knocking down leads, Shaffer could do that as well as anybody. Still, images of the murder scene kept popping up in his mind. He'd seen some bad ones in the past, but this was among the worst. Anything with children . . .

He called the DEA and asked about unusual activity in the Minneapolis area. He was told they'd check. He called a dozen people in his private intelligence net, including six Latinos, and asked about anything unusual going on in the underground Latino community.

He tried to work up another credible story, beyond Mexican dopers and the Charlie Manson scenario. Stories cost nothing but time.

Not that the BCA would have a lot of time.

Wayzata, the town where the killings took place, was one of the richer places in the Twin Cities, filled with people who felt entitled to a lot of attention, as befitted their economic status. It was also a place where the news media could get in a hurry, and not have to pay much to do it. Every news outlet in town could send a reporter six times a day to ask the locals, "Is the killer living among you? And what about your children?"

The investigation would be pressured.

The BCA had eight people on it: the crime-scene people, plus four agents in the team led by Shaffer. Lucas didn't count: he was essentially working for himself. Because the agents generally considered themselves equal, and only occasionally worked a case under hard supervision, they mildly resented

Shaffer, though they understood the necessity of having a team coordinator.

Lucas was another matter: he was neither their boss nor their coordinator, and they didn't like being interrupted by his calls. He called anyway, from time to time, and learned very little. They'd found nothing incriminating at Sunnie Software. They did determine that the house hadn't been carefully robbed — the crime-scene people found two thousand dollars in a bathroom drawer.

Shaffer told him that they had one positive indication that something was wrong with the way the Brookses conducted their financial life. A forensic accountant — that's how he referred to himself, though his colleagues called him "Specs" — said that they didn't appear to spend any money on small stuff.

They didn't take much money from the bank in cash, but they didn't charge groceries or clothing or gasoline or consumer electronics. In fact, their credit cards were almost unused, except for a few big-ticket items, like airline tickets. They'd once flown to Orlando, spent five days there, possibly at Disney World, and didn't even show a motel bill.

Brooks had three cashmere jackets in his

closet, all newer-looking, probably fifteen hundred dollars each. His wife shopped at Nordstrom and Neiman Marcus, had a closet full of clothes from Barneys in New York. They didn't have credit cards at any of those places.

Shaffer suspected that they were spending cash where a credit card wasn't mandatory; cash that didn't show up anywhere else.

After the first half-day of investigation, that was it. It was way too early to say that the investigation was driving into a ditch, Lucas thought, but it might be true that the passenger-side tires had wandered onto the shoulder.

Lucas went to lunch at two o'clock, ate a couple of bagel sandwiches, alone, thinking about his murder stories, then went back to his office and found a phone message from the Los Angeles office of the Drug Enforcement Administration. He called back and was hooked up with an agent named Tomas O'Brien.

"I was told you're the guy I should talk to," O'Brien said. "I've got a Delta flight out late this afternoon, I'm bringing a couple guys with me. We'd like to look at the books on this Sunnie Software."

"I can fix that," Lucas said. "You know

something about Sunnie?"

"The name has come up a few times, but there's been nothing specific. Nothing criminal. We took a look, once, even bought some of their software, like Hable Gringo en Treinta Días. Sorta sucks and it ain't cheap."

"We've been wondering if it's a laundry," Lucas said.

"That's why our guy there in the Cities gave me a ring, after your call," O'Brien said. "Sunnie buys product from a company here in LA called Los Escritores, which got started with a lot of twenty-dollar bills . . . or so we've been told. The software isn't very good, but it sells like crazy. We'd like to look at what Sunnie's been doing with them. Look back down the money chain."

"You know the details on the murders?"

"Your people let our guy walk through," O'Brien said. "From what he says, it looks like the work of Los Criminales del Norte, one of the cross-border gangs. They do a lot of that revenge-rape stuff. Killing families, sexual mutilation. Chopping off fingers, one joint at a time. They tend to go down shooting."

"You definitely think it looks Mexican?"

"Oh, yeah, absolutely. Don't see it up here, much, but this would be routine in

Mexico," O'Brien said. "We'd love to get one of their killers alive, if we could. Turn him over to the Federales for questioning."

"We plan to do that up here," Lucas said. "The questioning."

"You'd get more answers from the Federales," O'Brien said, persisting with the thought. "The LCN supposedly caught a Federale undercover cop and skinned him alive. Sent his skin to his boss, by FedEx, with a movie of the guy getting skinned. If we extradite one of these guys, to the right Federales, we will definitely get some answers."

"I don't think we'd want to do that," Lucas said.

"Whatever, it's your call," O'Brien said. "Anyway, we're gonna get there a little late. Maybe talk tomorrow?"

"I'll fix things up with the lead investigator," Lucas said. "See you then."

Thinking about the ATM robbers, Lucas called a list of county agents, missed a couple who were out of their offices, finally connected with one, and was told that there might be a list of some commercial riding stables, but a lot of stables were run off the books, as side ventures, and coming up with a complete list would be tough.

An opaque piece of the underground economy, Lucas thought, when he hung up. He ran into it all the time now; small businessmen had told him that government taxation and regulation had become so rapacious that cheating was often the only way they could survive.

Another step down to a third-world economy.

Del came back at three o'clock from a surveillance job in Apple Valley, pulled a chair around, and asked, "Why don't you turn on a light?"

"Forgot," Lucas said. "Anything happening with Anderson?"

"Not on my shift. Maybe he knows we're watching."

Terrill Anderson was suspected of stealing a three-ton Paul Manship bronze art-deco sculpture, *Naiads of the North,* from the front driveway circle of a home in Sunfish Lake, a town just south of St. Paul. The sculpture depicted three larger-than-life-sized nymphs dancing, flowers in their hair, hands joined overhead, standing in a kind of swirl, or whirlpool, of walleyes.

The owner of the sculpture, the fifth-generation heir of a railroad family, was massively rich, and had a daughter who chaired the state arts council. He wanted his sculpture back — the estimated worth, as a sculpture, was four million dollars. Looked at another way, three tons of bronze, which was mostly copper, was worth roughly eighteen thousand dollars if it had been in ingot form, or fifteen thousand or so on the scrap metal market.

The sculpture had been fitted to a granite base with six large steel bolts. Anderson had unbolted the statues and lifted the whole thing onto a flatbed trailer with a trailer-mounted crane, one night while the owner was inspecting a new home in Rio. The operation had been caught on a murky piece of low-res surveillance video from a house across the street — the heir's own camera lenses had been covered with pink goop before the removal began.

Phone calls were made, and the hunt for the statues, or, more realistically now, the bronze scrap metal, which had been some-what desultory, had sharpened. Somewhere, out there, maybe, Anderson was hiding a flatbed trailer and a lot of heavy metal. Del was watching him, waiting for him to go fetch it.

Lucas yawned, scratched the back of his head. "Hope he didn't drop it in a lake."

"He's probably already shipped it to

China," Del said. "It's possible that he had a boxcar waiting, loaded it right off the flatbed, and shipped it out. I've been talking to the railroad, but those guys have got no idea where most of their cars are, or what's in them. Which I guess is a good thing."

"Yeah?"

"Yeah. If a terrorist ever wants to blow up New York, he can't just build a time bomb and put it in a railway car 'cause nobody would have any idea of exactly when it'd get to New York, or how it'd get there," Del said. "More likely to blow up a cornfield than a city."

"Or a riding stable," Lucas said.

"What?"

Lucas told him about the Northfield robbery, and Del said, "Well, you can't say it's a horseshit clue."

"I thought of that joke about fifteen seconds after the guy called me," Lucas said. "I was embarrassed just thinking of it, and I never said it out loud."

"You're not going to ask me to look into it, are you? I mean, I got enough boring horseshit —"

"No, I'm just making phone calls to these county agent guys. See what turns up."

"Might be better than watching Anderson," Del said. "The guy is a slug. Never does anything, goes anywhere. I was sitting out there so long my ass got sore. But then, I read another hundred pages in the Deon Meyer, had four ideas for new iPhone apps, realized I could have had a career in Hollywood as a character actor, and tried to remember all the names of the women I could have slept with but didn't. How about you?"

"I slept with all the women I could have slept with," Lucas said. "Not being a complete fool. You think about the Brooks family?"

"I tried not to."

Lucas filled him in on the investigation, and finished with ". . . so it's gonna be slow and methodical. Lots of paperwork."

"But a big deal — unlike Anderson and his statue."

"Mmm. I called some of the people on my list, put out some lines in the Latino community," Lucas said. "Haven't gotten anything back yet. We need to be careful not to step on Shaffer's toes. We'll all be talking to the DEA tomorrow, we can figure out who's doing what."

Del stood up and stretched: "So, we go home and eat dinner with the kids?"

"Nothing wrong with that," Lucas said. He thought about the bodies in the Brooks house.

Lucas went home, watched the Brooks murder coverage on Channel Three; played with his son, Sam, throwing a Nerf ball at a basket; got a smile from his infant daughter, Gabrielle, who was now almost a toddler; and had a long, complicated discussion with his daughter Letty about television news.

Letty was between her junior and senior years in high school and had worked part-time at a TV station for three years. She'd met a politician that day, in the green room off the studio, who shook her hand and asked her what she wanted to be when she grew up. She said she was thinking about being a TV reporter, and the politician shook his head and said, "The thing about TV is, every single story is wrong. Nothing is ever quite right. If you go into TV work, you'll spend your life telling lies."

"Then what are *you* doing here?" she'd asked.

"I'm selling my side," he'd said. "Television isn't news — it's *sales.* I'm selling my ideas."

The conversation had troubled her and she'd expected some reassurance from Lucas. He failed to give it to her. So they talked about that for a while, and then she said, "I dunno. I like it, TV. But . . ."

"Don't tell me you want to be a lawyer," Lucas said. "And not a cop."

"This politician guy, when he came back out, I asked him what I should be. He said, 'If I were a kid, about to go to college, and was smart, and knew what I know now . . . I'd study economics.' "

"I wouldn't know anything about that," Lucas confessed. "Sounds kinda . . . dry. Maybe you oughta talk to your mom."

"You know what she thinks," Letty said. "She's already writing my essay for medical school. She wants me to take some surgical assistant classes at the VoTech and assist her in some surgeries next summer. She says she can fix it. But I just, uh, I like getting in the truck and running around town."

"You like watching surgery."

"Yeah, but in a *news* way," she said. "I'm not sure I'd be interested in doing it," she said. "Mom says every case is different, but to me, they all look a lot alike. I can't see myself doing that for forty years."

"So talk to your pals at Channel Three," Lucas said. "My feeling is, TV's like the cops: it's interesting, but it can get old, and pretty quick."

"Maybe I could be an actress," she suggested.

"Ohhh . . . shit."

At ten o'clock that night, Lucas got a call from a Mexican guy who'd been hassled by St. Paul cops for running an unlicensed, backroom bar out of his house. Lucas heard about it through a friend, one thing led to another, Lucas talked to the cops, and the pressure went away: the Mexican guy knew everybody, and was too valuable to hassle about a little under-the-counter tequila.

He said, "I talked to a guy today who talks to everybody, like I do, and he said there were some bad people in town from Mexico."

"Yeah? Who's this guy?"

"His name is Daniel. I think his last name is Castle. Something like that. But he knows the St. Paul police. . . ."

The caller didn't know much more than that, so Lucas rang off and called a St. Paul cop named Billy Andrews. "I'm looking for a guy named Daniel Castle, some kind of hustler around town —"

"That'd be Daniel Castells. What'd he do?"

"Nothing but talk. But we're looking around for some bad Mexicans, and he told a friend of mine that there were some bad Mexicans in town. I understand you guys know him."

"This about the Brooks case?"

"Yeah."

"Let me check around. You don't want him spooked."

"No. All we want at this point is a quiet chat."

"I'll get back to you. Probably tomorrow morning," Andrews said.

Lucas went to bed, thinking about the phone call. A little movement?

Maybe.

But he didn't dream about the killers. He dreamed about the tweekers.

3

Weather was always out of the house by six-thirty in the morning. The housekeeper got breakfast for the kids and saw Letty off to summer school. Lucas rolled out a little after eight o'clock, which was early for him.

He'd put a small flat-panel TV in the bathroom and watched the morning news programs as he cleaned up. There was a story about the DEA coming in on the Brooks murders, and the anchorwoman seemed to think the DEA's presence meant that every thing would be okay.

He turned off the TV, spent a few minutes choosing a suit, shirt, and tie, had a quick breakfast of oatmeal and orange juice, called the office, found out that he was supposed to be at a nine-o'clock meeting with the DEA. Because he was hoping for a break on the "bad Mexicans," and might be traveling around town with more than one other person, he left the Porsche in the garage and took his Lexus SUV.

He got to the meeting only a little late.

The three DEA agents were smart, bulky guys in sport coats, golf shirts, and cotton slacks. All of them had mustaches. O'Brien was a dark-complected Texan, complete with hand-tooled cowboy boots, shoe-polish-black hair and eyes, apparently of Latino heritage. When Shaffer asked him about his last name, he shrugged and said, "My great-grandfather was Irish. He married my great-grandmother, who was Indio. My grandfather immigrated to Texas, but we kept marrying Mexicans. Lot of Irish in Mexico. The Mexican name, Obregon? It comes from O'Brien."

"I didn't know that," Shaffer said. "Never heard the name Obregon."

"He was a president of Mexico," O'Brien said. "Got his ass assassinated. Like Lincoln, up here."

"Didn't know that," Shaffer said. He nodded at Lucas, who'd paused at the doorway to listen.

Lucas took a chair and said, "Sorry I'm late — had a late night. Where are we?"

"Getting introduced," Shaffer said. "I'm going to take them over to the house when we're done here. We still haven't moved the bodies. The crime-scene people are going over everything with microscopes."

"We want to look at Sunnie's books, is the main thing," O'Brien said. "These two guys" — he nodded at his colleagues — "are accountants. We'd really be interested in seeing what banks the company is using, and who they're in touch with at the banks."

"We don't even know that this has anything to do with you guys," Shaffer said. "Not for sure."

"Maybe not for sure," O'Brien said. "But it looks to us like these folks were killed by the Los Criminales del Norte, the LCN."

"Where'd they get that name?" Lucas asked. "Not particularly subtle."

O'Brien shrugged. "I don't know. Maybe they gave it to themselves. They usually do."

LCN, he said, specialized in the importation of marijuana and cocaine into the U.S., through New Mexico and Texas. Nobody knew what happened to the money they collected, and there was a lot of it. The theory had always been that it went to offshore banks, and from there to Europe or Asia, but nobody knew for sure how it got there.

"The thing is," O'Brien said, "when one of their big shots gets killed, he's always off in the sticks in Coahuila or Tamaulipas. No place near Europe or Asia. So where the money goes and what they do with it is really a mystery. If we could figure that out, and find out which banks are involved, we could hurt them."

He said that the LCN had an alliance with growers in Colombia and Venezuela, and may have used some of the South Americans' financial expertise to move the cash.

"They are not subordinates of the Colombia guys — they're independent. The Colombians tried to get them under their thumbs, and a whole bunch of Colombians got their thumbs cut off," O'Brien said. "Now the Colombians provide the product, and the LCN gets it across the border to their own retailers on this side. But they've got the same trouble everybody does who winds up with bales of hundred-dollar bills — how to get the money clean. We don't know how they do that, either."

"We can't find it at Sunnie," Shaffer said. "We've got an accountant of our own looking at the books and talking to Sunnie's accountants, and it doesn't look like much money was running through their accounts."

"Maybe we'll have to look at their accountants," O'Brien said.

"They're a pretty big company, been here a long time, and clean, as far as anybody knows," Shaffer said. "It'd be hard to believe that they'd take on something as risky as a Mexican gang account."

"It's there somewhere," one of the other DEA agents said. "Gotta be."

Lucas nodded: he'd said the same thing himself.

Lucas said, "Our big question is, why did they do it this way, this massacre, and turn it into a sensation? Maybe you can get away with that in Mexico, and maybe they do it when somebody needs public disciplining. But this . . . they're not taking credit for it, so it wasn't disciplinary. It looks like they were trying to extract some information from the Brookses, and not getting it."

"And if the Brookses were knowingly dealing with these guys, it doesn't seem likely that they'd be crazy enough to steal from them," Shaffer said.

"Or not talk when they showed up," Lucas added.

"It's gotta be money," O'Brien said. "Maybe they're killing two birds with one stone — looking for their money and making a point."

"What are the chances that it's a rogue element?" Shaffer asked. "Some smaller group inside the Criminales knew about

Brooks, and they came up to hijack the money stream?"

O'Brien shrugged. "Dunno," he said. "I guess it's possible." His voice said that it wasn't possible, and that Shaffer should hang his head in shame for having suggested it.

Shaffer, his face slightly red, began to tap-dance. "Or maybe the Brookses just really pissed them off, or threatened them some-how, and they came up, you know, to shut them down."

"But then, why the whole torture scene?" O'Brien asked. "These guys are brutal, but they're not stupid. They really don't do crimes of passion. They kill for business reasons. If they just wanted to shut Brooks down, they could have come up here, shot Brooks on the street, and gone back home. You guys would be scratching your heads. Nobody would even suspect anything other than a robbery. . . . Now, you're gonna be chasing Mexicans all over town. The DEA gets involved, the Justice Department calls up the Mexican government, and they get more pressure put on them. . . . They're not impervious to pressure, you know. They don't want a battalion of Federales up their ass that might have gone up somebody else's ass."

■ ■ ■ ■

They all thought about that for a minute, then Lucas asked O'Brien, "You're not really here to catch the killers, are you?"

"We'd certainly like to," O'Brien said. There was a tentative note in his voice.

"But basically, you're here to see if you can find a way to mess with the business," Lucas said. "From that perspective, the guys who did the actual killing are probably small potatoes. You're here to look at the books, not to track somebody down in Minneapolis."

O'Brien nodded. "Yeah. That's pretty much the case. We're not equipped to go chasing after individual murderers. We want to bust up their *system*. We'd like to find the cash that Brooks stole, and take it away from them. That'll amount to a bunch of legal writs, freezing bank accounts somewhere. The street stuff — that's you guys."

The BCA guys all glanced at each other, and Shaffer said, "Well, that's clear enough. We'll be glad to cooperate on that."

Lucas asked a few more questions, the most critical one, for his immediate future, being "Can these guys pass as Americans?"

O'Brien said, "Probably not. In the border states, their retailers are mostly Hispanic, recruited out of the prison system in California, Arizona, New Mexico, and Texas. Some of them are native English speakers, grew up in Los Angeles or Phoenix. Some of them hardly speak a word of English, and settle down in the barrios in LA. Up north, here, they use a lot of Anglo prison gangs — just a straight money deal. But their gunmen, their hit men, they almost all come from Mexico. They grow up with the gangs."

"So the guys we're looking for, they're probably Mexican."

O'Brien nodded. "Yeah. If we've got this right. If it's not some kind of . . . French connection."

They talked around for a while, and then Shaffer said he'd put all the accountants together after the DEA agents walked through the murder scene.

Lucas went back to his office and found a call from Billy Andrews, the St. Paul cop, who said they'd located the guy who knew about bad Mexicans in town. Lucas called Del, who was still in the building, and recruited him to go along for the ride.

Before he left, he called Virgil Flowers, an agent who worked southern Minnesota, and told him about the horse shit clue to the ATM robbers.

"Sounds like it's right up my alley," Flowers said. "Horseshit."

"I've been told that we could call around to county agents to see if they might know about riding stables, and who'd have hired hands as cleanup people . . . or some such. I'd do it myself, but now I'm all tangled up in this Wayzata murder. We're talking Mexican drug killers."

"Lot more eye-catching than horse shit," Flowers observed.

"Well, I'm a lot more important than you are," Lucas said. "So . . ."

"I'll do it, but I'm working on the Partridge Plastics thing, so there'll be extra hours involved," Flowers said. "If I get them, I'll want to work a little undertime in the next couple of weeks."

"Just locate them," Lucas said. "You don't have to *get* them. I want to be there for the *get*. We can talk about the undertime . . . if you find them."

"Oh, I'll find them," Flowers said.

Andrews was a detective with St. Paul narcotics/vice. He was so large that he was hard to miss: six seven or six eight, maybe 240 pounds, with over-the-ears blond hair and gold-rimmed glasses. He looked like a tight end with a PhD in European literature. He dressed in dark sport coats over black golf shirts because, he thought, they made him look smaller. They didn't; they made him look like a hole in space. His nose had been broken a couple of times, and maybe his teeth: he had an improbably even white smile.

They picked him up at the St. Paul police headquarters. He got in the backseat of the Lexus and said, "Okay, this guy's name is Daniel Castells."

"Dope dealer?" Del asked.

"Don't think so. He just sort of hangs out," Andrews said. "It's not real clear where his money comes from. He buys and sells, we hear . . . maybe, like stuff that's fallen off a truck. Maybe. If a pound of coke came along, with no strings attached, he might find a place to put it. Or he might put that guy who had the coke with a guy who wanted it. Or maybe he'd run like hell. I dunno. People say he's a smart guy."

"Where is he?"

"He's got a booth at McDonald's, over at Snelling and University," Andrews said. "Drinks a lot of coffee. Eats French fries. Talks to people on a cell phone. He's there now. Dan Walker is keeping an eye on him."

"Does he know we're coming?" Lucas asked.

"We haven't mentioned it," Andrews said.

"Sounds like the guy to know," Lucas said. "I'm surprised I haven't heard of him."

"Showed up here a couple of years ago, keeps his head down," Andrews said. "I've thought about watching him, to see what he's got going. I'd like to get some prints, or even some DNA, maybe track him down somewhere else."

"Not a bad idea," Lucas said.

They took ten minutes getting to the McDonald's, and Andrews called his watchman, Walker, on a handset and confirmed that Castells was still in his booth.

"He is," he told Lucas, after he'd rung off. "He's been talking on his cell phone for the last hour."

University and Snelling was a mess because of construction for a light-rail right-of-way, and Lucas had to dodge around traffic barriers to get into the parking lot. When they were parked, they walked across the blacktop to the McDonald's, past the window where Castells was sitting. He saw them coming, making eye contact with all three of them, one after the other. He looked at his phone and pushed a button, and Lucas nodded to him.

Inside, they walked over to his booth, and Castells said, "Officers," and Lucas gestured at the other seats in the booth and asked, "Do you mind?"

Castells had sun-bleached eyebrows and sandy hair, over a well-tanned face. His face was thin, like a runner's, his eyes pale gray. He was wearing a lavender short-sleeved shirt with a collar, and narrow jeans, with black running shoes. "Would it make any difference if I did?"

Lucas said, "Sure. Then we'd all stand up and talk to you, and pretty soon everybody in the place would be looking at us."

"So sit down," Castells said, waving at the booth.

Although he was the only one in it, he'd taken the biggest booth in the place, and had his phone charger plugged into a wall outlet below the table. A dealer of some kind, Lucas thought, with his own table at McDonald's.

Andrews fitted in next to Castells, with Lucas and Del sitting across the table. Lucas said, "So, a couple cops from St. Paul were talking to some dope dealers, and one of them said you told him to look out because there were some bad Mexican people in town. Is that right?"

Castells didn't answer immediately. Instead, he seemed to think for a moment, and then showed a thin flicker of a smile. He'd just figured out who'd talked to the cops, Lucas realized. Castells asked, "Does this have anything to do with those people who got killed on the other side of town?"

Del said, "Maybe."

Castells said, "I gotta change my name. People keep thinking I'm a Mexicano."

Lucas asked, "What kind of name is Castells?"

"Catalan," Castells said. The three cops looked at one another, and Andrews shrugged, and Castells said, "Catalonia is a country currently occupied by Spain."

"You some kind of radical?" Del asked.

Castells laughed and said, "No. I'm an antiquities dealer. You know — statues and stuff."

"Who talks to dope dealers," Andrews said.

"I talk to everybody," Castells said. "I'm a friendly guy."

"You never know who might need a statue," Del offered.

"That's right," Castells said, smiling at Del. "You just put your finger on the core of the business, Officer Capslock."

Del leaned back: "Where do you know me from?"

"You were pointed out to me once," Castells said. "I was told that I shouldn't be misled by the fact that you were wearing a trucker's hat backwards."

"Mmm," Del said. Castells had pushed him off-balance. He asked, pushing back, "You haven't seen a big bronze statue, have you? Some women dancing on some fish?"

"The *Naiads*," Castells said. "No, I haven't, and neither has anybody else in the statue business. There wouldn't be any way to sell it. Your statue is now a bunch of little bronze pieces, if it's not already been turned into ingots."

"I hate it when people say things like that," Del said.

Lucas jumped in: "So what about these bad Mexicans?"

"The thing about cops is, cops blab," Castells said to Lucas. "They bullshit with everybody. If somebody's talking about a particular group of bad Mexicans, well . . . you could get your head cut off on television."

"Not us," Lucas said. "We've all worked in intelligence. We keep our mouths shut."

Castells made an open-hand gesture, as if to say, "Whatever," and asked, "Which one of you is the boss?"

"We don't actually have bosses," Lucas said, but Andrews pointed a finger at Lucas and said, "He is."

Castells looked at Lucas and said, "I don't know very much, but I was talking to a couple of Mexicanos over in West St. Paul and one of them said to the other that it'd be best to stay away from the Wee Blue Inn, because there were some heavy hitters going through, supposedly from Dallas, but actually, he said, from Mexico. That is the sum total of what I know. I passed it on to another guy I know, because he is also a Mexicano. I didn't know he was a drug dealer."

"Why'd you think about the killings on the other side of town?" Andrews asked.

" 'Cause I watched the TV news last night. Sounded like Mexican dopers to me."

They talked for a couple more minutes, and when asked where he'd come from, Castells said, "Washington, D.C."

"You were a congressman, or something?" Del asked.

Castells said, "Something like that."

"You speak Spanish?" Del asked.

"Yes."

Lucas asked, "French?"

"Mm-hmm. You looking for a language teacher?"

"No. German?" Lucas asked.

"Maybe a little. I travel on business."

"Antiquities."

"Yes. And high-end furniture."

He did not, he said, have any more relevant information, but he'd keep his ear to the ground, his nose to the grindstone, and his feet on the fence. If he heard anything more, he'd call Lucas. Lucas gave him a card and stood up. "Stay in touch. We could be a valuable contact for a hardworking antique dealer."

"Antiquities, not antiques. Antiques were made in Queen Victoria's time. Antiquities were made by the Greeks and Romans and Egyptians. Entirely different market," Castells said, as he put the card in his pocket. He was, Lucas thought, exactly the kind of guy who would keep it.

Outside, Lucas said to Andrews, "Interesting guy."

Del said, "Yeah. So are we going down to the Wee Blue Inn?"

"Thought we might," Lucas said.

The Wee Blue Inn was a hole-in-the-wall motel and bar on Robert Street in West St. Paul. All three of them knew it, and Del and Andrews had been inside. "The owner is a guy named John Poe, like in Edgar Allan, but he doesn't write poetry," Del said. "He sells the occasional gun, and he'll rent you a room for an hour at a time."

"He sweats a lot," Andrews said. "He usually smells like onion sweat. I think he eats those 'everything' bagels."

"Can we jack him up without anybody looking in a window at us?" Lucas asked. "I'd rather talk to Poe straight up, see what he has to say, than go in with the whole SWAT squad."

"I could go in and look around," Del said. He looked nothing like a cop, a major asset in his job.

"Except that Poe knows you," Lucas said.

"He won't tell anybody," Del said. "He doesn't want his clientele knowing that cops are hanging around."

"Let's do that," Lucas said. "If there are three bad Mexicans in there, we'll call up the SWAT."

They talked about Poe on the way over, and Andrews called headquarters and got them to put a couple squads in a dry cleaner's lot two blocks away, no stoplights between them and the Wee Blue Inn. "Just in case," he said.

At the Wee Blue Inn, they dropped Del and went on their way, around the block. Del called one minute later and said, "I talked to Poe. He says the Mexicans were here, but they're gone. Checked out yesterday morning. They said they were going back to Dallas."

"Did he *ask* them where they were going, or did they volunteer it?"

Del went away for a moment, then came back: "They volunteered it."

"So they're not going back to Dallas," Lucas said.

"I wouldn't think so," Del said.

"Huh. Be back in one minute."

The Wee Blue Inn was an earth-colored stucco place with a blue-tile roof. The earth color came from dirt.

The floors inside were made of dark wood and squeaked underfoot, not from polish, but from rot, and the whole place smelled of old cigar smoke and something that might have been swimming-pool chlorine, or possibly old semen. Lucas tried not to touch anything, just in case; no swimming pool was visible.

Poe was a short fat man with a bad toupee and a three-day beard, whose lips formed a small but perfect O. Del had him in his office, where he sat sweating. He fit in the place like a finger in a glove, Lucas thought; or a dick in a condom. Andrews nodded to him, then pointed at him and said to Lucas, "This is Poe."

Poe was adamant about the Mexicans leaving. "They had duffel bags, and they took off. Loaded up, said, 'Thank you,' and they were out of here."

"Speak good English?" Lucas asked.

"So-so. They was Mexican, no doubt about that."

"What, they were wearing sombreros?" Del asked.

"No, they just looked like Mexicans," Poe said. "Mexican boxers. Welterweights. Small guys, good shape. Mean-looking. Most Mexicans around here don't look mean."

"Couldn't have been, like, Colombians?" Del asked.

Poe was exasperated: "They was Mexicans. They was fuckin' Mexicans, Del. What can I tell you?"

"They carrying guns?" Del asked.

"Don't know. We have a strict privacy policy about entering our guests' rooms."

"That's a little hard to believe," Lucas said. "No offense."

Poe said, "Well, we do. We got it when my ex entered a room and found the city council president banging his secretary. Who was of the same sex. Not that I got anything against fudge-punchers, in particular."

"You always have been sort of a liberal," Andrews said.

"I do what I can," Poe said.

"In other news," Del said, "you got an ex. She around somewhere?"

"No. We agreed that she should stay in the southern states, and I'd stay in the north. We stick to that pretty close. And I got Vegas."

Lucas: "These Mexicans, they said they were going back to Dallas?"

"That's what they said."

"You think they did?" Lucas asked.

"Well, they all told me that," Poe said, "All of them. So that made me think that they weren't. Really going back to Dallas."

Lucas said, "Mmmm," and they all looked at Poe for a while, and Poe sweated some more. "You didn't get their tag number?"

"No, we don't require it."

"Credit cards?"

"They paid cash, up front, so we don't require a credit card," Poe said.

"Security photos?"

Poe wagged his head. "Too expensive."

"Used glasses that might have finger-prints?"

"Cleaned up their rooms right after they left," Poe said. "In this business, we live on turnover."

"So really . . . you don't know nothing about nothing," Del said.

"That's about it," Poe said, sweating. "Thank God."

"Yeah?"

He nodded and wiped his forehead. "They looked like the kind of little fuckers you don't want to fuck with."

They were still talking to Poe when Lucas got a call from Shaffer, who was at the crime scene with the DEA agents. "Got a call from the patrol. They found that SKY van. They ran us around a little bit. After they stole the van, they stole some tags off another van that looked just like it."

"So they wouldn't get stopped for a stolen van."

"Yeah, that's right. We finally got it straight, and a highway patrol guy found the actual stolen van at a rest stop up I-35."

"Anything good?"

"As a matter of fact, there was. They wiped everything down, but they left a CD by a guy named El Shaka in the CD player,"

Shaffer said. "The van's owner doesn't speak Spanish and says he never heard of the singer or the record. He listens to Springsteen. Anyway, you can see what looks like a partial thumbprint on the top side of the disc."

"You running it?"

"No, no, I thought I'd just admire it for a few days," Shaffer said.

"All right, stupid question," Lucas said. "When you gonna see a return?"

"This afternoon, I hope. You doing any good?"

Lucas told him about the three Mexicans at the Wee Blue Inn, and Shaffer said he'd send an Identi-Kit guy over to build some pictures. Lucas looked across the room at Poe and said, quietly, to Shaffer, "You better do it quick. The guy who saw them is shaking in his shoes. He could take off."

Shaffer said he'd have a couple of people there in a half hour. "I'm going to send along a crime-scene crew, too. A dump like the Wee Blue Inn didn't scrub down *all* the surfaces: maybe we'll get some more prints."

Lucas turned back to the group and found Poe explaining where he got the name for the motel. "I stole it from a place up in Duluth," he said. "It's not like there aren't six hundred of them."

"Could have named it Dunrovin," Del suggested.

"Yeah, or the Duck Inn. I thought about it, but I didn't," Poe said. To Lucas: "We done?"

Lucas said, "I may come back in the next couple of hours. Nobody's gonna find out about this chat before then, so there's no point in you running out the door. Hang around."

"I was thinking Vegas," Poe said.

"Vegas is too hot at this time of year," Del said. "Stay here."

Out in the parking lot, Andrews hitched up his pants and said, "There are two hundred thousand Latinos in Minnesota. I know that because I'm married to one. So all we have to do is eliminate a hundred and ninety-nine thousand, nine hundred and ninety-six of them, counting out my old lady, and we got them."

"You're saying we ain't got much," Del said.

"That's right."

"But we got *something*," Lucas said. "Maybe we'll get some prints and some pictures, and we'll start putting some pressure on them. Betcha we get them by tomorrow night."

"Exactly how much would you be willing to bet?" Andrews asked, as they climbed into the truck.

Lucas shook his head. "I was using a common cliché intended to express optimism," he said. "But gambling in Minnesota is illegal, outside the Indian casinos and the state numbers racket, so I would be unable to actually put any money on the line."

"That's what I thought," Andrews said.

On the way back to St. Paul, Andrews asked whether Lucas had ever gotten a line on the robbers who'd broken his wrist. "Just did, last couple of days," Lucas said. "I was never able to generate much interest in the whole thing, and I thought I was gonna lose them."

He told him about the horse shit clue. "I got Flowers working it."

"That's pretty high-priced talent for a couple guys who get a hundred bucks at a time, and nobody gets hurt," Andrews said.

"*I* got hurt," Lucas said. "Some poor college kid got his arm broken."

"I mean hurt bad, not getting your little snowflake wrist cracked," Andrews said.

"Thank you," Lucas said.

"Whatever," Andrews said. "If that fuckin' Flowers can't find them, nobody can."

"Especially with a USDA-certified clue like he's got," Del said.

At the office, Lucas had a message from Rose Marie Roux: *Call me.*

He called her, and she said, "I got a call from Washington, a young boy from the Department of Justice said *they* got a call from Mexico. The Mexicans want to send an observer up here to look at the Brooks case. Apparently they've been talking to the DEA about it, and they want to watch. The DOJ said sure, send them along."

"Did you thank them for consulting with us?" Lucas asked.

"You got a problem with it?"

Lucas told her about the DEA agent's suggestion that they send any Brooks murder suspect to Mexico for questioning — and why, including the story about the agent who was flayed alive.

"You think that's a true story?" Rose Marie asked.

"Who knows? You hear all kinds of shit coming out of the border. Wouldn't surprise me, one way or the other," Lucas said.

"Well, we're not turning anybody over to Mexico," Rose Marie said. "But be nice with these people. They've got problems."

"You said they wanted to send an observer, but then you kept saying 'they.' How many are there?"

"One cop and his assistant," Rose Marie said. "Cop's name is David Rivera. I don't know the assistant's name."

"Okay. When do they get here?"

"If their plane's on time . . . they're coming Delta from LA . . . about forty-five minutes," she said. "It'd be really, really nice if some senior BCA agent was there to meet them."

Lucas called Shaffer, who'd heard about the Mexicans coming in but had no details. "I'm going over to pick them up and run them out there," Lucas said. "Have the bodies been moved?"

"Pretty soon now. Alex is talking to the ME's guys now."

"Hold off. If everything works, I'll be out there in a couple of hours," Lucas said.

"Why don't you just have . . . you know . . . somebody else pick them up?"

" 'Cause I want to talk to them about this whole Criminales business," Lucas said. "Hope they speak English."

Besides, he liked driving around town, looking out the window. You could never tell what you might learn. In this case, though, it wasn't much — a few leaves turning yellow on maple trees. At the airport, Lucas locked his pistol in the truck's gun safe, went inside, identified himself to the airport police, and got a piece of typing paper from them. He wrote "David Rivera" on it with a Magic Marker, and the airport cops walked him through security and out to the arrivals gate. The cop said, "With that sign, you're gonna look like a limo driver."

"But a very high-rent limo driver," Lucas said.

"Well, yeah."

They talked to the gate agent about the arrival, then Lucas found a seat while the airport cop wandered away. When the plane was parked, the agent came over and said, "They're here," and Lucas got up with his sign.

Rivera was one of the first passengers off the plane. He was a man of middle height, but more than middle breadth, with dark hair and a short, carefully trimmed mustache. He was wearing what looked like an expensive but ill-cared-for blue suit and a dress shirt open at the throat.

He looked at Lucas's sign and said, in good English, "You don't look like a limousine driver."

Lucas introduced himself, and Rivera

thanked him for coming and said they had to wait for his assistant, who had been riding in coach. His assistant was female, a pretty woman with dark hair and dark eyes, carrying an oversized briefcase and pulling a rolling carry-on suitcase. Lucas took the briefcase from her, and Rivera said, "She can take it," and Lucas said, "That's okay," and led them down to Baggage Claim, carrying the briefcase.

There was a big bag for Rivera, and a second small bag for the woman, and since Rivera had made no effort to introduce them, Lucas said to the woman, "I'm Lucas Davenport. I'm an agent with the Minnesota Bureau of Criminal Apprehension." She bobbed her head and gave him a quick smile and said her name was Ana Martínez. Lucas left them at the curb outside Baggage Claim, retrieved the Lexus, pulled around and loaded them up.

"I need to know about the Criminales," Lucas said as they left the terminal. "Who they are, what they want. What their reach is."

As he was talking, Martínez pulled an iPad out of her bag and began typing into it.

Rivera said, "They are not quite the worst of the worst, but they are close. They began with a family, or a clan, in Sonora. At first, they were cross-border smugglers, mostly people, not drugs. What drugs they did smuggle, they took the other way, from the U.S. back to Mexico. Prescription medicine that was hard to get out in the countryside. Then, they began with the cocaine, going into the U.S. There were wars with other gangs, and their leadership got wiped out a few times, and they kept getting lower, and lower, and now they are like mad dogs. They will bite anything that moves. They have several hundred members, two-thirds on this side of the border, in distribution, one-third on our side, for acquisition, smuggling, and enforcement. There are still some members of the original family, but most of those are dead. It is not hard to find new management."

Lucas mentioned the agent who was allegedly skinned alive and asked, "Did they really do that? Or is that mostly an urban legend?"

"The skin was sent to my superior — I saw it," Rivera said. "Along with a movie. They did it, really."

"Jesus."

"He was not involved," Rivera said. "I can tell you something else. You never want to smell a skin that has been three days in the mail."

"So then what?" Lucas asked. "You went to war with the Criminales?"

"We were already at war — if we don't kill them soon, the whole snake, they will be coming for me." He looked out the window at the lush August landscape of the Minnesota River Valley. "I come here to the States as often as I can, to stretch out my life."

Martínez passed the iPad over the seat and said, "E-mail from Luis."

Rivera looked at it, then said, "I'll call him later."

She took the iPad back and typed something else into it.

Rivera had more background on the LCN, but it was all fairly standard gang stuff. "They are not innovative," Rivera said. "They are just crazy, and what can you say about that? They don't seem to care whether they live or die."

His real information was not sociological or anthropological, but factual: he had names, fingerprints, DNA profiles in a few cases. "I can tell you who is who, what rank they hold, where they usually are, and what their job is, when we know that. I don't have any secrets. I want everybody to know them."

"I've got people from St. Paul shaking out

Latino gang members. Let's see if we can figure out who belongs to who," Lucas said. "If we find a Criminales clique, that'd be a step in the right direction."

"If these killers were doing what we think they were doing, they won't be local, and the local clique won't know them," Rivera said. "They will be from Mexico, and they'll go back to Mexico when they are finished here."

"You don't think they're finished?"

"I hope not," Rivera said. "If they're not, you might catch some of them. If you do, we will ask for extradition through our embassy. Or, if there is no proof, we will ask that you deport them. Illegal aliens."

Lucas said, "Huh."

Rivera smiled at him. "We don't get rough with them."

"Good to hear it," Lucas said. There was a little doubt in his voice.

"We pull down their trousers, then we bring in the garbage disposal," Rivera said. "They always talk. Mexican men are very adverse . . . adverse, correct? . . . adverse to having their personal parts placed in a garbage disposal. So, as we work to get it plugged in and operating . . . we always have to work at it, we invent problems, to invent time for them to watch the machine . . .

drop some walnuts in, to test it . . . They start talking. We never have to get rough."

Lucas said, "Hmm." Then, "We had three Mexican guys check into a hotel here a couple days ago, and then they took off."

Rivera was interested.

At the Brooks house, Rivera wandered away from the driveway, to walk slowly around to the back of the house to look out at the lake. "This is very nice. I could retire here, on this lake."

"You'd freeze in the winter."

"So, I go to Argentina in the winter." He looked at Lucas and added, "I speak Spanish." He looked back at the lake. "In the summer, this would be very pleasant. Sit on the grass with a fishing pole, catch some fish, throw them back. Get a hammock, take a siesta. Drink some Cuba Libres. Many Cuba Libres."

Lucas let him talk, then followed him back around the house. Martínez, the assistant, was always three steps behind them.

The doors of the house were closed against the summer heat, and when the Wayzata cop pushed the door open to let them in, they were hit by the odor, and by the cold. The odor was purely one of old blood and death,

not decomposition — the inside tempera-
ture, Lucas thought, must be down in the
fifties — but it stank anyway.

The dead looked as though they'd been
carved from wax, all the blood having
drained to the bottom of the bodies, that
blood that wasn't soaked into the carpet
around them. As they stepped inside, Martínez took some tissues from her purse and
passed two to Rivera, who held them to his
nose. Martínez did the same, and Lucas
could smell the thin floral scent of perfumed
bathroom tissues.

Rivera and Martínez had some experience
of mass murder: neither one of them
flinched at the sight of the four dead. Lucas
introduced Rivera to Shaffer, who said he
was pleased to meet them, and then took
the two of them around the room, to the
individual bodies, working through the
established murder sequence.

When they were done, Rivera asked Martínez, "Criminales?"

She nodded. "Yes, I believe so. That work
that they did in Agua Prieta. That looked
like this. Very exactly." She pinched the tissue to her nose.

"What was Agua Prieta?" Shaffer asked.

"Agua Prieta is a city near the border,"
she said. "There was another family killed

like this. The Criminales learned, or thought they learned, that the family was spotting for another gang, and so they made an example of them."

"You have any names associated with that?"

Rivera nodded. "Six names, although we think there were only three killers. We think it was three of the six, but we don't know which three."

"You have photos? Mug shots?"

"Of four, but we don't know how many are correct," Rivera said.

"We'll take them all, put them on TV," Lucas said. "If anybody shows up to object, we apologize and deport them."

"That would be excellent," Rivera said.

Rivera spent a half hour prowling through the murder scene, and watched when the ME's people pried the bodies off the floor and bagged them. Martínez turned away from that and went outside. Lucas followed and said, "It's ugly," and then, because TV Mexicans usually added it to their affirmative sentences, he added, "No?"

"Yes. I see so much. Inspector Rivera is called to many of these."

"How long have you worked together?" Lucas asked.

"Well . . . four years. But we don't work together. He works, I assist. I am good with the laptop and the iPad. He is the thinker."

"Are you a policewoman?" Lucas asked.

"Technically. I am a sergeant, mm, how do you say it? First class, I think. But I do not arrest people. I have my iPad and a MacBook."

"Like a researcher." Lucas thought of his researcher, Sandy, who had little interest in street work, or becoming a certified cop.

"Yes."

"Inspector Rivera . . . sounds like he really has some personal antagonism . . . for these Criminales."

"Yes," she said. She looked as though she might say something more, but then just smiled. Rivera came out the door at that moment and walked over. "I hope my hotel has a dry cleaning. I now smell like yesterday's blood."

Lucas walked them back to the truck and walked around to get in, but Shaffer shouted at him and called him back. When Lucas got close, Shaffer asked, "We know anything about the inspector?"

"No. I was going to ask the DEA guys," Lucas said. "Where'd they go?"

"Conferring. The accountants are going

to look at the books, and O'Brien is over at Sunnie," Shaffer said. He glanced past Lucas at the two Mexicans. "Anyway, you know, you read that half these Mexican cops are owned by the narcos. I'm a little reluctant to pass on any real secrets."

"I hear you," Lucas said. "You got any secrets that you're reluctant about?"

"Not yet," Shaffer said. "But I will have."

Rivera was on his cell phone, speaking in Spanish. A moment later he hung up and asked Lucas, "I don't want to ask too much, but could we go to a Hertz car rental business in downtown St. Paul? Ana has the address and a map on the iPad."

"Not a problem," Lucas said. "I live in St. Paul, and our headquarters is there. Where are you staying?"

"In Minneapolis, by the university," Rivera said. "The St. Paul Hertz has the car we require, with a, ah, autopilot?"

"Navigation system."

"Yes. We were awake much of the night last night and have traveled all day, so we would like to get the car and then go to our hotel. Agent Shaffer has invited us to a strategy meeting tomorrow at nine o'clock."

"Good. I'd like to get those names and photos from you, however we do that. I'll get them out to the television stations."

"Ana has a USB drive, with files translated into English," Rivera said.

A moment later, she passed it over the seat-back. Lucas glanced at it and stuck it in his shirt pocket. "Mac or Windows?"

"Both," Martínez said. "They are in the file called Agua Prieta. The other files, you can look in them, they are what we know about Los Criminales del Norte."

"Gracias," Lucas said.

4

The three Mexican killers were driving an Alamo rental car they'd gotten at El Paso International Airport. They'd driven it hard, two days straight, north out of El Paso, up I-25 through Albuquerque and Santa Fe and Denver, then I-76 to I-80 to Des Moines, and I-35 north, the only car on the highway that never exceeded the speed limit. They'd stopped only for gas and to pee and eat at McDonald's; they had a trunk full of guns and a couple of spare license plates. If a cop had stopped them and gotten too curious, they'd have killed him and gotten off the highway and changed the plates.

When they got to St. Paul they had intended to stay with a man who came from a village in Sonora, but when they got to the man's home, the house was dark and locked up. Not knowing the neighborhood, or the level of local police surveillance, they walked away, made some phone calls, and wound up at the Wee Blue Inn.

The next day, they stole a van and switched plates with a similar van, as an extra layer of security, and the day after that, slaughtered the Brooks family. Nothing came of the murders, and they were told to sit tight.

They had been trying to get in touch with the Sonoran, and when they did, he was in Georgia, delivering some workers to a tire-recapping company. He said he'd misunderstood their arrival date. These things happen, hey? He told them a key was hidden under a rock to the right of the front door, and they were welcome to the house. They moved in after dark on their third day in the Twin Cities, the day after they'd slaughtered the Brooks family.

Then they sat and waited for more instructions. Every few hours, they'd go out to the backyard, turn on a satellite phone, and talk to a man they called the Big Voice. The Brooks family, they told the Big Voice from Mexico, hadn't known where the money went. They were quite certain of that. If the Brookses didn't know, they were confronted with a mystery. How should they work that out? They weren't exactly detectives. Big Voice got back to them and said, "Stay out of sight, but be ready. We will send help."

The three — El Uno, El Dos, and El Tres — had all been named Juan by their parents, and were all cousins to one another. Because they had the same job at the same time and place, they became El Juan Uno, El Juan Dos, and El Juan Tres, or One, Two, and Three.

They were young men, the youngest still in his teens, the oldest only twenty-four, but even the youngest had been killing for five years. They were not overly bright, were poorly educated and a long way from sophisticated. They knew four things well: guns, cars, road maps, and video games. In their temporary living quarters, they had a theater-quality television equipped with a PlayStation, and two cases of Budweiser.

They gathered around the PlayStation and wrecked a lot of cars, and shot up a lot of aliens, hooting and laughing at the chaos. They didn't talk about the Brooks family, because the Brooks family was dead, and therefore irrelevant. Uno and Dos and Tres simply waited, in the cool of the air-conditioning, washed by the slightly stale breezes of *Real Housewives of New Jersey* and *Dancing with the Stars* reruns, the artificial excitement of the shooter games, a bagful of real guns by their feet.

■ ■ ■ ■

Tres was the odd one out, the youngest, and the one for whom both the others had the greatest affection. Tres was not entirely of the world. He could kill as efficiently as anyone else, but he talked with God and other spirits, and went to church when he could.

The spirits lived in churches. All churches. He could find his dead baby sister in Dallas as easily as in Juárez. She was always there, playing around the feet of the plaster Virgin.

There were evil spirits in the churches as well, mean old priests and nuns ready to stick their claws in your neck. Tres was afraid of them, but he went anyway, and always to confession on Saturday afternoons. He confessed all of his sins, down to the smallest verbal transgression, with the exception of those committed on behalf of the LCN. Always, "I took the Lord's name in vain, three times," but never "I carved his eyeballs out with a pocketknife."

When he was done, he scuttled out of the churches, sweating and shaking, but clean.

His uncle had brought him to the LCN when he was fourteen, said that he could do anything, but "This boy is a little crazy. Not a problem, but something you should know."

A little craziness was not a problem with the LCN. So he talked to ghosts? There were worse things in the world. And, with a good pistol, the boy could shoot the heart out of a peso coin at twenty feet. Also, he loved his mother greatly, and knew that if he ever said a word to the Federales, his employers would cut his mother's head off. He was ultimately trustworthy.

So the three Mexicans sat and played with the toys, and Tres would take his personal pistol out sometimes and stroke it and speak to it, and then Big Voice called and said they had another target.

"A gay boy," Big Voice said.

Inspector David Rivera inspected his room at the Radisson Plaza. It was okay, he decided, not great; a faint odor of disinfectant lingered in the air, mixed with the scent of thousands of Golden Gopher supporters, their beer and potato chips.

He had checked both himself and Martínez into separate rooms. After he'd looked at the first one, he turned and handed the other key to her and said, "I won't need you anymore tonight."

She'd nodded and left.

When she was gone, Rivera went to the window and looked out, then stepped back to his bag, unzipped the top compartment, and took out a cell phone. He carried it to the window, waited for it to come up: and he could see a satellite. He punched in a number and a man on the other end said, "David."

Rivera said, in Spanish, "I'm here. I was taken to the crime scene. The Americans already are looking for Mexican involvement, and Martínez told them that it looks like LCN. We've given them the six faces, which they will put on television."

"Do they have any solid leads?"

"No. Not that they told me about," Rivera said. "The team leader on the investigation does not like us. He thinks we are talking to the cartels. I think he will hold back information."

"I have two names for you. Good people, I'm told. They will meet you at the Garzas'. They might have useful information, if you can get away from the Americans."

"Getting away won't be a problem," Rivera said. "The Americans are polite, but they know almost nothing. They don't care if we're around, or not. I will go to any crime scenes they find, and to meetings in the morning. Otherwise, I will work on my own."

"Call me often," the man said. "The names, addresses, and telephone numbers of the contacts will be in your home file."

"I'll see to it."

He rang off, plugged in his laptop, went online, went to a Facebook location, copied the names, addresses, and phone numbers to an encrypted file on the laptop. When he was done, he looked in the minibar, took out miniature bottles of rum and blended whiskey, and a bottle of Coca-Cola, mixed himself two drinks, and drank them both. Looked at the telephone.

The alcohol slowed him down a bit; he was hungry, he thought. He called room service, ordered a steak and salad, then went into the bathroom and showered. The food came, and he ate it, looked at the telephone, lay on the bed, and finally picked up the phone.

And sighed.

Another sin, he thought.

He called Martínez's room and said, "I've changed my mind. I'll need you tonight."

Kristina Sanderson looked at Jacob Kline, who was lying facedown on his bed, wearing nothing but a grayed pair of white Jockey briefs. His bed smelled like sweat and other bodily fluids. She said, "I can't possibly know what it's like from the inside, but I can tell you that there isn't any doubt about it, looking at you from the outside. You're more cheerful, you get around, you eat —"

"Can't think," Kline said. They were talking about the possibility that he might go back on his antidepressant meds.

"You don't have to think," she said. "All you have to do is be there. Skipping work could make it look like you're hiding something. Like you're guilty. If the police came down on you, do you really think you're in any shape to resist?"

"Yeah, I could. I think they'd look at me and talk to me and give up," Kline said. "I can handle it. I'm like one of those demonstrators who goes limp in the street. I go mentally limp. And, I *am* guilty." They both thought about that for a few seconds, and then Kline added, "I could kill myself."

"I don't see it," Sanderson said. She sometimes thought he played with his own depression, deliberately deepening it, walking right up to the edge of the pit and looking in. If he looked too long, he *might* kill himself, and she couldn't have that, not at

117

the moment. "The thing is, if you kill yourself, that'd look like guilt, too, and then they'd get all over the rest of us. So if you're going to kill yourself, do it on your own time."

Kline groaned, and did a low crawl across the bed to the top end, which was pushed against the bottom of a window. He parted the venetian blinds and looked out. "Still light," he said. And, "I'm not going to kill myself, yet. Though, I have to say, it's an attractive option. I just don't want to hurt myself when I do it, or screw up and turn myself into a vegetable. All the painless and safe ways, like pills, are such a drag to organize."

He let go of the blind, rolled onto his back, and scratched his balls. "I guess I better get up."

"Get cleaned up, a little bit anyway. Okay? Get downtown in time for Don to see you tonight. He'll be there until eight. Give him the whole depression bit, tell him you'll work your regular shift tomorrow."

Jacob pulled the briefs off, scratched himself again. Sanderson and Kline had done a couple of overnights, and, in any case, she had slept with a large enough number of men that she was no longer impressed by the sight of a dangling penis;

118

nor was Jacob trying to impress her. He was just the kind of a guy who didn't much care if he was naked or not. "Ah, Christ," he said. "The idea of going in there . . ."

"Three more weeks, and you can quit," she said. "We worked it all out. You tell them you've got to get treatment, and you check into a facility. Nobody will argue with you. Sit there for a month. Talk to a shrink, and get better. When you get out, you tell Don that you're going to quit to travel through Europe. Then, quit and travel through Europe. You always talk about it."

"Yeah, but when I actually get to planning it, it seems like such a drag."

"So go somewhere else. Like *not* Mexico. And get dressed. You need to talk to Don tonight. He has to see you. We can cover for you, if he sees you." Don was their mutual supervisor.

Kline had helped steal the money because the theft was an intellectual challenge. He didn't really care much about getting rich. He was too depressed to care — what would he do, go shopping? He didn't even drive.

To the others, he was beginning to look like a threat, a loose cannon. What can you do with a crook who, if caught, wouldn't even try to run?

Sanderson, on the other hand, was a woman with a plan. Her mother had early Alzheimer's and lived in a crappy nursing home paid for by the state. If Sanderson had the money, she'd like to spend a few hundred dollars a month for an upgrade in her care.

Then there were the animals. She had her eye on a 160-acre semi-wooded acreage in southeast Minnesota. The owners wanted a half-million dollars for it, which she didn't have. She actually didn't have half of a thousand dollars, not at the moment. If she *could* get the half-million dollars, or even qualify for a mortgage on it, she would start a farm for rescue horses and rescue dogs. Maybe rescue chickens — she had a soft spot for good-looking chickens.

She lay awake at night, thinking of herself as a kind of saint, surrounded by the animals, and the souls of the animals, she'd saved. With her various instabilities, her schizophrenia, her OCD, she could actually experience the farm, the animals, and her impending sainthood.

Like, the karma cash-out was enormous.

So she didn't want the money for herself . . . it wasn't like she was *greedy.*

■ ■ ■ ■

The movement toward the theft began casually, when Kline noticed the odd ebb and flow of cash in the Bois Brule account while he was working at Polaris National. Money would flow in from Bois Brule, but always in individual amounts of less than ten thousand dollars, which made him suspicious. Amounts of less than ten thousand were not reportable to the government.

Then the money would leave again, in much larger amounts, on its way to a variety of obscure investment funds. Where it went from there, he didn't know — but he did know that as much as twenty-five million dollars a month flowed into and out of the account. He also noticed other oddities: the money was dead for each calendar month, earning minimal interest. The large amounts moving out always moved on the last business day of the month.

Almost, he thought, as if everything were on autopilot.

He did an experiment, which would have gotten him fired if he'd been caught. He deliberately entered an error on the account, sending money to a fake account he set up inside the bank. He heard nothing —

and a week before the usual transfer, he put the money back.

The next month, he moved more money, a lot of it, into the fake account. He waited even deeper into the month before replacing it. Again he heard nothing. He carefully erased his tracks and thought it over.

Interesting. The account *was* on some kind of autopilot. He could think of only one reason that might be: it was being run with an eye to minimal involvement.

He filed the information in the back of his head. The idea of stealing some of the money occurred to him right away, but planning a theft, working out all the contingencies, all the details, was a total drag. So he didn't do it.

A few weeks later, he realized he was about to be fired for absenteeism and general neglect of duties. Before they could do it, he set up a back door into the bank accounts that would allow him to come in from the outside. He had no specific plan in mind, he just did it.

During the exit interview, the firing supervisor was kind but firm. Kline was the one who showed a streak of nastiness. "I will not be fired," he said. "I will resign. I want decent recommendations when I go for a new job. If you don't agree, I'll sue you for firing me, claiming you did it because of my well-documented disability. I will get my disabled friends to march naked outside the bank. I will shit in the revolving door. I am not joking."

After considering their options, they gave him a decent severance and a good-enough, if not hearty, letter of recommendation. After he spent the severance, he got a job at Hennepin National, where he met Turicek, who'd had a previous life as a minor Lithuanian criminal while studying computer programming at Kaunas University of Technology, and Sanderson.

Turicek had mostly done credit-card scams around Western Europe, and thought it was criminal not to steal what you could. Turicek didn't think that working out a huge theft was a drag. Not at all. He came from a country with a glorious history in chess-playing.

Turicek and Kline worked out the details, lounging about the office, and after work, in bars. Turicek would propose a method, Kline would shoot it down; if he couldn't shoot it down, it was listed as a possibility. Sanderson had to be brought in because there was no way she wouldn't know what was happening, and the two men were pleased to learn of her animal-rescue dreams.

The problem was moving the stolen money into a form they could use, and could get at. Turicek knew a man who knew a man who'd once led a raid on an American prepaid credit-card company, stealing some thirty-two million dollars over a weekend. They'd hacked into the company and changed the withdrawal limit on the cards to the highest level allowed, which was nine hundred and ninety-nine dollars, and when the limit was reached, simply did an automatic refill.

They then used hundreds of zombie cards, and after business hours on a Friday, began the withdrawals.

"A cool deal," Turicek said, "but the problem is, you need a major gang to pull it off. To get that money over the weekend, they had to make thirty-two thousand withdrawals. How would the four of us do that? They used hundreds of people. We've got four."

He brought in Albitis, whom he'd met at a job in Ukraine. She had some experience in moving money around the Middle East, from accounts in Lebanon, Syria, and Jordan through Israeli banks, which was not commonly done. She also had an acquisitive streak. When Turicek called her and mentioned an amount, she started a list, headed by names like Malibu and Le Marais, like Porsche and Mercedes and Harry Winston and Cartier.

Albitis was their professional, the one who knew how to do it.

She told them, "Stealing this money is like kidnapping. The big problem is, collecting the take — where the money goes from legal to illegal. Somebody has to be there, with his hand out, and that's where you will get caught. If you try to take this money in cash, people will notice. Bank tellers notice you if you take twenty-five hundred in cash. If we steal twenty million, as you say we can, and we put it in a bank, or lots of banks, and then if we withdraw twenty-five hundred each time, we'd have to go to a bank eight thousand times to get the money out. And we'd be on camera. And even if you got it, what would you do with it? If you want to buy a million-dollar house, you can't show up with a suitcase full of hundred-dollar bills. They'd call the FBI."

"So what do we do?" Sanderson asked.

"We funnel the money into a few big accounts that look like businesses, and we use those accounts to buy gold."

"Gold?"

Minnesotans don't know gold, Albitis thought.

Albitis was a little impatient, explaining the fundamentals. "Look. We take the money out of this bank account, twenty million dollars, which I'll only believe when I see it."

"You'll see it," Turicek said.

"Okay. When we get it, we have to move it. Move it fast. We send it through a line of accounts we've set up in advance. Onshore banks, offshore banks, Lebanese banks. From there, we send it to Wells Fargo, to some made-up account. Syrian Investments Limited, International Marketing of Lebanon. The problem is, the FBI can walk right down that chain. The longer we make the chain, the longer it will take them to do it, but they can do it."

"If we make the chain too long, wouldn't it take us a long time to get the money to Wells Fargo?" Kline had asked.

Albitis poked a finger at him. "Don't interrupt — but you are correct. So we send the money to Florida, then jump to the Caymans, then to Lebanon, then back to the U.S., to the fake account. With the right banks, we can do that in four days, and it will take the FBI two weeks to walk down it. But, in the end, we can't take the money as a check, because we still have to cash it, and nobody is going to cash a check for twenty million dollars. Nobody. Or even twenty checks for a million each. They're going to want to see all kinds of ID and background details and fingerprints. They'll take pictures, they'll record serial numbers, they'll inform the feds. There just isn't a convenient way to get twenty million dollars in cash."

"What difference does gold make?" Sanderson asked.

"Okay. Gold. All kinds of people buy it and move it around for their own reasons, a lot of them legitimate. Like making gold jewelry. Women in India keep their wealth hanging around their necks and wrists. People in the United States put it in their basement because they think the end of the world is coming. People in Russia put it in their basement because the end of the world is already here. The thing about gold coins is, they can't be tracked. There's no real paper trail, any more than there is for candy bars. Gold coins have no serial numbers. And, there are gold dealers all over the United States, and everyplace else. If you have the money, they give you the gold. They're dealers, not banks. When we get the gold, we've broken the chain."

"Gonna be a lot of gold," Kline said.

Albitis nodded, and her eyes turned up as she ran the numbers. "Mmm . . . three hundred and sixty kilos of gold, about eight hundred of your pounds, which, right now, is worth a little less than sixty thousand dollars a kilo."

"But then we've got to sell the gold," Sanderson said. "And we're stuck with dollars again."

Albitis shook her head. "No. We've got the gold, and our trail goes cold. We're free of the banking system, and the paperwork. Then we start businesses in, say, Nigeria, or maybe Brazil —"

"I don't want to go to Nigeria," Kline said.

"You won't have to," Albitis said. "I know the man who'll set it up. You'll make up a job with a fancy name, with fancy letterhead paper and business cards — Kline Petroleum Futures, Kline Oil Mobilities. Whatever. You'll set up a bank account and then start selling the gold through a merchant in Lagos, who will feed dollars into your business account in return for your gold coins, at a slight discount of, say, five percent."

"So the merchant gets a mil," Turicek said.

"Correct. We take out twenty million, and nineteen million shows up in our bank accounts, which have no connection whatever to the accounts used to take the original money."

"But we have to live in Nigeria?" Kline asked. He was stuck on the idea.

"No. No. Listen to me. You can live anywhere you want. Look: we won't even have to get the gold to Lagos. My guy has contacts here in the U.S. We drop the coins with them, the dollars pop up in the Lagos account."

"Why couldn't we do that with cash?" Sanderson asked.

Albitis looked at her as though she were retarded. "We could, if we had the cash. But I keep telling you, it's *getting* the cash that's impossible. It's getting from a bank account to dollar bills that we can't do. But we can get from a bank account to gold. A gold dealer is a store. Buying gold is like buying a toaster. There's no trail. That's all we're talking about: killing the trail."

"Okay," Sanderson said. It'd take a while. "I guess."

"Anyway, when we've moved the gold, you hire some legitimate accountants to repatriate your money," Albitis said. "In the end, you have several million apparently legitimate dollars in your bank account. You pay whatever taxes you need to pay. The gold disappears into the souks. Nobody ever sees it again, except in rings and bracelets and so on."

"What soup?" Sanderson asked.

"Soup?" Albitis frowned.

"You said the gold would disappear into the soup."

"Souk," Albitis said. "Souk. A market." She looked at Turicek. "What kind of people are these two? Have they ever been out of Minneapolis?"

Turicek nodded at Kline and said, "Sleepy," and then at Sanderson and said, "Dopey," and tapped his own chest. "Grumpy."

"And I'm Greedy," Albitis said. "Okay. Now all we need is Snow White."

Albitis and Turicek were solid with the deal. Sanderson and Kline were a little shaky. Kline had been somewhat satisfied by simply knowing that he *could* do it; he didn't necessarily *need* to do it. The money was attractive, not mandatory. But they were not particularly strong people, and in the end, despite misgivings, they went along.

Now, with that family dead out in Wayzata, things looked a little bleaker. Before, Sanderson had mostly thought of ways they could do it; now she began to think of ways they could get caught. Turicek and Albitis could disappear into the former Soviet Union and probably be safe enough. But where would she go? Duluth?

Kline was another problem, she thought. He was erratic, and it was hard to tell what he might do, if the cops came around to talk to him. He had a weird sense of humor, a grotesque sense of humor. If he started trying to play games with the cops . . . And who knew, maybe he'd find prison *comforting.* He always said he never had a real home.

She had to think about all of that.

Lucas copied David Rivera's LCN files and photos to his computer, then gave the thumb drive to Shaffer to read. Shaffer said he'd put the six LCN mug shots on television that night and ask people to keep an eye out. When Lucas was done with that, he made a few more calls on the case, learned nothing useful, then went home early and collected Letty and a couple of pistols.

Lucas was an excellent shot. Part of that came from being a good athlete, with the kind of long-term training in hockey and basketball that allowed him to quickly grasp the essentials of accurate rifle and pistol work. Just as, in basketball, there had to be an instant of focus before the ball was released, a focus that excluded almost everything but the basket itself, good shooting required that same moment of mental exclusion, that moment when you saw nothing but the target. The athletic background also taught him that patience was needed to get good in any difficult endeavor. He developed the patience.

He wasn't particularly fond of guns, but he was effective, and he believed that since guns were one of the ubiquitous tools of violence in the late twentieth and early twenty-first centuries, it behooved one to know how to use them.

Weather disagreed; Letty did not.

Letty, in her previous life, had been severely neglected. She'd grown up in an isolated house, far out in the countryside in northwestern Minnesota. She had, at times, literally been required to hunt for her dinner. She also had been a fur trapper, a preteen wandering in rubber boots and a Goodwill parka around the muskrat swamps of northwest Minnesota, trying to make a buck. Then her mother was murdered, and she met Lucas, who eventually adopted her; in the course of that case, Letty had shot a cop. On two different occasions — the same crooked cop. She had no regrets or second thoughts whatsoever.

On this afternoon, they got Lucas's Colt .45 Gold Cup and Beretta 92F, and drove up to the St. Paul police pistol range in Maplewood, where a half dozen guys were going through annual testing. Lucas had a standing arrangement with the department to use the range, and had gotten a quiet okay to bring Letty along.

On the way up, they talked about her school, and about the Wayzata case, and Lucas gave her the details that he had.

"Nothing there for me," she said, thinking about the possibilities for her television job. "The cop reporters got all that stuff."

"I talked to Jen, and she said you were working on some Apple computer thing."

"Yeah, boring, boring," she said. "I'm doing a review of favorite laptops of the rich and fashionable kids, for the next school year." She pitched up her voice, "Oh, my God, she's got only four gigs of RAM."

"Girls don't talk like that," Lucas ventured.

"They do now. Everybody's got a Mac, an iPhone, and maybe an iPad, and God help you if you show up with a Dell," Letty said. "Then you're really socially f-worded."

"Really."

At the range, they put on ear and eye protection, got the okay from the range officer, and began working with the .45, and then the Beretta. The Beretta offered more firepower, in terms of sheer number of rounds, but Lucas had sent the .45 to a Kansas gunsmith to be tuned, and it was more accurate. Because of the relatively mild recoil, and smaller grip, Letty had no problem handling it.

"If you're shooting for real, shoot at the smallest spot you can see clearly," Lucas said, as he was looking at one of her targets. The bullet holes were scattered in a loose group around the center of the target. "A button is good. The smaller the aiming point, the tighter your group will be, but you still want a substantial target behind the aim point. Like the chest triangle: nipples and navel. An eye is small, and you naturally look at an eye, but the overall target, the head, is small, and it's always moving. The nipple-navel triangle doesn't move so much. Whatever you do, you don't want to just start whaling away, because if you do, you'll have a whaled-away group."

"I knew that," she said. "When I'd kill a

rat, I'd always aim at that little white spot in their eye. 'Course, I was using a twenty-two, from two inches. Still like that gun."

"Lot to like about it," Lucas agreed. "Saved your life."

He got into his gun bag and brought out a round red sticker about the size of a dime and stuck it to the center of the target. "Shoot at that. Focus on it. Even try to focus on the middle of the spot, if you can."

She did, and her group tightened up dramatically. "Interesting," she said.

"Let's do it again," Lucas said. "Then we'll run through the slap, rack, and fire."

"Always hurts my hand."

"You need the training," he said. "And what's a little pain?"

5

Lucas again arrived late for the morning briefing, and found a tense tableau: Shaffer was standing behind his chair, his arms braced on the top bar, his body rigid. Rivera sat across the table from him, half-turned away, but his face was red and he was shaking a chubby finger at Shaffer's face.

The three DEA guys sat at the far end of the table, looking back and forth between the two as though they were at a tennis match. Four additional BCA agents, part of Shaffer's team, were scattered around the room, two of them standing with their arms crossed defensively, looking down at Rivera.

Lucas came in behind Rivera, in time to hear him say, ". . . so I don't want to hear about Mexicans this and Mexicans that. These people are criminals and they are rats and the United States of America created them with this drug market, and with these guns that you ship across the border to the

136

narcos. Thousands of guns, black rifles that they change one part, and they have machine guns. Huh?" He patted his chest and said, "It's my people who are dying in hundreds and thousands so your rich people can put this cocaine up their noses and smoke their Colombians, so don't tell me about Mexicans this and Mexicans that."

He was shaking with anger. Behind him, Martínez was standing with her back to the wall, holding a briefcase. She glanced at Lucas and tipped her head, as if to apologize.

Shaffer, as angry as Rivera, said, "I wasn't trying to lecture you. I was trying to point out the obvious. You've apparently shipped a batch of insane killers up here from Mexico and they're butchering children and women."

"*I* didn't ship them. *Mexico* didn't ship them. They came here because this is where the money is. Because of *your* market. Because you do the money laundry, huh? Why do you think we are here? This Sunnie Software was the Criminales' bank, huh? It's a *bank*. So you provide the market, you provide the bank, you provide the distribution, but it's the Mexicanos who are at fault for all this? Bullshit."

Shaffer stuttered, "I — I — I just don't want to have this debate. We're all on the same side here. We're just trying to clear up this murder. At least I am."

Lucas cleared his throat and said, "Sorry I'm late. Any returns from the TV photos last night?"

Shaffer nodded, grateful for the interruption. He said, "Not yet. Nothing so far."

Lucas, looking over at the DEA agents, asked, "What about Sunnie's accountants? What about the bank? Anything there?"

"We're looking at eight years' worth of paper, trying to spot where the leak is," said O'Brien. "Haven't found it so far. Still interviewing the employees. Whatever Brooks was doing, it was complicated. But that . . . maybe that's what we should have expected. It wouldn't be right out there in the open."

Another one of the DEA agents, whose name Lucas didn't remember, said, "Our thinking now is, he was running a computer program that diverts incoming payments, depending on where they're coming from, to some other place. An automatic diversion. In other words, he's not actually collecting the money, he's simply set up a mechanism for collecting it. When it comes through, it carries a . . . signal of some sort . . . that simply moves the money elsewhere. If that's the way it works, and that's what we're starting to think, then we won't find it with an audit. We need a software guy to look at their programming."

Shaffer asked, "You got one of those?"

"We could probably find one," O'Brien said.

Lucas said to Shaffer, "We could bring in ICE. We really need to get on top of this. We don't need to wait a week for somebody to show up."

Shaffer: "She's pretty expensive."

"But she'd find it," Lucas said.

O'Brien asked, "Who's this ICE?"

Lucas: "Ingrid Caroline Eccols. She was one of the people who worked with me when I was running a software company, back in the nineties. Programmer, hacker, gamer, really smart. If she's not doing much, we could probably get her for two hundred."

"If you guys say she's good, I think the federal government could come up with a couple hundred bucks," O'Brien said.

Lucas said, "Ah, that'd be two hundred bucks *an hour.* Sometimes she works sixteen or eighteen hours straight . . . so it could be like three grand a day. Or four. If she's available and if she likes the idea."

O'Brien's eyebrows went up: "That, I'd

have to get approved," he said. "I can probably do it, for a couple days, anyway, if you guys say she's really good."

"She's really good," Shaffer said, and Lucas added, "She's as good as they get."

"So I'll make a call," O'Brien said. "Why don't you guys line her up?"

The rest of the meeting was a review of crime-scene evidence; one of the BCA cops passed Lucas a file of printouts of all the reports made so far. "We've got some prints, and we've got DNA, so . . . if we can find them, we've got them," Shaffer said, summing up.

"But, you don't really have them," Rivera said. "You have the instruments, but you don't have the men who ordered this done."

"Just for the time being, I'll take the instruments," Shaffer snapped. "I'll worry about the big chief after I get the guys I know about."

Rivera shrugged and muttered something to Martínez in Spanish. Whatever it was, it made a couple of the DEA guys swallow smiles.

Out in the hallway, after the meeting, Rivera caught up with Lucas, who'd been the first man out the door. He said, quietly, "This

Shaffer. He's not so smart. I was hoping for somebody smarter."

"He's . . . effective," Lucas said. "When he gets done, there'll be no stone unturned."

"Do you think he'll catch these killers, or the people who ordered this done?"

"I don't know," Lucas said. He added, "The meeting seemed a little tense. What happened?"

Rivera stopped in the hallway and did some straightening-out motions, shooting out his shirtsleeves, pulling his suit together. "When I came up here, I was told by your Justice Department that I could be involved in the investigation. Otherwise, what's the point for me to come? But Shaffer will not give me copies of your reports. He says it's for your agency only, that he has no authority to give them to me. So we sit here and tickle our thumbs. Is that right? Tickle? It makes no sense."

"Twiddle your thumbs," Lucas said. "That makes no sense either, but it means this." He put the report file under one arm and twiddled his thumbs for a few seconds; the cast made it difficult, since his left thumb was immobilized, but he got the idea across.

"Exactly," Rivera said. "I had the right idea, but not the word. Twiddle?"

141

Lucas looked back down the hall. Shaffer and another agent were just turning the corner, and Lucas said to Rivera, "Listen, I can't give you the report if Shaffer thinks it'd be improper. But if you want to sit in my office for a while, I'd let you read it. If you keep it under your hat. . . . I mean, don't talk about it."

"I knew you were the bright one," Rivera said. "Lead us to your office."

So they sat in Lucas's office for an hour, passing reports back and forth, and Lucas went out once to buy Cokes, which would give Rivera a chance to make a few notes if he needed to. When he returned, he noticed a book with a foiled cover, that had slid, facedown, out of Rivera's briefcase.

"What're you reading? The novel?" Lucas asked.

Rivera looked down, saw the book, and said, "Ah. Yes. It's bullshit. In English, I only read bullshit. I got it at the airport in San Diego."

Lucas couldn't help but smile. "What kind of bullshit?"

Rivera reached down and picked up the novel and turned it faceup. "In this one, the angels of the Lord and the devils of Hell — the fallen angels — are fighting each other, to control the future of humanity. The key to this struggle is an American CIA agent and this beautiful woman —"

"Of course."

"Of course, and the agents save the world at the last minute, and we don't all fall in the pit. It's all bullshit. But I finish it and I think, 'Okay, the good guys win.' That's wonderful. That's why I read it. The good guys win."

"You don't think the good guys are going to win?"

"I see no evidence of it. Even worse, I don't know who the good guys are," Rivera said. Lucas sat down again and put his heels up on his desk, as Rivera continued: "I always look at real estate when I come to the U.S. The first day here, when we were at the Brooks house, I looked at the real estate before I went inside. You know why?"

"Why is that?" Lucas asked.

"Because I have this dream. I hear about this narco, he has ten million dollars in hundred-dollar bills, in his backpack, and I find him. He tries to shoot me, and I righteously shoot first. But then I open the backpack and here is all this money. I do not hesitate. I take the backpack, I go to Ciudad Juárez, where nobody knows me. I hire a coyote to get me across the border to

Texas," Rivera said. "In El Paso, I get on a bus with my backpack, I go to Kansas, or Minnesota, or Montana, to some small town. I buy a nice house with a span of land, ten hectares, twenty hectares. I plant some fruit trees, I plant a garden, I marry a fat white American farm woman. We live on the farm and I raise goats and maybe a cow, maybe some pigs, some corn. . . . Sometimes, I have a small boat, and we take it to a lake on a wheeler. Hey? I dream this all the time. My fantasy. I live in these fantasy books, where the good guys win. I live in my fantasy dream, where I win. . . . It's all bullshit, but that's what I do."

Lucas said, "Well, if you make it across the border, you can stay at my house until you find the farm."

Rivera smiled and slapped the desktop. "Thank you. If I make it across the border, I will come here, for sure. But this won't happen. They'll kill me first. For the last three years, I have thought I have perhaps a year to live, probably less. So far, I defy the odds. But one of these years, I won't. They'll kill me. I hate them. I hate the motherfuckers. This is correct in English, right? Motherfuckers?"

"Yup, motherfuckers," Lucas said. "But it's trailers, not wheelers. You put a boat on a trailer."

"Because it goes on trails?"

"No, because . . . never mind. So . . . why don't you just quit and come up north?" Lucas asked.

"I can't. I am a patriot. These mother-fuckers are destroying my country," Rivera said. "I have to help stop them. But in the end, I lose. This is not a fantasy."

"That's pretty goddamn bitter," Lucas said.

Rivera nodded, held Lucas's eyes for a second, then turned to Martínez and said, "We have to go."

Lucas asked, "What are you up to? Is there anything I can do for you?"

"Your only, mmm, report of interest is your visit to this hotel, the Wee Blue Inn," Rivera said. "There are Mexicans there. I have introductions here in St. Paul, I will be able to find people who know the people in this town. . . . Maybe I'll find something."

"Be careful," Lucas said.

"That is my name," Rivera said. "Careful Rivera."

Martínez shook her head. "Careless Rivera, I think." She wasn't being funny; she was absolutely morose.

As they were walking away down the hall, Lucas stuck his head out and called, "Hey, wait a minute." He walked down to them and asked, "Could you guys come to my house tonight? For dinner?"

Rivera smiled and said, "This is very nice of you, but . . . I am afraid we have another dinner, with friends. If we could do it some other time?"

"Sure," Lucas said.

When they were gone, Lucas went back to reading the reports and found an enormous amount of detail, but nothing he considered important — not yet, anyway. The techs thought they'd probably get all kinds of DNA, which meant that after they caught the killers, they could convict them. Unfortunately, they had to catch them first.

He was still reading when Ingrid Caroline Eccols called. Lucas's secretary stuck her head in the door and said, "ICE is on line one."

Lucas picked it up and said, "Hey, Ingy."

"If I was there, and had a gun, I'd shoot you for calling me that," ICE said.

"Yeah, I know, but you're not," Lucas said. "So how you doin', CE?"

"Good. I just heard a funny joke. You want me to tell it to you?"

"Not especially," Lucas said. "You have a very limited sense of humor, and you don't tell a joke very well. You tell me one every time I see you, and they're never funny."

"Fuck you, Lucas. My rate just went up to two and a half."

"Tell the joke," Lucas said. "Come back down to two hundred, and I might even laugh."

She told the joke in what was supposed to be a heavy southern accent, but actually sounded more like deep Minnesota country hick:

Mary Sue, Brenda Sue, and Linda Sue were sitting on their front porch in Tifton, Georgia, on a hot afternoon, drinking lemon drops with a little extra vodka. After a while, Mary Sue said, "When I had my first baby, my husband gave me a brand-new Cadillac ragtop automobile."

Brenda Sue said, "What a marvelous, generous man he is," and Linda Sue said, "Well, ain't that nice?"

And they drank some more lemon drops, with a little extra vodka, and then Brenda Sue said, "When I had my first baby, my husband gave me a brand-new split-level house, with central air." Mary Sue said, "That's such a magnificent gesture. You must've been so proud." And Linda Sue said, "Well, ain't that nice?"

And they had a few more lemon drops, with a little extra vodka, and Mary Sue asked Linda Sue, "What'd you get when you had your first baby, Linda Sue?" And Linda Sue said, "When I had my first baby, my husband sent me off to Switzerland, to go to charm school."

Mary Sue said, "Charm school? Well, did you find that helpful, Linda Sue?"

Linda Sue said, "Oh, ever so much. I used to just say, 'Fuck you.' Now I say, 'Well, ain't that nice?' "

Lucas faked a fake laugh — he actually thought the joke was kinda funny, and that she told it well — and ICE said, "Well, ain't you nice," and then, "Listen, I'm taking the deal. I told Shaffer that it was only as a favor for you, because you used to be my employer. Which means, you owe me."

"Not much, if you get two hundred bucks an hour. I might buy you a cheeseburger someday," Lucas said.

"It'll be more than that, I promise you," ICE said. "Anyway, I'm in. I need somebody to meet me at Sunnie and get me online."

"I'll have somebody do that," Lucas said. "When do you want to hook up?"

"I'm gonna buy a bag of sliders and then I'm on my way," she said. "An hour."

"Somebody will be waiting," Lucas said.

Lucas called Shaffer to tell him that ICE was on the way, went to the murder book, but only briefly. Then he tossed it on his desk and kicked back, and considered the problem.

He'd had a thought when he was talking to Rivera, and Rivera and Martínez were going through all the papers, and not finding any more than he had.

The torture of the Brookses had continued until they were all dead: the last of them had apparently died as the torture was continuing. Which probably meant that the torturers hadn't gotten what they wanted.

What nobody had considered was the possibility that the Brookses had no idea what they were talking about. That they hadn't given anything up because there was nothing to give up. That Sunnie was not involved with the narcos.

He thought about that for a moment, but couldn't twist a story around so that it made sense. The narcos had to know who they were dealing with . . . didn't they?

But why had the Brookses taken it down to the bitter end?

Why?

149

Virgil Flowers called. "I've been talking to victims, and we have one more report of horse shit odor. Wasn't mentioned in the police report because the victim didn't think to do it. The pattern is what you said it was — I think they're out of a triangle with the bottom line from Mankato to Owatonna to Rochester, with the point up in the Twin Cities. Or a big circle around Faribault. Somewhere in there. But there's something else going on, too."

"Yeah?"

"A guy who runs a stable out by Waterville came home a year ago, after a weekend up in the Cities, and found out somebody had stolen a big pile of horse shit."

"You're joking," Lucas said.

"I'm not joking. There's rumors that somebody else is missing a pile of horse shit, too, but I haven't run that down, yet," Flowers said. "Anyway, a couple that sounds like the pair who jumped you were in Waterville just before this shit was stolen. They were driving a big old beat-up Ford flatbed with side panels, the sort of thing you'd want if you were stealing horse shit. People say they were sort of at loose ends."

"Virgil, if you're fucking with me . . ."

"I knew you'd think that, but I'm not," Flowers said.

"All right. But if you *are* fuckin' with me . . ."

"Lucas . . . listen, this isn't going to take long. These aren't big-time crooks. I'll get something in the next few days."

"Keep me up," Lucas said.

He hung up with the feeling that Flowers was fucking with him. Horse shit thieves?

He was pushing paper again when Del called. He was talking fast: "What're you doing? Right this minute?"

"Trying to choose between Caspian mocha and Castilian Café au Lait when I paint the hallway."

"All right. Listen, can you get down to South St. Paul? Anderson just pulled into a junkyard by the river. I think he's going for it, and I need some backup."

"The sculpture?"

"The sculpture. You still keep your running gear in the office? The shoes and pants?"

"Sure. You think —"

"Change into it and get your ass down here," Del said. "Bring somebody else, too, if you can find anybody. Down by the river,

151

by that little airport."

Lucas got specific directions, then went out to the main office and found an agent named Jenkins, who wasn't too busy, got him moving. Back in his office, he took his gym bag out of a file cabinet, sniffed it — not bad, he must've washed it after his last run — closed the office door, changed into gray sweatpants and a dark blue hoodie over an Iowa Hawkeyes T-shirt, and running shoes. His Beretta went under the hoodie.

Jenkins was a very large man who, with his sidekick, Shrake, had a reputation for asking questions later. They took Jenkins's personal car, a three-year-old Crown Vic that Lucas felt would work better with the riverside gestalt than would a Lexus.

"Is there gonna be any shooting?" Jenkins wanted to know.

"Nooo . . . probably not," Lucas said. "I just needed somebody large to load up this sculpture, if we find them. They weigh like three tons, it's gonna take some work. A crane or forklift or something."

"Screw that," Jenkins said. "My hands were made for love, not for heavy labor."

They took twenty minutes getting south, and found Del waiting in a beat-up Jeep Wrangler in a park off Concord Street.

"I'll drive," Del said.

"You sure you got them?" Lucas asked.

"Eighty-three percent," Del said. "There's a big old metal shed down there, used to be a barge terminal. It's big enough to hide the low-boy with the crane. And the thing is, before he came over, he drove around for a while, like he was trying to figure out if anybody was tailing him."

"And you being a genius tracker, he never saw you," Jenkins said.

"That's right. We wound up down here," Del said.

"Unless he's chumping you, and we go running in there, and he says, 'Aha, you were following me,' " Lucas said. " 'No copper here, copper.' "

"It's bronze. Like I said, I'm eighty-three percent," Del said. "The other seventeen percent is what you just said."

They left Jenkins's Crown Vic on the street and took the Jeep back into the tangle of streets and tracks that ran along the river, Del at the wheel. He eventually took them down a muddy dirt road, then off onto a branching track that ran down to the water. He parked and said, "We walk from here. Bring the camera. I got some glasses."

They walked back to the dirt road, then

farther along it, another hundred yards, then Del led the way through some low brushy trees to the top of a dirt levee that smelled like beached carp and dead clams. "Watch the snakes," he said.

Lucas: "Really?"

"Yeah, I almost stepped on a great big fucker when I came up here. Bull snake, I think."

"What do you know about snakes?" Jenkins asked. He was watching his ankles.

"Not much. Just garter, bull, and rattle. Wasn't a rattlesnake, I don't think, and too big to be a garter."

"Yeah, well . . . I don't fuck with snakes," Lucas said, with a shudder.

"Neither do I," Del said. "That thing scared the shit out of me."

At the top of the levee, Lucas could see what Del called a junkyard, but was really a long raw-dirt clearing with five chunks of wrecked, rusting machinery of uncertain purpose, and a couple of abandoned cars and trucks, some of which looked like they'd been submerged by past floods. The shed sat in the middle of it: dull-silver corrugated steel, the same thing farmers once used to build silos, but this structure was probably a hundred and fifty feet long and sixty feet wide, in the domed shape of a Quonset hut.

There were two sliding doors, closed tight, but big enough to accommodate a light airplane; Lucas thought the building might have been designed as a hangar. Although the big doors were closed, tracks in the dirt outside suggested that trucks had been coming and going. A black Cadillac sedan and an older twin-cab Chevy pickup sat outside the only human-scale door on the building. There were four windows down the length of the building, but all looked dark and dirty.

"Now what?" Jenkins asked.

"We watch for a couple minutes, then we run like hell down there and find a window clean enough to see inside."

"We're not going to get shot, are we?" Jenkins asked.

"I don't think so," Del said. "You ready?"

The three of them ran like hell down the levee and across a hundred feet of open dirt driveway, trying to be quiet about it, past the doorway, to the side of the building and the first of the windows. Del peeked and whispered, "I can't see a thing."

"Next window."

They couldn't see anything in the other windows, either. All were encrusted with what looked like several decades of dirt. Around in the back, they found a rotten door, and when Jenkins gently tried the rusty knob, the knob pulled out in his hand. He knelt and looked in the knob hole, shook his head, and said, "Nothing."

On the far side, they found a cracked window. "Don't tell the court I did this," Del said, and using a pocketknife, pried out a shard of dirty glass. He dropped it under the window and pressed his eyes to the hole, looked for a moment, then turned to Lucas and whispered, "Got them. I can see the truck. There's a pile of stuff off to the side. It could be a cut-up statue. It's too dark to see."

Lucas looked, and saw the truck first, then close to the entrance door, a pile of what might have been junk, except that it looked too manufactured, somehow. Too regular for junk. He pulled back and turned his ear to the door and could hear distant voices.

"Still in there," he whispered.

"We could wait at the front door, get them when they come out, see if they say enough that we can go in," Del whispered back. "I'm not sure about crashing in without a warrant."

"What if somebody comes?" Jenkins asked.

"Then we tap-dance," Lucas said.

They walked quietly around to the front and waited, and six or seven minutes later, sure as God made little green apples, they heard a truck coming down the road. There was no time to run and hide, so Del and Jenkins propped their butts against the Cadillac's bumper, and Lucas faced them, gesturing with one hand, as though they were arguing. Del said, "Don't wave your hand around so much . . . it looks fake."

"What the fuck am I supposed to do with it?" Lucas asked.

"Just cross your arms and take a step back and then turn around and look at the truck coming in," Jenkins said. "You're supposed to be curious."

Lucas did that, and the truck pulled up. Del muttered, "Check the bumper sticker." The bumper sticker said: "My other auto is a .45." A middle-aged man, balding with gray hair pulled back in a stubby ponytail, got out of the truck and asked, "You the guys with Middleton?"

"Who're you?" Del asked.

"I'm the guy with the copper," the man said.

"Anderson's the guy with the copper," Del said. "We've been sitting here arguing . . . never mind. Whose copper is it?"

157

"Mine. C'mon, we'll get it straight," the guy said.

Jenkins nodded: "Thanks for the invite."

An invitation was all they needed.

They followed ponytail inside. The sculpture was right there, on the floor, but in a thousand pieces: the first thing Lucas saw was a streamlined hand at the top of the pile. Anderson was talking to a guy in jeans and jean jacket, with dirty blond hair and black plastic-rimmed glasses like people wore in Europe. They walked up and Anderson looked at the ponytail guy, and then at the three cops, and asked, "Who're these guys?"

Del held up a badge in one hand, a gun in the other, and said, "The BCA. You're under arrest."

"Shit," said the guy with the glasses, and with no further ado, he began running, three feet, four feet, and then, as he would have passed Lucas, Lucas reached out with his fiberglass cast and swatted the guy on the nose, and he went down, his glasses, still intact, spinning away.

"Don't do that," Del said. "Next guy who runs, I'm gonna shoot him."

"I gotta get a cast," Jenkins said, impressed by the impact.

"I didn't do nothing," said the guy who'd led them inside. He looked at Anderson and said, "Tell them — I didn't do nothing."

Anderson shrugged and said, "It's your copper."

Del said, "Bronze."

The guy on the floor moaned, "Man, that smarts. That really fuckin' hurts."

They sat all three of them down and read them their rights, and gave the glasses guy a bunch of paper shop towels to squeeze against his bloody nose. Jenkins wandered over to the pile of metal, peered at it for a moment, then pulled out a semi-sphere the size of a soccer ball and said, "Look, a tit." To Anderson, "How could you do that?"

Anderson said, "With a Sawzall."

Del called for help from South St. Paul, and five minutes later two squads were parked outside. The three would be booked into the Ramsey County Jail.

"Four million bucks," Del said, looking at the scrap. "State Farm is gonna be really unhappy. They're holding the policy on it."

They were going through the rigmarole of handing the guys off to South St. Paul when Lucas's phone rang, and he looked at the screen and saw that it was from an old friend, James T. Bone.

159

Bone was president of the third-largest bank in Minneapolis, after Wells Fargo and U.S. Bank. Lucas touched the answer button and said, "Hey, T-Bone. What's up?"

"I've got a problem, and it could be serious," Bone said. "Are you at your office?"

"No, I'm down in South St. Paul, arresting some guys," Lucas said.

"Damnit. Well, this is the thing. I saw on television that you're involved in this murder out in Wayzata," Bone said.

"Some," Lucas said. "I'm not running it."

"That's good enough," Bone said. "I've got a vice president named Richard Pruess. He's about six tiers down and he's involved in a bunch of investment funds. Basically, he's a salesman. If a customer is big enough, and wants an investment adviser, Richard sets that up."

"What does that have to do with Wayzata?" Lucas asked.

"Pruess is missing," Bone said. "He didn't come to work today. He's been sick some, I guess — I don't see him much, myself. Anyway, he's been under the weather for a few days, but still working. Today he didn't show up at all, and he didn't call in. He had a couple of meetings scheduled and hung up some customers. His supervisor tried to contact him, but couldn't. His cell phone keeps kicking us over to the answering service. He's gay, somebody in the office knew his partner, and his partner said Pruess was getting ready for work this morning, he was fine, when the partner left. The partner went back to their apartment and Pruess isn't there."

"You call the cops? I mean, other cops?" Lucas asked.

"No, I decided to come straight to you. The reason is, you know . . . Pruess used to work with Candace Brooks. She was his assistant."

"What?" Lucas had been watching the copper thieves being put into the back of the squads, but now he walked away, across the oily dirt outside the shed.

"That's why I decided to call you," Bone said. "Candace Brooks worked here until a year ago, or fifteen months. Something like that — I don't have her file yet. She had an assistant VP job in Pruess's office. I didn't know that myself — I just heard it from Sandy Bernstein, who runs that end of things. Anyway, I'm wondering if there might be something going on."

"Jesus, Jim, I hope not, but there might be," Lucas said. "Listen, we're going to a full-court press on this. If you hear from this guy, call me right away. I'll be there quick as I can. Another guy's actually running the investigation, his name is Bob Shaffer. I'm gonna call him, I'm sure he'll want to be there. And some DEA guys, and even a Mexican Federale."

"You think it's dope?" Bone asked.

"I'm afraid it could be. I don't want to get ahead of ourselves, here, maybe your guy's just out getting a haircut, but this business out in Wayzata . . . it's bad as it can get," Lucas said. "We can't let this go, we can't wait. We've got to find out if it's related."

"I really don't need any of this money-laundering bullshit dropped on us," Bone said.

"I can't help what falls on you, if it's anything," Lucas said. "But this Pruess guy could be in the worst kind of trouble. The worst kind. I can't even begin to tell you. . . . Listen, I'll see you in an hour or so."

"See you then," Bone said. "I'll do some poking around, maybe I'll turn something up."

Lucas got off the phone and told Del, "I gotta go, man, I gotta run."

"Bad?"

"Yeah. Feels bad. Like, really bad."

6

Lucas called everybody on the way back to the office, and once there, got a quick rinse in the men's room, dried off with paper towels, and changed back into his suit. As he went out the door, Weather phoned and asked if he was interested in going to dinner.

"Probably, if it's like routine. I don't want to do a big deal."

"I'll call the Lex."

"Fine. I've gotta go over and talk to T-Bone. I'll probably be six o'clock." He told her, briefly, what had happened.

"I hope Jim doesn't get hurt," Weather said.

"If his bank's been laundering, he's probably gonna get hurt," Lucas said.

"I can't believe that he'd know about it."

"Neither can I," Lucas said. "But it's open season on bankers right now. Maybe . . . He's a smart guy. He'll figure a way to handle it."

On the way over to the bank, Bone called again and asked how long he'd be.

"Ten more minutes," Lucas said. "Something happen?"

"Yeah. Your guy Shaffer is here and he's pissed because I won't talk until you get here. And 'cause I got a lawyer to sit in."

"Nine minutes," Lucas said.

Polaris National Bank was in downtown Minneapolis, a skyscraper of pale yellow stone and blue glass. Bone's corner office was on the fiftieth floor, from where he could look crosstown at the slightly higher IDS Center. Lucas had been in Bone's office probably fifty times, after men's league basketball games, to drink a glass of bourbon or a G&T, if it was hot, and talk about money.

Lucas pushed through the revolving door into the lobby a little after five o'clock and found Rivera and Martínez talking to the security guards. Lucas walked over, showed his BCA identification, and they went up together.

In the privacy of the elevator, Rivera said, a question in his voice, *"Mrs. Brooks?"*

"Could be a false alarm," Lucas said.

"Do you *think* it's a false alarm?" Martínez asked.

"No, I don't," Lucas said. "But I've been wrong before."

"She was the first to die."

Lucas said, "We assumed they'd torture the main target last — let him see the others suffer. They didn't. They went right after her, and when she died, they tried to get what they wanted out of the husband, by torturing the daughter, and then the husband himself. He had nothing to give them."

"Again, this is a guess," Rivera said.

"Yes. Absolutely. A guess," Lucas said. "Except that we haven't found anything at Sunnie so far. We're really having some problems nailing down anything that looks like a laundry. So maybe it isn't."

"You know the president of this bank?" Martínez asked.

"Yeah. Good guy. I really believe that," Lucas said. "If there's a money laundry here, he didn't know about it."

"We'll see," Martínez said. "If this vice president is missing, and if he worked with Mrs. Brooks, there must be a connection."

"Or the Criminales think there is," said Rivera.

"There must be," Martínez said to her boss. "For somebody so high up to be in-

165

volved."

Lucas said, "He wasn't that high up. Americans . . . banks especially . . . sometimes give titles instead of money. You could ask Bone, but I wouldn't be surprised if there were dozens of vice presidents. It impresses the clients, to be dealing with somebody . . . so high up."

Shaffer and O'Brien, the DEA agent, were sitting on a narrow red designer couch in Bone's office. Bone and a tough-looking woman, who Lucas thought must be the lawyer, were facing each other across a cocktail table, on separate red chairs that matched the couch.

Two other men, who Lucas didn't know, one short and bald, the other tall and long-haired, both in good suits and ties, sat on the third side of the table, while three empty non-matching chairs were at the fourth side. Lucas, Rivera, and Martínez took the empty chairs and Lucas said, "Thanks for waiting."

Shaffer, who already looked unhappy, registered another few degrees of unhappiness when he saw Rivera and Martínez, but he didn't say anything.

Bone, a thin athletic man with a strong nose and thick black hair, introduced the unknowns — the woman was the lawyer, the two men worked as an account manager and a systems director — and then said to Lucas, "We've already been over a few of the ground rules here. Kate will jump in if you ask any questions that would suggest that I, or the bank as an institution, were knowingly involved in any kind of illegal activity. Other than that, I need to get this figured out as badly as you do."

Shaffer: "You said you found something."

"I did," Bone said. "We went through all of the accounts that Pruess helped sell, and I found one called Bois Brule Software. When I spoke to Agent O'Brien after I talked to Lucas, he said the name has some significance to the Brooks murders."

"Nothing direct," O'Brien put in. "The Brookses had a cabin on the Bois Brule River up in northern Wisconsin. We saw it when we were going through their assets."

Lucas nodded, looked at Bone. "And?"

Bone nodded to the man whom he'd introduced as Martin Brown, the account manager.

Brown said, "I took the account apart. The notation on the account said that it was designed to hold monthly receipts from software sales, and that the money would be dispersed at the end of each month to

Bois Brule's creditors, with some of it going to a tax holding fund and other amounts going to investment accounts. There's nothing unusual about any of that, except the amount flowing through the account. Some months as much as thirty million dollars would go through it."

"Holy shit," O'Brien said. "I need to get my guys over here."

"What else?" Lucas asked.

"A couple of things," Brown said. "First, it doesn't look to us, after we took a really close look, like any money was dispersed to creditors. All of it went to stock or bond mutual funds. The second thing is, while the money was always dispersed at the end of the month, with a few small exceptions, this month, and only this month, the money was moved almost as soon as it came in. There's an additional problem here: when I tried to find out where it went, I couldn't. When I try, I get a system error. The people down in Systems don't know what's going on, either. We can't find out where the money went. Somehow, the wire numbers have been sequestered."

"What are the bond funds that it usually went to?" O'Brien asked.

Brown picked up a yellow legal pad and rattled off a bunch of techie-sounding names. "I'm having my secretary type up a full list, with account numbers and so on. That would be the place for your guys to start," he said, and passed the paper over to O'Brien.

"How much did they get?" Lucas asked.

"Twenty-two million," Bone said. "Something else: the last withdrawals were the day before the murders. At first, I was thinking, well, they knew about them. But then I thought, maybe, maybe, what happened was that they heard about the murders on the morning news and bailed out. Didn't come back for the rest."

Shaffer said, "Huh," and Rivera said, "Is it possible that your Pruess was involved in this money movement, and now is running?"

Bone spread his hands: "He had no direct access to the account. He was a salesman, not a manager. It's more likely that, God help us . . ."

"What?" Shaffer asked.

"That the people who killed the Brookses knew about him, and have taken him away," Bone said.

Shaffer said, "They've taken him away because . . ."

"Because they think he was involved in stealing that money," Bone said. "He wasn't,

169

but because he sold the account, or he and Mrs. Brooks sold the account, they thought he was. They may not know the difference between the salesman and the account manager. But if they've got Pruess, they probably know now."

Lucas looked at Brown: "You got a wife and kids?"

Brown's Adam's apple bobbed and he said, "Yeah."

"Get them out of town. Take them to a resort somewhere. Jim will pay your expenses," Lucas said.

"Absolutely," Bone said. "Find a nice place."

"You don't think they can find us?" Brown asked. His voice was shaky.

"No. These guys are a bunch of hoodlums, not the FBI," Lucas said. "Not even the FBI could find you, if you're careful. Find a place where you can get back here in a hurry if you need to. A few hours . . ."

"If it's all right to fly . . ." Brown looked at Bone.

Bone said, "Marty, you can go anywhere in the country. Go to a resort near a big airport with direct flights back. We'll pick up every nickel."

Brown nodded, looked at the paper in front of him. "I will."

■ ■ ■ ■

O'Brien looked at Lucas, then Shaffer, and said, "You know what's strange? We can't find any sign of this over at Sunnie. They must have separate books out in a cloud somewhere. They use their system to take the money in, and kick it back out."

"We've got ICE looking at it," Lucas said. "If it's there, she'll find it."

O'Brien asked Brown, "Doesn't somebody have to direct the dispersal of the funds? Don't you deal with somebody from Bois Brule? I mean, who was that?"

Brown looked into a file folder, a bunch of paper torn from yellow legal pads. "A person named Sandor Gutierrez, who apparently has been in to the bank only once, to set up the account, through Pruess," he said. He was sweating, Lucas thought. "Since then, he's operated on the basis of encrypted instructions sent via the Internet, along with a code word as verification. This was all very routine."

"And profitable, for you," Shaffer said.

Bone jumped in: "Of course — we've made several tens of thousands of dollars on the account every year. We've made about as much on the account as we drop

171

around the cash register every day."

"You're saying that the money was no big deal," O'Brien offered.

"It wasn't a big deal. Not for us. It's chicken feed," Bone said. "The fact is, we were used. We'll cooperate with any law enforcement agency that wants in. We will press charges against anyone involved, and we will cover any loss claims."

The attorney nodded, and added, "We don't expect to see any of this in the media. We won't, will we?"

"Not from us," Shaffer said.

"I'd like to see a loss claim," Rivera said, picking up on Bone's comment. "A loss claim would be very interesting — but I can promise, this is one claim you won't see."

Shaffer asked Brown, "Wasn't this all very unusual? Didn't you flag . . . ?"

Brown was shaking his head. "Looking at it the way we did — the way we do — it was simply a successful business, processing bills. Pruess was supposed to have vetted him, and after that, it ran on autopilot. Bois Brule would accept credit charges, would run them through us, money would come in, and at the end of the month, they'd move their money out."

"And it's not nearly the biggest account

we do that for," Bone said. "Best Buy runs more money through here in a day than Bois Brule did in a month."

The long-haired man, who'd been introduced as Ron Vaughn, held up a finger. Everybody looked at him, and he said, "We're tearing the system down now. Like Mr. Bone said, Pruess sold the account, but he had no access to it. As far as we know, anyway. They may have trusted him with the dispersal codes, of course, which would explain just about everything —"

"Everything except why they didn't snatch him *first,*" Shaffer said. "If you've got a guy handling the money for you, and the money disappears, wouldn't you talk to him first?"

Lucas: "We don't know the details. We just don't know. Maybe they called Pruess to ask what the hell was going on, and he convinced them it had to be the Brookses. Maybe the Brookses passed it back to him . . . we just don't know, and there's no real way to find out."

"And if you were handling the money, and you knew that the Brookses had been slaughtered, maybe you'd just run," O'Brien said. "Maybe Pruess is on his way to Italy."

"No. Not Italy, anyway," said Bone. "When we had his partner look for him, he called back to say that Pruess's wallet and

173

car keys were in his bedside table, along with a money clip. I asked his partner to look, and Pruess had two hundred in the clip, and four hundred in the wallet. He didn't take his cash card, either, his debit card, and he has sixteen thousand in his account. He also said that Pruess's passport was there. So not Italy."

"Is sixteen thousand a lot, for a vice president?" Shaffer asked.

Bone shook his head. "No, I wouldn't think so. He had an account that allowed you to move money around online, and most of it was in a cash investment account, the rest in what was a bill-paying account. It looked okay . . . at least, superficially."

"Let me go back to this guy," Lucas said, pointing at Vaughn, the systems manager. "Were you about to say that whatever happened, it had to go through your computer system?"

"Yes. And Pruess didn't have that kind of access — the access needed to move that money directly."

"Who did?"

Vaughn chewed his upper lip for a moment, like men do when they've just shaved off a mustache, then said, "About a dozen people in Systems. In my department. There's a vice president named Tiger Mann,

I don't know his real first name. . . . He and his assistant could do it, but their access is also very limited, and they'd leave tracks. Everything is designed to make sure that people leave tracks. We haven't had time to look, but if it was either of them, we'll know in an hour. We're looking now. If it was somebody in my department, I don't know how they would have found out about the account. Maybe just stumbled on it. The important thing is: somebody had to have access."

Rivera frowned and said, "Wait. Could it not be that this money man, who moves the money, the man who talked to you, this Gutierrez. Could not somebody have spoken to Gutierrez with, say, a blowtorch in his hand, and convinced him to give up the codes?"

Vaughn seemed to go a whiter shade of pale: "Yes. That would be another way. But . . ."

"What?" asked Shaffer.

"Then, wouldn't Gutierrez be dead? If somebody forced him to give up the codes? And if he was killed or disappeared a month ago, wouldn't the narcos have done something to protect their account? Maybe even stop putting money in it?" Vaughn was tentative, uncertain of his ground when talking about criminal behavior. He added, "If Gutierrez himself was stealing it, would he do it this way — actually depositing it in an account, then stealing it back? That seems way too complicated . . . too risky, when you'd have other ways of doing the same thing. You could just send it out to your regular investment accounts, but then divert a check to an anonymous account somewhere."

"These are very good points. I congratulate you," Rivera said. "But it seems that you are arguing that the criminal here is in your department."

"I'm not arguing for it, I'm *afraid* of it," Vaughn said. "These killers . . . do you think they're after all of us?"

Rivera smiled and said, "Yes, that's likely. If twenty-two million dollars went away, plus more money that they can't ask about, I believe they would be very angry, and would continue their investigation until they got to the bottom of it."

Martínez said, quietly, "I think they would have some reason to come after a specific person. These people are somewhat crazy, but not entirely stupid. If they were stupid, all we'd have to do is watch each of you, and they would come to us. This, I do not think will happen."

That was the first time that she'd ever said anything that in the slightest way contradicted her boss, as far as Lucas remembered. He looked at her for a few seconds, then turned back to Vaughn. "So let's rip up the systems department. Mr. . . . ?"

"Vaughn."

Lucas continued, "Let's get a list of names, addresses, and phone numbers for the systems people, from Mr. Vaughn, and start running them through the mill. If he says that somebody must have known, I'm willing to believe that."

Shaffer said, "My guys can handle it."

"Okay," Lucas said. "You might want to work out some kind of cross-checking strategy, get them to rat on each other."

"We can handle an interrogation," Shaffer said.

"Great," Lucas said. "Let's get it on the road."

The whole discussion circled around Richard Pruess, but it would do Pruess no good at all. As they sat and talked, Richard Pruess was already dead. He'd been effectively chopped to pieces by Uno, Dos, and Tres, and now the three killers sat and looked at the remains of the banker's body and Dos sighed and said, "The cleaning up is always the hardest."

"True, but we have to do it," Uno said. "The owner here, he's a friend of the Big Voice. We cannot just leave it."

They'd killed Pruess in the basement, on a blue plastic tarp that they'd bought at a Home Depot. That kept the mess somewhat confined. Dos, who was sitting on the basement steps, pushed himself onto his feet and said, "So, let's get it done. He is making a stink."

Uno was sitting in a lawn chair, a blood-spattered pruning saw next to his feet. He'd used it to cut deep grooves in Pruess's shins. "They don't know, do they?"

Tres said, "They don't know anything. Nobody could be this brave."

Pruess had denied knowing anything about the stolen money. Then, after a while, he'd agreed that he'd taken it, but they knew he was lying, to make the pain stop. So they continued the pain and he went back to denial, and all through the pain and the death, they got absolutely nothing useful.

"If he knew nothing, and if the family knew nothing . . ." Dos began.

"They knew nothing," Tres said.

"Then what happened to the money?

Somebody knows something," Dos concluded.

"This is not really our problem," Uno said. "We call Big Voice and report. We do what he tells us. Knowing where to send us, and what we ask, this is the Big Voice's problem."

They were all wearing gloves, to avoid the slop of the butchery, rather than to prevent fingerprints. They wrapped Pruess's body in the tarp and bound the tarp up with duct tape, and when they were done, the body looked like an enormous blue joint. After dark, they would throw the body in one of the garbage dumpsters that seemed to be everywhere. After finishing some minor cleanup with paper towels and Lysol, they carried the body up to the kitchen and washed their hands and started talking about dinner.

"Pizza?" Tres asked.

"If you go get it," Uno said.

They'd happened across a pizza place a few blocks away, on an avenue called Selby; a pizza place that had two Mexicans working behind the counter. They'd eaten there twice.

"I will go," Tres said. "Anchovies?"

So Tres went down to Zapp's Pizza and

ordered two extra-large pizzas, one anchovy with mushrooms and olives, and one pepperoni, sausage, and corn. The man behind the counter told him that because of the dinnertime backup, it would be thirty minutes, and would that be okay?

"Is there a church where I can pray?" Tres asked.

The man behind the counter, who wasn't Mexican, but was extremely white and wide across the shoulders, gave him a smile and said, "Man, you are a five-minute walk from one of the phattest churches in the United States of America."

"Yes? Fat?"

"Yes. St. Paul's Cathedral. They'd be happy to have you come and pray."

That the church should be so close was like a sign, Tres thought, as he walked along the street. In five minutes, like the pizza man said, he came to a large but ugly church, sitting on the edge of a hill, like a frog ready to jump into a pond. There were thousands of churches in Mexico, and he was not intimidated either by the cathedral's size or by its holiness, although the gray, stark walls were somewhat forbidding. He found the heavy fort-like doors open, and people walking out, trailing the scent of incense. A religious service had just ended, he thought.

He stepped inside, intending to find a pew, to recite an Ave Maria or two, and perhaps a Gloria Patri, and to check the place out. And inside, he found the most glorious vision of his life:

Three rose stained-glass windows glowed like fire, the Jesus and the saints and the martyrs reached down to him. He turned and turned and turned, in the church aisle, looking at first one and then another, then stopped, breathless, transfixed, as the saints began to move, like willow trees in the wind, gracefully, a dance even.

And Jesus called, "Juan . . ."

Tres got back to the pizza place an hour later, and the man behind the counter still smiled, but he was annoyed. Although the pizza was still warm, he said, "The crust may be a little crispy because you're so late," and Tres said, "I went to the church. Like you said. Jesus called my name."

"Hey, that's really awesome," the pizza man said. "That'll be thirty-eight ninety."

Tres fumbled a couple of twenties out of his jeans pockets. He was still distracted, dazzled by the procession of Jesus and the saints. The pizza man handed him the boxes, and Tres went toward the door and turned to the pizza man and said, "Jesus said I will die soon."

The pizza man stepped back, and when Tres went out the door, thought, *Jeez. Is that a big goddamn gun in his pants?*

He watched Tres as he walked past the front window, and then turned to his pizza-maker and said, "Man, that kid had a big goddamned gun in his pants."

"All the better to shoot you Anglos with. Need a big gun to shoot a big fat man like you," said the pizza-maker, whose name was Ochoa.

"Fuck you," the counter man said. "Tell you what: no fuckin' Sweeney is any fuckin' Anglo."

When Tres got back, the others were unhappy with the delay — they were really hungry, and tired of watching *fútbol* reruns on the Spanish-language channels. He explained about the backup, and his trip to the church, how Jesus said he would die soon, and then they fell on the pizzas and ate them in five minutes.

When they finished, Dos gathered up the empty boxes and took them into the kitchen, where they'd left Pruess's bundled-up body. Blood had leaked out of the package onto the kitchen floor, like red sauce out of a burrito. Dos made a *sttt* sound with his tongue and palate, and bent and wiped it up and looked for somewhere to throw the napkin. Didn't want to put it in the garbage, in case somebody found the hideout; the blood could be used to tie the home owner, Big Voice's friend, to the murder.

As he was looking around, he heard Uno call, sharply, "Look at this! Look at this!"

Dos went into the front room and looked at his own face on the television; then a moment later, Uno's, and then the faces of two other men he knew, one who was dead and one who was somewhere around, in Sonora, both shooters, and then two more faces he didn't know. The local Latina anchorwoman was talking about them, about the killings in Wayzata.

"They know us," Uno said, unbelieving, staring at the screen.

"Don't know about me," said Tres.

"How did this happen?" asked Dos.

"Don't know. We have to call Big Voice."

"This is very bad," Dos said. "Very, very bad."

Instead of throwing the bloody napkin in the garbage as he went back through the kitchen, he did something *really* stupid, without even thinking about it.

183

■ ■ ■ ■

At the end of the meeting with Bone, Lucas headed back home, and to dinner with Weather.

Rivera, with Martínez driving, went to St. Paul, to a house off Robert Street. Four men were sitting around a kitchen table, drinking Budweiser. Rivera and Martínez were shown inside by the wife of one of the men, who led them through a living room with a sixty-inch television set up like a shrine, down a hall, to the kitchen.

Rivera stepped in and one of the men stood up and smiled and said, "David, good to see you," in Spanish. He introduced the other three, and they all stood to shake hands, and then Rivera took a chair and a beer while Martínez leaned against the refrigerator.

The man who greeted Rivera was named Garza, and he said, "So, Miguel here" — he nodded to one of the other men — "talked to this man Flores, who has a cleaning crew and cleans up at the Wee Blue Inn. He saw these three men, and he believes that one or two of them were among those photographs that you put on television."

Rivera grunted and said, "Excellent. Now,

does he know where they were going?"

Miguel shook his head. "No. But he recognized the kind they were, narcos. He didn't want to be around when they were, so he left work. Before he left, he saw their car, which he thinks was rented. It was a new Chevrolet Tahoe, silver. He thinks it had Texas license plates. That's all he could say."

"More than I hoped for," Rivera said. "I will call home and ask for help — if it was rented at the border, and since we know the type, we might find the number."

"What else can we do?" asked one of the other men.

"The basic thing, we need to find these three men," Rivera said. "We don't want anyone to be hurt. So, if you ask, ask gently. People who might see three small Mexicanos driving in a new Chevrolet Tahoe, they'll remember."

The men all looked at each other, and nodded, and then Rivera said to Garza, "So, Tomas, you have four more Garzas since I last saw you," and the meeting turned into a party, and Garza's wife brought in some very good mole poblano and roast turkey, and tortillas, and Martínez helped serve it around and then the kids came down and they had a very good evening. . . .

At the end, when the others had left, and Garza was taking them to the door, Rivera asked him, "Did you —"

"Yes." He reached behind a couch table and produced a yellow envelope and handed it to Rivera, who bounced its heft and said, "I am in your debt, Tomas. If you need anything, call me."

In the car, Rivera took the pistol out of the sack, checked it, cycled it: a well-used but nice Browning Hi Power, not a modern gun, but one he knew and liked. He put it in his belt and sighed.

"Ah. I feel right for the first time since I got here."

"If the Americans find out . . ." Martínez began.

"Fuck them," Rivera said, as he started the car. "They treat us like children or traitors. So . . . fuck them."

7

Tres couldn't stop talking about his conversation with Jesus and the saints, and his continual reflection began to get on the others' nerves, and finally Dos told him to shut up. Tres smiled and said, "I'm to die soon, why should I listen to you?"

"Because if you don't, you will die immediately." They all laughed at that, and Tres shut up.

They hung out and watched television until midnight, then carried Pruess's body out through the side door to the driveway, and heaved it into the back of the Tahoe. They planned to go out far enough that the body, if discovered, wouldn't bring the police into their neighborhood, and then throw it in a dumpster, and hope that it was hauled away to the dump, or the incinerator, or wherever the *yanquis* got rid of their trash.

Nothing worked quite right for them.

There were dumpsters everywhere, but it was hard to find one where they could safely and discreetly lift the lid and deposit a two-hundred-pound body. Especially since the body, wrapped in its blue tarp, looked more like a dead body than it would have if it'd been in a coffin. Somebody would look at the bundle and say, "Well, there's the head, and there's the feet, and that thick part is the butt. . . ."

Another problem was that the body wasn't easy to handle: it carried like two hundred pounds of Jell-O. They found an obscure dumpster behind an office building, but after pulling up in the car, realized that none of them were tall enough to lift the lid on the dumpster. That got them laughing, but didn't make things any smoother.

They laughed less when they found one short enough that they could lift the lid — barely — and then found they couldn't both hold the lid up and lift the mushy body high enough to get it inside. They were strong little guys, but it was two hundred pounds of mushy dead weight. They kept looking.

Eventually they found a shorter dumpster on Upper St. Dennis Road, outside a drive-way where a house was being remodeled. After driving past a few times, they quickly hopped out, in the deep dark night, popped open the lid, and threw the body in.

Five seconds later, they were gone.

Five hours later, Muffy St. Clair, a dog, stopped just down the street to poop. Her owner, Bonnie St. Clair, picked the poop up in a plastic baggie and carried it over to the dumpster to throw it in. Pruess's body-bundle was folded into the dumpster, feet and head up, butt down, bent in the middle. It took a few seconds, then Bonnie said, "Jesus fuckin' Christ, Muffy, it's a body."

She ran home to call the cops, and after a while, a St. Paul homicide cop named Roger Morris called Lucas, who had planned to sleep in late on a Saturday morning.

"Somebody tore the guy to pieces," Morris said. "It looks like what happened to those people in Wayzata, if those rumors are true."

"Half hour," Lucas said. "Did you call Bob Shaffer?"

"Naw, he's an asshole," Morris said. "You can call him if you want."

"Did the dead guy have any ID on him?"

"We haven't completely unwrapped him yet. He's wrapped in a plastic tarp."

"Well, his name is probably Richard Pruess, and he was a vice president for Polaris National Bank over in Minneapolis.

He was probably killed because some Mexican narcos think he stole a bunch of money from them."

"Huh. So I got nothing left to detect," Morris said.

"You could detect where the killers are," Lucas said. "We have no idea."

"Okay. Get your ass over here. And call Shaffer."

Lucas did, but Shaffer lived in one of the far north suburbs, and his wife said he was out running. "He left his cell phone here. He doesn't like to be disturbed," Shaffer's wife said.

"Well, tell him to call me," Lucas said. "I need to disturb him."

Then he called Rivera, who was eating breakfast, and gave him an address, and headed for the shower. Thirty-one minutes after he took the call, he pulled up to the St. Paul crime-scene tape and got out of the Porsche, held his ID up for the rookie who was minding the tape, and went through the line.

Morris, a fat black guy in a pink dress shirt and black slacks, was looking with discouragement into the dumpster, while a crime-scene guy walked around the area with a video camera. Morris's partner, who was standing on a nearby front porch, talking to the home owner, raised a hand, and Lucas waved back. Lucas walked up to Morris and said, "I really like you in pink, sweetie."

"Fuck you. You don't look this good in your dreams." He tipped his head toward the dumpster. The body was still folded inside, but had been partially unwrapped.

Lucas looked in, winced, turned back to Morris and said, "Same guys."

"Yeah, I thought maybe. I saw all that stuff on TV. They cut his fingers off at the joints, and the pieces are rolling around like unchewed chunks of Dubble Bubble gum."

"Nice simile," Lucas said. "Kinda literary."

"I'm a literary kind of guy, but . . . who're *these* people?" Morris was looking back over Lucas's shoulder.

Lucas turned and saw Rivera and Martínez walking up to the crime-scene line. He shouted down to the cop, *"Let them in,"* and said to Morris, "Mexican cops. They're up here to observe, see what they can pick up."

Rivera walked up, looking unsettled: a kind of after-sex look, and Lucas glanced at Martínez, who looked a little glassy herself, and thought, *Hmm.* Rivera had told him he was married to a nice hometown girl.

Rivera said, "Thank you for the call," and Lucas introduced him to Morris. Rivera looked in the dumpster, then called Martínez up with a crook of his finger, and they both looked in for a moment. Then Martínez turned to Morris and said, "This is the Agua Prieta group. The same people."

"Mexicans?" Morris asked.

Rivera nodded and said, "Yes. We think somebody robbed one of their drug laundries, and they are either trying to get their money back, or are on a punishment mission."

"Well, hell. I am definitely nonplussed," Morris said.

"As we all are," Lucas said. "Let's find a place to sit down, and we'll fill you in."

"One thing," Morris said. "We found a clue."

"Really?"

"Yeah. Really. C'mere." He led the way to his car, opened the door, took out a big plastic bag. "This was inside the wrapper right by the face. It's a napkin with a smear of blood on it, and what smells like a little dog shit."

"Dog shit?" Lucas, Rivera, and Martínez were looking through the transparent plastic.

"The body was found when a woman

opened the dumpster to throw in a bag of dog shit. I guess they all go around picking up dog shit in this neighborhood," Morris said. "Anyway, she threw it in, and it landed on the head part . . . but when we unwrapped, we found this. Looks like somebody used it to wipe up some blood or something. It's a napkin from Zapp's."

Lucas said, "Jesus, it *is*. It's like a *clue*. Like somebody dropped a matchbook from a bar."

"Whatever," Morris said. "Anyway, the crime-scene guys are gonna work this, and I'm gonna run over to Zapp's. You're welcome to come, if you want. It's as much your case as mine."

Lucas was in Zapp's every month or so. He looked at his watch. "Not open yet."

"I called John Sappolini, he's gonna meet us there. He's calling his crews in."

"Let's go," Lucas said.

Morris rode over with Lucas, and Lucas filled him in on the murders in Wayzata. "I'll send you the book. But it's the same guys."

"I don't want that shit starting up here," Morris said.

"I hear you," Lucas said.

Shaffer called, Lucas told him about

Pruess, and Shaffer said he'd be down as soon as he could make it. Lucas gave him Morris's cell phone number, but didn't mention that he was riding along.

When he got off, Morris said, "I wish I wasn't gonna be working with him."

"Something personal?"

"Just style. He's one of those ball-bearing guys, who goes ricocheting around banging into people," Morris said. "He's got no sense of humor. No style."

"He's sort of a cowboy guy," Lucas said. "He and his wife used to teach line dancing. They came down to the office a few times and gave lessons to guys who wanted them, and their wives. Everybody was wearing cowboy boots."

"Now, see, that's something I didn't know," Morris said. "I can't believe that guy can dance. Not that line dancing is really dancing."

"Of course it is, and it's very romantic," Lucas said. "I actually got addicted to it, for a while."

Morris bit: "Really? I never would've thought you were that kind of guy."

Lucas nodded. "Got so bad my shrink put me in a two-step program."

Morris tried not to laugh, but finally let it

out, and they laughed for a block or two, until Lucas's cell phone rang. He looked at the screen: Virgil Flowers.

"What's up?" Lucas asked.

"Got a minute?"

"Yeah, I'm just riding around with Roger Morris. He's wearing a hot-pink short-sleeved dress shirt."

"Tell him he looks fabulous," Flowers said.

Lucas passed the word, then said, "Roger gives you the sign of the horns, and knowing your second ex-wife, he's probably right. Anyhow . . ."

"I found out that there are roughly a million riding stables out here, or people with horses, anyway," Flowers said. "Using my quick intellect, I called up everybody I knew, and I'm starting to get some serious vibes from the Waseca area. Horse people there have seen them. Hauling horse shit on an old Ford flatbed."

"Man, that's terrific," Lucas said. "What's next?"

"I'm going over there, talk to the various sheriffs, the county agents, anybody else. I don't have anything definite, though — I'm basically checking in. Wanted you to know I'm not out fishing, even though it is Saturday, and my day off."

"Hey, Virgil — find them for me. Honest

to God, I'll introduce you to one of my old girlfriends."

"Thanks anyway," Flowers said. "But she'd be too old for me. I'll call you tonight or tomorrow, soon as I get anything."

"Too old? What the hell . . ." Flowers was gone.

"What's that?" Morris said, when Lucas rang off.

"Best news I've had all summer," Lucas said, as they turned into Zapp's parking lot.

Zapp's Pizza was a tightly run ship, with good pizza and bread, a bunch of red-vinyl booths in the back, along with a half dozen tables, and, this early in the morning, an empty salad bar. The owner, John Sappolini, was not happy about the napkin, but had no trouble talking to police. "Half the cops in St. Paul eat here," he said.

He'd once told Lucas that he called the place Zapp's because his Wells Fargo small-business counselor suggested he not call it Sapp's.

Sappolini had two crews working eight-hour shifts, from ten o'clock in the morning until two o'clock in the morning, with the restaurant open from eleven o'clock until one. After the call from Morris, he'd called both crews in. He had the first ones brew

196

up a few gallons of coffee, and Lucas and Morris sat at one of the tables and everybody pulled chairs around to talk about the situation; Rivera and Martínez sat out on the edge.

They'd been talking for fifteen minutes, with late-arriving members of the crew straggling in as they talked. One of the last ones in was a short, wide-shouldered man who listened for one minute and then said, "There was a short Mexican kid in here yesterday afternoon with a gun in his belt. I think."

Lucas looked at him and asked, "You think?"

"Couldn't see it because he was wearing an iguana shirt," the man said.

"Guayabera," Morris said.

The guy shook his head. "No, iguana. It's like a golf shirt, but instead of like that polo pony, you know, it had an iguana on it."

"Yes, they sell them in Mexico, on the coast," Rivera said.

The pizza guy said, "See?"

"*Sí,*" Rivera said.

"So what else about him?" Lucas asked.

"He was just a kid, and he was looking for a place to pray while he waited for the pizzas, so I sent him down to the cathedral. He went, or at least he said he went, and he said he saw the big windows, and Jesus spoke to him."

"Spoke to him," Lucas repeated.

"Yeah, he said Jesus spoke to him, and Jesus told him he was going to die soon."

Morris looked at Lucas, and they simultaneously shrugged. From the back, Rivera asked, "How many pizzas did he buy?"

"Two. Extra large."

Rivera said, "Enough for three or four."

The pizza guy didn't know whether the kid had arrived on foot or had come by car, but had the impression that he'd been on foot. "I don't know why, it's just an impression."

Morris: "Is a cold-blooded killer going to church? I don't think so."

"But you'd be wrong," Rivera said. "Some of these bangers, they go to church every Sunday and pray for their souls. And because their mothers make them go."

"Then, if he is one of the guys, they'd be holed up around here somewhere," Morris said. They all looked out the window.

"I'll tell you what," Lucas said, when they looked back. "We've probably got DNA on these guys, we probably have at least one fingerprint and maybe more, they've committed at least five torture-murders of the worst kind. If we catch them, they're going

198

away forever, so they've got nothing to lose by shooting as many cops as they see. They've probably got an arsenal with them, and they've had lots of practice."

Morris said, "Huh. Better talk to SWAT."

"Better talk to everybody," Lucas said. "You don't want a lot of patrol cops rolling around sticking their noses into everything. If somebody finds them just sort of spontaneously, he'll probably be killed. I think you put together a good crew, start working the neighborhood, but you gotta be discreet. You don't want to scare them off, but you don't want to get anybody killed, either. No impetuosity."

"No impetuosity," Morris repeated.

When they'd extracted everything they could from the Zapp's crews, they broke up. Lucas headed over to the BCA, and Morris went back to the murder scene — from there he'd head to police headquarters, which was about five minutes away, to arrange for a careful survey of the neighborhoods around Zapp's.

Rivera and Martínez went back to their car, and Rivera dug his pistol out from under the front seat and said to Martínez, "You drive."

"To where?"

"Up and down these streets. If he walked, he is not far. We'll circle the streets, go out for a kilometer —"

She said, "This is crazy. We —"

"We know the car. This neighborhood, most of the cars are on the street," Rivera said. "I predict that we will find them."

"Then what?"

"Then we will see," Rivera said.

"You are too crazy," Martínez said. She bit her lip, as though she feared she'd gone too far.

All Rivera said was, "Drive."

The neighborhood around Zapp's Pizza was all old. From north to south, it varied from rich, south of Grand Avenue, to increasingly poor, north of Summit Avenue, to poor, next to I-94. Grand Avenue itself was mostly commercial and apartments.

Rivera didn't think the shooters would be in an apartment. Somebody, he thought, had probably arranged a house. The house wouldn't be on Summit, because those houses were basically mansions. This would be more discreet, in a neighborhood where people might be a bit more reluctant to ask questions.

The streets stepped back from the expressway were the most likely place, he told Martínez. The faces on the sidewalks were of every shade of black, brown, and white, from African to Scandinavian to Latino and American Indian. The Mexicanos would fit here, he said.

Even so, there were a lot of streets to look at, in the grid around Zapp's. They started a little after ten o'clock in the morning. Rivera was a little surprised when it took them only three hours to find them; or that they found them at all.

After several false alarms — it seemed that half the people in St. Paul drove oversized SUVs — and a stop for a quick lunch and to fill up the car's gas tank, they spotted the Tahoe sitting down a driveway, tight between two aging white houses.

"There it is," Rivera said suddenly. Martínez looked that way, and saw the truck. "There. Keep going, keep driving . . . Yes, Texas plates." He was sweating with excitement. "Go to the corner."

"What are you going to do?"

"Look in the window," Rivera said. "See what is what."

"Crazy," Martínez said. "David, don't do this."

"You sound like an American, like Shaffer," Rivera said. "Pull over, pull over."

She pulled over and Rivera jacked a round into the chamber of the single-action pistol, and said, "When you see me look at the window, call Lucas. Do not call before you see me look in."

"David, please, please don't do this. Let me call the police. You watch them. I will call —"

"I won't be made a fool. I will look before we call. I'll know that I am right."

"All you will do is look in?"

"The situation could develop," Rivera said. "Be ready."

"Ah, no, David . . ." She grabbed his jacket sleeve. "Don't go, don't go —"

"Call Lucas when you see me look in," Rivera said again, and he hopped out. She watched him down the street, a stout man with a dark face behind his sunglasses, his street-side hand under his jacket. He walked right past the house, only glancing at it, but she shook her head. He did not look like a pedestrian: he looked like a cop giving the place the once-over.

Rivera's heart was pounding like a trip hammer. He gave the house what he thought was a casual glance, went on by. The house was small, shabby, probably built after World War II. He'd seen houses like it in eastern California, in Riverside, in parts of San Diego, and down the coast in Baja.

The house would probably have a living room in the front, he thought, with a hall at one side leading back to a kitchen, a utility room, and a side door. A hall on the other side of the living room would lead back to two bedrooms and a single bath. There'd be a stairway leading to an attic, or a converted third bedroom, under the roof.

A large window looked out at the street from the left side of the front door, and a smaller one from the right. The window on the left had drapes, with a two-inch gap between them. The gap was dark, but there could have been somebody standing back, watching him. The window on the right had venetian blinds, fully lowered. He continued down the block, then came back in a hurry, walking across the lawns of the adjacent houses, close to the front of houses, the gun now in his hand.

He came into the house on the side with the venetian blind, and clambered up the concrete stoop. There was a small head-height window in the front door, and the door looked weak. He stood beside the door, unmoving, listening.

He heard laughter, and the sounds of a video game, not far behind the door. They were probably sitting on a couch in the living room, he thought. At least two, but from the jumble of voices, he thought probably three.

And the door looked *really* weak — dry rot in the wood, flaking paint. He risked a peek at the door window, just his left eye, drifting slowly across a corner of the glass. There was no entryway: the door opened directly on the living room, and he could see one man, and the shoulder of another, on the couch. The man he could see had a game remote in his hand and was looking to his right, at what must have been the TV. Then a third man, just his arm and shoulder, came into view, for a second or two. He was also watching the game. Two of the faces were from the mug shots.

He had them.

He turned and looked at the car, and saw Martínez looking at him. He put his hand to his ear, gesturing "phone," and she waved, a flash of her hand.

Rivera got his guts together, stood back, took a deep breath. He'd done this before. He was a large man, and strong, and he could kick like a horse.

With one quick move, he shifted back on his right foot, lifted his left, and kicked the door as hard as he could, two inches from the knob. The door exploded open and he was inside, behind the muzzle of the gun.

Inside was chaos, three men scrambling off the couch, a game console and cables and a bag of Cheetos flying, and Rivera screamed at them in Spanish, "Stop! Stop or I'll kill you! Stop!"

One of the men didn't stop: Dos had a gun on the back of the couch, and quick as a snake, he reached over for it and got his hand on it and started to swing back to Rivera, but he did it too fast and fumbled the pistol and it went up in the air and landed on the rug with a thump.

They all froze, looked first at the gun and then at Rivera, and Rivera said to Dos, "Too bad for you," and shot him twice in the heart. To the others: "Raise your hands."

Uno and Tres raised their hands, and Rivera heard footsteps behind him and saw Martínez coming and called, "Did you call . . . ?"

Martínez came up close behind and took a small revolver out of her purse and put it one inch behind Rivera's skull and pulled the trigger. The slug blew through the back of his head and emerged at the forehead and Rivera went down, dead as Dos.

Uno and Tres stood, hands still up,

stunned, and Martínez said, "You have one-half minute. Get all the guns and money you have, get the telephones, leave everything else, run out to the car and go. Find a motel, not the Wee Blue Inn, the police have been there. Check into a motel, put the guns inside, and your suitcases, and then abandon the car. I will find you one hour to do this. Call the Big Voice and he will tell you where to go after that, will tell you where to get a new car. Tell Big Voice that I will call tonight. Now run, children. RUN."

They were out of the house in thirty seconds, never looking at Dos's body, or Rivera's. As they went out the back door, she handed them the revolver and said, "Take this. Throw it where they'll never find it. A river." They took the revolver, threw the bag of guns in the back of the truck, along with their suitcases, backed out of the drive, and were gone.

Martínez took ten seconds, gathering herself, looked at Rivera, and said, "You idiot." If he'd called for backup, she would have found time to step away, to call the Big Voice to warn the children, to get them out. She shook her head, then turned and ran screaming out the front door, half fell down the steps, went down on the sidewalk, skinning her hands, ricocheted down the empty street. She landed a bit sideways on one of her heels and lost the shoe and let it go, and got on the cell phone and called Lucas and when he answered, screamed, "Help us. David is shot David is shot help us . . ."

Lucas was working the computer when the call came in, and he listened astonished to the screaming and then shouted at her, "Where? Where are you? Where?"

"I don't know, near the pizza, near the pizza . . ."

"Look for a street sign," he shouted. "Find a green sign at the end of a block."

She called back a minute later, "Marshall and Kent."

"I'm coming," Lucas said. He punched in 911 and shouted at the man who answered, "Davenport, BCA. We've got a cop down at Marshall and Kent in St. Paul. There's a woman there who was with him. Look for the woman. Tell everybody to be careful, there's three men with guns."

And he was running down the hall, the people in the offices around him looking after him because he was running like something very bad had happened.

8

The first St. Paul cop car got to the shooting scene in three minutes. Morris had been organizing the search of the streets around Zapp's Pizza, which had been going slowly, but it also meant that a dozen additional cops arrived in the next five minutes.

The first cops gathered up Martínez and locked her in their car, and posted watchers on the corners of the house, nobody going in or out. Martínez, apparently in shock, told them she thought the house was empty and she didn't know how badly Rivera was hurt, so the next cops went in and cleared the place.

One came out a minute later and told an arriving patrol sergeant, "Two down. Both of them are gone."

"You sure?"

"Oh, yeah. One of them's missing most of his brain. The other one took two shots in the heart."

"No sign of anybody?"

"Didn't clear the basement, but I think it's empty. I didn't recognize either of them, but one could be a cop. He's gotta be federal or something. Doesn't look local. He was shooting some big old automatic like you don't see anymore."

The sergeant nodded and saw Morris's car fishtail into the street. "Here comes the man. You get Rudy and block off the street."

The cop took off and then Morris was there. He nodded at the sergeant and walked up the steps, took a look at Rivera and said, "Shit. I was just talking to this guy."

"He's a cop?"

Morris nodded. He might have been Mexican, but a dead cop was a dead cop. The dead man in the dumpster was just another dead man in a dumpster.

Morris walked back outside and saw Davenport's Porsche curl into the curb up the street. Davenport jumped out and jogged toward them.

"He got here in a hurry," the sergeant said.

"He's gonna kill somebody," Morris said.

Lucas dumped the Porsche and jogged through the scene, past clusters of neighbors watching from the sidewalks. Morris was talking to a couple of other cops, and he waved Lucas toward the front door of the house, which stood open.

Lucas stepped up, looked inside, said, "Ah, man." He stepped inside, moved carefully around the body, squatted to look at it: Rivera was facedown, his brown eyes still open, but flat and dead. A pistol sat a few inches from his right hand, the hammer back, the safety off.

Across the room, a Mexican guy slumped half-on, half-off the couch, looking dead. Lucas had read of shooting victims looking surprised, but he hadn't seen that. They just looked dead. The Mexican's T-shirt was stained with blood, a circle at the heart with seepage lines down the front.

"Looks like he kicked the door," Morris said.

Lucas stood up, made a hand-dusting motion, glanced at the door handle, then looked back in the room. "Did you talk to Martínez?"

"For a minute, but she's fucked up. We're looking for a silver SUV of some kind. Don't know what kind, don't know the size, don't know the plates."

"Good luck with that," Lucas said.

"Yeah." Morris waved at the scene. "What do you think?"

"Looks like he kicked the door, landed on his feet, the guy on the couch pulled a gun and he shot him." Lucas looked at the front drapes. "I wouldn't be surprised if he made a little noise, a sound, coming up the steps. Another guy steps over to the window, to look, he's got a gun in his hand. . . ."

Morris nodded. "Rivera kicks the door, lands inside looking at the couch, the guy on the couch goes for his gun, Rivera shoots him, never sees it coming from the guy at the window. I'd buy that."

"The question is," Lucas said, "where are those fuckers now?"

"Not too far away. This only happened fifteen minutes ago."

Lucas looked around the living room. "We need to find out who owns this place and grab him. If we get to him quick enough, he might not know what happened."

Morris said, "We probably can't screw the scene up too much — we know what happened. There could be something that would tell us everything we need."

"So we'll walk easy," Lucas said.

The house seemed to be lightly lived-in — not much in the way of personal stuff, but on the kitchen counter they found a basket full of paid utility bills, which had been sent to a Ricardo Nuñez, and in the bedroom, a box of business cards, half of them in English, half in Spanish. Under Nuñez's name was a business name, "International ReCap, Inc." with a phone number, but no address.

Lucas called his researcher, Sandy, at home, told her he needed her to work despite the fact that she'd planned to go to a flea market that morning. He gave her the information he had about the house and said, "We need to know where International ReCap is, and what it does, and we need to get our hands on Nuñez."

"Sounds like some kind of finance company, International ReCapitalization, or something like that," she said. "I'll get back to you."

"Quick as you can," he said.

Lucas said to Morris, "Let's go talk to Martínez."

The neighboring house had a small covered porch, with two chairs behind a banister. Nobody home. Morris and Lucas took Martínez up onto the porch and sat her down, and Lucas leaned back against the banister: "You okay?"

"No, I'm not," Martínez said, though she looked fairly composed, sitting with her hands in her lap. No tears.

"I was under the . . . impression . . . that you and David had a personal relationship," Lucas said.

She nodded, and now Lucas saw the crystalline glimmer of a tear. "I hope this does not become official. He is married, he has four children."

Morris, in the chair to her right, said quietly, "Do you remember anything else about the vehicle?"

She shook her head. "No. A silver truck. David knew something more about it, I think, he didn't say anything to me. When he got out, he wasn't sure it was right . . . so he peeked in the window. I was parked there" — she pointed down the street to the car — "and I heard the gunshots and I got out. I was going to call . . ." She pointed at Lucas.

"Okay," Lucas said.

"I didn't know what happened inside, but I thought David probably succeeded. He was a, mmm, not devil, that's not right, I don't know the English, a daring devil . . ."

"Daredevil," Morris said.

"Yes. A daring devil. He has done this before. He is very proud of this, of taking down these Criminales. He calls it the American phrase, *going in hard,* from some

213

movie, I do not know which."

"That's when you called?"

"No, I heard shouting. . . . It didn't sound like David. I don't have a gun, I don't shoot, but I started to walk that way, and then I started to run, and I went to the steps and I saw him lying there, his shoes, anyway, and I knew it was him, he wears those white stockings, and I went up the steps and then the men ran out the back door, I think, and I heard the truck start and I ran up the steps so they couldn't see me, because I'm afraid they will . . . kill me . . . and David is there and I see he is dead and the car goes past the door, fast, and I run outside, I fell down."

She turned her wrists toward them, showing them the bloody scrapes. "And I tried to call you, but I couldn't push the button right. . . ." She brought her purse with her, like women do, unconscious of it, but always with them, and she dug inside and produced a cell phone. "The fuckin' telephone, this is a piece of shit, this telephone, this, this, Samsung shit . . ."

She stood suddenly and pitched the phone into the street, where it clattered across the blacktop, and she said to Lucas, "He is gone. I was waiting for this. I rehearsed this, sitting talking to the investigators, saying,

'David is gone.' " "

They worked through the details. Halfway through, she began to sob, and asked where they could find a bathroom. She didn't want to go back in the death house, so they walked her down to a neighbor's place, and asked, and the neighbor said she'd be welcome to use the bathroom.

She was in there for ten minutes, and Morris said, "Jesus, wonder what's going on in there."

"Crying out of sight," Lucas said. "She's got her pride."

When she finally came back out, they went back to the porch and walked her through the details: how they'd found the shooters' car, the meeting the night before. She said Rivera had gotten some information about the shooters' car from his friends, but she didn't know exactly what that information was.

"But he didn't tell you?" Lucas asked.

"He might have told me, but I don't remember. The name, I don't remember — but he said it was a silver SUV, and it was. I don't know cars. My job was to drive slowly up the streets, and his job was to look for the car."

"Why didn't he tell us?" Lucas asked.

She shrugged. "He might have told *you,* but this Shaffer . . . Shaffer runs this investigation, and David does not like how he is treated, like he is a stupid brown man up here in the white state. You know what I mean?"

"I got a small feel for that," said Morris.

"Yes, a Negro, yes, I suppose," she said, unself-consciously. "So this is how he is treated, and he told me that when he learned about the truck, and then this morning, with the Zapp's place . . . he thought they must be close, and that if we drove around . . ."

"You found them," Lucas said.

"It took a long time," she said. "Three hours."

"Hell of a lot better than we did," Morris said. "We hardly got started in three hours."

Morris's partner showed up, and leaned against the banister with Lucas, and they walked through it all over again. When they were finished, Morris and Lucas walked off a bit and Morris said, "You know what the British say, this 'fuck-all' thing that they say? 'You don't know fuck-all about whatever'?"

"Sure," Lucas said.

Morris looked back at Martínez sitting on the porch, still talking with his partner.

"That's what we got from her," he said. "We got fuck-all."

"I'm gonna go find this Latino guy he talked to last night," Lucas said. "You want to come?"

"Let me talk to Larry, I'll be right with you," Morris said. Larry was his partner. While Morris was doing that, Lucas went back up the porch steps and looked at Rivera's body. Martínez said he'd done this before, but Lucas thought that it didn't look like he'd done it before. Why he thought that, he couldn't say: but he thought it.

He walked back out to Martínez and said, "We have to notify the Mexican police. Can you do that informally, and then we could follow up? We need to know the official contact. Preferably somebody who speaks English."

She nodded: "I will arrange that."

And he asked, "Did David bring that pistol with him? On the plane?"

She shook her head. "No, he got it last night. If he hadn't gotten it, he would be alive now."

She'd driven to the meeting the night before, and the address was still on the car's GPS. Lucas took it down and then said, "I'm sorry. I'm really, really sorry."

Red-eyed, she started snuffling into another Kleenex, and he went to get Morris.

Morris drove a city sedan so bland that Lucas could barely see it, even when he was sitting inside it.

"Better than the death trap you're driving around in," Morris said.

Tomas Garza lived south of downtown St. Paul, just off one of the main commercial streets, amid a clutter of food, shoe, and auto franchises, mom-and-pop restaurants, carpet stores, remodeling contractors, and a couple of big box stores and supermarkets.

He wasn't home, but his wife was, and worried when they showed her their IDs. "He is gone. I don't know when he'll be back," she said.

"We don't have anything to do with immigration," Lucas said. "We need to talk to him about David Rivera. We need to talk to him right away."

Morris played the bad guy: "If we don't find him right away, we'll have to ask the immigration people to get involved. They've got more sources than we do."

Her face went blank, and Lucas added hastily, "We don't want to do that. Rivera was hurt. We need to find out what was said at the meeting last night. Miz Martínez is cooperating with us, she's back . . . uh . . . ."

"How bad hurt?" she asked.

"Ah, he's dead, Miz Garza. He was shot to death an hour or so ago, when he found these bandits who murdered the family over in Wayzata."

She put a hand to her face: "He is dead? He was just here."

"We know, Miz Martínez told us," Lucas said. "That's why we need to talk to Tomas. Somebody last night told him the kind of car and maybe the license plate numbers of the bandits. . . . We desperately need that information."

She said, "Nobody knew the license plate numbers. But it was a silver Chevrolet Tahoe with Texas license plates, and they thought it was a rental car. This came from somebody else — not Tomas. I don't know who."

"I'm going to call that in," Morris said.

"Let me do it," Lucas said. "My researcher's looking for that Nuñez guy. She can switch over to this. She'll have it for us in twenty minutes."

Morris nodded and went back to Garza: "We still need to talk to your husband."

"He works very hard for his family," she said.

"We really don't care about his status,"

Morris said. "We really don't."

"He works at Europa Car," she said.

Lucas got on the phone and called his office, got switched to Sandy, and told her what he needed. "How long?"

"Not too," she said. "Fifteen minutes. Half an hour."

"Fifteen minutes," he said. "The shooters may still be in the car. Push Nuñez."

"I can't push both of them," she said.

"Sure you can."

Europa Car was a repair shop a half-mile down the street, a bunch of older BMWs, Mercedeses, and an ancient Porsche, covered with gray primer paint, in its parking lot, which was surrounded by a chain-link fence with concertina wire on top.

Garza was sitting in the outer office, nervously smoking a cigarette, when they arrived: his wife had called, and he'd decided to talk.

"We know the Tahoe and the Texas plates. What else?"

Garza took them through the meeting, didn't mention the gun until Lucas asked. He looked away, then back and said, "David said you treated him like a child. This is a man who'd been fighting the gangs in a way you Americans just don't know. You have nothing like this, except, maybe Afghanistan."

Lucas and Morris looked at him, but he turned away again, and Lucas decided, what the hell, and said, "Okay. He needed the weapon. I'll buy that."

"If anybody pushes it, it could be a problem, later on," Morris said. "I'm not saying it will be, but it could be."

"Whatever," Garza said, in what was almost a valley accent.

They talked for a few more minutes, then Sandy called back and said, "There's a silver Tahoe out on the road from El Paso, been gone a week, to a man named Simon Perez, who showed a Texas driver's license and credit card. It looked good, so I called this Perez in El Paso, and he answered and he says he doesn't know anything about a car rental. Says he's never rented a Hertz in his whole life."

"That's it," Lucas said. "Put that out to every agency in the state, the description and the plate, and get the highway patrol looking down the interstates. They might be running for home. Tell everybody for God's sakes be careful: they've now killed six people that we know about, and another two or three won't make any difference to them. Put an alert out on that credit card. I want to know where and when they use it."

"I'll do that. About that International Re-Cap — I'm not sure, but I think it's a tire place. They buy used tires here in the U.S., recap them, and ship them south, across the border."

"Where's their headquarters?"

"Brownsville, Texas."

"Call them up and find out about Nuñez — where he might be."

"I did that, but I got a woman who says she's an answering service," Sandy said. "She can take messages, but that's all she does. She won't give me Nuñez's phone number."

"So call the Brownsville cops, have them drop in and ask her. Those places don't like cop trouble."

"I'll try," Sandy said.

Lucas went back to Morris and told him about the car: "All right. Now we're getting some traction," Morris said. "They're either riding in a car we know, or they're walking around with a bunch of suitcases."

"No traction on Nuñez," Lucas said.

He explained, and then they said good-bye to Garza — told him to stay away from street guns — and headed back to the crime scene. On the way, Lucas took a call from the BCA duty officer who said he had a Mexican cop on the line. "He says he's Rivera's boss. You want the call?"

"Yeah, give him the number," Lucas said.

The phone rang again a minute later. A Comisario General Jorge Espinoza, a secretary said, and Espinoza came on a minute later. "David is gone, I'm told."

"I'm afraid so," Lucas said. "He located the shooters in our case, and he went after them himself. He shot one of them, but was shot himself. The shooters are running, and we're trying to track them."

"I can give you a probable car and license plate number for them," Espinoza said. "David called in to our office last night and asked us to trace a late-model Chevrolet Tahoe with Texas license plates. We were waiting to call the information to him, but then we could not reach him this morning. . . ."

Lucas took down the information, which matched the information he'd gotten from Sandy; and that made Lucas feel that Espinoza could be trusted, to some extent. He gave Espinoza the details of the investigation, including the discovery of the pizza napkin, and told him how Rivera and Martínez had used the car information to track the killers.

"This is typical: I have told him at least one hundred times that someday he would be killed kicking down doors like this. He did it anyway. I think he got some kind of pleasure from it, going in with a gun, naked, so to speak."

"So he's done it a lot," Lucas said, thinking again of Rivera's body.

"More than anybody else," Espinoza said. "Ah, David, this is so stupid. So stupid, to get killed like this. . . ."

Back at the Nuñez house, the St. Paul crime-scene people were at work. Martínez was still sitting on the porch of the house next door, but when she saw Lucas and Morris arrive, she came down and asked, "Did you find them?"

"Got the plates and make and model," Lucas said. "We're looking for them now. Couldn't find Nuñez, but we found his answering service in Brownsville. We're going to ask the Brownsville cops to check for a cell number. That should give us his location."

She nodded, then said, "I'm going back to my room, if you don't need me."

"I'll drop you," Lucas said.

224

She shook her head: "No. You stay here and do what you do. I have a taxi on the way."

"What a day," Lucas said. "What a sad day. I'm sorry for David and for you. So sorry."

9

Uno and Tres were freaked, not so much about the death of Dos — that was going to happen, sooner or later, to all of them, and probably sooner than later, part of the business — as the *morra* who shot him. She'd done it as well as either of them might have, had come out of nowhere, like a vision behind the muzzle blast of the Federale, when they'd been caught cold, and Dos had been shot. . . .

She'd known the Big Voice and they'd said to each other, as they sped away, heading for the Rosedale mall, their bailout site, "The Big Voice is everywhere. Did you see this *morra* with the baby gun, she goes *boom . . .*"

She'd given them one hour to get rid of the car. That wouldn't be a problem, they'd worked it out in advance. *But did you see her with the baby gun . . . ?*

At the mall they found a space in a thickly

occupied corner of the parking lot between Macy's and JCPenney. They had a box of Handi Wipes and used them to wipe the plastic surfaces of the car, everything they could reach, although they knew there'd probably be a few prints remaining when they finished. Still, no reason to make it easy for the gringo cops.

When they finished, they got out and began wiping the exterior door handles and under the back hatch release; that done, they got back in the car and turned it on, and found a radio station that played Mexican music and sat and waited.

They'd taken less than fifteen minutes to drive to the mall, and they'd waited almost another fifteen, passing on a number of shoppers who came and went, until Uno said, "There. That one."

Ferat Chakkour came out of the shopping center twirling his car keys on his index finger. He worked in one of the Rosedale kiosks, selling oversized soft pretzels, for which he made seven dollars an hour. Which was okay. The job brought in extra money, on top of money sent by his parents back in Egypt, while he studied advertising and business management at Metro State.

He was a happy enough young man until

he stepped around the corner of his four-year-old Subaru and popped the door. Immediately, a thin young brown-skinned man was behind him, with a handgun, and he said, with a Latino accent, "Give me the keys."

Then another brown-skinned man came around the nose of the car and said, "The keys," and he also had a gun.

Chakkour handed over the keys and said, "Let me go," but the smaller of the two men backed away from him and said, "Get in the backseat. We will let you go, but we need your car for a while. Get in or I will shoot."

Chakkour got in without a struggle: for one thing, he hoped he might get the car back.

Once in the car, Tres told him to slide across, then Tres got in beside him with the handgun pointed at Chakkour's stomach.

Uno got the bags from the Tahoe, threw them in the trunk of the Subaru, and they headed out of the parking lot and onto I-35W north. Chakkour began pleading: "Don't hurt me. I'm like you, I come from another country, I come from Egypt, my family sent me here to work to get an education. . . . I'm brown like you, we're brothers. . . ."

Tres laughed and said, "I think you are

228

even browner. But you are like a terrorist, huh? Like an Arab terrorist."

Chakkour picked up on the joke and got the two Mexicans talking, and twenty miles north, they took an exit, chosen just at random, drove four miles and then took a side road, and another mile, and another side road. No houses around. Uno stopped and said, "We leave you here. When you walk to a house, you don't tell anybody who took you. We need one hour. One hour, and you never see us again."

"Okay. Okay."

Tres got out first, and Chakkour scrambled out after him and moved to the side of the road. Tres said, "Good-bye," and shot Chakkour in the heart, and when he'd fallen, put a shot in his head.

Some red-winged blackbirds startled out of a cattail swamp in the ditch and flew away, but the Mexicans could see or hear nothing else but the breeze; this was in the best part of Minnesota's August, with the roadsides turning golden brown, and the wind carrying the scent of ripening grain.

"In the weeds," Uno said, getting out of the car.

They took Chakkour's wallet, with his driver's license, then picked him up by the hands and feet and threw him back into a tall stand of reeds. The body disappeared as effectively as if it'd been thrown into quicksand.

"So. We have a car. Now we need a house," Uno said. "We need to talk to Big Voice."

They got back in the car and turned around and headed back out toward the interstate. On the way, Uno looked at the photo on Chakkour's driver's license. "He's the right age, the picture, it could almost be me."

"We are all brown together," Tres said, and then he giggled. "All brown brothers."

"What a moron," Uno said in English. Then back to Spanish: "Brown brothers."

At the hotel, Martínez went first to Rivera's room, for which he'd given her a key. She knew the St. Paul police would eventually show up, so she went quickly to his suitcase, opened it, pulled up a seam at the bottom, and slipped out an envelope. She thumbed the flap on the envelope, saw the sheath of fifty- and hundred-dollar bills, and put it in her purse. Moving to the closet, she checked his suits, then his shoes, for a second envelope. She eventually found it in a bundle of dirty underwear. Altogether, six thousand dollars.

In her own room, she stashed the money, then undressed, except for her underpants, and pulled on a man's T-shirt, which she used as a nightgown. Then she lay on the floor, her hands at her sides, her eyes closed, in a yoga position called the Corpse Pose. The pose was useful for eliminating tension. Breathing through her nose only, willing her breathing to slow, and then her mind, then letting go even of her will, she felt herself clearing. . . .

Martínez had been born in the same kind of village that had given birth to Uno, Dos, and Tres. She had no more hope than they had, no more possibilities, but something primal, something in her soul, kept her going to school when most everybody else had given up. She learned very early, though, that while she was smarter than most men, men were stronger.

That was a very simple equation where she came from: you could be a young Einstein, but that wouldn't keep you from getting beaten bloody, or worse, if you said something unwise to the wrong narco. She learned to keep her head down.

When her father went to the U.S. to work, her mother moved them to a slum in Ciudad Juárez. Drugs were everywhere, and gangs.

She got back into school, drawn by one belief: that if you could graduate, you would "have it made." She worked, kept her head down, a pretty young woman who was raped one Friday night by a low-ranking narco named Bueno Suerte, and then, for a while, was passed around the gang, beaten regularly, raped even more often.

Still, she was good at math, at numbers, at bookkeeping, and a year before she graduated, went to work as an accountant of sorts, for a mid-level marijuana exporter, a fat man named Chanos. While Chanos raped her occasionally, he protected her from anyone of lower rank. Sometime after she started with Chanos, she confessed to Bueno Suerte that she desperately missed his attentions. She would like to slip back in his bed, but if Chanos or anybody else found out . . .

Bueno Suerte was transfixed by the possibility of putting the horns on Chanos, and they conspired to meet one night when Chanos was traveling. She went to Bueno Suerte's bed, and when he was done with her, and asleep, she took a hammer out of her purse and smashed his head with it. She was told later that someone had hit the boy twenty or thirty times with a pipe, or something, and that his head had looked like a pizza. She didn't remember hitting him that often, but she did remember how purely wonderful it felt, as she did it.

She stayed with Chanos, and did well enough that the narco had a word with the school principal, and when graduation day came, she walked across the stage with the few of her schoolmates who'd gotten that far, and got the precious paper.

Later that year, Chanos committed suicide by cutting off his own head and putting it on his chest, and she was inherited by the new boss. Seven years later, when she was twenty-five, a narco named Cabeza de Madera, a member of the Criminales, suggested that she might have another potential. She listened to his suggestion and applied for a job as a clerk with the Federales. The skids had been greased, and she got the job, a short, quiet, pretty, head-down young woman.

Two years after that, at the suggestion of the Big Voice — Cabeza de Madera had had an unfortunate encounter with *un bate de béisbol* — she took some law enforcement courses, learned to shoot a pistol, and became, in name only, a policewoman. In reality, she was a secretary and a book-keeper, paid a little better than the other female secretaries and bookkeepers.

She'd become a person of some value to the narcos, a chunky, humble, almost unnoticeable spy at the center of a Federale headquarters. And she continued taking classes, increasing her value to the Federales. She moved into a decent apartment, went to better restaurants, even signed up at a health club, where she did the stair-climber, became an exerciser-dancer, and went to yoga classes.

All of this taught her one great lesson: money was everything. *Everything.* Safety, privilege, a roof over your head, good clothes, decent food.

With the payments from the Criminales, she could even have afforded a car, although she wasn't allowed to buy one — her Federale pay wouldn't support it, and the purchase of a car might be looked upon with suspicion. Still, she took driving lessons and was eventually approved to drive government cars.

And one day, the Big Voice said to her, "There is an inspector, named Rivera. You know him. He is an unhappy man, we hear, with a loveless marriage. . . ."

She allowed herself to be seduced. The sex meant nothing to her — she'd become numb to it as a teenager. Rivera, as it turned out, was an intelligent man, but harsh, and sometimes foolish. He deluded himself into believing that she loved him, or at least regarded him with great fondness. In fact, she disliked him, and that feeling grew over the years.

She had no trouble concealing that from Rivera. He believed, with great certainty, that women admired him without reservation. By the time she killed him, she was very, very tired of Rivera's whole act.

In her room, Martínez sat up and let her eyes and mind readjust to the world. Five minutes later, she was reporting to the Big Voice. He said, "I will talk with the others. We did not see this possibility, though the death of Rivera had been expected for some time. But not by our hand."

"A decision was required," Martínez said. "I felt for some time that I was coming to the end with David. He had much guilt about me, and about his wife."

"If it was going to end, then, better to have saved the children," Big Voice said. "So: we will consult, and I will call back."

When she hung up, she worried: Big Voice had not been approving. Had, in fact, seemed a bit chilly. Had she miscalculated? She had felt that she was coming to an end with Rivera. Was she coming to an end with the Criminales, as well?

Ivan Turicek drove to St. Paul, turned north on I-35E, then exited to an office that he'd rented in St. Paul under a phony name. He'd been willing to do that because he never expected to see the landlord a second time, and he planned to sterilize the place when he left it. It was a package drop, pure and simple. A dozen deliveries were coming that morning, another dozen in the afternoon.

There'd been no questions at the bank, nobody snooping around, but the cops were moving. Kristina had friends at Polaris, and on Friday afternoon had arranged to bump into them at their regular lunch spot, sat with them, and all the talk was of accountants looking at the computer system.

So the cops had gotten that far. Taking the step to Hennepin would be difficult, but not impossible. In the meantime, the gold harvest was under way.

The instructions on the FedEx boxes simply said to leave the boxes outside the door if there was no answer. There'd be no answer, but Turicek would be waiting behind the door for the FedEx man to leave. Four of the boxes were coming in First Overnight, eight more Priority Overnight.

Twelve more should arrive in the afternoon on Standard Overnight, Saturday delivery. Albitis was shipping them with a variety of priorities, hoping that they'd be delivered by different FedEx men, in separate vans, to confuse the issue of how many boxes were suddenly arriving at a place that had never before gotten any. None of them would require a signature.

Turicek was moving early in the day because he didn't know where he'd fall on the FedEx delivery list. At the office complex, he parked in the lot, down a bit from the office, and spent a few minutes watching. The only activity was at a carpet place, where a couple of people came and went. Turicek sighed, got out of the car with his briefcase, and walked over to the office and let himself in. Waiting for the handcuffs, but they never came.

The office smelled like carpet cleaner and contained a cheap wooden desk, three inexpensive chairs, an old computer with a keyboard that Turicek got at a rehab store, and a TV set that sat on a built-in bookcase shelf. Whiteboards hung on two walls, with phony scrawled appointments they changed every time somebody was able to stop by.

That was usually at night to avoid contact with other tenants.

There was no telephone.

Turicek locked the door, pulled on a pair of cotton gloves, and took a seat at the computer. The computer contained no files, but it was hooked into the Internet, paid through the same dead-end account that paid the condo rent. Turicek signed on and began looking for news on the murders in Wayzata: there was a lot of it, but everything he found he'd already seen. The cops were still focusing on Sunnie Software.

Killing time . . .

The first spate of the FedEx packages arrived an hour later. Turicek had been pacing back and forth between the front window blinds and the computer, saw the truck pull in. The driver knocked, perfunctorily, and started dropping the packages outside the door. He made two trips, and when he put his truck in gear after the last one, Turicek opened the door and scooped up the packages.

The biggest of the boxes looked like it might contain books, but was too light — it was a cube eighteen inches or so on each side, and weighed 9.6 pounds, according to the label. Everybody knew that gold was heavy, so they wanted boxes that felt light. Turicek took a box cutter out of his pocket and slashed the box open. Inside were wads of newspaper — the *Los Angeles Times* — and six rolls of American Eagle gold coins wrapped in flexible plastic tubes, taped on the ends.

He shook the coins out of one of the taped tubes onto the desktop. Twenty coins in each roll, each an ounce of gold, one hundred twenty coins in all. That morning, each coin was worth about sixteen hundred dollars. Together, they were worth a little less than $200,000, give or take.

He looked at the coins for a moment, thinking how useless and ridiculous gold was, except for the two things it did. The first was to store value, the second was to look good around the necks of rich women. In some places, as in the Middle East and India, both of those things. He picked up one of the coins, carried it to the window, and looked at it in a pencil-thin beam of light. The gold shimmered, and the eagle looked alive. He shook his head and began opening the other packages.

In the course of the morning, the rest of the packages showed up in a second delivery. Twelve in all, with a hundred to a hundred and fifty coins in each.

All together, by the end of the morning, he had two and a half million dollars in gold in the car, repacked into the three smallest of the delivery boxes — almost a hundred pounds in all.

Not enough: it was coming in too slowly. If the cops had gotten to Polaris, they'd eventually track the cash into the buying accounts. But they'd have a way to go before they could do that — a lot of wire transfers in and out of Cayman Island banks, and then back to the U.S. That would take some time. Turicek was sure they had another two days, but after that . . .

Turicek was hypersensitive about surveillance, and so when he called Albitis, he called her on a disposable phone. She answered on the same kind of phone, standing outside a gold shop in Duarte, California.

She said, "Yes?" and Turicek asked, "How's it going?"

"Fast, but risky. I committed fifty thousand to Clark Lewis at Venice City and he tried to bullshit me a little. He's getting curious. I put him off by saying my folks in Syria were moving money," she said.

"I like that. I like the Syria story," Turicek said.

"So do I. Lots of people trying to get their money out of Syria," Albitis said. "Did you get today's deliveries?"

"Yeah, the morning boxes are all here. We're at what, nineteen?"

"A little more than that," Albitis said. "We'll be close to the end. It'll take another three days to get the last of it. As soon as I've arranged the Vegas wires, I'm flying to New York, and I should put the rest of the money down in New York, New Jersey, and Philadelphia. Then I'm back to Vegas for the pickup and ship, and then back to New York for the pickup there. How are we doing on time? Have you heard anything?"

"Yeah, and it's not good. The cops are at Polaris," Turicek said. "You've got to hurry."

"I'm hurrying — I'm hurrying," she said. "We're doing it way too fast as it is. I'm getting scared. You gotta tell me if anything happens. I don't want to ditch three million, but I'll do it if it means we don't get busted."

"Absolutely. I will tell you the instant I hear," Turicek said.

"And, Ivan — don't run on me. I know you're thinking about it, but honest to God, if you dump me, I'll tell the fuckin' Vory that you've got twenty million in gold and no protection. They'll cut you up like fish bait."

"I'm not running —"

"But you've thought about it," Albitis said.

"I thought about it, but I'm not running," Turicek admitted. "I've done the numbers, and I wouldn't make it."

"That's right: you wouldn't," Albitis said. "So keep talking to me. Call me every hour."

"I'll call you . . . but I'll tell you, you'd be less frightened if you could see the gold we've got here, all together," Turicek said. "I've never seen anything like this. Sixteen hundred dollars for every single coin, and we've got a river of them. It's like a pile of oyster shells."

"Sixteen-twelve an hour ago," Albitis said. "And going nowhere but up. I'm moving as fast as I can."

"Keep moving," Turicek said. "Keep it coming."

Lucas sat outside the Nuñez house, watching Morris direct traffic, until the medical examiner's people moved Rivera's body out. Sandy called to say that the Brownsville cops had come through, had jacked up the answering service for the ReCap guy. Nuñez was supposedly in Atlanta, Georgia, buying

242

old tires, but nobody answered his cell phone.

If he was a bad guy, Lucas thought, looking at his watch as he talked to Sandy, and if the shooters had called home, and if Nuñez had been tipped . . . He could already be in the air, on the way to Mexico.

"See if you can get a license tag for him. Call Atlanta, see if they can find him."

"I wouldn't hold my breath," she said. He could hear her typing on her keyboard. "Atlanta's got . . . uh, better'n five million people in the metro area."

"So we need to get lucky," Lucas said.

He had little faith in luck.

As Rivera's body was wheeled out of the house, strapped to a gurney, inside a black plastic body bag, the crime-scene boss walked over to say to Lucas and Morris, "We got something in the basement."

"Like what?" Morris asked.

"We think it's blood."

They followed him inside and down the stairs into what amounted to a hollow concrete cube with gray-painted walls. A furnace and water heater stood in one corner, with a stack of furnace filters and a circle of dusty hoses. The basement was almost too clean, particularly the floor.

"Bernie noticed how clean the floor was, so we started looking around. We think we've got blood here." He pointed at a dark speck on one of the walls. "And over here, on the water heater. You can see the color of it against the white."

Lucas squatted to look at the water heater. The spatters, if that's what they were, were small: smaller than a black ant, close to the size and color of a flea.

"Looks like blood to me," Lucas said. He looked at the opposite wall, which was eight or ten feet away. "If blood was getting spattered that far . . . I bet it was Pruess. I bet they brought him down here and went to work on him."

"We oughta know, ninety percent, in an hour or so," the crime-scene boss said.

"It was him," Lucas said. "Goddamnit, I'd like to get my hands on those little fuckers."

"We know that they're little?"

"That's what I was told," Lucas said. "Three of them. Two now."

"At least he got one," Morris said.

Lucas nodded but said, "One-for-one isn't the kind of ratio we want. We've really got to be careful with these guys."

Back upstairs, he looked at the entryway,

where Rivera had gone down, and shook his head. Something was nagging at him, but he couldn't quite put his finger on it. . . .

He was still trying to figure it out when Bone, the banker, called: "This ICE you sent over, she thinks she's found a back door into our computer system, but she's afraid it's booby-trapped."

"I'll be there," Lucas said.

He'd told Morris about the DEA accountants and the possibility of pulling information out of the bank computers, and Morris had asked to be kept current: "But I don't know shit about computers. I'll leave it to you guys."

So Lucas told him he was leaving, and why, and drove across town, in heavy afternoon traffic, and into Minneapolis's loop. He found a space in the bank's parking structure and took the elevator to the systems center. A guard took his ID, made a call, and let him in.

ICE was sitting on an office chair in one corner, with six regular employees scattered around the room, peering at oversized computer screens. Her feet were up on a desk. She was talking on her cell phone when Lucas walked in, said something in it, and rang off. "I heard about the Rivera guy," she said.

ICE was somewhere in her early thirties, slender, medium height with long legs, blond short-cut hair, tight but not spiky, and the finest pale Scandinavian complexion. Lucas had known her since she was seventeen or eighteen, a girl geek at what was then called the Institute of Technology at the University of Minnesota; he'd hired her to do some programming at his newly launched Davenport Simulations, the company that made him rich.

"A complete goddamn disaster," Lucas said, about Rivera. He pulled an office chair around to face her, and asked, "Where's Bone? And what'd you get?"

"He said he'd be down when you got here," she said. She turned back to her desk and tapped a few keys on a keyboard. The computer screen, which had been dark, came up, showing a palm-sized patch of neatly ranked numbers.

"Since you don't know anything about computers . . ."

"Though I sold my computer company for eighteen million bucks," Lucas said.

"Blind luck and perfect timing," ICE said. "But you never did know shit about computers, so what I'll say is, see this bunch of green gobbledygook right here?"

"Yeah."

"What that is, is the beginning of a little programmer's doily, which, among other things, I think, would allow somebody to call in from the outside and take control of a computer. When he comes in, he's automatically got root, so he can start moving money around. There are lots of alarms, and when he started messing with money, they should have gone off. So I think they were turned off for this one account."

"You keep saying 'I think.' Is this for sure?"

She shook her head. "I'm pretty sure, but the only way to know for sure is to run the program and see what happens. . . . And there's some other stuff in here that looks like it might be parts of a booby trap. That's why I called it a programmer's doily — you pull on the wrong string, and the whole doily unravels, and you'll never figure it out."

From behind Lucas, Bone said, "The important points are, he had administrator's privileges, and he had to know enough about the security system to turn off the alarm."

Lucas swiveled around and, with a question mark in his voice, asked, "Pruess?"

"Not unless he took some serious programming classes somewhere, and then figured out how to get in from a remote terminal. I don't believe it — there's nothing on his record that would suggest that he knew anything about programming. He was a sales guy," Bone said.

"The programming here isn't particularly hard," ICE said. "There's a lot *of* it — finding this little knot was essentially a problem of finding a needle in a haystack — but the knot itself is pretty simple."

"To simplify all the techie bullshit," Lucas said, "you're telling me that somebody here set up this . . . doily . . . and then he could call in from the outside and loot the account."

"You're smarter than you look," ICE said.

"Thank you," Lucas said. "But what you've given us here, I could have figured out myself, eventually, even though I don't know anything about computers. We need you to give us some details, not this sort of, excuse me, generalized bullshit."

ICE turned her palms up and said, "We might need a warrant for that. The Bonester is seriously unhappy. He's dragging his feet."

Bone said, "Look, we'll get it done — but I can't have you setting off some logic bomb that's going to blow up the bank's accounts. I've got three hundred billion dollars in assets floating around in there. I need to know what's going to blow if you touch the wrong wire."

"You've got multiple redundancies —" ICE began.

"But there might be multiple bombs," Bone said. "What's the point of taking us down, if we go back online in ten minutes? If there's one bomb, there could be lots of them."

ICE stuck out a lip and tilted her head: "It's a thought."

Lucas asked ICE, "How long would it take you to evaluate the situation? In detail?"

"A day, maybe," she said. "Depends on how tangled up the knitting gets."

"Too long, too long," Lucas said. "They're killing people every day. You have to move faster."

Bone said to ICE, "No. No. If you gotta go slow, go slow. And I want my computer security people looking over your shoulder while you're doing it. I'm not bullshitting you two —"

Lucas interrupted: "Jim. People are being killed —"

Bone said, "Look. Lucas. Ol' buddy. If she touches off a string of bombs and brings down the bank, Wall Street dumps two thousand points and the economy goes into recession. You'd kill more people than a whole bunch of Mexican gangbangers."

Lucas grunted, a short laugh, and ICE put on her mildly amused look, but Bone wasn't laughing. He was snarling: "You think I'm joking? I'm not. This bank crashes, and the first thing everybody thinks is, 'Terrorists. Gotta get out.' And they run for the doors. Lucas, I'm not fucking you around here. Miz ICE is wearing a suicide vest, she just doesn't know it."

Lucas said, "All right." To ICE, "Fast as you can, without blowing anything up. These guys, they're crazy, and they're going to kill again."

"Gonna take a lot of high-priced speed," ICE said.

"I don't want to hear about it," Lucas said. "I just want to get it done."

10

That night, Weather and Letty sat around and talked about the murder of Rivera, and Lucas worried that he'd messed things up.

"I knew something was up with him. I knew he was running around talking to the Latino community, and I might have figured he'd go hunting them on his own. . . . I just couldn't imagine that he'd actually find them. I've been hung up on the horse shit gang. I wanted to get them, so I let him go. Now he's dead."

"You think you can know everything, but you can't. You think you can anticipate everything, but you can't," Weather said. "I didn't tell you my John Greene story, did I? What happened yesterday?"

"No." Greene was a friend of theirs, a cardiac surgeon.

"Yesterday morning, he takes a sixty-five-year-old guy into bypass surgery. Vietnam vet, this is down at the VA hospital. They've done a huge workup on the guy, everything is perfect, he's an excellent candidate, hasn't smoked in thirty years, a little overweight but not terrible, always had high cholesterol but he's gone on the reversal diet and he's bringing it down. . . . But he's having trouble breathing from all those years of eating pork chops. So it looks like if they do the operation, he's good for twenty or thirty years. They do the work, the op is fine . . . but his heart won't start. Nothing they can do — they try everything. Guy's dead."

"Jeez," Letty said, her face going white.

"Bad day," Lucas said, "But that doesn't have —"

"Sure it does," Weather said. "You can't know everything. You're walking through a fog, all the time. Even in situations where you think you know just about everything, like with John, something can go wrong. He's devastated, because he's the same kind of guy you are, a control freak. The patient had a nice wife and four kids, couple grandchildren . . . and he's dead. But it's not John's fault. Same with this Rivera. Shit happens. That's what everybody was telling John. He *knows* that, but he doesn't *feel* like that. You've got the same problem."

So he thought about it, and didn't sleep

well. Weather had planned a morning at the Minneapolis Institute of Art with Letty and Sam, and Lucas was invited, though he told them not to count on it. He slept through the phone when it rang early the next morning, but Weather, who was used to getting up early, picked it up, and then woke him by pulling on his big toe.

"What?" He was groggy, and pushed himself up.

She was still in her pajamas. "Your phone was buzzing, so I looked at it. It's Ingrid. She says she needs to talk to you." Weather held out his phone.

"Uhh . . ."

"Man, you sound like you're dead," ICE said.

"Just asleep. What happened?"

"You better come over here and interview a couple guys," ICE said.

"You figure it out?" Lucas asked.

"I'm still working through the software," ICE said. "This, I got with chitchat. Come over here and talk with these guys."

"Who?"

"The pizza guy and one of the computer security guys. I'm serious, you need to talk to them. They're waiting for you."

"Ah, Jesus."

"C'mon. Skip the mascara, just rinse off

253

your face and run on over here," ICE said.

He took the time to stand in the shower for three minutes, put on jeans and a T-shirt and a jacket to cover the Beretta, headed downstairs, unshaven. Weather got some coffee going, and Lucas made himself an egg sandwich, two eggs fried hard inside two slices of white Wonder bread. He borrowed one of Weather's travel cups for the coffee, and was out of the house five minutes later.

The day was cool, though the cold front that had come with the initial killings had blown through, and it looked like the day would be sunny and reasonably warm. He took Mississippi River Boulevard north to the point where it leaked onto Cretin Avenue, by the St. Thomas University stadium, took Cretin to I-94, drove across the river and into downtown Minneapolis.

ICE was sitting on a granite post outside the bank, smoking a cigarette. When she saw him coming, she flagged him down, walked around to the passenger side, and got in the Porsche. "This is pure detective work on my part," she said. "What happened was, it's six o'clock and I'm stoned on speed and caffeine and I'm starving to death, so we order out for pizzas at the bank guys' regular place, and the pizza guy comes by."

"The bank guys work on Sunday morning?"

"This Sunday they do. Anyway . . ."

The pizza guy brought in a load of pies, she said as Lucas parked the Porsche, and she and the pizza guy and one of the computer guys started chatting, and the computer guy said that he hardly saw the pizza guys anymore after this guy named Jacob quit. And they said, yeah, he was more of a pizza eater than anyone else, came from all those years as a midnight writer . . . meaning a hacker.

"So I say, 'Jacob who?' This overnight computer guy, Jon, says, 'Jacob Kline,' and I say, 'Holy shit, there's your leak, right there. There's your money.' That's when we decided I better get you out of bed."

In the secure area, the pizza guy, who wore a little white paper hat like the ones that U.S. Marines called cunt hats, said, "Dude," and a computer guy turned from his terminal and asked, "You Lucas?"

"So tell me," Lucas said, taking a chair.

The pizza guy said, "Jacob was like this total stoner, slacker, bullshit artist, I don't know how he kept the job."

"Good programmer," ICE said. "Smart."

"But messed up," said the computer guy named Jon. "He was depressed. I mean, like mentally ill, not like bummed out."

"Okay," Lucas said.

"And he wouldn't take his meds, even when he was going down. He'd just sit there and get worse," Jon said. "Said he couldn't program when he was taking his meds, said it screwed up his head."

"His head was totally screwed up," said the pizza guy.

"So why does that make you think . . . ?" Lucas let the question hang.

"He used to talk about making a killing with some computer app and then getting out, so he wouldn't have to work," Jon said. "He said work was what was killing him. It was so boring. So stupid. He couldn't stand it. He said he went out to Silicon Valley one time, thinking it might be better, but it was worse, they treated people like robots. Anyway, he got fired for nonperformance. He knew it was coming . . . and this stuff that ICE has been looking at, it *feels* like his work. It works and all, but it's got these little flourishes. . . ."

ICE nodded. "I know him from gamer work. He's both fucked up and good. I don't know his style well enough to pick it out, but I believe Jon when he says he can."

"Like a writing style," Lucas said. "Like a book-writing style."

"Exactly," said ICE. "The other thing that we didn't think about long enough . . . whoever stole this money knew a lot about banking and how to set up accounts. So it had to be inside, right? But if it was inside, why did they set up this back door to get in? It'd be easier and less visible if they moved the money from in here. You wouldn't have this *doily* to untangle."

"But that would pin it down to somebody here," Lucas said. "If you were in here, and you built a back door, it'd look like it was done by an outsider. The back door could function as a decoy."

"True, I didn't think of that," ICE said. She looked at Jon. "I guess you're fucked."

"Not recently," he said, and waggled his eyebrows at her.

"In your dreams," she said.

"Okay, kids, calm down," Lucas said. "You're saying the main reason that Jacob did it is, he's messed up."

"Not exactly," Jon said. "Because this almost has to be an inside job, which has everybody worried. But the people working here now are the straightest, most-insured, most 401k'd, middle-class . . ." He paused, then pointed at ICE. "She's the biggest criminal who's ever been in here. Except for Jacob. What I'm saying is, Jacob would do this. Nobody else would."

"I agree except for one thing," the pizza guy said. "He's the laziest motherfucker in the world. He's too lazy to steal. He's too lazy to learn how to drive a car — he used to order pizzas at the end of his shift because he knew the store was down near where he lives, and he'd bum a ride home. That's what I don't see: he doesn't give a shit, not enough to steal a billion dollars or whatever it is."

"Also true," ICE said. "And it's not because he's depressed. He's just fuckin' lazy."

Jon and ICE said that whoever had built the back door had, in fact, created a little group of booby traps and alarms, but they were taking them out and should be done by the middle of the day. "I never did finish over at Sunnie, so after we're done here, I'm gonna go home and get a few hours of sleep, then get some sliders and go back to Sunnie. When I get done with *that,* I'm going to Paris."

"Where do I find this Jacob guy?" Lucas asked.

"I know the answer to that," Jon said.

■ ■ ■ ■

When Lucas left the bank, it was still before eight o'clock, and there was no reason to expect that Del would be awake. But there was no reason to expect that Lucas would be awake, either, and there was no reason that he should have to suffer alone, so he called Del, got his wife, and told her that he was on his way and to pull Del out of bed.

Del was not happy when Lucas arrived: "There's a nuclear weapon somewhere in the Twin Cities and we only have a half hour to find it," he said. He was sitting on his bed, pulling on his socks.

"No, there's a guy named Jacob in an apartment off Lyndale who may have stolen twenty-two million dollars, and we have to shake it out of him," Lucas said.

Del: "Jesus, couldn't you have gotten a flunky to go with you?"

"Uh, Del . . ."

"I know, I *am* a flunky." He got a pistol from under the bed, already in a holster, and stuck it in his belt. "I'm good."

Del lived in St. Paul. Lucas filled him in as they drove back to Minneapolis, then turned south.

"What you're telling me," Del said, "is that we got nothing but what some pizza guy suspects."

"No. We've got solid judgments from two computer people that the work looks like Kline's, and that he has voiced some inclination to make a killing, somehow. And that he was fired, and he was pissed about it. According to the Polaris computer guy, when they fired him, he threatened to shit in their revolving door."

"Another Dillinger, no doubt about it," Del said.

They were at the apartment by eight-thirty. Most of the parking around Kline's apartment was on-street, but they found a space without much trouble. They walked around a corner past a basement-level mystery bookstore, and Del asked, "You read that stuff?"

Lucas nodded. "Sure. We've got a bunch of detective novels up at the cabin. I read them on rainy days. They're mostly full of shit."

"That's because they have to combine Hollywood and the cops. An author told me that," Del said. "He said if a book described what the cops really do, everybody would fall asleep. So they have to stick in some

Hollywood. Maybe a lot of Hollywood."

"What about true-crime books? Those sell pretty well."

"Yeah, but . . . those aren't about the cops," Del said. "Those are about the criminals, and what they do. The bloodier the better."

"You ever read that book about Ted Bundy?" Lucas asked, as they waited by the door to the apartment.

"No, but I saw the movie. He was cute as a button, Ted was."

A guy came out of the apartment and Del hooked the door while it was open. The guy turned and looked at Del, frowned and asked, "Do you live here?"

"Would I be going in if I didn't?" Del asked.

Lucas pulled his ID and said, "It's okay, we're cops."

The guy nodded and took another look at Del, and went on his way.

"People are just too goddamn suspicious," Del said.

According to the building directory, Kline was in 204. They took one flight of steps, turned right, and were looking at the door, one of twenty or thirty running down a long dim hallway. Lucas knocked. They waited.

No response, so he knocked louder. No response, so he knocked louder yet, and they heard what sounded like a groan from the apartment, and heard somebody call, "I'm coming."

They could tell before he got to the door that he was barefoot, from the soft footfalls. A chain rattled on the back of the door, and the man opened it. He was as tall as Lucas, or maybe an inch taller, white, with a curly black semi-Afro. He had thin, wispy whiskers on a face that probably wouldn't need much shaving. He was wearing a pair of jockey shorts and nothing else. He said, "I don't want any."

"We're with the Bureau of Criminal Apprehension," Lucas began.

"I don't want any of that, either," the man said.

"Are you Mr. Kline?" Del asked.

"Yeah. I think so. I was last night." He pulled on the top of his underpants, peered into the opening, then looked up and said, "Yep. Still am. What do you want?"

"We need to talk to you," Lucas said.

"Oh, right," Kline said. "I let you in, you toss my apartment, take my stash."

"Not interested in your stash," Del said. "We don't have a search warrant, so we won't toss the apartment. We just need to talk to you about a problem at Polaris National."

Kline snorted, "They got more than one problem."

A young blond woman came out of her apartment down the hall, wearing what might have been a churchgoing dress, and as she pulled her door closed she called, "Jacob, you put some pants on or I swear to God I'll call the cops."

"These *are* the cops," he said.

The woman was coming along the hall, slowed, and said to Lucas, "I was joking. He plays with it, but he never wags it."

"Doesn't necessarily qualify him for an honorary degree," Lucas said. She was pretty, and he was always up for a chat with a pretty woman.

"No, but . . . he's not actually a pervert," the woman said. "Well, he *is* a pervert, but not a dangerous one."

"They say they're not looking for my stash," Kline told the woman.

"Then they must not be," she said. "The police never lie. It would be against their ethics."

"You're my witness," Kline said to her. Then, to Lucas and Del, "You can come in, but you can't search the place."

"Okay, I'm your witness," the woman said,

and went on her way.

"Good-bye," Lucas said, and she twiddled her fingers over her shoulder, but didn't look back.

Kline's apartment stank of tomato-based food-like products, ramen noodles, pepperoni, and maybe some spilled Two-Buck Chuck with an underlying whiff of ganj. Two wooden chairs faced each other across a tiny table in the compact kitchen; in the living room, a couch faced a huge television that was wired into three different game systems, the consoles of which sat on a plywood coffee table; and straight through, they could see the foot of an unmade bed.

Kline flopped full-length on the couch and said, "So, get the kitchen chairs."

Del picked them up, handed one to Lucas, and they put them in the living room facing the couch, their backs to the TV, and Lucas asked, "Did you steal twenty-two million dollars from an account at Polaris National Bank through a back door you put into the system before you were fired?"

Kline looked from Lucas to Del and back, then said, "Noooo . . . Do they think I did?"

"Some of them do," Lucas said.

"That's right, blame it on the handicapped guy," Kline said. Then, in what seemed a genuine question, "They lost twenty-two mil?"

"They didn't exactly lose it," Del said. "Somebody took it. We thought maybe it was you."

"I confess, Ossifer, it was me," Kline said. He waved his arm at his living quarters. "The first thing I did when I got the money is, I went out and rented this beautiful apartment, so I could live a life of leisure and luxury with a lot of high-price hookers."

"If you didn't do it, who did?" Lucas asked.

Kline pushed himself up, looked under the coffee table, came up with a pack of cigarettes and a Bic lighter, lit one, and blew smoke. "Good question. I mean, I didn't do it, so it must be somebody else. But they're all so fuckin' straight . . . on the surface, anyway. I suspect Angela . . . have you met her?"

"No."

"Blond chick, big headlights." He cupped his hands on his chest, to indicate the size of the headlights. "One of the analysts down there. I suspect her of being a secret rubber freak. She denies it. Anyway, I don't know who would take it. The money. I sort of can't believe that anybody did. If *somebody* did, of the people who work down there, or used to work down there, it'd most likely be . . . me. That's who I'd suspect. But let me tell you a secret: their security isn't as good as it looks. You've got the cameras and the doors and all that, but if you've got administrator's status, you can actually get in from a couple of places around the building. Did they tell you that?"

"Yeah, but we've got a pro checking it out, and it doesn't look like that to her," Lucas said. He hadn't known about the other entries, and that worried him. "It looks like it took a pretty heavy programmer, who really knew the system. This wasn't some casual hack from a secretary who took a college course in C."

"Her?" Kline blew more smoke. "Would I know her? Your pro?"

Lucas said, "Ingrid —"

"ICE. Well, well." Kline blew more smoke, and then laughed up at the ceiling. "They let little ICE into the security section, huh? Fuckin' morons. They'll be missing a lot more than twenty-two million before she gets out of there. She's not gonna build in a back door, she's gonna build in a fucking Holland Tunnel. How'd you ever hook up with a crook like ICE?"

"She used to work for me," Lucas said.

"Oh, yeah," Kline said. He shook a finger at Lucas. "Now I know the name. Davenport Simulations, right? Nice little gig. I heard you were a cop. Okay, I want to get really clear with you. A: I didn't do it. Didn't build a back door, didn't take any money out. B: I don't know who did it, but I find it hard to believe that it was one of my former associates, may their treacherous little souls burn in hell, anyway. C: I really need to light up a fatty, so if you guys are done . . ."

"I understand you've been a little depressed, from time to time," Lucas said.

"No, I've been a lot depressed," Kline snapped. "It's not what you think it is. It's not being bummed out. It's . . ."

"I know what it is," Lucas said.

"Ah." Something softened in Kline's face. "Well then, you know like Snoop says, I need my medicine."

They worked him for a while, recycling the same questions, looking for holes, pushing him on other suspects. "So where're you working now?" Lucas eventually asked.

Kline said, "Same ol' same ol'. Hennepin National Bank, doing the same old shit."

"They took you after you were fired by Polaris?" Lucas asked, surprised.

"I wasn't fired. I resigned, with a good

recommendation," Kline said.

"And if they hadn't let you do that, you would have shit in their revolving door," Del said.

Kline smiled. "So you heard that, huh? I thought it was colorful."

Twenty minutes later, they were back out on the street, walking past the mystery bookstore. Del said, "The guy is unhinged. But I think he might know something about the money."

"Yeah. He was a little too unconfused about the questions," Lucas said. "I'm gonna get Jenkins and Shrake over here. Keep an eye on him for a few hours. Let's just sit for a while, see if he moves."

They found a no-parking zone where they could watch both of the building's exits. They were still watching, an hour and a half later, when Jenkins and Shrake pulled up behind them. Lucas got out of the Porsche and went and sat in Jenkins's backseat.

"We got a photo, but we can't find a car," Shrake said. "He must either borrow one, or get around on buses. So what are we looking for, other than time and a half?"

Lucas told them, and gave them a thorough description to go with the photo: "Figure out where he goes, if anywhere. We need to know who he talks to, and where. You've got the camera?"

"Yeah." Jenkins held up a compact camera with a super-telephoto.

"If he meets somebody, when they split, make sure you get the other guy's license tag or take him home, or something. If Kline is on foot, maybe one of you can follow him on foot."

"We can do that," Jenkins said. "By the way, Shaffer says he's calling his whole crew in. They'll be meeting in a bit. You're invited."

When Lucas and Del got to the BCA, the meeting was over. Lucas stopped at Shaffer's office, intending to fill him in on the morning's developments, and was told by another cop that Shaffer had gone to Sunnie Software, where the DEA accountants were still at work, and planned to go to Polaris after that.

Lucas walked back to his office and found Martínez sitting outside the door. Shaffer had told her that Lucas was on his way in, and she'd decided to wait. "I hoped to speak with you."

"Sure, but I've got to make a phone call. Come on in."

She took a visitor's chair, and he settled

behind his desk, got Shaffer's phone number, and when Shaffer came on, filled him in. At the end, he said, "It could be a wild-goose chase, but Shrake and Jenkins weren't doing much anyway, they're not real churchy, so they'll tag him around for a while."

"That's fine," Shaffer said. "And you think Kline knows something that we don't?"

"Yeah, I do. I don't know what, or how much," Lucas said. "It's also possible that he suspects a particular person, and maybe's gonna ask for a piece of the action. I was told that he's too lazy to steal, so . . . take it for what it's worth."

When he got off, Martínez said, "My superior wishes that I stay here until we can send David's body back to Mexico, and to come to the meetings in his place so I can relay the news back home. If that is okay. I am a certified police officer."

"I don't think anybody will have a problem with that," Lucas said.

"You have been making progress, but I understand from this morning's meeting that Agent Shaffer has not," she said.

She already knew about the back door at Polaris, but not about Kline. He filled in what she hadn't overheard in the phone conversation, then said, "It could be a complete waste of time. This guy is a slacker. . . . You know slacker . . . ?"

"Yes, I know this," she said.

"He's a slacker and a depressive and he apparently smokes a lot of dope and doesn't care who knows about it. He says this theft is way too ambitious for him, and I halfway believe him. But he's all we've got, at the moment."

"Okay," she said, and stood up. "So now I go see your medical inspector, and they will tell me about the autopsy. You will call me if something happens?"

"Absolutely," Lucas said.

He called ICE, who told him she couldn't talk for a couple minutes. "I'm right in the middle of something. Call you back in three minutes."

He looked at his watch, and again five minutes later when she called. "What I was right in the middle of, was a bunch of bank systems security people. The thing is, we cleared out the problems in the main system, and now that they've seen it, the security people can take care of the back-ups."

"So you're done there?"

"Pretty much. But you've got these accountants here, the DEA people?"

"What about them?" Lucas asked.

"Once we broke through on the back door, and the booby traps, I let the Polaris security people take it, and I started looking around the system. The thing is, I isolated at least some of the wire numbers where the thieves sent the money. The last of it went out three days ago, and it went to four different accounts in four different banks, all of it to either the east or west coasts, the big cities, LA, New York, Philadelphia. I don't know where it went from there."

"So get the DEA guys on it."

"I told them, but that's not what they're here for," ICE said. "They're hot on the trail of this drug money, the big money, and they don't give a rat's ass about your twenty-two million. They say they do, but they don't. You need to get your own people over here, or Bone's people, or somebody, if you want to start running down where this money went, and who's got it, and who's going to get killed next."

"Yes," Lucas said. "That's what I need to do."

He called Shaffer, and Shaffer exploded and said, "Those fuckin' feds . . . All right, I'll get somebody there. I'll get Specs over there."

"Tell him to talk to Bone. Bone will help."

"Listen, I heard two minutes ago — I swear to God, two minutes — the Roseville cops got the shooters' SUV up at the Rosedale parking lot. I don't think they're shopping, I think they went there to get a new ride. I'm going up there. What about you? Heard anything back from Shrake and Jenkins?"

"No. They're pretty good about updating me, so I suspect Kline is still holed up in his apartment."

"Okay. I'm outa here," Shaffer said. But just before he hung up, he said, "Things are moving."

"Yeah, they are," Lucas said.

Martínez talked to the Big Voice a few minutes after she left Lucas's office. She had known him when she was a child, and though his name was Sebastian, she'd always called him Sebas as a kid, and still did. "I think the money is gone," she told him.

"Tell me why," he said.

She explained about the DEA accountants and the two teams, one following the shooters and the stolen money, the other going after the main accounts where they'd been sending money for three years. "They know it is going through Sunnie, but they haven't found the pathway yet. They will, it's a matter of time. So, that is finished."

"They won't get the main money. It's filtered three times, and then it goes poof, and disappears," the Big Voice said. "The money stolen, this is a shame. I'll talk to Javier, but I think you're correct. It's gone."

"So, will you call back the children?"

"I'll talk to Javier," the Big Voice said. "To tell the truth, I think that since we've already made so much noise, it would not hurt to make a little more. To send the message. Also, this Kline. If there's any chance . . ."

"They would have to be very careful. I know he is being watched," she said.

"We will think about it," the Big Voice said.

"So that's up to you . . . and Javier," Martínez said. "What do you want me to do?"

"Come back with the body. But be careful, Ana. This killing of Rivera, this was brilliant but dangerous. It frightens me. If we cut the money loose, there is no reason to stay."

"Okay. I will go to these morning meetings, to hear what I can, and when they release Rivera's body, I'll come with it. You do want me to continue to work with the Federales?"

"I believe so. I will talk with Javier about

this, also. If you wish to get out, we will consider it — this would not be a bad time to go, after Rivera's death. You could claim that you are too frightened to continue."

"I prefer to stay," Martínez said. "A small raise would not be unwelcome."

The Big Voice laughed and said, "Perhaps a big raise. I will talk with Javier."

Shrake called Lucas a half hour after he talked to Shaffer and said, "Our boy's on the street. He's on foot, and Jenkins is tagging him. We'll keep you up."

He called back twenty minutes later and said, "He took a bus, and he just dragged his sorry ass into Hennepin National."

"Didn't talk to anyone?"

"Not unless the other guy was on the bus," Shrake said.

"Wonder why he's going in there today?"

"I do not know the answer to that question," Shrake said. "But it's a big bank. Maybe they have a Sunday crew?"

"All right. If he's working, you might as well come back in," Lucas said. "Pretty much a fool's errand, anyway. We're not going to take him like that."

11

Two days after stealing the car from Ferat Chakkour, Uno abandoned it at Minneapolis–St. Paul International Airport, in the hopes that if Chakkour was reported missing, his car would be found at the airport and the police would assume he was traveling.

After leaving the car in a long-term lot, Uno, wearing a suit and tie, and with a good Mexican passport, made a call to a number given him by Big Voice, then went and stood on the curb in front of the airport baggage claim.

Five minutes later, a Toyota Camry, with a blond man at the wheel, pulled over in front of him, and Uno got in.

The blond man, who had a dragon tattoo on his neck, said nothing at all; he was wearing black wraparound sunglasses, nodded at Uno, and drove out to a pancake house, got out, and walked away. Uno walked around to the driver's seat, got in, and drove back to the Holiday Inn where they'd been hiding out.

Tres was waiting. He brought the bags out, threw them in the backseat, and they took off. They drove east on I-494, then south on Highway 61 to Newport, then through back streets until the refinery loomed in the windshield. The new house was little more than a cottage, with a one-car garage and a dark picture window looking out at the lawn. They got the garage door opener out of the mailbox and drove into the garage. They had no key, but the garage had a door that opened into the house.

The house was a step down from the last one, with one small television and no cable hookup, empty cupboards, a single bed in a back bedroom — nothing in the other bedroom except some scraps of paper — and a broken-down couch. The place smelled of beer and cigarettes.

They turned the television on, and found they could get three over-the-air channels pretty well, if they manipulated the rabbit ears. The television was full of talk about two small Mexican men. Uno's mug shot was there, but Tres was still clear.

Uno said nothing about it, but he was

afraid that Tres had become unhinged. He walked around muttering to himself, crossing himself, smiling and waving his arms, talking to unseen saints. He wanted another church, so he could pray, but Uno worried about being seen; when they were in the car, he made Tres slip down in the passenger seat so other drivers wouldn't see two Mexican men together.

When they'd carried their bags inside the new house, Uno took the satellite phone outside, told Big Voice about the problem with Tres. Big Voice asked if Tres was a risk. Uno confessed that he did not know. "He will do his work, but he . . . I don't know him anymore. He is a different person. I'm not sure if I can rely on him. He says I can."

"Watch him. If he endangers you, you may have to settle him," the Big Voice said. "Do not just leave him, he knows too much about you, and he has seen Martínez."

Martínez, they'd learned, was the name of the woman who'd saved them from the Federale.

The Big Voice also told them that the trip might be near its end — they should be prepared to run south to the border. "It may be that we've lost the money."

"Very much money," Uno said.

"Yes, but if it's gone, it's gone. There's no point in crying over spilled milk: *No llores por leche derramada*."

At a later phone check, the Big Voice said that one of the thieves may have been identified. He told Uno, "It is possible, likely, that he is being watched by the American police. When you go after him, be very, very careful. Examine the ground, inch by inch. If you see anything, walk away from this man."

The Big Voice gave him the address, and Jacob Kline's name.

They went after him at dark. Spent an hour driving slowly through the streets around Kline's apartment, looking at every car where a cop might be stationed, checking anyone who seemed to be loitering. After the hour, they decided that if somebody was there, watching, they wouldn't find them.

The other possibility, they agreed, was that the cops were already inside the apartment, maybe in an adjacent room, and would not come out until they had jumped Kline.

They decided to reconnoiter, without making a definite move until they had a better idea of the interior terrain.

Kline's apartment, they found, was one

door down from a stairway. They made a plan: "I go in for him," Uno said. "You stay here in the stairway with your phone. If you hear people running down, you tell me, then you wait below, and after they go through the door, you tell me when, and then you take them, and I will come out the door at the same time and take them from the other direction."

"This could work," Tres said.

"It *will* work if you don't shoot me when I come out the door."

"I'll be careful," Tres said. "If they are in the next apartment, instead of above or below . . ."

"You'll still hear them when they come out. Same thing. Tell me on the phone, then take them."

Tres nodded.

"And be careful. Don't shoot me," Uno said.

"And you also," Tres said.

"It's not much of a plan," Uno said.

"Well, what else do we have?"

So they did it. They went to his apartment, knocked, waited, knocked . . . nobody answered. "He's not home."

"Come back later."

"Go to church now," Uno said.

■ ■ ■ ■

So they found a church, Uno dropping Tres in front of the place, and then waiting for a half hour, until he came back out. As he had before, Tres came out deep in conversation with somebody not there. The most worrisome thing, Uno thought as he watched his friend coming down the sidewalk, was the possibility that whatever saint Tres was talking to would turn him against the killing. Tres said they were not that kind of saints, but how could you tell?

Tres got back in the car with that quiet, unfocused look that Uno had come to recognize, and said, "Go now. I think he's back."

"Why do you think that?"

"A saint told me," Tres said.

Uno crossed himself. But when they got back, the apartment windows were still dark, and their knock went unanswered. "I think your saint, uh, has bad information," Uno said. He didn't want to say that the saint was full of shit.

Tres shrugged.

They had no photo of Kline, but they had a description: tall, thin, dark hair worn in an

281

Afro. They waited another hour and a half, saw a bus pull to the corner stop, and a man of that description stepped off the bus, carrying a brown paper grocery bag.

"Here," Uno said.

"*Sí*," said Tres.

The man disappeared into the apartment building, and a moment later, the lights came on in his apartment.

"Let's go," Uno said.

Kline had brought back six packs of ramen, two large quart jars of apple cider, two packs of spaghetti, and a jar of Newman's Own All-Natural Italian Sausage & Peppers pasta sauce. He put them on the kitchen counter, opened the jar of pasta sauce and dropped it in a saucepan, put it on the stove, lit a cigarette, blew smoke at his reflected image in the kitchen window, and thought about Turicek.

He'd told Turicek and Sanderson about the cops. He'd been cool about it, getting them back in an isolated hallway at the bank, in case there were monitors they didn't know about.

"They think it might be me, but they've got no idea about you two, or Edie," he said. "They think it might be me because those assholes at Polaris tried to shift the blame onto me."

"Correctly," Sanderson observed.

"Still a fucked-up thing to do," Kline said. "Anyway, they may be watching. I may get another visit. I'm not going to talk to you or call you outside of work, and you better stay away from me, too. I can't help with the gold."

Both Turicek and Sanderson said that he'd done well, but he could see that both were sweating. He'd seen Turicek studying him, past his computer monitor, during the afternoon, and it occurred to him that if something should happen to him — call it like it is, he thought: if somebody killed him — then there would be no connecting thread between the theft at Polaris and Turicek and Sanderson.

Would Turicek be capable of killing someone?

He didn't know. He suspected, though, from stories Turicek had told about his life in post-Soviet eastern Europe, that he'd know somebody who would not only be capable of it, but would do it for ten bucks and a pair of hubcaps.

Huh.

He got a kettle out and dropped in a package of spaghetti, blew more smoke. He could just begin to smell the sauce starting to get hot when there was a knock at the door.

He went and asked, "Who is it?" and a voice said, "Police."

He opened it and started to say, "Hey —"

Not careful enough.

The two Mexicans blew through the door and smashed Kline back across his kitchen table, over the chairs, into the living room, and when he finally stopped rolling and twisted to look up, there was a gun in his face.

"Do not say a thing."

Kline's jaw worked but no sound came out. His mind was working, though: and his mind told him that these two Mexicans would find a way to get him out of his apartment, and then they'd cut him into sausages. Getting shot would be far preferable, and the only rational way out, if he couldn't think of anything else.

The second Mexican had shut the door; he had a small backpack and took out a roll of tape, and Kline figured that if they taped him up, he was dead. He loosened his bowels as much as he could, and tightened his stomach, and cried at the Mexican over him, "I shit my pants. Oh, God, I shit my pants."

The stench confirmed the fact; the two

Mexicans were disgusted at this sign of abject cowardice, and Kline thought, *Gotta get in the bathroom.*

The Mexican with the tape said, "Put your hands up," and Kline sobbed, "I shit my pants, man. I got a load in my pants. . . . Oh, God, I'm still shitting myself. . . ."

The older of the two Mexicans looked around and said, "The bathroom," and Kline thought, *Please, Br'er Fox, don't throw me in the bathroom,* and he sobbed, "Aw, Jesus, it's still running out of me. . . ."

"Get in the bathroom," said the Mexican with the gun. The muzzle was four inches from Kline's eyes, and, still sobbing, and now holding the seat of his pants, he pushed himself to his feet and hobbled toward the tiny bath. The toilet sat directly in front of the door. To the left, there was a vanity counter with an absolutely critical drawer, part of an incompetent remodel: the vanity was too big for the tiny bathroom, but had been on sale at Home Depot.

To the right of the sink, a tiny window, no bigger than Kline's head, which might once have been intended to provide ventilation, was sealed shut with years of paint and silicone. The window looked out over the bookstore; or would have looked out, if somebody hadn't painted the glass yellow.

To the left of the door, an old cast-iron bathtub.

Kline hobbled into the bathroom and turned and undid his belt, and dropped his pants, and the stench got worse, and Uno frowned and stepped back, but kept the gun pointing at Kline. Kline kicked off his jeans, and then his underpants, and then unrolled about ten feet of paper from the toilet paper roll, and looked down between his legs.

The Mexican looked away, not wanting to witness this, and quick as a snake, Kline kicked the door closed and pulled the drawer out of the vanity.

The open drawer blocked the door as effectively as a chain lock; Kline threw himself into the bathtub as the Mexican outside kicked the door, once, twice, and then Kline reached across with the handle of the toilet plunger and punched out the small window and began screaming for help.

He screamed, at the top of his lungs, "MURDER! THEY'RE MURDERING ME! HELP! FIRE! FIRE! THEY HAVE GUNS! MURDER! . . ."

The first bullets punched through the door and took out the toilet tank, and Kline dropped lower in the tub, but the tub was short, and his knees stuck up, and the Mexican, still kicking the door as Kline screamed, finally simply sprayed the bathroom with bullets, one of which went through both of Kline's thighs and he began screaming even louder, "I'M SHOT, THEY SHOT ME, MURDER . . ."

Uno fired the whole magazine through the door, angling the gun around, heard the *whank-whank-whank* as a few of them hit the tub, but he didn't know what the sound was. He was using hollow-points, which began coming apart as they went through the old-fashioned oak-paneled door, and didn't have enough residual energy to pierce the tub. He continued to kick, but the door wasn't moving, and finally Tres shouted at him, "We go, we go, the police . . ."

They were making a lot of noise; and the sound of Uno's silenced pistol still sounded like a gun when it was fired quickly: it went *bop-bop-bop-bop,* and while it was quieter than an unsilenced weapon, it still sounded like a gun and nothing else. In the meantime, Kline was screaming for help.

Uno shouted, "Son of a whore," at Kline, and he and Tres turned and ran out of the apartment and away from the direct stairway down, to the back of the building. They came out in an alley and heard sirens, sprinted to the end of the alley, walked a hundred feet down to their car, did a

U-turn, and rolled away through the dark streets.

Kline, in the bathtub, was bleeding from four through-and-through holes caused by one slug, and from about a hundred oak splinters. When the shooting stopped and he thought he heard the Mexicans running, he continued to scream and managed to reach over the side of the tub to his pants. He fumbled out his cell phone and called 911.

"I'm shot, it's the Mexicans, it's the fucking Mexicans."

The woman on the other end sounded almost robotically calm. "Sir, please tell me where you are and the situation there."

"Get me some help! I'm shot, I'm shot, you stupid shit!" He screamed the address at her, and then screamed, "Get that cop Davenport. Davenport knows, it's the Mexicans, they shot me, I'm bleeding, I'm shot. . . ."

The firemen who eventually got him out had to use an ax to open the door, and the paramedics wearing yellow toxic-waste gloves lifted him out of the tub and bundled him onto a stretcher and off to the hospital.

Both the cops and the paramedics were talking to him as they went, the paramedics asking about street drugs he may have ingested, the cops wanting to know who did it. Kline, in deeper pain than any he'd previously experienced, managed to say, "It's those Mexicans. The ones everybody wants. Davenport the cop was here today. They think I took that money. . . . Call Davenport."

Eventually, the cops did.

Lucas found Kline sedated but still conscious at Hennepin County Medical Center, conscious but woozy, but not so woozy that he still wasn't pissed, and when Lucas came through the door, the doc trailing behind, Kline asked, "Who told them about me? Who told them?"

Lucas said, "We're trying to figure that out. We're thinking that they may have an insider at Polaris."

"Man, I gotta get out of here," Kline said. "You know what happens. They'll come in here while I'm sedated and they'll put some shit into my drip bag and that'll be it. That'll be it! Game over, man! Game over!"

"That's mostly in the movies, where they do that," Lucas said. "There's about fifteen people right outside your door, including a couple of cops. Nobody's coming in here that we don't know about."

"Aw, Jesus, they killed my legs." Kline began weeping. "You guys did this. I don't know anything about any money. You guys sicced them right on me. I'm suing you guys for everything you got."

Lucas calmed him down enough to get him to describe the shooting, and when Kline was done, Lucas said, "That's the smartest goddamn thing I ever heard of. You're the only one who survived these guys, and you did it with a gun in your face. . . . Man . . ."

"They would have cut me up like a summer sausage," Kline said.

"Yeah, probably — but most people would have frozen," Lucas said. "You came up with a plan."

"I shit my pants," Kline said.

"You're still here, it was a hell of a move," Lucas said. He patted Kline on the arm. "You look like a stoner and wastoid, but you got some major balls."

"I'm still gonna sue you," Kline said. His eyelids dipped. "They're giving me the good stuff, but when I come out of it, I'm gonna hurt. If the Mexicans don't get me first . . ."

Two minutes later, he was gone, sound asleep.

The doc said, "He'll be gone for a while. You get what you wanted?"

Lucas looked down at Kline, then shook his head. "There wasn't much. They crashed his door, he got them to put him in the toilet, and he started screaming. . . . Hell of a thing, but he doesn't know anything."

"Well . . . want somebody to call you when he wakes up?"

Lucas shook his head. "If you don't mind, I'm just going to sit here with him for a minute, until I'm sure he's not going to wake up."

"He won't."

"If you don't mind."

"I don't mind, but you're wasting your time."

Not really, Lucas thought, as the doc moved on. He sat looking at Kline for a couple minutes, then peeked out of the room at the nurses' station. There were four or five people there, all busy with paperwork. In the other direction, the hall was empty. Lucas walked around the bed, around the monitoring equipment and the drip-bag rack, and pulled open the top drawer of the bedside table.

The first thing he saw was Kline's wallet, and next to that, his cell phone. Excellent. He picked up the cell phone and carried it back around the bed to the chair he'd been sitting in, got out his notebook, turned the phone on, and started going through the call log.

He got an instant hit: starting the day of the murders, there were two dozen phone calls from a Kristina and just as many from an Ivan; there were other calls from a Kristina and Ivan before the murders, but only a couple. The murders, he thought, had caused a ripple.

He took down the phone numbers of Kristina and Ivan, went looking for their last names, and failed to find them.

Going back into the call log, he looked for more telltale contacts, but nothing jumped out at him. He moved to the contact directory, touched Kristina, went to History, found a list of messages, and clicked to them.

All very short:

Call me. Urgent. Urgent.

Jacob, call me.

Jacob, look at TV news. Call Ivan.

Jacob, you need to take an office shift tomorrow. Call me.

Not much information, but he'd learned that Kristina knew Ivan. There were no outgoing messages to Kristina, but Kline had made calls in response to a couple of them.

He made one in response to the "office shift."

He got a break with Ivan. His messages were also short and cryptic, but one said, *See you at the office.*

Lucas thought: *Ah. They all work with him.*

The phone might have more information, but he didn't know how to get at it — Kline listed dozens of contacts, far too many to copy in a short time, but listed no information other than names and phone numbers.

He checked the apps, looking for photos, found none. He also found a password vault, and it was operational, but he had no idea what the password might be.

Lucas closed down the phone, slipped it back in the drawer.

He listened, heard only distant chatter from the nurses. He took Kline's wallet out of the drawer, went through it quickly. He found only one thing of interest: a card from Sirius satellite radio, and on the back, an apparent password, 6rattata6.

He noted it and replaced the wallet.

There was not much chance that the Sirius password also would be the password for the vault. Most vaults, Lucas knew, gave you a prescribed number of chances to enter the password. If you got it wrong, it would then warn you about the number of remaining chances before it scrambled the contents. If he tried entering a password and it didn't work, then Kline would know that somebody had been working on his phone.

Not worth it, he thought.

He looked down at Kline, now sleeping deeply, said, "Huh," and headed for the door.

ICE had left Polaris National after she and the security people cleaned the booby traps out of the computer system, and she'd gone back to Sunnie to see if she could find the incoming system.

In the meantime, the DEA agents were trying to track money that, in earlier months and years, had been shipped out of the Bois Brule account . . . and to find out how it got to Bois Brule.

Not much for Lucas to do but let them work. Still, he was right there, at the hospital, two blocks away . . .

Lucas walked over to the bank, identified himself to the guard, and got him to call O'Brien in the systems center. Bone actually came to collect him.

"Working late, for a Sunday," Lucas said, as they went through the big glass doors to the elevator.

"I'm having trouble getting across how

serious this is," Bone said. "We'll talk about it sometime — but I have to tell you, it's a hell of a relief to hear that it's probably an inside job."

"ICE told you that?"

"Everybody tells me that. It's somebody in the company, or it's this guy Kline," Bone said. "If it were somebody in Russia, or China, which would suggest that we had a major undetected system vulnerability, I'd be sweating bullets."

"Kline just got jumped by the Mexicans."

"What!" Bone almost missed a step, caught himself and turned. "Is he dead?"

"No, he managed to get out of it. But he got shot." He told the story as they went through the door at the bottom of the stairs and started down the hall to Systems.

"How'd they find out about him?" Bone asked.

"Don't know. ICE said a bunch of people in Systems had been talking about Kline. It's probably all over the bank by now, and it's possible that somebody here is monitoring things for this Mexican gang."

"Ah, Jesus. But you don't know that."

"No."

O'Brien and his accountants were busy with two bank computer-security experts. When

O'Brien saw Lucas come in, he broke away and said, "This Bois Brule account is a ghost. The money comes in, but we can't backtrack it. From here, the money goes out to the Islands, the Caymans, where we're temporarily bogged down. We won't get any information from them before tomorrow morning at the earliest."

Bone said, "We gotta talk," and pointed them to a cluster of furniture at the end of the room, and they went over and sat down.

Lucas: "What's up?"

Bone said, "We've got a management problem. I don't care so much about the dope money coming in, or going out, because I understand it now: we were scammed about the source of the money, but all of our systems stayed intact and worked as they're supposed to. We might figure out some way to do a statistical study of our accounts, to isolate odd behavior, but that's off in the future. I'm more worried about these hackers — if they attacked one account, they could attack more. We don't even know for sure that they haven't. I really need to get them caught."

"We're working on it," Lucas said.

"But not so hard. What *you're* really interested in are these killers," Bone said. "In the meantime, the DEA is up to its ass in killers, and *they* don't care that much about individual gangbangers who'll be dead in a year, anyway. What *they* want to do is break into the gang's banks. So they want the banks, you want the killers, and I need to stop the hackers. But I'll tell you, Lucas, if the BCA catches these killers, you personally won't have much to do with it. Somebody will see them, somebody will rat them out. It'll be luck or routine, not brains."

"Maybe," Lucas agreed.

"I'll make it even simpler," Bone said. "You've got three crimes here. First, you've got the dopers laundering their money. The DEA's covering that. Second, you've got the killers murdering people. Shaffer's got that. Third, you've got the thieves who took the money out of the bank. Nobody's interested. But that's the most important one — I can't seem to make that sink in. Somebody has to cover it — I mean, like you."

"What am I supposed to do?" Lucas asked.

"Let the other cops, this Shaffer guy, let them do the routine work," Bone said. "Let the DEA do the accountancy, you don't know anything about that anyway. You should be going after the thieves, not the gangbangers."

"I don't know any more about them than I do about the shooters," Lucas said.

Bone disagreed. "Sure you do. They're thieves. They had to have some access inside the bank, so you do whatever it is you do when you're looking for any thieves. Look for opportunity, motive, all that shit you see on TV. I can tell you a few things about them — I can tell you what they're doing right now, for one thing."

"Yeah?"

"Yeah. Not the small details, but I can probably get close even to that. At some point, after running through five or six banks, the Caymans, the Dominican Republic, Venezuela, Panama . . . at some point, they have to get cash or an equivalent. Gold, silver, diamonds, rare stamps or coins. Probably not silver, come to think of it, because it'd be too big to move. But they're going to have to get something to break the paper trail, and it'll have some intrinsic value. Can't be unique — can't buy a Picasso, because that would have its own kind of trail. So it's probably gold, in some form. Coins, ingots, something. Or maybe diamonds, if the paper trail ends in Amsterdam or Tel Aviv. And . . ."

"And?"

"And they're buying it right now," Bone said. "Whatever it is. They know you're coming after them, they know the Mexicans are out there. They're moving as fast as they can. But you can't buy that much coin that fast without somebody noticing. So find those people. Find the people who are selling. You're looking for somebody, maybe several somebodies, who are selling a lot of gold or diamonds or stamps or coins. You've got no time — no time. Once they finish buying whatever it is, they'll bury it and go back to their day jobs. Nothing'll move. Then, in a year or two, they'll find a way to bring the money back in, probably in some other city or some other country, and we'll never know. And I won't know whether they can come back to the bank for another round."

Lucas and O'Brien were sitting back, taking it in. When Bone finished, O'Brien turned to Lucas and said, "He's right. Finding those gangbangers gonna be mostly a matter of luck, if they haven't already taken off. As far as we know, they're driving through Kansas City right now. If they're still here, you won't get them . . . unless. . . ."

He paused, and Lucas prompted him, "Unless . . ."

299

"Unless you find a way to suck them in," O'Brien said. "They went after Kline. If you'd been there, you could have trapped them. If you could get them to come after somebody, if you were ready for that . . ."

Lucas thought, *Hell, if I'd left Shrake and Jenkins on Kline . . .*

Bone said, "Aw, c'mon. He's not gonna suck them in. They're not reacting to Lucas — they're doing what they're told."

Lucas nodded. "Probably."

"So work on the thieves," Bone said. He was leaning toward Lucas, intent with the sales pitch. "It's really urgent. I'll give you every scrap of information we come up with at the bank, I'll make all of our people available to you, anything you want. Anything. If the BCA needs more budget for overtime, I'll work that out, make a donation to the state. *I need these thieves.*"

Lucas said, "I'd really like to get the shooters. But you might be right."

"If you get them, these fuckin' thieves, the next time we play basketball — I'll throw the game to you," Bone said.

"You'll be a very old man before that could happen," Lucas said. But he slapped Bone on the knee and said, "Let me think about it."

12

Sam and the baby were asleep when Lucas got home. Letty was reading a fantasy novel involving vampires, and when Lucas tried to talk to her, she gently shooed him away — somebody was about to get kissed. Weather was getting ready for bed: "Anything good?" she asked.

"Jim got on my case. He's worried that the people who stole the money might somehow be able to get back in — that there might still be an inside man, and they'll come back and hit him again."

"Is there an inside man?"

"Probably at least one, and maybe two." She knew about Kline getting shot, and he told her about the brief conversation in the hospital room. He didn't mention searching Kline's cell phone, because she had specific ethical viewpoints regarding the treatment of patients; a covert search of a patient's personal effects while he was drugged would almost certainly be an occasion for a major confrontation and possibly a reeducation program of the kind meted out by the Communist Chinese to capitalist running dogs during the Great Leap Forward.

So he kissed her good night and went down to the den and got out his Strathmore sketch pad and began doodling: names, connections, questions, possibilities laid out in boxes connected by dotted lines and arrows.

One thing that seemed quite clear, and fascinating in its own way, was that information was leaking back to the Criminales. That meant that the gang almost certainly had an observer inside the bank, and the observer was close to the investigators — close enough to pick up clues and tips as to where the investigation was going.

Lucas began working out some ideas about who that person would be: who inside a bank would have a connection with the Criminales. He (or she) must still be in place, because he (or she) sicced the killers on Kline.

It seemed likely that the person would be Mexican . . . wouldn't he?

He looked at his watch, went to his cell phone and called Bone's home phone. Bone's wife picked up, went to get him. Bone said: "You got them. Good work."

"Could be a while yet," Lucas said. "I have a question for you. Have you had anything weird happen with any of your people in the last few weeks? Say, people who would have been aware of an investigation of this account, so somebody up fairly high? Some unusual questions, or concerns . . . ?"

Bone was crunching on something that sounded like a carrot stick. He crunched and said, "What do you mean, weird?"

"I'm thinking that the Criminales might have been paying somebody to watch for unusual attention to the account — you know, in case the cops came around, or the DEA. I can see two possibilities. The first is somebody with contacts back in Mexico, who got pulled in somehow. Could be a previous association, could be threats to a family. Whatever. The second possibility is that they simply looked at who was working at the bank, picked somebody out, and paid him. So you'd be looking at somebody who might have had a drug problem, somebody who might have had big financial problems. There'd be rumors around . . ."

"I don't know of anything like that personally," Bone said. "We've got a few alcoholics in positions where they might pick up an investigation, but I don't know of any druggies. If we knew, we'd get rid of them. But let me ask."

"How about Mexicans? Or Central Americans?"

"I'll check that, too. I've already been thinking about that, and I can tell you, we've got quite a few people with Hispanic names. I don't know who's a Mexican, or whatever . . . Let me ask around."

"Try not to disturb anyone."

"Believe me, these guys I don't want to disturb."

"One more thing," Lucas said. "When you were talking about the fact that they'd have to change the wire transfers, or whatever, into some high-value form, like gold or diamonds . . . it seems to me that would be pretty much a full-time job. That the thief would have to have accomplices."

"Oh, sure," Bone said. "Getting this done would be a fulltime job. You'd have to buy whatever it is, make the payment, secure it. . . . Every purchase would involve several contacts with the sellers. These aren't people who will give you a million bucks in gold with the promise of a check in the mail. I imagine it would take a couple of people, or more than that."

"Gold or diamonds or stamps . . ."

"I thought about that some more when I got home," Bone said. "I'd be willing to bet it's gold. If you were trying to sneak out of Nazi Germany and needed to hide a lot of value, you might take a rare stamp or a bunch of stamps and hide it in a shoe or something. But stamps, and diamonds, and rare coins, have to be sold through specialists. Diamonds have to be evaluated, and that all takes time, and multiple contacts. But you could take a stack of American Eagles into any number of places — hundreds of places here in the States, thousands more in Europe or Asia — and walk away with cash. Say you set up a company called International Goober, and take your Eagles to a gold dealer, get a check made to International Goober, and who's to know what happened there?"

"So, gold."

"That's what I think."

After talking with Bone, Lucas turned to the problem of the thieves.

A reverse directory got him the full names of Ivan and Kristina — Ivan Turicek and Kristina Sanderson. A check with the NCIC showed no criminal history for either one of them. He got photos, ages, addresses, and car tags from the DMV and found that Turicek had used a Lithuanian passport and a Green Card as identification when he got his first Minnesota driver's license, five years earlier. Sanderson had held Minnesota licenses since she was sixteen, and so probably was a native.

He called ICE, got her on the first ring, and said, "In the Polaris computer system, you could see the back door they came through, but you couldn't see the computer system the instructions came from."

"That's right. What they apparently did was set up their back door, then they'd come in and move money, and each time they backed out, they touched off a little program that wiped the incoming addresses," ICE said. "If we'd had them, we might have been able to nail down which computers they'd been working from, what the IP addresses were, and so on. All that's gone — but it probably wouldn't have helped much anyway."

"Why not?"

"Because if they've got a brain in their heads, and they do, they would have gone to Best Buy and bought some cheap laptops with cash, and signed on from Starbucks. When they finished, they would have dropped the laptops in the river."

"You know Kline was attacked."

"Yeah, the DEA guys told me what happened," she said. "I feel kind of bad about it. Not too bad, because he's such an asshole."

"You kept telling me that he's too lazy to steal."

"He's pretty lazy," she agreed.

"So the question I have is this: From the time he found out he was going to be fired until he walked out the door, would he have had time to program in this back door? Those systems are supposed to be pretty secure."

"Hmm. Well, I don't know their work schedules down there. It's not something you'd do just casually. Usually, if you're going to be fired, they don't let you have access to the systems anymore. They don't want some pissed-off programmer bombing them out. On the other hand, programmers, by definition, are pretty smart, and would probably know they were going to be fired before they actually were. He might have been proactive, so to speak."

"Okay. Now answer me this: Could you get into Polaris's systems from another bank's secure systems? Without a back door?"

There was a long silence, then she said, "Damnit. You know, we didn't look at that. All the banks' systems have links between them. If you had the protocols for the target bank, you might be able to get in from a secure link from another bank. You'd need administrator's status, but, you know, people have ways to get that."

"So they could have gotten in without a back door?"

"But there was a back door," she said. "I found it."

"It just seems to me that if you were coming in from another bank, because you didn't have a back door . . ."

"You'd probably build one," she finished. "Genius. Yes. That's what I would have done . . . if I didn't have the back door to begin with. Do you have any reason to think that's what he did?"

"I'm not sure — it could go either way. I think he planned the theft with two other people he works with, from Hennepin National," Lucas said. "He knew about the account, but didn't move to steal from it until he got to Hennepin. He didn't steal while he was at Polaris, as far as we know, and he didn't start stealing until he'd been at Hennepin for quite a while. Didn't even try to steal when he was unemployed, and he was out of work for months, which makes me think he didn't have the back door then. Then he ran into these other people, at Hennepin. He's lazy, he's depressed, but somebody gave him a push."

"I'd buy that," ICE said. "I'll tell you what — if that's what happened, there won't be any sign of it anymore. They'll have taken everything out."

"Shoot. You're sure?"

"I would have. It wouldn't be hard."

When he got off the phone, Lucas spent some time thinking about Bone's theory that the thieves were buying gold or diamonds — probably gold. If they were, they'd have to send it somewhere to be collected, and that would probably be the Twin Cities, simply because they were based there. They couldn't just stick it in a suitcase and bring it on a plane. It'd be too heavy, and might bring questions from the TSA.

He didn't know how gold was normally delivered, though he'd been told once that the post office would handle it via registered mail. The problem with the post office, from the police point of view, was that you had to jump through your ass to get any information about deliveries — they seemed to delight in making sure every legal technicality was observed before they'd cooperate with the cops.

But once a package was delivered, all he'd need was a search warrant. If Kline was taking deliveries . . .

He thought about that, looked at his watch again. Getting late, but fuck it, people were being killed. He went to his black book, got the number of Martin Clark, the head of Minneapolis Homicide — Homicide would have covered the Kline shooting — and called him.

When Clark came up, Lucas asked, "Are you done with the crime scene at the Kline shooting?"

"Pretty much," Clark said. "Kline told us the story, and everything we saw jibed with what he said."

"Get anything I need to know about?"

"Wasn't much to get, other than a bunch of used-up slugs and brass," Clark said. "From talking to Kline, we know the shooters weren't in the apartment for more than a minute or two, and he thinks they were wearing gloves. So . . ."

"Could I get in there? Tonight?" Lucas asked.

"Ah, man . . ."

"Look, you don't have to have anything to do with it," Lucas said. "Get the watch guy downtown to get me the key. You got the key in an evidence locker?"

"Yeah."

"I'll go on down and get it, and you can

310

have a squad meet me at the door," Lucas said. "The thing is, I talked to Kline, and I don't like his story. I think he's involved in the theft of this money from Polaris. . . . I just want to see the scene."

After a moment, Clark said, "I'll get you the key — but don't get me in trouble."

"I won't," Lucas promised. "I'll be over at Homicide in twenty minutes, and over at Kline's in forty-five. You get a squad down there, I'll go in for ten minutes, and I'll drop the key off when I get finished walking through."

"Just leave the key with the uniform," Clark said.

"Good with me," Lucas said.

Lucas was at Homicide in fifteen minutes and signed for the key. Back on the street, he drove as quickly as he could to an all-night convenience store in North Minneapolis, known for its burglary support services, walked through to the back and got a once-and-future convict named Kevin to make a duplicate key for him.

"I keep losing mine," he said.

"They all say that," Kevin said.

By the time Lucas got to Kline's apartment building, it was after eleven o'clock, and the building was mostly dark, and quiet.

A cop was sitting out front, in his squad, the engine running and the internal light on, reading a hard-cover comic.

"Nice night," he said, as Lucas walked up, after parking the Porsche.

"Not bad," Lucas agreed.

Kline's apartment was the first one at the top of the landing. Lucas pulled off a piece of crime-scene tape, let himself in, turned on the lights, put his hands in his pockets, and walked through the place.

The uniform said, "Stinks."

Lucas spent fifteen minutes inside, looking at bullet holes, looking at angles. Finally he said, "Maybe."

"Maybe?"

"Maybe he's telling the truth. It sort of looks like he's telling the truth. Problem is, nobody saw the supposed Mexicans."

The cop shrugged. "He got shot, and they don't have a gun, right? Seems pretty straightforward."

"Nothing is straightforward in this," Lucas said. He took a last look around. "Okay. I'm done."

Outside, he passed the key to the cop and said, "I'd appreciate it if you'd sign it back in as quick as you could. Your boss didn't like the whole idea."

"I'll do that," the cop said.

Lucas sat in his car, his cell phone up to his face, faking a conversation, until the cop pulled away and a half dozen cars were between them. Then Lucas did a U-turn and followed, until he was sure the cop was headed downtown.

Five minutes later, he was back at Kline's door. He used the new key to unlock it, pulled on a pair of latex gloves, and began searching the place.

He needed, specifically, a stash of coins, or a discarded envelope or package wrapping that would connect him to a gold dealer, or anything that could suggest a conspiracy with Turicek and Sanderson.

The apartment was small and shabby, smelling of spaghetti sauce overlain with the scent of human waste and blood; there was minimal cooking gear, three large bookcases full of paperback books and DVDs, an oversized TV with a game console hooked to it. The floor was littered with medical detritus, the paper and plastic packaging for bandages and syringes and whatever. Though he went through each cupboard and drawer, rolled and poked the mattress, looked in the toilet tank, and even removed every electric-outlet cover plate — took his time — he came up empty.

Then, in a military-styled shirt-jac, the kind with zippers on the sleeve, he found a cheap cell phone. He brought it up, looked at the call log, found dozens of incoming and outgoing calls, but only to three numbers. He took the numbers down and put the phone back.

When he finished the general search, he sat at Kline's desk, going through the paper around the Mac Tower, and found a lot of litter and cryptic notes of the same kind Lucas had on his own desk. He turned on the computer and was asked for a password. He took out his notebook and looked up the password he'd found on the back of the Sirius Satellite Radio card, and typed it in: 6rattata6.

The computer shook him off, and he closed it down and turned away from the desk for a last look around the place.

There were two big framed posters on the wall opposite the desk, each showing multiple images of Japanese cartoon characters. He hadn't looked behind them, so he looked behind them and found the back side of posters. When he was straightening the second one, his eye caught a caption with the word *Rattata.*

He looked closer. The posters were composites of favorite cartoon characters, if *anime* meant "cartoon." There were a couple dozen of them, and if Kline was taking his passwords from anime characters . . .

He went back to the computer and brought it up and it occurred to him that most people didn't have large numbers of different passwords, but just a couple of passwords, with perhaps variations.

So instead of plugging in all the anime characters, he started with plain "rattata," and worked from 0rattata0 through 9rattata9, and was shaken off with each of them.

"Goddamnit."

He looked at the pictures again, then pulled the closest one off the wall. Forty minutes later, working from the names on the picture, he typed in "5pikachu5" — and he was in.

"Excellent," he said to himself.

He went to the Spotlight feature and typed in "Gold," and got dozens of hits. He said, "Gotcha," and then, a minute later, "Don't gotcha."

As he started working through the hits, he found that most of them were document and online files that included the word *Gold,* as in one place, Golden Artist Colors, and in another, WhatsUp Gold, some kind of network monitoring software. Then, as he was growing discouraged, he found Donleavy Precious Metals, and a website for a Chicago dealer in gold, silver, and platinum. A few minutes more got him a link to Las Vegas Numismatics, and he said, "Now I've gotcha."

When he shut down the computer an hour later, he had a list of twelve dealers on the west and east coasts.

Too late to do anything about it, he thought.

Somewhere along the line, it occurred to him that he hadn't spoken to Virgil Flowers. He'd probably taken the day off, and knowing Flowers, he'd done it in a boat. The thing about Flowers was, in Lucas's humble opinion, you could send him out for a loaf of bread and he'd find an illegal bread cartel smuggling in heroin-saturated wheat from Afghanistan. Either that, or he'd be fishing in a muskie tournament, on government time. You had to keep an eye on him.

In bed that night, he spent little time thinking about the tweekers — Flowers would get them — and more time thinking about the gold. The gold was interesting because it tied everything together. He also thought about Shaffer: the problem with Shaffer was that he was straight. Very straight. He had little sense of humor when it came to things like illegal searches, using unknowing innocent people as decoys, and so on.

He would have to use some finesse, he decided.

The next morning, before he left for work, he called Sandy, the researcher, and said, "I need to find the biggest gold dealers in the country. Maybe, like, the top one hundred."

"Do you have any idea how I'm supposed to figure that out?" she asked.

"No, I don't," he said. "I need the list this morning. Also, I have three phone numbers. I'd like to know who the subscribers are."

"Well, that part'll be easy enough," she said.

Outside, he found that Letty had parked the Lexus behind the Porsche, and instead of shuffling cars, he took the truck and headed downtown. They met at nine o'clock, the whole murder crew, and Shaffer reported that they had enough evidence to convict anybody they managed to arrest, with fingerprints and DNA from three suspects. "We've got everybody in the metro area on board, every single cop has the photos and the Identi-Kits, and we think

317

we may have a line on the car they're driving. It's a green Subaru Forester owned by a pretzel seller named Ferat Chakkour, who disappeared after he left his job at the Rosedale mall an hour or so after the shoot-out in St. Paul. He usually parked in the same lot where we found the Texas truck. We think they picked him up, probably killed him, dumped him somewhere, and are driving his car. This is confidential information — we've asked everybody to hold it close, make sure it doesn't get out to the media. We've talked to all the highway patrols all the way to the Mexican border."

"Gonna leak pretty quick," Lucas said. "This guy got any family?"

"He's got a housemate, another student, we've asked him to keep his mouth shut, but he's already been talking to Chakkour's parents in Cairo. Chakkour's from Egypt. The roommate's already talked to some classmates . . . but we're hoping to keep it close for a day or two, maybe pick up the car before it breaks out."

They'd already had four separate alerts, from cops who thought they might have spotted the suspects, but nothing had panned out; still, it kept them jumping.

The DEA, O'Brien said, was working the offshore banks but hadn't gotten anything yet. "Probably get it later today — we're talking to the state department and our own people, squeezing as hard as we can. It's not usually as hard to get it if we say it's drug money. The problem is, every time the IRS goes after some corporation for tax evasion, they start out by saying it's drug money, so the banks don't always believe us anymore."

Shaffer wrote a note and pushed it to another BCA agent while O'Brien was talking; Shaffer didn't care about the banks.

Lucas told them about his conversations with Kline and Bone, and his conclusions from those conversations: that the thieves who'd hijacked the bank account were probably buying gold, and that there were probably several of them. He mentioned that he was having a researcher get together a list of gold dealers who could be checked for suspicious gold sales. He also suggested that the Criminales must have had a contact at the bank who tipped them to the suspicions about Kline.

"So you keep doing that, working on the thieves, and we'll keep pushing people on the shooters," Shaffer said. "If anything comes up, for anybody, call us."

"The thing is, Kline's the best lead we've got for the thieves, and the Criminales apparently think the same thing. I'd love to find something we could use to serve a search warrant on his young ass," Lucas said. "If anybody thinks of anything . . ."

O'Brien asked, "Say, anybody seen Ana Martínez?"

Shaffer shrugged. "I know she was making arrangements to take Rivera's body back to Mexico. I talked to her last night. I thought she'd be here. I called her, but she didn't answer her phone."

Lucas said, "That's a little worrisome. I'll check on her."

As they were breaking up, O'Brien took a call, listened for a minute, then said, "We'll be right over. We're just leaving here, about twenty minutes."

He hung up and said, "That was ICE. She found the shadow books at Sunnie. She said they've been there right from the start, when the system was first put together."

"Bingo," Shaffer said. "That's large. I'm coming with you. Lucas?"

"I'll be around."

13

Lucas was sitting at his desk when Martin Clark, the Minneapolis homicide detective, called and demanded, "What the hell did you do in Kline's apartment last night?"

Lucas, confused, said, "What?"

"What'd you do to the computer?"

"I didn't do anything to the computer," Lucas said. "Your guy was there the whole time. What happened to it?"

"Somebody cracked it open and took the disk drive."

"Ah, shit . . . Marty, I didn't touch the goddamn computer. I was just sitting here trying to think of a way to get a search warrant. . . . Wait a minute, could I put you on hold for a minute? Or call you right back?"

Martínez stepped to the doorway, looked in; her face was drawn, her eyes puffy. Lucas held up a finger. Clark said, "Yeah, okay. What's going on?"

"Tell you in one minute," Lucas said.

Then, "Wait, wait, was the door forced? It wasn't, was it?"

"No, the door's fine."

"I'll get right back to you," Lucas said.

He hung up and pointed Martínez at a chair, said, "Ana, glad to see you. I was a little worried. I've been trying to get in touch."

"My phone was off," she said. "I'm sorry."

"Gotta make a call." Lucas called Hennepin Medical Center, was put through to the surgical intensive care ward, identified himself, and asked the nurse, "I really need to know if Mr. Kline had any visitors this morning. . . . Yeah, I'll hold."

When he was on hold, he said to Martínez, "Trying to get a line on the thieves . . ."

A woman came on the phone and identified herself as the charge nurse. Lucas told her that they were worried about possible interference with Kline, and asked if he'd had any visitors. She said that he had, apparently a coworker, a tall thin man with a sandy beard and a foreign accent — she thought he might be Russian. He'd visited very early, before seven o'clock, saying he was on his way to work.

Lucas thought: Ivan Turicek.

"Did you get a name?"

"No, I didn't ask. Mr. Kline knew him," the nurse said. "They were friendly. At least, when I was there."

"Is Mr. Kline awake?"

"Yes, for the time being. They'll be taking some drains out of his legs this morning, and he'll go to the OR for that. He'll be sleepy for a while." That, she said, would happen whenever the doc was ready for him — there were three patients in front of Kline, all getting minor procedures.

Lucas said, "If that man shows up again, could you not allow him into Mr. Kline's space by himself? It might be important to our investigation."

She said she would keep an eye on him.

Lucas got back on the phone to Clark.

"You know why these shooters hit Kline? Because we, and they, think Kline had something to do with hijacking the drug money account."

"I know that," Clark said.

"I don't know this for sure, but I think one of his accomplices is a coworker named Ivan Turicek. They work together at Hennepin National. Anyway, if they're the ones who did it, they got in through a computer . . . and Turicek visited Kline at the hospital, early this morning."

"Ah, man."

"Yeah. I talked to Kline yesterday, and the drawer was open on his bedside table. His keys were in there. Kline's going into the OR this morning. If you could have somebody go over and maybe just peek in that drawer while he's in the OR . . ."

"That would be legally questionable," Clark said.

"But morally correct," Lucas said. "Besides, maybe the drawer is still open . . . like it was yesterday."

"All right, you talked me into it," Clark said. "I'll send Potach over. He's a moral guy."

"Sneaky, too," Lucas said. "Good choice."

"If we dust the keyboard, we won't find any Davenport prints?"

"You will not," Lucas said, happy about the fact that he'd worn gloves the night before. "You might find some from Ivan Turicek. That would be useful. And he's an immigrant, so the feds will have his prints."

"Talk to you," Clark said.

Lucas turned to Martínez, who said, "It will be another two days before I can send David's ashes home. Your medical examiner has to complete some forms that I do not understand, and then we will cremate. In the meantime, my superiors wish to have reports on the progress of the investigation."

"As for the progress, we have every cop in the Twin Cities looking for the shooters, and there is reason to believe we know what kind of a car they're driving," Lucas said.

He told her about the disappearance of Ferat Chakkour, and about the interview with Kline, and about Bone's belief that the money was being converted to gold coin, about ICE's discovery of the shadow books at Sunnie, about the DEA's tracing of the Criminales' bank accounts through the Cayman Islands. He told her about everything except his search of Kline's apartment and the phone numbers from Kline's phone.

"So, you are questioning these people? These computer thieves?"

"Not yet — everything I've told you is conjecture . . . guesswork. Right now, we're trying to find out who's buying the gold, and where they're putting it."

"So somewhere, there is a thief with a large pile of gold."

"That's what I think. And the shooters are somewhere. And the drug money is somewhere, but we don't know where any of those things are."

"Very complicated," she said. She stood and said, "I am no David Rivera, I cannot help you with this investigation as he did. But if you can keep me, mmm, informed, this will be much appreciated by my superiors."

"I will keep you informed," Lucas promised.

Lucas called for Shrake and Jenkins, and got them pulled off some bullshit that involved the theft of ATM machines from convenience stores. They showed up together, Jenkins wearing a straw cowboy hat and western boots, which made him about six-eight.

Lucas explained Kline and Turicek, and said, "If Turicek's getting gold from somewhere, it would be nice to know where he's putting it, and where it's coming from."

When they were gone, he got his jacket, planning to head for Minneapolis: he wanted to talk to Kline again, and then to Bone. He opened his office door and saw Sandy, the researcher, coming down the hall. She was a tall woman, thin, introverted, bespectacled, a latter-day hippie in paisley dresses with an improbable talent for tracking crooks through her computer systems. Everybody in the BCA abused her talent, when they could, and Lucas and Virgil Flowers led the pack. She said, "I've got your list. I can't guarantee that they're exactly the top one hundred, but they're big."

Lucas said, "All right. Sit in Cheryl's chair." He pointed her to a chair where his secretary normally worked. "I'll be back in a minute."

"Wait," she said. "I also checked those three phone numbers — they're all to prepaid cell phones. No credit cards attached to them. Sold through Walmart. So you're outa luck, unless you actually find one of the phones."

He went back in his office, closed the door, got out the list of gold dealers he'd found in Kline's computer, and compared his list to Sandy's. All twelve of Kline's shops were on the list.

He made check marks next to the dealers he'd found in Kline's computer, put his list away, and carried Sandy's back to her.

"I want you to call the top twenty-five, plus the ones I've checked. Everybody should know about these killings, what's going on here. You can imply that we're calling because of that investigation."

"Are we?"

"Yeah — but we're chasing the people who took the money, not the killers," Lucas said.

"I'd like to get the killers," she said.

"So would I, but we do what we can."

"So what are we looking for?"

"We want physical descriptions of people who are making big buys, of gold coins, not bars with serial numbers. We only want people who started last month and have come back repeatedly. They want physical delivery of the coins, and they want fast delivery. We're talking buys in the hundreds of thousands of dollars. . . . Tell the dealers we don't necessarily need names, but we need the physical descriptions. If you find somebody making really big buys, at a lot of shops, somebody who sounds like the same guy, then call all one hundred dealers and see if you can figure out how much gold the guy is taking and anything else you can get — name, bank, whatever."

"That'll take me all day," she said.

"Probably." He put his jacket on. "Better get to work."

Martínez did not call the Big Voice immediately. Instead, she drove back to the St. Paul Hotel, lay on her bed, and thought about her next move. Twenty-two million dollars, or a large part of that, was sitting out there in gold. She was paid quite well by the Criminales, but the compensation was nothing like a million a year. Not even a tenth of that. Twenty-two million . . .

She considered several possibilities:

She might try to go for the gold herself. If Davenport would keep filling her in on the investigation, and if she could get to one of the thieves first, with Uno under control, she *would* find out where the gold was: Uno was the designated torturer. Then, if something happened to Uno, she would be there with the gold. If she weren't greedy, and took only part of it — say, five million — and let the police find the remainder, who would know, or be able to figure out, what happened to the rest?

Or, she could recover all the gold for the Criminales and suggest to the powers that she deserved a cut for her actions. They'd probably give her something — not five million, but something. Five percent? One million? Maybe. It wouldn't cost them much, compared to what they got back, and would demonstrate their generosity toward loyal employees.

Or, she could recommend that they cut the cord, with everybody pulling back to Mexico. That, she thought, was a problem for one big reason: she, Uno, and Tres weren't important enough to save, compared to the value of the gold. They'd want

329

her to risk everything in going for it — and if she lost, and was killed or imprisoned . . . well, she just wasn't that big a deal, to them.

She considered the possibilities and decided that whatever she eventually did, she didn't have to make a decision immediately.

So she called the Big Voice and filled him in: told him about the discovery of the shadow books at Sunnie, about Lucas's focus on Kline and Turicek, about the DEA: "I hope you have all the money out of the pipeline. The DEA is now in the Caymans and they have the account numbers."

"Don't be concerned about that — all the proper people know," the Big Voice said. "We are now more interested in the possibilities with this gold. Do you need help there? Is there anything to be done?"

"Mmm, the police have now put surveillance on this Turicek, and Kline is protected by more policemen at the hospital. Davenport believes there is at least one more accomplice, the person who does the buying. I cannot think of how to find that person. Turicek and Kline work in the computer department of another bank. If we could find a friend of theirs at the bank . . . we might learn something from the friend, but how do I find the friend?"

Big Voice said, "Let me see what I can do.

Maybe we can find something online, in Facebook perhaps. Perhaps we can find a directory for this Hennepin National. We will call you."

"I will be waiting."

Turicek was moving fast.

After talking with Kline early in the morning, he and Kline together had erased Kline's phone messages and phone log, and Turicek said, "Christ, you can't keep this stuff on here, this message from Kristina. It ties us all together."

Kline told him there was even more on his home computer, gave Turicek his key, and a list of files that needed to be erased.

"You don't have any cloud files?" Turicek asked.

"I'm not suicidal."

Turicek had driven straight to Kline's apartment, peeled off the police seal, which appeared to have already been tampered with, and let himself inside. He had no intention of erasing selected files: instead, he'd cracked the computer case and yanked out the two disk drives, and fled.

Back at his apartment, he used a ball-peen hammer to crack open the drive cases, removed the disks, beat the disks into fragments, and flushed them down the toilet.

At the rental office, where they took the gold deliveries, he'd waited until the morning packages came in. When Sanderson showed up, they talked for a couple minutes, then he passed the gold on to her and went to work.

He was picked up there by Jenkins and Shrake, who had his license tag and a description of his car.

Jenkins and Shrake had determined that he wasn't at work by calling and asking for him. They were told that he was working the afternoon shift, and would be in at one o'clock. He rolled into the parking garage at ten minutes to one, and when he was inside the bank, Shrake said, "Piece-of-shit old Chevy. We could crack it, no problem."

"No problem as long as we don't get caught," Jenkins said.

"But if we crack it and find a pile of gold, and tell Lucas, he'll find a way to do a search, and then we're . . . gold. If there's nothing in it, we're still cool."

"Okay, I'm bored," Jenkins said. "Let's do it."

They got in quickly enough. Jenkins blocked, standing by the car's trunk while Shrake slid his slim jim down the window and popped the door. The car was clean, and, when he popped the trunk latch, so was the trunk.

"Life is hard and then you die," Shrake said.

They closed up Turicek's car, went back to their own vehicle, and started the surveillance: doing it the hard way.

When Sanderson met Turicek at the rental office, she'd said, "We have to stop this. Jacob's in the hospital, they could be coming for us."

"Which *they?*" Turicek asked.

Sanderson shuddered: "Better the police than this crazy drug gang. My God, I can't believe we're doing this."

"Well, we can't stop now," Turicek said. "There are more packages in the air, and if they just get dropped here, and nobody picks them up, sooner or later somebody will get curious and open them. . . . If they find a big bunch of gold, and go to the cops . . ."

"We should tell Edie to stop. It's just too dangerous. If she stops, we pick up the last packages, and we're done."

"I'll talk to her," Turicek said. "There's only three more million to go. . . . I'd hate to cut it off, but I will if I have to."

"Ivan, the police are already on to Jacob.

What more do you need?"

"I'll talk to Edie about it," Turicek said.

Sanderson got four more packages that afternoon, unwrapped the gold, repacked it, and took it to her mom's home and hid it in a concealed closet where her daddy — now long gone — had hidden his gun safe. The gun safe was still there, though all the long guns had gone shortly after Daddy died, sold to his hunting buddies. A couple of handguns remained, which she hadn't bothered to get rid of.

Since she and her mom didn't share a last name, and her mother wouldn't have remembered her last name if asked, the gold was safe enough, at least for a while.

Standing in front of the safe, looking at the now substantial stacks of coin — fifteen million worth? eighteen million? — and the two guns, Sanderson, though a gentle person, couldn't help thinking:

If something happened to the other three, then she'd have it all. . . .

When Lucas got to Minneapolis, he stopped first at Polaris, and went up to Bone's office. Bone was in a meeting, but came out to talk: "What do you need?"

"Do you know anybody who'd do you a

favor at Hennepin National?"

"Sure. I know the boss, Bob McCollum," Bone said. "You're still looking at this Kline guy?"

"I think . . . I'm not sure . . . that another guy in the computer department might be in on it. I need to talk to somebody nice and quietly who knows the people in their systems department. All of the people. Somebody who can keep his mouth shut."

Bone tipped his head down the hall toward his office: "Come on. I'll call Bob."

Hennepin was only three or four blocks from Polaris, and Lucas walked over, went up to McCollum's office. McCollum was not particularly happy to see him, and less happy when Lucas finished outlining the problem.

"You think they've figured out a way to get into Polaris's systems from here?"

"I think it's a possibility. I'm most interested in Kline, Turicek, and Sanderson, but there might be others," Lucas said. "Is there somebody outside the department who'd know them all?"

McCollum scratched his head, then picked up his phone, pushed a button, and said, "Babs, could you come in here?" To Lucas, he said, "My assistant."

A woman stuck her head in a moment later and said, "Sir?" She was an older woman, with steel-gray hair; she did not, Lucas thought, look like a Babs.

"Come in and talk to this guy. This is Lucas Davenport, he's with the BCA."

Babs nodded. "I know the name."

"So tell her," McCollum said.

Lucas outlined the problem, and the woman thought for a moment and said, "Dave Duncan would be your best possibility. He's in HR and he vets all the computer people. He had systems management courses in college, he knows that language."

"Get him up here," McCollum said.

McCollum excused himself to go to his private bathroom, and Lucas sat and read a *Cowboys & Indians* magazine, and decided he needed some cowboy boots. McCollum came back, his face and hair damp, and a minute later Babs escorted Duncan through the door. Duncan was a nervous, narrow-shouldered man in a gray suit, some indeterminate age between twenty-eight and forty, Lucas thought; one of those men who looked like they'd never quite grown up, and didn't know what to do about it.

Lucas told him the story. Duncan rubbed his fingers together as he listened, looked away from Lucas out through office windows, across town toward the Polaris Tower, where, as far as Lucas knew, Bone might be staring back.

When Lucas finished, Duncan didn't say anything until McCollum grunted, "Well?"

"Turicek may be a criminal," he said. "There was a party once, a karaoke party over at the Raven, and he and Doris Abernathy got loaded and I think she may have gone home with him. May have continued to see him for a while. Anyway, Doris told me later that he'd get drunk and tell the most outrageous stories about himself, about the old days in computer school in Russia, or Lithuania. About hacking and so on. I did some careful research on him, but there was nothing to be found."

"What about Kline?" Lucas asked.

"He came with a good recommendation from Polaris, but he's not really a satisfactory employee. He's sick too often, and we believe he's faking it, but there's no question that he's been under treatment for depression. Firing him . . . becomes complicated. In any case, he's not really a satisfactory employee, though he's smart enough."

"Sanderson?"

"Quiet, but a little nutty? Nothing out of control, but, you know . . . a former girl nerd, so to speak, smart, does her work. The kind of person who, after a few years, might open a candle store."

"Any other potential criminals down there?" McCollum asked.

"I wouldn't call Sanderson a potential criminal. She's very quiet, and reclusive," Duncan said. "The other two . . . I just don't know well enough to say. Turicek, maybe, but Kline . . . he doesn't seem to have enough of an executive mind to run a big theft."

"Executive mind?" McCollum asked, drily.

"Able to make a plan, then execute it," Duncan said.

"If Turicek and Kline were going into another bank's computer system, using your system here, how many of the systems people here would have to know about it?" Lucas asked.

Duncan shook his head. "Hard to say. I don't know enough about computer programming, for one thing. Everything depends on the details of what you're doing. Normally, if you had a complicated piece of programming to do, you could do it all off-site, and then bring it in and load it. But our systems have protections against that kind of thing — of rogue programs being loaded without a lot of checks and warnings. So it'd probably have to be done here . . . and it would take a while."

"I know this is complicated, but make it as simple as possible for me: If this was being done in Systems, would everybody have to know about it?"

Duncan thought for a moment, then said, "Nooo . . . I don't think so. But probably all the full-time programmers would. They'd be the only ones who could do it, in the first place, and they're working there side by side, and their schedules are always overlapping. If somebody was doing some heavy programming, and working into another system from ours, they'd see it."

"And that would be who?" Lucas asked.

"Just who you're asking about — Kline, Turicek, and Sanderson. There's another man, Ken Gleason, a supervisor, who could cover for any of them, but he's actually in a different office. They could do this without him knowing."

"Have any of them been taking days off lately? Traveling?"

"I'd have to call downstairs and ask. Take me a minute," Duncan said.

Lucas: "If you could do that."

Duncan did; they sat watching him talk into his phone, and as he said, it took only a moment. He hung up and said, "Kline is gone, obviously, and Sanderson has been coming in early to cover his shift. Turicek has been coming in later to cover his shift and part of Sanderson's. There's a gap around noon, so they aren't overlapping at the moment. They're both working a little overtime right now, because Kline's out."

Lucas said, "Huh," and McCollum said, "Doesn't exactly fit your model."

Lucas disagreed: "It could. There's always somebody here, but there's always somebody not here. It's what they're doing when they're not here that interests me right now."

When he'd gotten as much as they knew, Lucas warned all of them not to talk. "This is a dangerous situation, and it's possible that this drug gang has people working for the banks. Watch the news: talking about this investigation could get people killed."

He took the elevator down with Duncan, went to Duncan's office, and got a printout of Turicek's and Sanderson's addresses. As he handed them over, Duncan said, "I have an observation, if you'd be interested."

"I'm always interested in observations," Lucas said.

"If I were a police officer, and if I wanted to shake one of these people by questioning them . . . I'd go after Kristina. She doesn't strike me either as the criminal type, or as a strong person. If she's involved, and she was pushed, she'd fall apart very quickly."

Lucas nodded and said, "I'll think about that."

Back on the street, he got a call from Shrake: "What're you doing here?"

"Talking to the bank president. Where're you guys?"

"Jenkins is in the Skyway, watching the elevators there. I'm in the garage across the street — I can see both ground-floor exits from up here, and his car's on the other side of the floor."

"His car, huh?"

"We're pretty sure a guy like that wouldn't put anything incriminating in his car," Shrake said.

Lucas said, "I trust your remarkable insight into the criminal mind."

"Into the criminal glove compartment, too," Shrake said. "Anyhoo . . . we're here."

Lucas knew where Turicek was, so he drove the Lexus south and west out of downtown, to Sanderson's place. On the way, he called in to the BCA duty officer and got the make and model of her car and the license tags, and, as a bonus, her home and cell phone numbers.

Sanderson lived in a small, yellow-brick apartment complex a short walk east of Lake Calhoun. The apartment had underground parking, with a gated entrance ramp, and he had no way into it. The place looked nice enough, without being rich — exactly the kind of place an orderly, intelligent, well-employed single woman would pick.

He sat for five minutes, working out the possibilities, then called her home phone number. It rang seven times, then clicked over to the answering service, and he hung up.

He was considering the possibility of trying to get into the building when his phone rang. Sandy. "Yeah?"

"Okay, I've been calling the gold dealers, and I think we've got a hit."

"Excellent. Who is it?"

"There's a woman who says she's Syrian, has been showing up at a lot of gold dealers, both on the left and right coasts, and buying gold coins, fifty, seventy, a hundred thousand dollars at a time. She says her family is Christian and is getting out of Syria, and they don't think anything is safe but gold. That's what she tells them. She's gone to *all* of the dealers you checked — I'd like to know how you did that — and a half dozen more places."

"Have they got a passport, a name, a description, a photograph, an address . . . ?"

"They've got a cheap business card, the kind you print on your home computer, with an address in Damascus, in English, and some Arabic writing that nobody understands but looks like the same address. That's it — we don't even have a description, because she wears one of those veils. All they've seen is her eyes. . . ."

As she was talking, two men walked down the sidewalk on the other side of the street. They were coming from up the block behind him, and he didn't notice them until they passed his car. He glanced at them, went back to Sandy, said, "I can't believe . . ." then trailed off, frowned, and looked at the men as they approached the sidewalk that led to the entrance of the apartment.

Two short men, slender, wearing baseball caps and T-shirts. Dark hair, athletic. Lucas said, "Holy shit," and Sandy said, "What?" and Lucas said, "I'll call you back," and he punched in 911 and watched as the men walked up to the apartment entrance. They were planning to do wrong, he thought, because they had that wary, check-it-out attitude, looking here and there, while pretending not to.

When the 911 operator came up he identified himself and half-shouted the address and said, "The two Mexican shooters, I think they're here. They're going into the apartment building where one of our suspects lives. I need help here, fast as you can get it. These guys are shooters. I need people with vests and shotguns, I need them flooded in here."

He was dealing with Minneapolis and expected a fast response, and a few seconds later the operator said, "We've got a car two minutes away. We've got another car five minutes out, we'll route them in there. What are you doing — ?"

Lucas was shouting back at him, "They're on foot, five-seven, five-eight, dark hair, jeans and running shoes, red T-shirt, blue T-shirt, worn outside their pants. I'm afraid they'll take somebody down. . . . If they get in, I'm going after them. Tell everybody I'm in there. . . ."

"Do you think —"

The two men disappeared behind the glass doors at the front of the apartment building, but he could see them behind the glass, apparently waiting to get through an inner door, and Lucas shouted over the operator, "They're inside, but they're stuck behind the inner door. Call that apartment if you can, tell them not to answer the — Shit, they're inside, I can see them going in. I'm going, I'm going."

He was fifty yards up the street and he gunned the car down the block, stopped just short of the sidewalk, and jumped out, pulling his Beretta as he did it. He couldn't see the Mexicans inside, in the outer lobby, so he ran up the four wide steps to the front door, staying to one side, remembering Rivera, peeked at the door, saw nothing, peeked again, then pushed through.

Inside the door was a fifteen-foot-square lobby with mailboxes and an intercom, and he saw a button labeled Management and he leaned on it, and leaned on it some more, and nothing happened, nobody answered, and he leaned on it some more, and finally took a look at the door.

The door was wooden, but had a long, narrow glass window down the middle. He looked through the glass and could see an empty atrium and an intersecting hallway, and the bottom of a curving stairway. He thought the chances of kicking the door in were remote — it was a solid chunk of wood with heavy brass hardware. Kicking it would make too much noise, anyway.

He leaned on the management doorbell

again, got no answer, then took the end of his gun, pressed it against the glass in the door, and pressed it until the glass cracked and finally fell away, inside. He broke out more glass until he could reach through to the inside handle, and popped the door open.

Sanderson's address said apartment 344, so she'd be up two flights. He ran up the first flight, looked both ways, and then a voice said, "Hey," and he turned and saw a square-faced woman, red glasses, dishwater-blond hair, who saw the gun and said, "No, no," and turned as though to run.

Lucas said, sharply but quietly, "I'm a cop. Did you just see two Mexican-looking guys come through, going to Kristina Sanderson's?"

"Yes, I just . . . Oh, my God, are they . . . ?" She looked up the stairs.

"Which way to her apartment?" Lucas asked. "Which way?"

"Top of the stairs, to the left." She pointed.

"Did they go in?"

"They were just going to knock. . . . I left them when they were walking down the hall."

"You're the manager?"

"Yes. I'm Pat."

Lucas went up the stairs, saying, as he went, "There are more cops on the way. Let them in."

He took the stairs in five seconds, peeked down the hall to the left. Nothing. He looked right. Nothing. Had they gone in? Was Sanderson home, maybe not answering her phone?

He hurried down the hall, checking off the numbers on the doors, got to 344. The door was closed, no sign that it had been forced. The door across the hall was also pristine. He continued down the hall, to an exit sign, went through a fire door, looked down the stairwell, heard and saw nothing at all.

He went back: Where had they gone? If they were in the apartment, they might be torturing her . . . although the place didn't look substantial enough to smother a scream. . . .

At the door, he stood quietly for just a second, then pressed his ear to it. He got back an almost unearthly silence. The whole building was quiet.

Kick the door? He looked at the door, and again, as with the door below, he doubted his ability to get through it. The door looked like it was metal, set in what was probably a concrete block wall.

He was still looking at it when he heard some scuffling on the stairway, and he padded back down the hall, and a cop peeked around the corner at him. Lucas held up a finger and continued that way and said, quietly, "Davenport, BCA," and the cop said, "I know you. They in there?"

Lucas recognized him, but didn't remember his name. "I don't know. I kind of . . . I'm just not sure."

"What do you want to do? We've got more guys on the way."

"Set up and wait five minutes, until we've got the place blocked off, and then knock and see what happens."

That's what they did. A SWAT team showed up, and Lucas was talking to the commander when Pat, the manager, said, "Kristina's out on the sidewalk. Do you want to talk to her?"

"Yes, I do," Lucas said. To the SWAT commander, he said, "If she didn't let them in, and if they didn't have a key . . . then they left. We missed them. We gotta check, but I think we're wasting our time."

"We'll get a key and check it," the SWAT guy said.

"I'll be outside," Lucas said. "Goddamnit, anyway."

14

Kristina Sanderson had left her car down the block and walked to the apartment, to see why the cops had blocked it off. But in her heart, she knew. "I live here," she told one of the uniformed cops, who'd used their squad cars to block the street. "What's happening?"

"We're looking for a couple of people," a cop said. "You'll have to wait awhile. If you have some shopping to do . . ."

Instead of shopping, she drifted to the side of the street with a cluster of other rubberneckers, including two that she recognized as other residents of the apartment building. They nodded to each other, agreed that they hadn't heard anything. The manager, Pat, walked out the front door with a police officer and talked to him for a moment. At one point, Pat looked across the street and saw them, and Kristina waved and Pat raised a hand, then held up a finger — one minute? — and went back inside.

A minute or two later, a tall, well-dressed man came out with Pat, looked across the street at them, and then started toward them. He could be a police officer, she thought, but he didn't look the part. She'd known a number of plainclothes cops, and even dated one. They generally wore jackets and pants that would not be a great loss should they get torn, vomited on, or grass-stained.

This man wore a suit that was in an entirely different league; he looked like a banker, she thought, and an athlete. One of the bankers from the top floor, with a particularly well-developed mean streak. He said, "Hello, Miz Sanderson? I'm Lucas Davenport."

They moved away from the crowd to talk, and Davenport asked her about Kline, about whether she'd seen him doing unauthorized programming while working in the secure area. She denied seeing anything like it, and internally, she fought down the rising panic. They were, she thought, really and truly fucked. She was going to prison.

Sanderson was a guilty woman, Lucas thought, more scared and less curious than she should have been. She knew what was going on: she knew about the theft, and what the Mexicans had wanted.

Lucas said to her, finally, "I have no idea whether you had any part in the transfer of funds out of the Polaris bank accounts —"

"That's ridiculous," she sputtered, "I don't even get traffic tickets."

She was lying, Lucas thought. He plied on. "If you do know about it, there's no way we can protect you against these drug people. They have very good intelligence about what's going on with the bank, and if they think you have their money . . . you've seen what happened to that family out in Wayzata, mother, father, both kids. Kristina, you've got to talk to me. You really do. This is your life we're talking about."

"I don't know anything," she wailed, and she thought about the pile of gold at Mom's, and Lucas saw it in her eyes.

Edie Albitis overnighted the last of the packages and walked away from the FedEx store, got a cab to EWR — said to the driver, "EWR," and he said, "Okay" — and not until she'd settled back in the cab did she consider how much of her life had come to be dominated by three-letter airport designations: LAX, MIA, ORD, MSP, PHX, DEN, SFO, ATL, LGA, MCO, DFW.

Yesterday she'd gone from LAX to ORD to LGA, and now from EWR to MSP; that is, from Los Angeles to Chicago to New York's LaGuardia airport, and now she'd be traveling from EWR in New Jersey to Minneapolis-St. Paul.

With any luck, from there it'd be from MSP to CDG, Charles de Gaulle outside Paris, or AMS, Schiphol International at Amsterdam, and from there into the apartments of any of a number of eastern European cities. Once she was there, once she was moving by train and car, it'd take the Stasi to sniff her out, and there was no Stasi, not anymore, not since East Germany ran off the rails.

She was not a sentimental woman, and she shed no tears for the Stasi, the East German State Security.

The ride from Manhattan to EWR took the best part of an hour, traffic stacked up around some kind of a strike, with honking car horns and screaming cops, a strike leader with a bullhorn leading chants that had something to do with hotel rooms and bedbugs. All the time her Somali driver chanted along with unusual tunes from the car radio.

Ten minutes out of the airport, she took a call from Turicek, who said, "Edie, the cops

352

are all over us. They've been asking about me, they've interviewed Jacob, and they'll get to Kristina sooner or later."

"How? How'd they do this?" she asked.

"Jacob. We think they just asked around Polaris, who did it, and the Polaris people blamed Jacob," Turicek said.

"They got that right," Albitis said.

"Yeah, but . . . we think they might be watching all of us, and we can't get to the office. You've got to go over there as soon as you get in. The day's packages are gonna start piling up at the door. If somebody steals one of them . . ."

"Ah shit, I'm five hours out, if the plane's on time, and I don't miss it."

"That's gonna have to do," Turicek said. "You're the only one we got. The rest of the stuff is stashed. There's no way they know about the office, but we can't go there."

"We're so close."

"What's that crazy sound I'm hearing?"

"Radio. Listen, when I get to the airport, I'm going to throw this phone away," she said. "I'll get another one at the airport, if I can. But if you get an unknown number coming in tonight, answer it."

"Okay, but —"

"I'll pick up the packages if it looks okay, and I'll get tomorrow's," Albitis said. "Can you get to Kristina?"

"I think so. She should be coming in," Turicek said. "There's been nobody here at work, so they haven't bugged us, I don't think."

"They'll figure out the gold, sooner or later, and come looking for it. So tell Kristina that I'm taking it out of her mom's place. I'll rent a van and drive down to Iowa, or to Wisconsin. Once it's safely stashed, we can figure out our next move."

"I'll tell Kristina. Call me when you get in."

Sanderson wouldn't move from her insistence that she knew nothing, and the SWAT team's search of the apartment building came up empty, so Lucas headed back to the office. He was confused: he knew why the Mexicans had gone after Sanderson, but where had they gone? And why had they gone? They'd casually walked in the front door, like a couple of tourists, so why had they apparently fled out the back like a couple of hunted killers?

There was an answer to that question, but he didn't know what it was.

Sandy was waiting at the office and asked, "What happened?"

"Aw, it was a clusterfuck. Wait for me, I've

got to go talk to Shaffer."

He'd called Shaffer after the SWAT team had begun its search, and though Shaffer was miffed by not hearing about it sooner, he relaxed when Lucas told him that nothing would be found.

"I can't tell you what happened," he now said, as he leaned against Shaffer's doorjamb.

"What are the chances, really, that they were the guys we're looking for? Our Mexicans?"

"About ninety-eight percent," Lucas said. "They were looking for Sanderson, and they took off. They got warned, somehow. Maybe they saw me running up the steps. . . . Anyway, we're no closer than we were before."

"Well, we know they're still here, anyway," Shaffer said. "We've still got a shot at finding them."

Lucas nodded. "So what did ICE find at Sunnie?"

"Ah — the shadow books. About a year after Brooks set up Sunnie, when they were struggling, he made a whole replicated set of books for a fake company called Bois Brule, which did the same thing Sunnie did — sold foreign language software, but a lot more successfully than Sunnie. Money

355

would come in, in all kinds of amounts, but all on big recognized credit cards, VISA and MasterCard. The VISA and MasterCard banks would collect the payments and credit Bois Brule's account with Polaris. They needed the Bois Brule system to make sure that whoever owed them actually paid."

"I'm not sure I see it yet," Lucas said.

"Okay. They sell a kilo of cocaine, collect, say, twenty K. They get it in cash. Eventually, they have this huge bundle of dollars, and no way to deposit it. You can't show up at a bank with thirty million in ten-dollar bills without somebody getting suspicious. Not even in Mexico," Shaffer said. "If nothing else, it'd be considered rude."

"Okay . . ."

"So what they do, they have a hundred people each with a hundred credit cards. Those people charge twenty-five hundred bucks each, every month, on every card, and buy bank drafts with cash to pay off the accounts. VISA collects the cash and credits Bois Brule. Now the money is in the bank system, and goes all over the place, and pays for all kinds of stuff. Real estate, gold, whatever . . ."

"And the DEA guys have broken it out?"

Shaffer nodded. "Some of it, anyway. They're over at Sunnie peeing themselves, out of pure excitement. They might be able to claw back six months of it, or a year, even. But after a while, with these kinds of deals, records get lost, accounts get closed and confused, companies turn out not to exist anymore . . . at least, that's what O'Brien says."

"Hmm. Well, better them than me. I'll stick to murder and theft," Lucas said.

Back at his office, Lucas said to Sandy, "All right: the Syrian woman."

"You heard the biggest part of it: that she exists," Sandy said. "Everybody who co-operated with me — not all of them co-operated, but of the ones who did, I couldn't find any buying pattern. I can't figure out where she'll show up next. All I could think of is that you get ahold of all the different police departments, and we get the gold dealers to tip us off, and we get a squad car around to the dealers —"

"To do what? We don't even know that she's committing a crime," Lucas said.

"They could talk to her," Sandy said. "Get a look at her. Check her ID. Maybe get some fingerprints. Uh, I remember seeing these signs that say you can't bring more than ten thousand dollars into the U.S. without registering, and she's got all this money."

"Okay, there's something in there," Lucas said. "Start calling the dealers, see who'll agree to tip us."

"I thought we might need your weight behind it."

"Sandy, I'm a goddamn voice on a telephone," Lucas said. "So are you. Tell them that you're Rose Marie, that you're the public safety commissioner."

"That'd help my career," Sandy said.

"Sooo . . . figure something out," Lucas said. "We need this woman."

"What are you going to do?"

"I'm gonna jack up Turicek. They know we're coming, so we might as well show up."

Albitis was about to drop her phone into a trash barrel at EWR, when it rang. Had to be Kline, Turicek, or Sanderson, since they were the only ones with the number for that phone, but when she looked at the screen, it said, "Delta Airlines."

"Oh, fuck me with a phone pole," she muttered. A man walking just ahead of her turned and looked at her, bewildered. She punched up the text message that said that her flight had been indefinitely delayed. She kept walking, through security, down to the gate, where a Delta attendant told her that the plane was broken, though she didn't use that exact word.

"So what are we doing?" Albitis asked.

"We're bringing another plane in from Atlanta," the attendant said. "It should be here by eight o'clock."

"Eight o'clock? I won't be in the Twin Cities until midnight," Albitis said.

"We apologize for any inconvenience. . . ."

Albitis thought the woman sounded insincere, but she turned away and punched up Turicek and told him what had happened. Turicek said, "The cops talked to Kristina. Some of the Mexicans turned up at her apartment. She's scared shitless."

"So what do you want to do?" Albitis asked.

"Let me think. I'll call you."

Turicek called Sanderson, who was holed up at her apartment, and told her to get down to the bank. "Perfectly safe," he assured her. "You're inside your own parking garage, you drive straight to the bank's parking garage, you call me just before you get here, and I'll meet you in the garage. But you gotta take over for me. I'm really sick — I say no more."

She recognized the "say no more." It was part of a Monty Python sketch that Kline and Turicek, when in nerd mode, could do in endless variations: *"Nudge nudge, wink wink, say no more."* It meant, in this context, that something was going on but Turicek couldn't talk about it on the phone.

"I'll come," she said. She added, "I don't want to go to prison."

Turicek couldn't think of how to answer, so he said, "Good."

When Sanderson showed up, an hour later, Turicek took the elevator down to the Skyway and walked over to Macy's, looking in windows and mirrors for familiar faces. Was he being watched? He had that familiar creepy feeling at the back of his neck, familiar from the old days back in Lithuania, when he was a fifteen-year-old school kid dealing in American cigarettes and British pornography.

In the Macy's men's store, he bought a pair of athletic shorts, a T-shirt, a pair of white socks, a black ball cap, and Nike cross-training shoes. He paid and carried the bag back out of the store, went to the office-supply store next door, bought a backpack, the kind kids wore to school. When he walked across the bridge between Macy's and the IDS Center, he risked a quick glance back and picked up a large man ambling along behind a fat woman, as though he were using her as a blind. He thought he'd seen the face earlier.

They were, he thought, tracking him.

Of course, they hadn't grown up in Vilnius.

He carried the clothes down to the security center, changed in the men's room, put his work clothes in the backpack, slipped his arms through it, and pulled the cap down over his eyes. "I'll be a couple of hours," he said, quietly, to Sanderson.

"Be careful . . ."

"If anybody asks, tell them I'm out jogging."

He walked out in the running gear, and when he hit the door — the first place the watchers could see him — he was running.

Jenkins was up in the public parking ramp where he could watch both Turicek's car and the street entrance to the bank, and Shrake was loitering in the Skyway. Jenkins had recently bought a chunk of blue goop that came in a plastic egg and was meant to be squeezed, to strengthen hands and forearms. It also had some bubble-gum-like qualities: a pinch of it could be stretched almost indefinitely, into long gummy strings, and doing that was oddly engrossing.

He was pulling out one of his longest strings when Turicek burst through the door and started running down the street. Jenkins shouted into his handset, "Shit, I think he's running, but I'm not sure it's him. He's on the street running south."

"Watch him," Shrake called back, and thirty seconds later, Shrake burst onto the same street and looked south, but Turicek was far down the next block, and Shrake couldn't see him through the people on the street. Jenkins shouted into the handset, "He turned left . . . he's gone."

Shrake ran that way, and Jenkins got the car, and they cruised, looking for a man in running shorts, but they never saw him again. Jenkins called the bank and asked for him, and the woman who answered the phone in the systems division said he'd gone jogging.

"Goddamnit," Jenkins said. He got on his cell phone and called Lucas. "I got bad news and bad news. Which do you want first?"

Lucas asked, "What happened?"

"Turicek must have spotted us, and then he ran. We never had a chance," Jenkins said. "He either knew we were here, or he assumed it."

"Goddamnit," Lucas said.

"That's just what I said." He described the circumstances, and Lucas asked, "You think he's really jogging?"

"Not unless he's practicing for the hundred-yard dash. He came out of there like he was being chased by the hound of the coupe de villes," Jenkins said. "What do you want us to do?"

"Drive around. Hang there. Call the cab companies, see if they picked up a jogger. Quit when it's quitting time. I mean, I don't know."

"All right. I'm sorry, man."

"Call me if anything changes. Goddamnit, again, we need to know where that guy goes," Lucas said.

Turicek ran four blocks, swerved into the Pillsbury Center and took the escalators up, watching the doors, then turned and walked quickly down toward the Government Center, ninety percent sure he'd lost the men behind him.

In the Government Center men's restroom, he changed into his street clothes, put the running clothes in the pack, and called a cab. Five minutes later, he was on his way to St. Paul. There, he directed the cabbie through a couple of back streets to a bar, paid off the cab, walked into the bar and out the back, called another cab. When that cab arrived, he took it to the rental office, picked up the packages, and took them to Sanderson's mom's house and stashed them in the closet.

He left the house on foot, called Albitis, told her what he'd done.

"This is the last time I can pull this off — they probably know I was on to them, but they can't be sure," Turicek said. "I can't do it again or they'll pick me up."

"Can they know for sure that we took the money?" she asked.

"No. They can believe it, but they can't *know*. We'll have to figure out what to do next — I think we're going to have to leave the gold for a while. You can get yours, and take off, but the other three of us, we're going to have to stash our shares and wait for a while."

"Quite a while. Years," she said.

"Maybe a couple of years," Turicek agreed. "We'll figure something out. Maybe we'll start a software company and get rich, in quotes."

"Yeah, well, good luck," Albitis said. "I'll see you in Pest. If you need to call me again, I'll be on the other phone. I'm sitting in the gate here, and I'm throwing this one away."

■ ■ ■ ■

When he got off the phone, Turicek called a fourth cab — he'd walked a half-mile from Mom's, by then — and took it to his apartment. If they picked him up again, so what? He was out of it, now. Albitis would pick up the last shipment, take it to Mom's. From here on out, it was the daily grind at the bank.

A year, or two . . . he could handle two years, if he knew he was getting paid a tax-free two and a half million a year to do it.

Boring, but manageable.

He was imagining himself in the new life when he got to his apartment door. He put the key in, pushed it open, and the Mexican hit him in the back. They'd been in the apartment across the hall and they took him down in a heap.

Turicek was strong, and he fought back, tried to scream, or shout, but managed nothing but a gargling sound as they rolled across the floor. One of the Mexicans had his arms and legs wrapped around him, while the other one stumbled over them, punching him in the face, then picked up a plaster lamp and whacked Turicek on the forehead and everything went gray. He heard them cursing, heard the door close, knew, vaguely, that he had to resist, but couldn't make anything work, felt them rolling him, his arms pinned, his hands taped, then his feet.

They picked him up, like a six-foot cigar, slung him over their shoulders, looked out in the hall, and then they were running, away from the entrance to the fire stairs. They went down the stairs, then they were outside and Turicek, coming back now, felt himself folded at the waist, and thrown in the trunk of a car. He heard two doors slam, and the car began rolling.

Turicek could feel himself bleeding, was sick with the impact of the lamp, but knew in a cold corner of his mind, just as Kline had, that he was a dead man, but not for a while — the time it took them to cut him to pieces.

When they'd thrown him in the trunk, they'd folded him at the waist, with his hands behind him. He realized then, cramped as he was, that he could touch the back of his feet, and the tape that bound them together. He tore at the tape, felt fingernails ripping, but caught an edge, and ripped at it frantically, now pulling whole fingernails loose. . . .

As he did it, he thrashed around, and saw a green-white glow, a small T-shaped plastic handle, with a pictogram of a stick-figure man jumping out of the trunk of a car. An emergency trunk release. The Mexicans must not have known it was there.

It was, as bad luck would have it, near his head, not far from his eyes, but he couldn't lever himself far enough up to catch it with his teeth. So he pulled at the tape, and he thrashed, and tried to turn around, thought he would break his neck, but finally one foot came free, though the other was wedged against something, and it took another ten seconds to wiggle it free, and another long two minutes to turn himself around.

Now he felt hope for the first time. The car suddenly slowed and pitched down, going down a hill, and he got a foot up near the emergency release, cocked himself as best he could: if he kicked it loose, he'd throw his legs over the back of the trunk, and then throw his body backward.

He took a breath, and did it: kicked the release. Nothing happened. He kicked it again, and again, then thought to hook it with his toe, and pulled, and then the trunk popped an inch. He kicked it open, and threw his legs out the back, and heaved himself out of the car.

The car was traveling thirty or forty miles an hour, and he hit with a terrific impact, unable to protect his head, felt and even heard a shoulder break, was clouted in the face, rolled forever and forever, bouncing; it was like being beaten by a bare-knuckle boxer, without defense, simply pounded, until finally . . . he stopped.

Still alive.

He heard the noise, the screaming noise, looked wildly back and at the very last instant realized that he'd thrown himself into the middle of a freeway ramp, and though he didn't have time to think it, or to recognize it, a Ford F-150 pickup was twenty feet away, slewing wildly as the driver tried to stop.

Then it hit him.

And Uno looked out the back window and said, *"Pinche hijo de . . ."* and said to Tres, "Faster now, faster."

Virgil Flowers called Lucas and said, "Things are getting interesting."

"Yeah?"

"There's a farm here, and your robbers are apparently going in and out of there with their loads of horse shit," Flowers said. "We can't figure out why anybody would need so much horse shit, but I've got Richie Jones interested. You know Richie?"

"Yeah." Richie was the sheriff.

"We're going to take a look at the farm," Virgil said. "Talk to some people around there. There might be something else going on."

"Virgil, goddamnit, all I want to do is bust these two. I don't need a fuckin' Shakespeare festival."

"Yeah, well, that's because you've got something to occupy your time up there. I'm just trying to drum up a little business, and Richie's got to run for reelection this fall."

"Just get on with it, okay?"

"Maybe," Flowers said. "I'll call you. Sometime."

Lucas heard about Turicek five minutes later, when, still brooding over Flowers's insubordination, he got a call from the duty officer at the BCA. "We got a woman who's trying to reach you. She says her name is Kristina Sanderson and it's an emergency. Sounds like she's freaking out."

Lucas thought, *Ah,* with some satisfaction. She was cracking. He had the call switched through and then Sanderson was screaming at him, "They took Ivan, they, I think he's

369

going to die, I think, he's oh, God, he looks like, oh God, he looks like a . . . like a . . . a stewed tomato."

15

Turicek had been taken to Regions Hospital, the major St. Paul public hospital. The cops who'd followed the ambulance didn't find a wallet, but did find his cell phone. His last call had been to a blocked number out of state, and when they called it, they got a ring but no answer.

The next number had been Sanderson's.

She'd driven herself across town to Regions, found that Turicek was in surgery, but had been walked into the OR, and identified him behind the tangle of breathing equipment. When she asked the surgeon how bad he was, the surgeon had said, "You'll have to leave now."

She followed the circulating nurse out of the room, and the St. Paul cops asked her if she knew what had happened, and she'd started blubbering. All she'd seen of Turicek was his head, which looked like an oversized raw turnip and was shaped all wrong, and a large patch on the abdominal covering, which showed a lot of blood and what she assumed was guts.

She told the cops, "The Mexicans, the Mexicans," and they said, *"The Mexicans?"* and she'd nodded and said, "There was a police officer, and agent, from the state . . ."

One of the cops said, "Davenport?" and she nodded again, and the cop said, "Let's give them a ring."

About that time, the surgeon walked out of the emergency OR, pulling off his bloody gloves, and one of the cops, looking past her, said, "Uh-oh."

Before heading down to Regions, Lucas called Shaffer to fill him in. He'd parked and was walking toward the emergency room entrance when he saw Shaffer pulling into the parking area, and he slowed and waited until the other agent caught up.

"What the fuck happened?" Shaffer demanded. "Shrake and Jenkins take the day off? They were supposed to be all over him."

"Take it easy," Lucas snapped. "The guy knew we were there, and he bolted. He knew where he was going. We could have had a whole team on him and he would have lost them."

"Wouldn't have lost my team," Shaffer

said. "For God's sakes, this was our big chance. We knew the Mexicans were looking for him."

"Having a little trouble finding the Mexicans, Bob? Don't lay it on us, that was *your* job."

They snarled at each other some more on the way to the ER; too much media, too much attention, too many people watching. Tempers were going to flare. . . .

"What about Turicek?" Shaffer asked.

"Last I heard, he was still breathing," Lucas said.

They pushed through the door and saw a woman in a surgeon's gown with blood at her waist, talking to Sanderson, one hand on Sanderson's shoulder, and Sanderson was sobbing, and Lucas said, "Maybe that changed."

Two St. Paul homicide cops told them the story, and they went outside, where the driver of the Ford pickup had been stashed, waiting, in his truck. His name was Robert Johnson, and he was with his girlfriend, whose name was Betty Johnson, no relation, yet, and Robert Johnson said, "I couldn't help it."

One of the St. Paul detectives said, "We understand that, Mr. Johnson. We believe it was a kidnapping. If you could just tell the agents what you saw."

The two Johnsons took turns: they'd just taken a left onto the freeway ramp at Snelling Avenue, not going fast at all — they agreed on that — and pulled up behind a white car that was accelerating even more slowly than they were. They were a truck length or two behind the white car when the trunk popped open and a man came flying out. He landed on the pavement directly in front of them, and Robert, who was at the wheel, swerved, but said that he didn't know if he hit the brakes before or after they hit the man.

"It sounded like we'd hit a watermelon, or a basketball, there was this awful *whump* sound," Betty said. "I knew we hit his head. . . ."

The white car sped away while the two Johnsons jumped out of their truck and found Turicek half under it, about halfway down the length of the truck. He had a tire track on his pants, and the Johnsons said they'd probably run over his body, just at the hips.

They'd stopped traffic and called 911 on Robert's cell phone. The ambulance had been there in five minutes, right behind a cop car. The ambulance attendants had pulled Turicek out from under the truck, and it seemed like he was dead, except that he kept blowing blood bubbles. They threw him on a gurney and rushed him back to the hospital. It was then, the responding St. Paul uniform said, that they saw that his arms were taped behind him.

Lucas turned to Shaffer and asked, "How'd they know where to find him? How did they know that?"

Shaffer shook his head: "Has to be a leak inside the bank. I mean, my team didn't even know he'd run, and if it was only you and Jenkins and Shrake and . . ."

They turned and looked at Sanderson. She said, "Not me. I didn't tell anybody." Then she remembered the phone call, put her fingers to her lips, and said, "Oh . . . wait."

Shaffer: "What?"

"Somebody called me and asked where he was. I told them he went jogging," she said.

Lucas said to Shaffer, "That was Jenkins."

"Who else did you mention it to?" Shaffer asked her.

"Nobody. Nobody else," she said. "Not a single person called me, except that one person, after he went jogging. Who cares if somebody goes jogging?"

Lucas: "Did he ever go jogging before?"

"No. No. He showed up with some bags from Macy's, went into the men's room, changed, and said he was going jogging. He'd never jogged before."

Shaffer looked at Lucas and conceded, "Okay. He knew."

Lucas looked at Sanderson for another long minute, then said, "Miz Sanderson, I need to talk privately with Agent Shaffer for a few seconds, then I need to speak privately with you."

She said, nervously, "Okay."

Lucas and Shaffer walked down the sidewalk and Lucas said, "Why don't you take off? You don't want to witness this."

"What're you going to do?"

"Push her around," Lucas said.

Shaffer said, "I'll see you at the meeting tomorrow."

Lucas took Sanderson to an empty hospital room, pointed her at a chair, then stood over her, and too close.

"You're going to prison for life."

"No . . ."

"Yes, I think so. I'm almost sure of it. The fact is, you've been withholding information from us, and that information could have led to the arrest of these Mexican killers. That makes you complicit in a whole series of first-degree murders. They have a source of information inside your bank, and you could probably tell us who it is. Instead, you keep passing along this bullshit about how you know nothing, it was all Turicek. Well, I don't believe it, and neither will a jury. I am going to arrest you. Just a matter of time, Kristina. It's a matter of time."

"But I don't know anything," she wailed. "I've tried to tell you everything —"

"You're going to prison," Lucas repeated. "But before I come over and arrest you, I want to tell you in some detail what they did to the Brooks children before they killed them."

And he did, telling her about the throat-cutting, the knuckle amputations, the rape of the little girl and the mother while their father was bound on the floor beside them, about the puddles of blood and the blue-bottle flies and the finger stumps used to write the bloody message on the wall.

Sanderson's head went down, her hands between her thighs, pressed together, her forehead nearly on her thumbs. "This is what you guys did, bringing these killers into town," Lucas said.

"It was all Ivan. It had to be," she said. "I didn't know."

Lucas got up, sighed, and said, "Well. Be

seeing you. Take care of yourself, these people are crazy."

Now her head came up and she shouted at him, spittle flying across the room: "I know they're crazy. You don't have to tell me. They almost killed that poor Jacob, who wouldn't hurt a fly, and they murdered Ivan, and they missed me just because I got lucky, and you know who brought them around to us? You police! You police dragged them in on top of us. That's why they're coming for us. You did this!"

"See ya," Lucas said, and he was out the door. As soon as he was out of sight, he jogged down the corridor and around the corner, and outside to the parking lot to the truck. From the door pocket, he retrieved his own prepaid cell phone and punched in the first of the numbers he'd taken from Kline's prepaid cell phone when he searched Kline's apartment. When Sanderson appeared at the emergency room door a moment later, he tapped the "call" icon. A phone rang, but she made no move to answer it.

He punched in a second number and, as she walked up to her car, let it ring. Nothing. He put in the third number, and on the fourth ring, a man answered with a soft southern accent.

"Hello?"

"I must have the wrong number," Lucas said. "Is this Jimmy?"

"No, this ain't Jimmy," the man said, with an amused chuckle. "This is the custodian who just took Jimmy's phone out of the trash can at Newark airport."

"I'll have to kick Jimmy's ass," Lucas said.

"What do you want me to do with the phone?" the custodian asked.

"Keep it," Lucas said. "It's a prepay. When it runs out, you can pay for more."

Sanderson was in her car, backing out of the parking space, but one thing that Lucas knew, as sure as sin and taxes, was that if somebody called a woman on a cell phone, she'd answer it. Or at least look at it. Was it possible she really wasn't part of the Kline-Turicek-Gold Buyer phone circle?

She took a left onto the road, heading down to I-35, and he followed, several cars back. She drove slowly across the Cities, all the way to her apartment, into her parking garage, and out of sight.

"Goddamnit," Lucas said aloud.

Was it possible that she really was innocent?

No, he decided. It wasn't. He did a U-turn and headed back home.

■ ■ ■ ■

Edie Albitis got into town just before midnight. She'd tried calling Turicek fifteen times on her second phone, hadn't gotten an answer. As the plane rolled across the tarmac at MSP, she tried Sanderson. Sanderson, she thought, was probably the weak link in the whole chain, the one most likely to cough them up. She'd talked to Turicek about it, and he'd suggested that she probably wouldn't screw up and talk until he and Albitis were safely in their respective bolt-holes in Lithuania, Ukraine, or Georgia. That had changed now, with all the attention from the cops.

She tried to get Turicek, failed, knew she couldn't get Kline, who was still in the hospital and apparently didn't have his prepaid phone with him, and so she went to Sanderson, who'd just walked in the door when she called, the phone ringing from where she'd left it, on the floor next to the living room couch.

"Yes?"

"It's me," Albitis said. They didn't use names on the phone.

"Oh, my God, have you heard?" Sanderson cried.

"Heard what?"

"Ivan's dead."

"What?" Albitis freaked; if it hadn't been for her lap belt, she might have leaped out of the airplane seat.

Sanderson told her about it, and Albitis listened, openmouthed, as they taxied up to the Jetway.

"All right," Albitis said. "I'll call you back in five minutes. I have to think."

It wasn't so much that she had to think, but she couldn't talk with the guy in the next seat leaning over her. Once inside the terminal, she found an empty space next to a window and called Sanderson back. She said, "Okay, you've got this cop threatening you. That means he suspects, but he doesn't *know.* He's got no proof, or he already would have popped you. If you and Jacob keep your mouths shut, you'll be okay."

"I'm sitting here shaking like a leaf," Sanderson said. "You should have seen poor Ivan's head. There was hardly any skin left on it. Like his nose had almost been scraped off."

"Okay, okay, I don't want to hear that," Albitis said. "I really don't."

"I had to *look* at it."

"Enough. I'm going to the office to pick up today's packages. I'll sleep there, on the floor. The last of the packages come in tomorrow. I'll pick them up, and then, we'll just wait. We'll have all the gold, and the cops'll have no clue. We'll split it up, and we're done."

"Will you call me?"

"I'll call you three times a day. . . . Anything you hear, call me, but only on the cold phone, okay? Only on the cold phone. They're probably monitoring your cell."

"Oh, God, this agent said I'm going to prison for life, I'm an accessory to murder because I won't help them."

"Just stay cool."

When Lucas got home, Weather was asleep, but Letty was still up. "Mom said to tell you she saw the autopsy stuff on your desk, and she says she's got a bad feeling about it. Something's not right. She says she can't imagine how Rivera got shot, if it happened the way you said it did."

Lucas frowned and said, "Did she say why?"

"No, she says she just couldn't imagine it," she said. "You know, if it was the way you said."

Lucas went to his desk, found the autopsy file, and thumbed through it. Letty, munching on a PowerBar, came to look over his shoulder.

"You don't have to see this," Lucas said.

"I already did," Letty said. "I couldn't figure out what she meant, either. Maybe we should go wake her up."

"Is she cutting tomorrow?"

"She's got a nose . . . rhinoplasty." Weather had outlawed the phrase "nose job" in the Davenport household.

"So we let her sleep," Lucas said.

He looked through the photos, of both the crime scene and the autopsy, along with the autopsy notes.

"You see it?" Letty asked.

"No, because I'm going to have to imagine it, and I can't do that with you crunching the PowerBar in my ear," Lucas said.

"Chill."

Lucas looked at the photos, closed his eyes. Simple enough. Rivera walked up the front steps, cocked his gun, made sure the safety was off, got his guts up, and kicked the door. He landed with one foot inside, saw the two men off to his right, turned that way. One of them went for his gun and he fired twice and the third man, whom he hadn't seen, who was standing next to the picture window to his left, peeking through the drapes, that man swivels with a gun and shoots. . . .

He looked at the pictures.

Closed his eyes. The man on the left shoots . . .

He shoots . . .

Lucas opened his eyes and said, "Houston, we've got a problem."

"I'm Letty," said Letty. "You had a stroke, or something?"

Lucas spent a restless night working through it, realized he should have seen it a lot sooner. He'd sensed it, back at the shooting scene, but hadn't been able to put his finger on the problem. But better late than never.

Weather's alarm went off at six o'clock. He usually slept right through it, but this time he rolled out of bed with her, shaved, gave her a good scrub in the shower, which might have grown interesting if they'd only had more time, but they were both in a hurry. He took the time to say, "Thanks for the tip on the autopsy."

"That's something?" she asked.

"I'm afraid it is."

16

Lucas began by calling Shaffer, taking a certain amount of satisfaction at the thought of blowing him out of bed. Shaffer answered the phone on the second ring and sounded unnaturally alert, saying, "Yeah? What's up?"

"You've been up for two hours and you've already done your yoga exercises and now you're drinking fresh-squeezed orange juice, aren't you?" Lucas asked.

"Carrot juice," Shaffer said. "Getting ready to run. You're calling for juice advice?"

"No. I need to meet with you at eight o'clock instead of nine, and out of sight. You drink coffee?"

"You broke something?"

"Maybe."

"Tell me where."

Del was not quite as alert. "Jesus. Is the sun up?"

"I need to talk to your brother-in-law, the real estate guy," Lucas said. "I need to talk to him right now."

"We're not an early-up family," Del said.

"Well, you're up, so why shouldn't your brother-in-law be up?" Lucas asked.

"That's a point. I'll call him," Del said.

When he got off the phone, Lucas went to his study and got out a yellow pad and started making a list. When he finished, after some thought, the list had only three items.

— Rivera choreography.

— Sanderson apartment.

— Insider information.

He worked through it all again and was convinced. He wasn't sure Shaffer would be.

Del's brother-in-law called. His name was Dominic and he worked the east side of St. Paul. "Dom, I need an empty east side house, a little run-down, not occupied. I can get you a thousand dollars for three days, starting today. You got somebody?"

"This for a sting?"

"Yeah."

"Let me call around."

Lucas and Shaffer met at an east side coffee

shop. They got a couple of cups of something that looked and tasted like Folgers, and found a corner where they could talk. Lucas pulled a legal pad out of his briefcase, pushed it across the table, and said, "I'm going to walk you through it." He used a pen to draw a sketch of the entry area of the house where Rivera had been shot to death.

"Here's the steps, here's the couch where the one Mexican was shot," he said, tapping his pen on the outline drawing. "Now, Rivera kicks the door, presumably having done a peek so he knows where the Mexicans are. Now, if you saw one out of three, or two out of three, when you peeked, would you kick the door? Or would you call for backup?"

"I'd call for backup under any conditions," Shaffer said. "If he'd called for backup, we'd have taken them all and he'd still be alive. He should have done what you did down at Sanderson's apartment."

"But he's got the macho gene, he's hot, he hates these guys," Lucas said. "They literally skinned one of his fellow agents alive, then mailed the guy's skin to his boss. So he sees two of them. Does he kick the door or not?"

Shaffer considered, then shook his head.

"He's gonna have trouble just with the two of them, unless he went in planning to kill them. If there's a third one, that he can't see, he's got a serious problem."

"The crime-scene guys say there was a shooter game plugged into the TV, with two consoles. Both were turned on. Probably two guys on the couch, one of them shot to death," Lucas said, tapping the sketch. "The third guy, they thought, was probably by this window, may have seen Rivera coming, at the last minute, and had his gun out. Maybe heard Rivera on the step or something. Rivera kicks the door, gets two shots off, and the guy by the window shoots *him.* Then the two who are still alive run for it."

Shaffer said, "Yup."

"But I'm saying, if he could only see two out of three, he probably wouldn't have kicked it," Lucas said. "But, just for argument's sake, let's say he's super-macho, so maybe he does kick it. Now you've done this. You've got a target off to the right that you know about. So you kick the door, your gun goes right, but you glance to the left, just an instant, to clear the rest of the room, and then you come back to the gun's sights. Okay?"

"Okay."

"Now, he got off two aimed shots, but he

apparently never looked left, never suspected anybody was to his left, and he apparently never saw the other guy coming. The other guy put the gun so close to Rivera's head that he burned his hair, tattooed his scalp," Lucas said. "To do that, he would have had to hold the gun out at arm's length and crank his hand to the left, to make that shot. And not be seen while he did it. The bullet went in at the right-side base of Rivera's skull, and came out of the top of his skull, above his left eye, having gone all the way through his brain."

"The guy couldn't have been by the window to his right because the door would be in the way," Shaffer said. Then, "Okay, I see what you're saying."

"Do you?"

"Yeah." Shaffer grimaced and shook his head. "You're saying he was probably shot by somebody standing behind him to the right, shorter than he was, or somebody standing one step down, somebody that he knew was there and maybe trusted."

Lucas nodded, and Shaffer continued: "You're saying that Martínez shot him in the back of the head."

"Attaboy," Lucas said.

"Sonofabitch. I knew you couldn't trust those people." Shaffer, agitated, got up and walked around a couple of tables, then came back and sat down again.

"You could trust Rivera. You couldn't trust Martínez," Lucas said. "It all depends on the individual. The goddamn gang planted her on him, knew every move he was making. She could do her 'research' and point him at other gangs, but tip off the Criminales if he ever went after them. I'm pretty sure she was sleeping with him. She was sleeping with him and when the time came, she swatted him like a fly. If I'm right."

Shaffer stared at the yellow pad, wiping his tongue across his bottom lip, and then, "I'm buying it, but it'd be nice if there was something else."

"There is," Lucas said. "I'm down at Sanderson's apartment, looking for Sanderson, and what happens? Two of the Mexicans come walking down the sidewalk. I can't believe it. For one thing, how'd they know so fast? How'd they figure that out? They go up to the front door and go inside, and I pull the car out and across the street, jump out and run up the steps," Lucas said. "I wasn't more than a minute behind them, going through the front door. I punch out the door panel, get inside. I know what her apartment number is, I run up the steps. They can't have gotten to her apartment as fast as I did — for one thing, they had to talk with the manager, at least for a second or two. So I run up the steps, and they're gone. *Gone.* Vanished. Nobody ever saw them again. Why is that?"

"Tell me," Shaffer said.

"First, because I semi-fucked up. We were always dealing with the idea of three Mexican men. One was dead, here were the other two. Why would I worry about another one? But, the thing is, I'd given Rivera and Martínez a ride in the Lexus. *She knew the car.* And guess what? She'd driven them over there, and was waiting up the street, behind me. I never saw her. That's where they were walking from. Her car. She saw the Lexus, saw me jump out, and she called them on their cell phones. They ran out the back way and around the building, and she picked them up and they were out of there. It's the only thing that works."

Shaffer thought about it for a minute, then said, "I'm buying that, too."

"Third," Lucas said. "We've known we had a leak. They weren't one step ahead of us or behind us — they were exactly in step with us. We thought it was in the bank — but why would a leak in the Polaris bank know about Sanderson over at Hennepin? At least, know that fast? But when we *sus-*

pected Kline or Sanderson had something to do with the theft, with no proof at all, we couldn't do anything about it. We just had to keep looking. But *they* could do something about it. They were right there, ready to go. They were all over Kline right after we told her about him."

"So what are we going to do about it?" Shaffer asked.

"We're gonna set them up," Lucas said. "I'm already moving on it. But I'm going to need you to do some acting."

Shaffer scratched his head. "I can do that."

Lucas laid out the rest of his plan, and when he finished, Shaffer said, "It bothers me that we don't tell the rest of the crew until later."

"Somebody will give it away," Lucas said. "I'll tell you what, Bob, she's both a major crook and a kind of a cop — she's worked both sides, and if she smells a rat, she's outa here. She'll just take Rivera's ashes and go home. So we don't tell anybody what we're doing. The whole discussion will be real, instead of phony."

"Some of the guys will be pissed," Shaffer said.

"Hey, a little rain, you know? Apologize later," Lucas said. "What worries me more is that some of them are going to argue that it's really stupid not to cover the house from the get-go. We gotta go with the idea that we just don't have the guys, and we don't have anything for a warrant. We say we're gonna put two on Kline, we're gonna put two on Sanderson, we're gonna put four out at the airport, wait for the plane and then follow her."

"What's her name? The chick we're following?"

"Martha . . . something?"

"Martha White," Shaffer said. "Like the biscuit mix."

"Good. So you want to do this?" Lucas asked.

"Got nothing to lose," Shaffer said. "If you're wrong, we pay some overtime. But if you're right, we get three killers."

Lucas got a call back from Dom, the brother-in-law, who'd found a house off East Margaret Street, owned by an absentee landlord who'd be happy to take a thousand dollars for three days, plus costs, if the cops did any damage. Lucas okayed the deal, Dom gave him the number for the realtor's lockbox on the front door and said he'd pull the For Sale sign.

"You could do the landlord a favor and fire a few shots through the roof," Dom said. "The place really needs a new roof before he can sell it."

"We'll do that for sure. You can count on it," Lucas said.

They were out of the coffee shop by eight-thirty, and since the house was not too far from the BCA, they went that way. The key was in the lockbox, as Dom had said, and they cracked the door and walked through. The house was probably eighty years old, Lucas thought, and thoroughly scuffed up, two stories, fifteen hundred square feet or so, with gritty hardwood floors and a refrigerator-stove combination that came from the fifties. It smelled like plaster, nicotine, and old rugs. There were three outside doors.

"You want to use it as a dummy, or do you want to put a couple of guys in here?" Shaffer asked.

"I don't have anybody to spare, but if we could get a couple of guys from the SWAT, that'd work," Lucas said.

O'Brien from the DEA was at the morning meeting, along with Shaffer and three members of his team, Lucas and Del, and Martínez. She arrived carrying her five-pound briefcase, pulled out several report books that appeared to run to a hundred pages or more, each, and said, "I spent last night printing these. This is a report from our central headquarters on known and suspected gang connections in St. Paul. We thought it might provide some information on where the fugitives have hidden themselves."

She handed a copy to Lucas, slid one across the table to O'Brien, walked around the table and passed one to Shaffer, and left another one in the middle of the table. Lucas, Shaffer, and O'Brien spent a few seconds flipping through the reports, which were in English, then Lucas put his copy aside and said, "That's gonna take some reading time."

"Why are they in English?" Shaffer asked.

"Because they are prepared with a DEA task force. They are both English and Spanish."

"Any specific contacts for the Criminales?" Lucas asked.

"Two possibilities, but we are not sure. They might be worthy of surveillance," Martínez said.

"We've had a break," Shaffer said, setting his copy aside, as Lucas had. "Lucas, do you want to tell us about it?"

Lucas nodded and said, "We know when

the money was taken from Polaris. We know when they stopped. We know that they will have to break the chain of checks and formal money transfers, which we are now tracing. Both the DEA and the bankers involved agreed that they would probably use the stolen money to buy gold coins, which would break the identification chain. They'd have to buy a lot of gold — twenty-two million dollars' worth. We figured they'd have to go to several major dealers, so I assigned my research assistant to track down all the major dealers in the U.S. She found a Syrian woman. . . ."

The woman had disguised herself by wearing a veil, and nobody had seen her face. Purely by coincidence, he said, one of the dealers had seen Delta airline tickets in her shoulder bag, and she'd said that she was in a hurry to get to the airport.

"We checked Delta flights around that time, out of Los Angeles to several major destinations, but there weren't many: one was to here. We got the names for all the female passengers on that trip and ran them against the other major gold sellers, in Los Angeles, Las Vegas, Denver, New York, Philadelphia, Miami, and so on. A Martha White shows up right after a purchase in each of those cities."

"So you got her," one of the agents said.

"Sort of," Lucas said. "The problem is, she looks nothing like an Arab woman. She was born here, and though she has a passport, it doesn't show her traveling to anywhere in the Middle East. She has no connection with either of the banks involved in this. She's got a house not far from here."

He looked at his notebook and read off the Margaret Street address. "That's a block or two south of East Seventh. It's a rental. She's had it for three months. We think . . . and I emphasize *think,* or *suspect* . . . that she's sending the gold back here, probably by FedEx or UPS or even registered mail, then flies back here to receive it. It's possible that it's in her house. But. We can't get a warrant. Our attorney says we're not even close. We need to show some connection between her and the other suspects — Kline, Sanderson, anything that would help. If we can build a solid enough case, without her knowing it, we can hit the house."

One of Shaffer's agents asked, "So we're surveilling the house?"

Lucas said, "Not yet. Not enough people, is what it comes to. She's coming into the airport today. In fact" — he looked at his watch — "she ought to be getting up in the air right now, out of Phoenix. We're putting six people on her, we'll keep her in a moving box. Once we ID her car, we'll get a tech to put a GPS on it. At the same time, with her coming in, we're going to have a couple guys each on Sanderson and Kline. Kline's getting out today. He's still screwed up, but he's getting out. If we're watching the house, and they meet somewhere . . . I mean, maybe we're wrong about the house, but I don't think we're wrong about her."

Shaffer said, "The house isn't going anywhere. The thing is this: they think they've kept Martha White out of sight. And now they've got lots of reasons to lie low for a while. I suspect what they're going to do is, they're gonna leave the gold alone."

"Seems kind of strange to leave twenty-two million in gold coins unguarded in a neighborhood like that," another of the agents said. "Seems more like they'd put it in a bunch of safe-deposit boxes."

Lucas nodded. "Bob and I considered that, and you're right. They might have done that: it's probably fifty-fifty. That's why we *cannot* lose her. We need to see everywhere she goes. If she goes into a bank, we can make inquiries. On the other hand, they've got to know that if they put it in a bank, and the smallest thing goes wrong, we can paper every bank in the country and keep them from getting the gold back. If she hides it in this old house, and she's smart about it, her biggest worry wouldn't be some crackhead finding it, it'd be that the house burns down."

They spent another five minutes talking about it, working through the equities, dismissing suggestions that they bring in more cops from St. Paul or Minneapolis.

Martínez hadn't said a word during the discussion, and during a lull in the arguments, Lucas turned to her and asked, "Rivera's remains . . ."

"I will get them today."

"We're so sorry about what happened."

"Before we start celebrating United Nations Day," one of the agents said, "I'm happy enough that we're getting these thieves, but what about the shooters?"

Shaffer said, "Well, it's mostly a snake hunt, now, Roy. I'm calling up every police chief between here and the border. We don't think these guys can move, but who knows? Maybe they had a private jet over in St. Paul, and they're now on the beach at Cabo, drinking cocktails with little umbrellas."

"It just seems like we're giving everything we've got to tracking down the thieves, and do we really care that much?" said another agent.

"There are a couple bankers who care that much," Lucas said.

"Is that what this is about? Bankers getting their money back? Did somebody make a phone call?"

"Hey, fuck you, George. We're not paying anybody off." Lucas was pissed, and let it show.

Shaffer held up his hands and said, "George, I'll talk to you in my office in just a bit. But that was bullshit. I agree with Lucas. I mean, what the hell are you planning to do, drive around town until you see them?"

"There's gotta be something."

"Well, I'm waiting," Shaffer said. "Tell me what it is. I'm more interested in the killers than the money, but I got nothing. So what do you have that we don't? That we could personally do? Come on. Tell me."

George had nothing, and, cornered, he admitted it. O'Brien said, "I'll tell you what, if we can get that gold, that's not going to wreck the Criminales, but it's going to give them a couple of flat tires. We're starting to see some places that they're taking their investments in Europe."

"What about the thieves?" Lucas asked. "You see where their money is going?"

"Yeah, but we're not getting to the end of

the line. We've got them in Europe, but it's coming out of there to somewhere else. We're talking to Interpol now, but that always takes time."

"We don't have time."

"Tell that to some time-wasting asshole in Lyon," O'Brien said. "They gotta cross every T twice."

"So we're doing a full-court press on Martha White," Shaffer said. "We keep our mouths *shut* on this. If anything leaks, somebody's gonna be learning the private detective trade, because his ass is gonna be outa here. We all clear?"

Everybody nodded, and the meeting broke up, with Shaffer saying, "We'll get back here in two hours. Everybody take a leak, get something to eat. We could be on her for a while."

Out in the hall, Martínez touched Lucas's arm and said, "If I get the ashes, and they say I will, I will not be here tomorrow morning. My flight leaves at nine o'clock. So, I thank you for your help."

"What can I say?" Lucas said. "It's a tragedy, but honestly . . . he brought it on himself. If he'd only called us . . ."

"I tried to get him to do it," she said. "But he was a very stubborn man, with very

401

big . . ." She hesitated, looking for the right word.

"*Cojones,*" Lucas said.

She smiled then and said, "Ah, your Hemingway. But yes, exactly. So . . ." She put out her hand, which was small and soft, and Lucas took it and said, "If I don't see you again, I thank you for coming and trying to help."

That conversation, Lucas thought as they parted, should just about cover the state of Minnesota's daily minimum requirements for hypocrisy.

From his office, he watched her walk across the parking lot to her car, and when she was rolling, he called Shaffer and said, "She's gone."

"You think she bit?"

"She was so straight that I'm beginning to worry that I could be wrong," Lucas said.

"She's been spying on the guy she's been working next to for, what, four, five years, and then she killed him? If she couldn't look you in the eye and sell you a lie, she would have been dead a long time ago," Shaffer said.

"Yeah, you're right. I know goddamn well she's the one," Lucas said.

"I'm calling my crew back. Get Del,

Jenkins, and Shrake over here, and let's put it together. She might be moving fast."

"Wish we'd had time to box her," Lucas said.

"Just no time," Shaffer said. "Besides, she'll be coming back."

Martínez was moving fast. After leaving the BCA head quarters on Maryland Avenue, she took Maryland west to a CVS pharmacy and got out in the parking lot with her sat phone. A few minutes later, she was speaking to the Big Voice, telling him what had happened at the meeting, reading off the address for Martha White. The Big Voice got it on his computer screen, asked her where she was, and said, "You are perhaps two kilometers away. A few minutes."

"I will find it on my iPad."

"I will alert Uno and Tres. Meet with them, go in there, see if the gold is there, and get out. Do you have your alternate ID?"

"Yes."

"I will have a car rental for you in . . . Bloomington, Minnesota," the Big Voice said. "This one is near the airport, on the same freeway, but farther west than the airport. I will send a map for your iPad."

"Thank you."

"I will have another car and a new ID for you in Kansas City, Missouri. If you drink enough coffee, you can be on the border tomorrow afternoon."

"Yes."

"You're not worried about entering the house?"

"Not if we do it fast enough," Martínez said. "They are deploying at the airport in two hours. . . . We have to be out in two hours, or sooner."

"Then go."

But she *was* worried. Her conscious mind had bought the charade at the BCA, but her unconscious, her intuition, nagged at her. She paid attention to that, the nagging feeling. Rational analysis argued that she had not given herself away, but there was something about the situation. . . .

And she still hadn't made up her mind about the gold. Keep it, or turn it over to the boss? If she kept it, she'd have to do something about Uno and Tres. She decided that she'd worry about that when the gold was in her car.

The phone rang a minute later, and it was Uno.

"Where do we meet?"

"There is a school here. In the parking

lot. I will tell you the directions. . . ."

They were fifteen minutes away.

She resented all fifteen of them.

17

Martínez's problem, which she'd recognized before she ever set foot in the U.S., was that none of her subordinates, Uno, Dos, and Tres, were particularly bright; they were the Mexican equivalent of the hapless American shitkicker who discovers the power of the gun. Which was fine when somebody needed to be killed right now, or chopped to pieces. Not so fine when subtlety was needed.

She waited for Uno and Tres in a Metro State University parking lot; when they arrived, they got out wearing jeans and black sport coats, and not-so-subtly armed with Mac-10s over their shoulders, nine-millimeter pistols tucked in their belts.

"How will you carry them if we have to go on the street?" she asked of the Mac-10s.

"Under a jacket," Uno said.

"It's warm. It's hot."

"So . . . if anybody asks, we shoot them."

Uno laughed to show that he was joking. Maybe.

They were in a hurry, but Martínez took five minutes to examine the target house, and the surrounding area, on a Google aerial photo that she pulled up on her iPad. When she was satisfied that she had the general lay of the land, they left, taking her car. If they were ahead of the BCA, then the car wouldn't matter. If it was a trap, and they had to run, the BCA agents knew Martínez's rental, but not the Toyota.

As she waited for traffic at the edge of the parking lot, she remembered her shock when Davenport had suddenly appeared at Sanderson's apartment, running up the apartment steps with the gun in his hand.

She began to sweat. Something about the feel of the thing.

The direct route to Margaret Street would be a left turn and straight ahead. She considered, checked her iPad again, and took a right. She turned right again on East Seventh, then left on Greenbrier, drove a block, and found herself looking out the driver's-side window, down a long, steep bluff, into a vast weedy hole in the ground. She'd seen it on the iPad, but hadn't been quite sure what she was looking at.

Another block and they came to Margaret Street, but five blocks from the target house, and across the four-lane East Seventh Street. Margaret dead-ended at the hole, which a sign said was Swede Hollow Park.

She looked at it for a moment, then turned around and drove back the way she came, again overshooting the direct route to Margaret.

Uno, who was now looking at the iPad, said, "No, you turned the wrong way."

"We're going another way," she said.

Uno turned the iPad in his hands, and the map image turned with him, frustrating him — he wanted to look at it sideways, and it wouldn't allow him to do that. "Shit," he said. "This machine is shit."

Martínez took the tablet away from him, propped it against her steering wheel, and followed the map along Mounds Boulevard to Third Street, took Third to Cypress, turned left on Cypress to Fremont, turned the corner on Fremont and pulled over.

"So now, one of you has a mission." She didn't care about which one — one was as dumb as the other.

Uno was querulous: "*¿Qué?*"

She explained: there was some small chance that the cops were watching this house. A small chance, but a chance. They nodded.

"There may be twenty-two million dollars inside," she told them. "Big Voice says that if we get the gold, I will get ten percent for taking the chance to get it, and each of you will get five percent. That's one million dollars in gold for each of you, if we take this chance. A million in gold will buy a very nice life for you and your mother and your wife, if you have one. A Toyota Tundra with a cap, running boards, brush guard, bush lights. Whatever you want. Ten of them, if you like, and you still won't have spent even half of the gold."

They nodded, listening closely now.

If the police were waiting up ahead, it would be better if only one of them was caught. The others could then try to rescue that one, or get away, and send money for lawyers and so on.

"So which one goes?" Uno asked.

"You decide," she said.

The two killers looked at each other and Uno finally lit up and said, *"Piedra, papel o tijera."* Rock, paper, scissors, best two out of three.

Tres laughed and nodded. Uno promptly won the first round, rock breaking scissors. Tres groaned with excitement, and they went again, and Tres won this time, paper covering rock, when Uno tried to get smart and do "rock" twice in a row. Tres pulled out a second victory with another paper over rock.

Uno giggled and said to Martínez, "I thought he would do scissors because he thought I would go to paper, but, I fail."

Martínez nodded, contained an impulse to smack them both, and said, "Look for people in cars, or people standing around not doing much, or even people hiding. Look in windows. Walk slowly. We will keep the telephone on, you and me. If you see something, tell me."

If he didn't see something, she told him, he was to check the house, and perhaps go in. "If you do see something, go this way on the same street, on Margaret. If they chase you, keep going, and you will come to that big hole we saw. They can't follow in their cars, and you are very fast, so you will lose them when you go through the hole."

"Ah," Uno said. He was, indeed, very fast. "Walk on to East Seventh Street, and then down the long hill to the city."

"We will be on this street, and will watch behind you." She tapped the iPad. "When you get here, in the city, you will call us and we will come and get you."

Uno looked at the iPad for a long moment, then said, "So I walk to this Margaret Street and then to the right number, and then, if I find the gold, I call you. If I don't, I call you, and then walk down the same street."

He repeated it all, tracing the route on the aerial photo. When she was satisfied that he had it, she cut him loose.

They watched as he walked back to Fremont, looked at the street sign, and took a right. In a moment he was out of sight.

Shrake had gotten permission from a Margaret Street homeowner to sit behind the slats of his old-fashioned front porch, a block east of the decoy house. Jenkins was two blocks away, also on Margaret, west of the decoy, on his stomach behind a hedge. Lucas was in Del's pickup with Del, parked a block over, north and west, toward East Seventh, where they expected she would come in. Shaffer was in a car with another agent, north and east.

The second meeting with the other agents had gone well enough, with a couple of them annoyed that they hadn't been let in on the secret about Martínez, but most agreeing that not knowing had given the meeting, with its flashes of anger, more authenticity. "Never would've guessed it," one of the agents said.

Shaffer found two members of the BCA SWAT team who weren't on any immediate assignment, and grabbed them, and assigned them to hide inside the decoy house.

In any case, it was Shrake who saw Uno coming. There'd been a half dozen false alarms, guys walking alone or in pairs along the street, but none of them looked right. Shrake checked Uno with a pair of compact, image-stabilized Canon binoculars, then called in on a handset that all the other teams would pick up.

"Got a small guy coming in, he looks right, he looks Mexican, he's small. Moving slow. He's on Cypress, coming up to Margaret. He's checking things out."

Lucas: "He's alone?"

"He's the only one I see."

"I'm moving over a block, to Margaret," Shaffer called. "Everybody else stay put."

A moment later Uno came up to the intersection and stopped on the corner, and with great, ostentatious nonchalance, stretched, yawned, took a good long look around, then turned toward the target. Shrake recognized that for what it was: "This is one of them," he said, excitement riding in his voice. "He's checking out the block. He's got a phone in his hand, he just said something into it, so it's turned on, or it's a walkie-talkie. He's turned toward the house."

"I see him," Shaffer said. Shaffer was a full block behind Uno, sitting at an intersection.

"She's sent him out here to look for us," Lucas said. "She's not sure we're here, but she's worried. And she's close. Not more than a few blocks away. I'm going to break off with Del and start turning blocks, see if we can spot her car."

"Go," said Shaffer. "John, come in a block. Look for people in cars."

"The guy's looking at the house," Jenkins called.

Jenkins, Shrake, and Shaffer took turns recounting Uno's progress down the block, and Lucas and Del started turning corners, looking for Martínez. They started north and west of the target house, while Martínez was south and east. As they went first south, and then east, they turned a block too soon and passed a block north of Martínez's position. They never saw her car, and she never saw their truck.

Martínez asked Uno, on the phone, "How close are you?"

"I'm crossing the street," he said. "I see nobody here. There is a porch. It's an old house. All the curtains are closed."

"All the curtains?" She tensed.

"Yes, all the curtains. I am at the front. Should I go up?"

"You see nobody?"

"Nobody."

She thought about it for a few seconds, but it was only Uno. "Go up," she said.

Uno walked up the porch to the door. The door had a glass panel in it, at head height. He peeked. He didn't see anybody, but he saw a shadow, and the shadow moved.

He stepped back and put the phone to his mouth. "There is somebody inside," he said.

Martínez closed her eyes. She said, "Is there a doorbell button?"

Uno said, *"Sí."*

"Push the button, then count to thirty. If they don't answer, it is the police. Then, fast as you can, run down Margaret Street toward the big hole," she said. "We will catch you on the other side."

"Push the button and count to thirty," Uno repeated.

"Like you were waiting for an answer. Then run like the wind."

As she talked to him, she'd made a U-turn on Fremont and headed west, following the aerial photo on the iPad. She jogged onto Fourth Street, turned left on Hope, and as Uno shouted, "I'm running," she pulled into a Laundromat parking lot on West Seventh.

Uno shouted, "I am one block."

"Faster," she shouted back. "Run faster."

There was one car out in front of Uno, and others following on parallel streets. Jenkins ran sideways out to Cypress, jumped in his car, pulled onto Margaret with Uno now a full block ahead, drove down to Shrake, closing the gap a bit, opened the door so Shrake could climb in.

"That motherfucker has legs," Shrake said.

"But we got wheels," Jenkins said.

"Easy, easy," Shaffer called. "Keep him boxed, but let him run."

"I'm coming up to East Seventh," Lucas said. "You want me up the hill?"

"Come up partway."

"He's coming up to Seventh," one of the other agents said, from a car in front of Uno, on Margaret. "I've got to get out of his way. You want me to cross, or turn, or what?"

"Take a right and pull over," Shaffer said.

"Taking the right."

"I see you," Lucas called. "We got him this way."

At that moment, Uno bolted straight across the four-lane street, through traffic, and on down Margaret. "Holy shit, he ran straight across, he could lose us," an agent called.

"We're on it," Lucas said. Del accelerated up the hill, ready to take a left on Margaret.

"I can't see him anymore," Jenkins said. "There's a jog at the intersection."

Del made the left, and up ahead they could see Uno running hard as he could, straight up the street. "Got him," Lucas said. "He's heading straight for Swede Hollow. Shit, he's going down the Hollow. I bet they set this up. We need to get somebody on the other side. If he runs down, we'll spot him from up on top."

Uno had done his job. From the Laundromat parking lot, Martínez had seen Uno bolt across the street, and then, as he ran out of sight, the car swerving out from a curb into the turn lane, and then down Margaret.

She saw Lucas quite clearly, a handset to his mouth.

She turned to Tres and said, "Ah, well."

"¿Qué?"

Lucas and Del parked at the top of the park bluff, and ten seconds later Shrake and Jenkins arrived, Shrake with his binoculars, and they followed the flight of Uno down the hill, through the trees, and across the park. It was a long, hard run, and Uno fell at one point, and apparently lost his phone. He scrambled back to pick it up, and then ran on.

Shaffer's team was out in front of him. As Lucas called out his location on the handset, another of the agents came back and said, "We got him. We see him. We're out of the car, we're going to run down the track here, try to keep him in sight."

Shaffer asked, "You see anybody following him?"

"Nobody. There's no way anybody could, unless they were waiting in here. I think they're probably on the other side of East Seventh."

"I don't think you'll see them," Lucas said. "She broke us out. She knows we're on to her."

"Should we take him?" one of the agents asked.

"Where's he headed?" Shaffer asked.

"He's running down the track alongside the creek. He'll be coming out at East Seventh in a minute or so. He's really motoring. I can't keep up, but he's not running off into the trees, anyway."

Lucas called, "He's out of sight from here. We're coming your way."

Another agent: "I'm out of the car on East Seventh. I saw him, he's still on the track."

Shaffer said, "Keep out of sight. Let him run for a minute. Let's box him again at East Seventh."

Uno was in good shape and a fast runner, but as the track led under a bridge, he paused, caught his breath, got on the phone and called for help, but got no answer. He thought that perhaps Martínez and Tres had been caught, somehow, and that he might be on his own. He thought about it, saw the tall buildings ahead, remembered what Martínez had said about finding him downtown, and turned that way.

He came to a fence at a railroad track, tried to climb it, got his jacket snagged, pulled the jacket off and threw it over, then climbed over after it. The jacket was a mess from a couple of falls he'd taken while running through the park, but he picked it up, ran across the tracks, careful not to break an ankle in the rough gravel, threw the jacket over another fence, climbed the fence, pulled the jacket back on, and jogged toward a car wash.

Lucas and Del, in Del's car, followed by Shrake and Jenkins, were rolling down East Seventh, pulled in by Shaffer's agents, when one of the agents called, shouting, and said, "We got a problem. We got a problem. He just jumped the fence around the railroad track, and I'm not sure, but it looks like he's got a fuckin' Uzi slung over his back."

Shaffer came back: "An Uzi? You're sure?"

"It's a short black gun with what looks like a thirty-mag hanging under it. Hang on, hang on, Jack is coming up, he's got glasses."

A moment later, a new voice: "This is Jack. He jumped another fence and he's running up toward that car wash place, and I'm looking at him, and it — That's a Mac-10, not an Uzi."

Shaffer said, "Lucas? What do you think?"

"We're busted. She sent him out there to see what would happen. If he's got a Mac-10, I don't think we can let him get into town. There's some big parking lots on the other side of the car wash. If he runs across those, we'd have him out in the open."

"I agree." Shaffer began directing traffic, sending four cars on the other side of the parking lot, calling, "We're coming, Jack. You and Roy follow on foot, come up behind him so he can't run back into the park."

Jack called, "He's walking now. He's walking around the car wash."

Uno was looking around, saw nobody. He stopped, put the phone, which was still open, to his ear and asked, "Can you hear me? Can you hear me, Mama?"

There was nobody on the other end. He heard what might have been traffic, but no human being.

He looked around, and started walking, out onto a huge parking lot, toward a squat five- or six-story redbrick office building. He was thinking, now, *They have left me.* Not that they had been caught, or that they were waiting, but that he'd been abandoned. He felt like crying, but hadn't cried since he was six, and so he didn't. And there glimmered in his heart the possibility that they were waiting for him, just around the redbrick building. . . .

The glimmer of possibility died as he came up to it, and a man emerged at the side of the building and shouted, "Police. Stop."

Another man, in a dark uniform, stepped out with a long arm of some kind, a rifle.

Uno had been born to have this moment happen. There had been other possibilities, that he might have wound up as a dirt farmer, or stuck in a barrio, scratching out a small life, but he'd chosen the narcos and they'd chosen him, and this moment was always going to come.

He stripped off his jacket and threw it on the ground.

The man out in front of him was shouting, "Stop! Stop!"

Uno shouted back: *"Chingate!"*

Then with a single motion, long practice, he swept the Mac-10 from behind his back up into the shooting position, raking off the safety and tightening his finger against the trigger, the stuttering burst beginning as the muzzle came up. . . .

They'd seen the move and the man who'd first shouted at him dropped behind a car, and Uno saw him dropping and then the first impacts came, in his chest, turning him, and then . . .

Nothing.

■ ■ ■ ■

Shaffer was screaming, "He's down, he's down, everybody okay? Everybody okay?"

Uno's burst from the Mac-10 had mostly spattered off the parking lot, ricocheting nobody knew where, but nobody, other than Uno, had been hurt.

Uno was dead; the cops stood back, in a circle around his short, thin crumpled body, and a couple of sirens started — St. Paul cops responding to reports of a shooting. Lucas arrived with Del, Jenkins, and Shrake, and as they walked across the parking lot, they could see his face, looking up at the blue sky and the summer clouds. Shaffer said, "Mac-10. Haven't seen one for a while."

And Shrake said, "The kid had legs."

18

They were all still standing around the parking lot, looking at the body, when Sandy, the researcher, called Lucas and said, "All that bullshit you said at the meeting this morning, about the Martha White woman on the airplane?"

"Yeah?"

"You were right. Except that her name is Edie Albitis and she flew in here last night from Newark," Sandy said. "She'd just picked up two hundred thousand dollars in gold at Biedermann's in Manhattan, and another two hundred thousand at Scone's in Brooklyn."

"You're sure?"

"Well, every time we get a sale or a pickup, the TSA says we've got Albitis flying in and out of the local airport," Sandy said. "Another thing — she's an immigrant, from the same neck of the woods as Turicek."

"Call the TSA," Lucas said. "We want her

held the next time she goes through airport security, if we don't get her first."

"I talked to Rudy, and we've already started the process."

"Excellent. Be nice if we could find an address."

"I'm looking for all that," Sandy said. "Nothing so far, anywhere in the metro area. I wouldn't be surprised if she's using another name, or staying with somebody. I'm trying for her credit cards, to see if we can pick up hotels or whatever."

Lucas told her to keep pushing it and rang off, told Del about it.

"Almost done," Del said.

The shooting scene was shut down, and the media showed up, and after a while Lucas went back to the office to start writing his piece of the after-shooting report. Shaffer's team had gotten a warrant and had gone into Martínez's hotel room, and found it empty. Security tapes from BCA cameras covering the parking lot got them a description of her car, and the number on its plate. The TV stations were running photos of her every fifteen minutes or so, along with photos of two other Mexican suspects.

Lucas suggested that Shaffer, in the inevitable press conference after the killing of

Uno, tell the reporters a strategic lie. Shaffer thought about it for a while, then demurred, saying that it felt unethical.

"But I won't give you up, if you tell it," he said.

So Lucas, speaking last, told the assembled reporters that the fleeing Mexicans were believed to have escaped with millions of dollars in gold coins, taken from the thieves who had stolen from the drug gang's account. The gold, he said, had been taken from Turicek's apartment at the time the gang had kidnapped him.

Lucas watched tapes of his performance, with Shaffer standing next to him, and Shaffer said, "You lie really well."

"If I have to," Lucas said. "I figured it was too important to pussy out on."

"Hey . . ."

"Ana's got a problem, now," Lucas said. "Can't stay here — and if she goes back to Mexico, the gang's gonna want the gold, and the Federales are gonna want her ass."

"I didn't pussy out."

"Yeah, you did, Bob. Pretty amazing — you've got no problem shooting it out with a Mexican hit man, but you puss out when it comes to lying to reporters. Listen: everything you see on TV news is bullshit," Lucas said. "You would have added a teaspoon of bullshit to an ocean of it. Nobody would have noticed, and it'll help catch a couple more killers. So fuck your qualms, and your ethics."

Del got between them and said, mildly, "Let's agree to disagree. At least while there are cameras around."

Virgil Flowers called a while later and said he didn't have much to report. "We're trying to figure out how to get some surveillance on the farm. I might have actually seen the truck that your two robbers drive around, but we didn't want to stop them. We're afraid we might give something away."

"Like what?"

"Dunno," Flowers said. "Something."

Martínez knew the police would be looking for her car, so they dumped it for the Toyota and headed back to the Newport house, and put the car in the garage.

Tres hadn't asked about Uno: he knew what had happened. When they got inside, they turned on the television and saw the breaking news story. Tres said, "I thought I would be the one to go. The saints said so." Martínez patted him on the shoulder, went out in the backyard, sat on the ground between a couple of bridal wreath bushes,

426

and called the Big Voice.

"They know about me, my photo is on the television. We have lost the car, but still have the truck. We are safe for now, I think, but I'm afraid to move."

"Stay there. One day, two days, we can get you out. If they have your face, and the Federales have it, then the only safe place for you is farther south. If we can pick you up, arrangements can be made — Venezuela, perhaps. Ecuador. So. Hide. Call me every four hours."

Two hours later, eating tomato soup and microwave tacos, and clicking compulsively through the cable channels, they caught Davenport: ". . . believe she has twenty-two million dollars in American gold eagles. That's a lot of money and it's also a lot of weight, so we think they're moving it by car or truck. We've alerted every gas station and truck stop between here and the border. . . ."

"Oh, no," she said.

Tres didn't understand. He looked from her stricken face to the TV: "*¿Qué?*"

Early in the afternoon, Sanderson went to Mom's house. She'd been worrying obsessively about the gold — with Turicek dead and Kline incapacitated, with the Mexicans visiting her apartment, with the cops all over her, she began experiencing the symptoms of what her doctors had previously described as a schizophrenic break; she'd experienced them a few times before, but not for a few years. She hadn't been able to eat or sleep at all, a ragged headache was a constant companion, and her normal mental playacting had become dominant, the plays more real than the world around her.

One of the plays ran over and over, a sequence in which Edie Albitis went to Mom's house and stole all the gold, and then Sanderson, seeing herself standing in the house with an empty bag, peeked out the window and saw Davenport and more cops gathering on her lawn, with guns. . . .

She kept trying to rerun the vision to eliminate the cops, to get the gold back, but none of it worked: the vision was assertive, and inescapable.

So she went to Mom's: the presence of the gold, she thought, would be curative: if she had it in her hands, it couldn't have gone with Albitis. If she had the gold in her hands, the vision would go away.

And she should move the gold, she thought. Take it somewhere nobody would know, for safekeeping. Out in the countryside. She could get a shovel. . . .

■ ■ ■ ■

As was the case with paranoia, a little schizophrenia could work for you, if it wasn't too severe. In her most acute episodes, Sanderson's visions were actually tactile. When the visions involved conflict with threatening people, she'd worked out all kinds of evasive tactics. She would evade the threats on foot and in her car, in airplanes, on horseback, on snowmobiles, and in boats. . . . She'd worked all through it, in her dreams.

Now, with an actual threat of police surveillance, she went down to the garage and carefully looked around, until she was confident that she was alone, then looked under her car for suspect boxes and wires. She'd seen GPS trackers on some cop show on TV, though she wasn't sure whether they were real or fictional.

Finding nothing, she got in her car and went through an evasive routine imagined many times in the past; it took a while, and involved twisting routes through the parking ramps at the Mall of America, followed by a trip through country lanes south of the Cities, and finally, unable to discover the slightest sign that she was being followed, she drove back into town, to Mom's.

Calmer now, after her journey through the real world, she pulled into the driveway, lifted the garage door, and drove in. The gold was packed into small cardboard boxes, and made a fairly compact stack. But then, dumbbells were also fairly compact: gold is heavier than lead, and though the gold pile was not particularly impressive, it weighed something like 860 pounds.

She looked at it for a few minutes, snapped to the vision of the cops arriving outside, and ran to the front window and peeked: the street was empty. Breathing hard, and struggling to calm herself, she went to the kitchen, got a glass of water, then went back to the gold. She tried picking up three boxes, but together they were heavier than a car battery, and she dropped the bottom one. Two at a time were more manageable, and she took two the first and second trips, shuttling out to the garage, but after that, she slowed down, taking one box at a time.

She was two-thirds of the way down the stack when she heard a car in the driveway. She was standing next to her own car, having just dropped another box in front of the backseat, when she heard it, and there was no doubt about it.

But then, what she heard and saw wasn't

necessarily what was out there, and she knew that: she was mildly schizophrenic, and fully aware of that fact. She went back to the front window and peeked again.

Edie Albitis was getting out of a car parked at the curb.

Albitis had spent the night sleeping at the office condo, on a blow-up mattress she'd bought at an all-night Walmart. She had her suitcase with her, and in the morning had managed to clean up using a six-pack of bottled water she'd gotten at the same Walmart.

She was frightened: the drug gang and the police had been all over Turicek, Kline, and Sanderson. It was unclear to her whether the Mexicans had had Turicek for any length of time, if he might have given away Mom's house, and her name. It was unclear if the police had been able to track her through something said by one of the others. In any case, she'd decided not to risk the Ramada, and had gone to the rental office.

FedEx made two separate deliveries that morning, totaling more than a half million dollars. She moved the gold out to her car, and headed for Mom's.

The thing about Mom's was, you could see the driveway from a long way out. She stopped at a convenience store, peed one last time, got three bottles of water and a submarine sandwich, went to Mom's, but stopped five blocks short and parked.

She was patient. There was too much involved to be hasty, and she took the quiet time, with the sandwich, to plot out her next moves. If either the gang or the police had her name, and she'd have to assume they did, she'd have to drive out to New York with her share of the gold. Turicek's share, too. That was only fair, she thought: he was *her* partner, not Sanderson's or Kline's.

With that much gold, an ID would not be a problem. There were several Eastern European consulates where she could buy a completely legitimate passport for a couple thousand dollars. Just a matter of locating the right guy, and again, with the gold, that would be simple enough.

Then where? Prague, she thought. Maybe Budapest. Romania . . . maybe not. She wanted a solid legal system, with at least some respect for the privacy of safe-deposit boxes. Latvia?

She'd been there three hours and was beginning to feel a little bladder pressure when she saw Sanderson arrive. She sat up, watching intently. Nothing moved. Nothing moved . . .

Sanderson opened the door and Albitis stepped inside and asked, "What's going on?"

Sanderson thought it would look bad, so she stuttered, "Ah, mmm, I'm moving the gold. I'm afraid the police are going to find this place. They're just everywhere."

"How do you know they're not watching you?"

"I was very careful," Sanderson said. "Unless they had an airplane, they couldn't have followed me." She explained about driving down the dusty gravel roads, and Albitis came around.

"All right," she said. "But: I want our share of the gold right now. Mine and Ivan's. I'm leaving. I'm heading for California, and I'm getting a boat out of San Francisco. So let's start dividing it up."

Sanderson said, "But . . . that's not fair. Ivan's dead. You get one-third now —"

"Ivan was my partner. I get his," she said. "You still get plenty." "Oh, no . . ."

Sanderson was bigger and stronger than Albitis, but Albitis had a kind of feral toughness that frightened Sanderson; and Albitis

433

began crowding the other woman, not realizing that Sanderson was experiencing the schizophrenic break, and finally, when Albitis reached out and pushed Sanderson, Sanderson struck back with a wild roundhouse punch that bounced off the back of Albitis's head, not having much effect, and Albitis screamed and launched herself at Sanderson, fingernails flashing, and they went right to the floor, punching and screaming.

Sanderson was better on the floor, since she was stronger. Albitis finally managed to wrench herself free and, being quicker, got to her feet and ran into the bedroom where the safe was: Daddy's guns.

Sanderson knew exactly where she was going, looked at the back door. The door was locked, and she'd have to fit a key into it. Albitis was between her and the front door. She panicked and pulled open the nearest door, the one that went to the attic, and as she heard the mechanical ratcheting as the .45 was cocked, she ran up the stairs.

The stairs were a straight shot, eighteen steps straight up: the entry into the attic was simply a hole in the floor, wrapped on three sides by a banister. The attic, which had been Sanderson's bedroom when she was a teenager, was full of junk. She looked around wildly, anything that she could use to defend herself, heard Albitis start up the stairs, shouting, "Kris! Kris!"

Daddy's golf clubs, nearly twenty years old and covered with dust, were poking out of his old Golden Golphers–themed golf bag, propped against the wall behind the back banister. She pulled out the biggest one, an original Big Bertha, raised it over her head, looked over the banister, and Albitis was right there, nearly at the top of the stairs with the .45 in her hand.

Albitis shouted, "Kris! I don't want —"

Sanderson didn't hear any of that: she just saw a killer coming for her, and she swung the club in a long arc. Albitis either sensed the motion or heard it, cocked her head upward, and caught the face of the Big Bertha on her forehead.

Crunch.

It sounded bad. It sounded like somebody had broken a board over his knee.

Albitis stiffened, looked right at Sanderson with blank eyes, and then toppled and fell down the stairs in three stages. She went *thumpa-thump,* and stopped, then *thumpa-thumpa-thump,* and stopped a couple of steps from the bottom, then turned one last time, *thumpa-thump,* and hit the floor at the bottom.

Sanderson cried, "Oh, my God, Edie, are you hurt?"

She ran down the stairs and found Albitis in a heap; still breathing, her eyes still open, and blank as a sheet of paper. There was no blood, but there was a major dent where the crown of her head met her forehead.

"Oh, my God," Sanderson cried again. She tried to get Albitis to sit upright, but Albitis was as loose as a bag of laundry.

Sanderson ran to the front door and looked out, and then to the back door and looked out, and then to the garage. She frantically threw the boxes of gold onto the garage floor, then half-carried, half-dragged Albitis to the car and across the backseat.

"Are you all right?" she sobbed.

No answer.

She ran back into the house, got Albitis's shoulder bag, and threw it on the other woman's body.

As she backed out of the garage, she saw the boxes of gold lying on the garage floor and got out and ran back up the driveway, pulled the door down, making sure it latched. She was five minutes from Regions Hospital. She didn't dare take Albitis all the way in because there would be questions. Instead, she drove around on side streets until she found a place where she couldn't easily be seen, dragged Albitis out of the car, and propped her against a tree.

She got Albitis's bag and propped it against her side: What's a woman without her bag? Albitis was still as loose as death, but she wasn't dead: she was now snoring. As Sanderson turned away from the body, she saw Albitis's cell phone on the ground, where it had fallen out of a pocket. She picked it up, looked at it, and thought, Keys. She went back to Albitis's bag and got the car keys. With the keys in her pocket, she drove out to the end of the street and called 911.

The 911 dispatcher asked, "Is this an emergency?"

A St. Paul cop called Lucas through the BCA switchboard.

"Uh, you guys had that pickup request on an Edie Albitis?"

"Yeah! You got her?"

"Well, sort of . . ."

Albitis was being prepped for surgery when Lucas arrived at the emergency room. He talked briefly to a neurosurgeon who said that Albitis had not regained consciousness since she'd arrived, and had a significant depressive fracture of the frontal bone.

"The imaging shows we've got significant epidural bleeding under the impact site, and there appears to be some rebound bleeding on the opposite side of her head," he said. "We need to relieve the pressure from the bleeding as quickly as we can, so we're going in right now. She was lucky in that whatever hit her didn't break the skin, so the wound is closed."

"She gonna make it?" Lucas asked.

The surgeon shrugged. "I'd say she should, but I don't know how bad she's been scrambled. She took a terrific whack with something. Something smooth, no edges to rip the skin. I was almost thinking it might be something like a fender, but the radius of a fender is too large. This was a small-radius impact, and nearly symmetrical. It's like somebody whacked her with one of those iron balls they use in the shot put."

"An iron ball?"

"Just an example," the doc said. "But like that. I'd say small radius, metal, smooth, moving fast. The frontal bone is tough. This took a lot of energy."

A St. Paul cop was in the waiting room, one of the first responders, and he described the scene where they picked her up. "Got a nine-one-one call, and we were close and went over there and found her. Her purse was there, but nothing else."

There was no sign of an accident, no glass in the street. She was propped up against a tree, completely out of it, when the cops arrived. "We could see something was wrong with her head, so we called for an ambulance. Talked to some of the neighbors, but nobody had seen anything. Where she was . . . wasn't like concealed, or anything, she was right out in the open, but she would have been hard to see from any of the houses. The place was picked."

"What about the call to nine-one-one?"

"Woman caller, gave the exact location, sounded freaked out. The call came from a no-name phone. Didn't find a phone with Albitis, so it may have been her own phone."

"Shoot."

After thinking about it, Lucas called the dispatch center and had them play the 911 call for him. He couldn't have proven it, not in a court, but he recognized the trembling panic of the caller. "That fuckin' Sanderson. Kristina Sanderson," he said aloud, and he went to find her.

After dropping Albitis and making the call to 911, Sanderson wiped the phone with a

Kleenex and dropped it out the window onto the freeway, where it was run over several hundred times in the next hour or so, before the biggest chunk of the finely ground remnant made it to the shoulder.

She was worried about Albitis, but was now more focused on the gold. Albitis, she thought, really couldn't turn her in, without implicating herself. So, however that turned out, it was something for the future. For now, she had to take care of the gold, which was the only remaining reason for doing any of this.

Back at the house, she threw the boxes of gold back in the car. Since she'd already moved them once, by the time she was finished, she'd moved seventeen hundred pounds of heavy metal, almost as though she'd been stacking car batteries all day.

When the gold was loaded, she went out to Albitis's car and found more gold in the trunk. She backed Albitis's car up to the garage and transferred the gold to her car. Then she got a bunch of garbage bags from under the kitchen sink, a spade, and a blue plastic tarp from the garage, put them in her car, and pulled out to the street. Albitis's car went into the garage: she'd move it later.

With all that done, she headed out into the countryside. Out to the farm.

She'd never really expected to have the money to buy the place, but she'd visited it a dozen times, touring her dream. Dog kennels over here, a stable over there. Chicken coops to the right.

The drive south took a bit more than an hour, into the Cannon River Valley south of Farmington. The farm was barely a farm anymore — forty acres were planted with a ragged cornfield, but the other forty were nothing but weeds and a scattering of saplings sprouted from windblown seed. A line of taller timber marked the north side, where the land started to fold as it dropped down to the river. The acreage didn't border on the river itself, but was close. She could walk to a bridge. . . .

She got to the farm as the sun was hovering above the horizon, turning the overhead clouds a gorgeous lavender-and-salmon. She pulled open the gate — the owner of the land had told her she could stop by anytime — and pulled in, closed the gate behind herself, and drove slowly along a thin track toward the timber.

She dug carefully, throwing the dirt onto the blue tarp. By the time she finished, it was nearly dark, the sun long gone; she put one of the plastic bags in the hole, filled it with boxes of gold, then cinched up the bag so it would be as waterproof as possible, then did the same with a second bag. She refilled the hole, replaced a few pieces of sod by flashlight, then threw her equipment back in the car. If anybody were to come by before the next rain, they might find themselves some gold. But that was unlikely: one in a million.

When she was done, she examined the site one last time with the flashlight, then drove carefully back across the field to the gate, drove through, replaced the gate, and drove home.

She missed Lucas by ten minutes.

19

The dimensions of the problem were now clear.

Lucas went back to the BCA offices, spoke briefly with Shaffer, who was directing a regional search for Martínez and the third shooter, talking to DEA officials and Mexican Federales, all of whom would love to get their hands on her. Shaffer could plainly see that if he got the bust, he'd be hero of the week; and even if he didn't, he was getting the credit for breaking her out, and he was taking it.

Lucas no longer cared about her: now it was a matter of locating her, and whatever happened would happen. Most likely, he thought, it'd be a couple highway patrolmen, in their funny blue hats, chasing them down in rural Kansas, after they were spotted at a gas station. Lucas had his differences with various state highway patrols, based on what the Porsche management referred to as "spirited driving," but conceded that when it came to the chase-and-shoot business, they were pretty good at it.

But: there remained the problem of the thieves who set off the whole episode, and most notably, Sanderson. If Albitis died, Sanderson would be a murderer, Lucas thought. That was not allowed in the state of Minnesota.

When he left Shaffer, he called Del: "I'll be in my office. Come on up, we've got to do some plotting."

Del showed up a half hour later. He was wearing a double-knit blue blazer, a white shirt with a red polyester necktie, gray slacks, and dress shoes. All of the clothing was slightly too large for him, his thin neck sticking out of the shirt collar like a turtle's. Taken all together, he looked like a security guard at a movie theater.

"You going to court?"

"Just came back," he said. He unclipped the necktie and put it in his pocket.

Lucas watched him do that, then said, "Let me see the tie for a minute."

"Huh?"

"Let me see the tie."

Del took it out of his pocket and passed it over. Lucas turned and dropped it in his wastebasket. "I'll buy you a new one," he said.

Del looked wistfully at the wastebasket and said, "I sorta liked that one."

"I'm doing this for your own good. You remember Bertha Swenson? You remember what I did for you there?"

"Ahhhh . . ."

"This is the necktie equivalent of Bertha Swenson. Think about it."

"She wouldn't have shot *me*. . . ."

They plotted:

"We need a way to get Sanderson out in the open. The way I read her, she's a hippie, a little flaky, probably got dragged into it against her will, but in the end, she winds up whacking Albitis."

"And you say Albitis is really the only thing we've got on the rest of the group?"

"Now that Turicek is dead," Lucas said. "Sandy says every time there was a big gold sale at one of the dealers we were looking at, Albitis was getting off and on a plane. The DEA has followed the money trail to a supposedly Syrian company, and it was supposedly a Syrian woman who was buying the gold."

"But you can't tie Albitis to the Syrian woman — not directly."

"No, and it doesn't matter much, if Albitis dies. Actually, we're probably better off if she dies, because we can build our case, and she won't be around to deny it."

"As long as a Syrian woman doesn't show up."

"That won't happen," Lucas said. "Albitis is the Syrian woman. I know it."

"Then where's the gold?"

"I don't know. Maybe Sanderson's got it."

They worked around that question, and Del finally suggested that what they knew wasn't adding up to much of a court case. "We've got Kline getting shot, and Sanderson was looked at, but they could be completely innocent. In fact, we're the ones who sicced the Mexicans on them."

"That's true."

"We may *know* they were involved in the theft, somehow, but all they have to do is deny it," Del said. "If they get a decent lawyer, the lawyer will pin the theft on Turicek and Albitis. I mean, Turicek was apparently some kind of criminal over in Lithuania, and he brings in Albitis — we're pretty sure of that."

"Yeah." Lucas spun around in his chair, looked out at the parking lot. Then, "Kline was involved. But he got shot, and that's some kind of punishment. Maybe we let him go: work a deal, get Sanderson. She's a killer, or close to it."

"How do we cut him out?"

Kline had checked out of the hospital, in a rental wheelchair, and had gone back to his apartment. Lucas and Del arrived at ten o'clock the next morning, Lucas carrying a briefcase full of paper, including the murder book on the Brooks killings, as well as files on Pruess, the Polaris vice president who'd been thrown in the dumpster, on the killing of Rivera, and the shootings of Uno and Dos.

He planned to take the whole mass, as he told Del, sharpen it to a fine point, and shove it up Kline's ass.

When they arrived at Kline's apartment building, they could see, from the street, a light on in the bathroom through the new window. They went up and pounded on the door.

Nothing.

They pounded again, and then a weak, nervous answer: "Who is it?"

"Lucas Davenport, BCA. I spoke to you before."

After a long pause, Kline called back, "How do I know it's you?"

"You could look out the peephole," Lucas said.

"But if it's not really you, as soon as I look out the peephole, you could shoot me again."

"Ah, for Christ's sakes, Kline, it's me," Lucas said. "Call your building manager and ask her to come up and look."

There was another long silence, then the peephole darkened, and finally a chain rattled on the inside. Kline, unshaven, white-faced, peeked out, saw Del, looked up and down the hall, and said, "All right."

He'd been on his feet, and now he settled back, in the wheelchair, and rolled himself backward into the apartment. He'd been watching a morning talk show: a man stood behind a microphone, turned to a stunned-looking young man, and said, "Sean, you are . . . NOT . . . the father." The crowd cheered, or jeered, and Kline clicked it off.

"Trying to keep from going insane," he mumbled, apparently embarrassed to be caught watching the show. "What do you want?"

"We need to talk to you about this whole case," Lucas said.

"I talked to a guy in the hospital," Kline said, "And he told me that one thing I shouldn't do is talk to the cops. You're probably recording all of this."

"We're not recording it, and we don't want you to say much anyway. We're here more to make a presentation," Lucas said.

"A presentation?"

"Yes. All you have to do is sit there and listen."

Kline looked from Lucas to Del, and back and forth a couple of times, and then, "I guess I can do that. But I'm not answering any questions."

"Just listen," Lucas said.

Kline said to Del, "Nice tie, dude."

"Hermès," Del said, in his best French.

The place smelled weird, like hot dogs and sweat, brittle yellowed wallpaper and dry rot, with a little old-bathroom smell thrown in. The couch was covered with newspapers, and when Lucas looked for a place to sit, Kline said, "Throw those papers on the floor," and Del did that, making a stack and dropping it beside one couch arm.

Lucas took the paper out of his briefcase, put the case between his feet, and started talking:

"Don't say anything. Don't argue with me, just listen," he said. "Now, we know you were involved in this theft from Polaris.

There's no question in our minds about that."

"Oh, bullshit, you're —"

"Shut up," Lucas said. "Just listen to the case."

Lucas laid it out piece by piece. How ICE had found two back doors into Polaris and had documented them before she took them out. How they had to be done from the inside. How Kline had migrated to Hennepin National, where he'd hooked up with three other people for the theft: Turicek, Sanderson, and eventually, Albitis.

"We can tie you to the other three. We can tie Turicek to Albitis, and Albitis to the gold purchases. We believe we can tie Sanderson to the attack on Albitis — she called nine-one-one on a phone Albitis used to call Turicek, and I recognized her voice on the tape. The tape is being analyzed in our laboratories now, and after we get the forensic voice analysis done, we'll be able to hook that to Sanderson. So, we've got you all in a bundle."

Kline broke in, shaking his head: "You don't have me. All you have on me is that I sat in the same office. And I'll tell you what: banks deal with each other all the time, system to system. I think Ivan found a way into Polaris from our system, picked out an account to loot, and did it. He never told me about it. I think it was him and Albitis, and everything else you're telling me is bullshit."

Lucas shook a finger at him: "Not bullshit. I think we can make a powerful case. But you're right about one thing — our case against you is the weakest. We don't care about Turicek, because he's dead. So it comes down to you and Albitis and Sanderson. We've decided to settle for two out of the three. We're going to give somebody partial immunity, in return for testimony against the other two."

"Partial immunity," Kline scoffed. "That's worth a lot. Go to prison and get killed for being an informer . . . get banged by a bunch of faggot convicts . . . that's an attractive deal."

Del said, "Listen, Jake, you know what happened here. The Brookses, David Rivera, the cop from Mexico, Pruess, the VP from Polaris . . . we're not going to come after you for stealing a little money. We're coming after you for multiple murder. You and the others touched this off. How old are you? Close to thirty? You'll be sixty years old, under Minnesota law, before you'd have your first chance to see the outside again."

"But I'm innocent," Kline said.

"Oh, bullshit, Jake," Lucas said. Then, into a moment of deadlocked silence, "But there's something else. And I brought some stuff to show you."

"I need to talk to a lawyer."

"You do, but for now, listen another two minutes," Lucas said. "Have you been watching television? All the news reports about these Mexican gangsters?"

"Yeah, I've seen it."

"I'll tell you what — they don't have the gold. We're lying about that, hoping to confuse things."

"So they can't go back," Kline said. "The killers. That's cruel. Funny, but cruel."

"Sooner or later, the truth is going to come out," Lucas said. "When it comes out, these gangsters are going to say to themselves, 'Jacob Kline and Kristina Sanderson and Edie Albitis have our twenty-two million dollars.' They're going to come after you. They're going to want their money. You understand?"

"I understand what you're saying, I'm not sure I believe it. There seems to be a lot of bullshit going on here."

"So look at this," Lucas said. "Does this look like bullshit?"

He reached down between his feet, got the color prints of the murder scenes, the

Brookses, Rivera lying in a puddle of blood, the Mexican guys shot on the couch and in the middle of the parking lot, Pruess folded like an old banana in the dumpster, and then lying on the street partially unwrapped, one butchered hand sticking out on the blacktop.

Lucas pushed out a close-up of a finger joint. "This belonged to Patrick Brooks. Cut them off one at a time. Used them to write a message on the wall."

Pulled out the "Were coming" scrawl.

Kline looked at the photos, first in fascination, then in revulsion, and finally he turned away and said, "I don't want to see that shit."

Del said, "This is what they were going to do to you, dude. You were smart enough to get away, but you might not get away the next time."

Lucas added, "They'll get you, unless you get some protection. . . . If we get that gold back, and make a news story out of it, that'll take away any reason for them to come after you."

"What about revenge?" Kline asked. "They'll still want revenge."

"Listen, the average life span of these guys, these gangsters, is a couple of years," Lucas said. "We cover you for a couple of years . . . we could make that part of a deal. Eventually, they'll forget about it. It'll seem pointless, if the money's gone."

"I've got no idea about the money," Kline said.

"If you help us out with Sanderson and Albitis, one of them will cough up the money," Del said. "We think Sanderson took out Albitis because of the gold."

Kline put his head down, seeming to think about it, reached out and pushed one of the photographs aside, to expose a shot of the dead Brooks children, and said, finally, "I'm innocent. But maybe I can find a way to help you. I've got to talk to a lawyer first. I'll start calling around today, see when I can get one. Maybe this afternoon."

"You need to move fast," Lucas said. "I'll tell you what, if Albitis wakes up, and if she's willing to cooperate . . . then our deal with you is off. She gets the protection, you get the thirty years."

"You can guarantee this deal?" Kline asked.

"You get your attorney, you work through the terms, and we'll put you with a county attorney to get the deal in writing," Lucas said.

"I'll start looking for a guy right now," Kline said.

Lucas said, "Good." He started gathering the murder pictures.

Del smoothed down his new silk tie and said, "Let me tell you something, Jake. You're a smart guy. If you think really hard about this, you'll realize it's the best deal you'll get. It might be the best deal of a lifetime. Don't fuck it up."

Kline whined and prevaricated and lied some more, wheeling around the apartment, and eventually Lucas and Del picked up the pictures, gave him a last warning about how little time he had to act, and left.

Out on the street, Lucas asked, "Did he buy it?"

Del said, "I don't know. I can usually tell, but he . . . I don't know."

Lucas said, "I guess we'll find out this afternoon." He looked back up at the apartment and caught a flash of movement in the bathroom window.

They walked back down the street and around the corner to the Lexus, and on the way, Lucas called the hospital about Albitis's condition. The charge nurse said that she was still unconscious, but that the operation the night before had gone well, the bleeding had been less severe than expected, and she was now expected to recover "to some extent."

"What does that mean?" Lucas asked. "To some extent?"

"Can't ever tell, with cases like this," the nurse said. "She could be fine. On the other hand, she could be a wreck. What usually happens is that they lose something, at the start, then they get most of it back. But you just can't tell in advance."

Up in the apartment, Kline stood next to the bathroom window, looking down, and saw the two cops come out of the apartment door and stand talking on the street. Then Davenport looked up at the window, and Kline pulled his head back. A few seconds later, he peeked from behind the shade and saw them walking away down the street. He couldn't see them turn the corner, but they didn't come back, either.

When he was sure they were gone, he went to the bedroom and asked the bed, "Did you hear that?"

The bed said, "Yes. Are you sure they're gone?"

"They're gone. The door's locked."

Sanderson edged out from under the bed and said, "It smelled like something died under there. You might have mice."

"I'd be shocked if I didn't," Kline said.

"So now what?"

"First, I swear to God, I swear to God, I didn't just attack Edie. She came after me with Daddy's gun, for Christ's sakes. I was lucky to get away from her."

"I believe you — but the cops won't believe it," Kline said.

"I still don't think they have enough to take me to trial," Sanderson said.

"We need to get lawyers."

"We can get lawyers, but I swear to God, if you drag me into this, I'll take you with me," Sanderson said. "I'll tell everybody that you knew you were stealing drug money and that you've got it all hidden. Then these Mexicans *will* come after you. They *will* chop you to pieces."

"You don't have to threaten me," Kline said.

"Yes, I do," Sanderson said. "I can see you're thinking about it, about a way out. I promise you, that's not the way."

Kline wheeled himself around the apartment, ran both hands through his long oily hair. "Christ, I go around telling everybody that I don't care how it comes out. I'm cool. I'm cold. Now, they're talking about prison. . . . You know what I found out? I don't want to go to prison. I mean, I *really* don't want to go to prison."

"Davenport's just mean," Sanderson said. "Mean and smart. But we're as smart as he is, and we've got more to work with. We just have to fix things so he can't get us."

"What about Edie?" Kline asked. "What if she wakes up and says, 'Kristina hit me'?"

"Then I'll have to deal with that then. But I don't think she will. Anything she says brings it back to her. Anything she says gets her deeper in trouble. Right now, she could say that she was buying gold for a Syrian buyer, some guy trying to get his fortune out of the country. She didn't know who he was . . . nothing illegal with any of that."

Kline said, "For Christ's sakes, Kris, nobody's gonna believe that."

"They don't have to," Sanderson said. "All we need is for them to not have enough to put us on trial. Or not enough to convict us, if they do put us on trial."

"We need to get lawyers," Kline said.

"But what we really need to do, you and me, is sit down and figure out how we can get out of this mess. We're smart. Let's use it."

Kline cocked his head and said, "You don't sound like a hippie anymore."

"And you don't sound like a cynical depressive," Sanderson said. "We've changed. We've become criminals."

458

20

When Lucas looked at his phone on the way back to the office, a note popped up on his calendar software: Cast, tomorrow, 9 am.

The cast was coming off. Hallelujah.

Kline called Lucas after lunch and said, "I've got an appointment with an attorney this afternoon. He said there's no possibility that we can talk to you before tomorrow morning. Don't do anything before then."

"I can't promise," Lucas said. "Whatever happens, happens."

"Please, don't do anything. I gotta talk to the lawyer."

"Who is it?"

"His name is Jay Keisler. I got a recommendation from a friend."

"I don't know him," Lucas said. "But you tell him, there isn't much time."

"I'll tell him," Kline promised. "Please don't do anything."

Lucas clicked off and called an attorney

named Annie Wolf, who had once been a prosecutor and was still big in the Bar Association, and asked about Jay Keisler.

"Yeah, used to be an Anoka County public defender," she said. "Has a general-law practice in Minneapolis. Does some criminal and personal injury."

"Good trial lawyer?" Lucas asked.

"As a trial lawyer, on a scale of one to ten, I'd give him about a seven."

"Not the sharpest arrow in the quiver, huh?"

"It's not that — it's that he looks like a fourteen-year-old Albert Einstein, with this fright-wig hair," Wolf said. "He's just no damn good with juries. I understand that he is *excellent* in pretrial negotiation, and trial prep. Excellent with insurance companies, where nobody wants to go to trial. When they *do* go to trial, he has an associate, Don Pew, who'll usually handle it. Pew looks and acts like Jimmy Stewart. Between the two of them, they get the job done."

"So, if we're trying to work a deal, get a guy to turn state's evidence in return for a reduced charge . . ."

"That's how Jay made his living for a decade or so. He's done hundreds of them. Be ready for him."

"Thanks, Annie."

■ ■ ■ ■

Satisfied that he'd stampeded Kline, but a
little worried about Kline's choice of attorney, Lucas called the Ramsey County attorney they'd be working with and told him
about Keisler.

"Not the best news, but not the worst,"
the prosecutor said. "He'll wring every inch
out of us . . . but in the end, he'll deal."

"That's what I wanted to hear," Lucas
said. "You'll be around tomorrow?"

"All day. Give me a call."

Lucas checked with Shaffer, learned that
there was nothing new with Martínez or the
last shooter, but Shaffer said, "The hunt's
gone viral. Everybody in the country's looking for her. You see the thing about Brooks,
the last hour or so?"

"No . . ."

Lucas was standing in the doorway of
Shaffer's office, and Shaffer leaned back in
his chair and put his feet up on his desk.
Lucas had never seen him do that before;
had never seen him look quite as pleased
with himself.

"Sunnie will now be owned by Brooks's
brother, Stan. Stan was the final disaster
inheritor in Brooks's will. You know, one of

461

those provisions that lawyers put into wills in case the whole family dies in a plane crash?"

"I know about those," Lucas said. "I got one."

"Anyway, he's also on the company board of directors," Shaffer said. "He got the board to offer a hundred-thousand-dollar reward for anyone who *spots* Martínez. *Anyone who spots her.* Don't even have to convict her. Just call the cops on her. It's like a nationwide Easter-egg hunt with a hundred-thousand-dollar egg. Plus, everybody's talking about all that gold they think she has."

"Easter egg with a Mac-10," Lucas said. "Hope nobody gets killed."

Shaffer pulled his feet down. "Well, yeah . . ."

"I wonder if this Stan had anything to do with setting up the fake Bois Brule account? Seems to me that there are going to be a lot of claims on Sunnie. Maybe it'd be better not to get too enthusiastic about Stan's reward offer."

Shaffer rubbed his chin. "You could be right."

"We're still going with the press conference tomorrow? Ten o'clock?" Lucas asked.

"Still scheduled," Shaffer said.

"My daughter Letty works part-time as an intern at Channel Three," Lucas said. "She said Ralph Richter is coming over. He's going to do his media-asshole thing on us. Don't worry about it, and don't let him get under your skin. That's just his gig, you know? Playing the tough guy."

Shaffer suddenly looked worried again.

His job there done, and not feeling at all guilty, Lucas went back to his own office.

Loose ends: He called Virgil Flowers.

"What's taking so long?" he asked.

"I gotta tell you," Virgil said. "I think I've got them spotted. I'm talking to Richie. He's got a deputy with a big fucking pair of binoculars and a radio, hiding out in an oat field, watching the farm. We think your robbers work out of the place, but there're ten other people out there. Something's up. Could be a big meth operation. We're tracking people coming out of there, running their plates, all kinds of different places, Missouri, Colorado, lot of drug busts. Richie's all excited. When we know something, I'll call you."

"I want to be there when you take my two," Lucas said.

"I'll call you. I gotta say, we don't know how horse shit ties into meth, but we're researching it."

While Lucas was calling around, Martínez and Tres lay low. Tres's face wasn't on television, so Martínez gave him two hundred dollars and a shopping list and sent him out for food. When he came back, he said that a Xerox picture of her was on a bulletin board at the supermarket.

"They have put out a reward," Martínez said. She felt a little like a fool for confiding in a child. "One hundred thousand dollars for anyone who finds us."

"So, we hide. I one time, with Dos, hid for ten days in an attic, fifty degrees every day, we could smell our skin cooking up there, it's so hot. Better than getting shot, you know?"

One way or another, she thought, they had a good chance of making it across the border. If she could make it to El Paso, she could make the last mile. The problem was that Davenport had told everybody that she had the gold . . . and that Big Voice had heard about it.

"You have the gold safe?" Big Voice asked.

"No. We don't have any gold at all," she'd said. She explained Davenport, how he was trying to keep her nailed down.

"Very clever," Big Voice said. Then, with

464

disappointment plain in his big voice, he said, "You have no gold at all?"

And in that, she sensed doubt.

The next time he talked to her, he mentioned that the "powers" had heard that she had the gold and had been upset when they heard that she denied it.

"We have never seen the gold. I can let you talk to Tres —"

"Tres is a child," the Big Voice said. "You could hide the gold from him."

"If I had the gold, I would not come back to you," she said. "If I had the gold, I would disappear. But I am coming back to you."

"That is a point in your favor," the Big Voice said. "When will you come?"

The "powers" wanted the gold. They weren't sure about her. They were looking for somebody to blame for its loss.

This would not, she thought, end well for her.

She saw the tape again, of Davenport talking about the gold.

It was his fault, she thought.

He was squeezing her, squeezing her. Squeezing her to death.

While Lucas called around, and Martínez watched the television, Sanderson was in her car, doing her frantic escape-and-evasion routine, worried that she was being tracked. Eventually, she decided that if anyone was following her, they were just too smart for her, and she drove around to a half dozen Walmart and Target stores, where she bought small flattened cardboard shipping boxes and packaging tape. Scared to death of fingerprints and DNA, she bought two extra boxes at each store, and touched only the top and bottom boxes in the stack.

Once she had them to her car, she separated the boxes with the fingerprints from the boxes without, and put the boxes with prints in the front seat. She also bought a bottle of Windex and some kitchen gloves.

An hour after she left the last of the stores, she was back at the farm. She made sure she was alone, then she drove through the gate, closed it behind her, and bounced across the field to the spot where she'd buried the gold. She parked thirty feet away from it, not wanting to make new car tracks through the weeds that might lead somebody to the burial spot.

Digging up the gold was a bit less hot and sweaty than putting it in the ground, but not much. Then, when the gold was uncovered, she had to pull it out of the hole and run it back to the car, eight hundred–plus pounds of heavy metal. She was frightened that she might be seen, and so did it as fast as she could, laboring like a ditchdigger with a short deadline. When she was done, she was more angry than scared, and breathing hard: all of this work, and all of this blood, and they were taking it away from her.

She *deserved* this gold. Now the cops would get it.

Well: most of it.

Some of it, she carefully rewrapped and left at the bottom of the hole. She filled the hole again, replaced the chunks of sod and weed, and spent a half hour cleaning up the area around it. When she was done, it looked better than it had the first time. She got in the car, bounced back across the field, out through the gate, which she carefully closed, and down the dusty road toward the Cities. She still had work to do at the office.

Lucas called Flowers: "Anything yet?"

"Won't be today. But Richie says they're doing drugs, one way or another. So probably tomorrow afternoon. Next day at the latest. Your two guys, the guys who robbed you, are probably named Duane Bird and Bernice Waters. Both have a long trail, but all minor stuff, not counting these robberies. Bernice stole sixteen thousand dollars from the Full Bible Church of Darby five years ago, and spent some time out at the women's prison. . . . That's about as big as they've gotten."

"All right. Keep talking to me," Lucas said.

Lucas went home, and Weather, who always got home earlier, said, "Cast is coming off."

"Which is good," Lucas said. "Which is about time."

"For such a big lug, you're such a baby," she said. "You got anything else tomorrow?"

He told her about the press conference, and about Virgil's investigation, and she said, "So you're going to have to get up early."

"Eight o'clock."

"Maybe we ought to go to bed early. We could get this week's sex out of the way."

"I'll have to look at my calendar again, and maybe have an extra glass of milk," he said, "but it's a possibility."

He barely thought about Martínez, except to wonder where she might be. Still in the Cities? In Missouri or Oklahoma? Back in Mexico already?

Whatever. He no longer much cared —

she was Shaffer's Easter egg.

Lucas's eyes popped open at six o'clock, when he felt Weather stirring around. She said, quietly, "The alarm is set for eight."

"See you tonight," he said. He tried to go back to sleep, dozed for a while, but at seven he got up; there was too much going on for sleep. He cleaned up, dressed for the press conference in a blue suit and a white shirt with a thin blue stripe, saw the Martínez photo again on the morning news, and a promo for the ten-o'clock news conference. Letty was kicking around in the kitchen getting some cereal when he got downstairs, and he chatted with her about Channel Three and asked her about a kid named Tom who'd been hanging around the driveway, and was told that he was just a friend.

Further efforts to elicit information were fruitless, but he decided that Tom would bear watching.

He was out of the house at eight-thirty, at Hennepin Medical Center at nine, where he checked with Weather's secretary and was told that she was already doing a scar revision. He went down to the clinic, stated his business, and was told to take a seat.

He was reading a home furnishings magazine when his name was called. He took a seat in an examination room, and five minutes later a small fussy middle-aged man showed up, said he was a doctor, and showed Lucas what he, the doctor, called "a specialized kind of saw." The saw looked a little like a Dremel tool with a sanding disk. "It will cut the cast with a vibration. It will not cut your arm," the doctor said.

"Sounds good to me," Lucas said.

The doctor peered at the tool, as though he was unsure exactly how to turn it on, then said, "I don't usually do this — a nurse practitioner usually does it, but she's not here right now."

"Just glad to get it off," Lucas said.

The doctor began cutting, and it went quickly enough, but an inch down the foot-long cast, Lucas felt a cutting pain, and flinched. The doctor said, "Just hold on, you may feel a few twitches, but it won't cut."

He started again, and another inch or two along the way, there was another slicing pain, and Lucas flinched away again.

"Don't do that," the doc said impatiently. He took the head of the tool and pressed it against his palm, where it buzzed away. No cut.

"You think it's cutting, but it's not," he said. "Let's not break the cutting head."

Another inch, and Lucas said, "Ahhhh . . ." but didn't flinch; another inch, and he did flinch, and the doctor said, "Hold on, hold on." To Lucas, it didn't seem like his imagination. . . . One more searing pain, and the cast popped loose.

The doctor carefully pulled it off and said, "See, no cuts."

Lucas could still feel something like cuts, and looked closely at his arm. There were five inch-long white lines on the fresh pink skin.

"What're these things?" he asked. "They hurt like hell."

Del said, "Burns?"

Lucas: "Yeah. I've got five burns, each one an inch long, gonna be scars, right up my arm. What he didn't know was, the saw doesn't cut you, but if you go through the cast slowly enough, like he did, the blade gets red hot. He was branding me, and telling me the pain was just my imagination, the silly asshole."

Del said, "Ah, well . . . you know. Accidents happen."

"Accidents? The guy was supposed to be a medical doctor."

"You're getting to be a sissy, man. . . ."

"Sissy?"

471

■ ■ ■ ■

At the press conference, Shaffer spent fifteen minutes describing and discussing the extent of the hunt for Martínez and the last of the Mexican shooters, and Lucas said that the BCA was expecting some kind of movement in regard to the thieves who'd started the chain reaction that led to the murders.

"Any more about the gold?" he was asked.

"I just want to say that anyone who sees Martínez should not get any ideas about this gold — that will get you killed," Lucas said. "We believe she has it, as much as twenty-two million in untraceable gold coins, but that should not be a motive to go after her. Let the law handle this. No amount of gold is worth losing your life, and these two people are professional killers. So stay clear."

Virgil Flowers called fifteen minutes after the press conference. "You looked good. Nice suit."

"You know what I was doing? I was saying 'gold,' " Lucas said. "Gold, gold, gold, gold. I want everybody thinking gold, and that Martínez has it."

"Whatever works," Flowers said. "Listen, Richie wants to pop these guys at the farm so bad that he walks around with his legs crossed. He can't wait — I think we'll be going in this afternoon. Everybody coming out of there has had a drug problem. He's talking to his favorite judge about a warrant, and probably Channel Three. Did I mention that he's up for reelection this fall?"

"Yeah, you did. What time you want me there?" Lucas asked.

"I don't know. I'll call you. Be ready. It's about an hour out of town."

Kline's attorney, Jay Keisler, called: "Can we get together?"

"If you make it worth our while," Lucas said.

"I think we can, but maybe not exactly the way you want it," Keisler said. "We've run into a bump in the road."

"If I hear about bumps, we might have to go with what we've got," Lucas said.

"Who're we talking to over at the county?"

"Dave Morgan," Lucas said.

"So let's let Dave decide," Keisler said. "What time's good for you? I've got to be in court at eleven-thirty, but only for a motion, take five minutes."

"One?" Lucas suggested.

"One's good," Keisler said.

"I'll check with Dave and get back to you."

Lucas checked with Morgan, who said try for twelve-forty-five, because that's what lawyers do, and Keisler sighed as though it were the end of the world, but agreed.

Lucas, Del, Shrake, and Jenkins went out for an early lunch, much of it spent in a thoroughly despicable gossip session about another agent and an extraordinarily attractive female tech, both in their early forties, both married with children, who may or may not have been having a hot affair, that may or may not have included sex on the upstairs gun-testing range.

By the time they got back to the office, Lucas had to hurry to make the appointment at the prosecutor's office. Morgan's office was in the Ramsey County courthouse, and Lucas parked kitty-corner in the Victory parking garage. As he hustled across the street, something felt wrong, but he wasn't sure what it was, so he kept going.

A secretary showed him into a conference room, where Kline was waiting with a man who looked as though he'd just been electrocuted: the Einstein hair. Lucas said, "You must be Jay," and they shook hands, and then Morgan bustled into the office and said, to Lucas, "We've been talking for a couple of minutes in the hallway. . . . It's not quite what I thought."

Lucas looked at Kline: "What's up?"

Keisler answered. "We have a small problem. My client is innocent. I try not ever to get into that question, but he told me before I could stop him. Then, you know, he convinced me. He also convinced me that even if he isn't innocent, you could never convict him. So, we don't have a basis for a bargain. But we do have something."

Morgan: "What?" He was not at all perturbed; just another workday.

"There's the possibility that my client might be able to provide you with some information about an accomplice of the real criminal in this matter, Ivan Turicek," Keisler said.

"If your client is innocent, he has the obligation to provide us with any information he has," Morgan said.

"But not misinformation. Let me put it this way. This is more of a feeling than hard information, and while it includes a name, it's possible that he would be implicating a completely innocent person. He wants to cooperate, and if he cooperates, and you guys, from some misplaced sense of vengeance, go after him, we want the court to know that he cooperated."

After a lot of to-ing and fro-ing, which took the best part of fifteen minutes, a name was spat out: Mohammed Ibriz.

Lucas: "This guy, Mohammed Ibriz, is an accomplice?"

"I can't swear to it," Kline said. "But I heard Ivan talking to the guy several times, when we were working down there in Systems. I was over on the other side of the computers, and you know how you listen to somebody when they're trying to be confidential and quiet? I heard him call him Mohammed several times, and you know now, how you notice Islamic names because of all the trouble?"

"Where did the Ibriz guy come from?" Lucas asked.

"From Ivan's cell phone. It was sitting on the work table, and it rang, and I looked down at it and it said, 'Mohammed Ibriz' on the display," Kline said. He thought Ibriz might be an accomplice, he said, because the calls started just about the time the money was stolen, and continued off and on through the month.

"And you just remembered the name, like that?" Morgan asked.

"Well, I heard *Mohammed* a lot, so that

was already in my head, and then Ibriz . . . I guess it just stuck," Kline said. "Then Officer Davenport asked me these questions about some Syrian moving gold coins. . . . It popped into my head."

"You wouldn't know where we could find this guy, would you?" Lucas asked.

"Well, I know what I did, this morning," Kline said.

"What was that?" Lucas asked.

"I looked in the phone book. There's an office listing for a Mohammed Ibriz over in Galtier Plaza. How many Mohammed Ibrizes can there be?"

Galtier Plaza was maybe six blocks away.

There was more lawyer talk, but Morgan had agreed that no matter what happened, if there should be a prosecution, the court would be told of Kline's cooperation . . . if, in fact, it turned out to be anything.

When they were gone, Lucas asked Morgan, "What do you think?"

"Keisler's a dealer. That's what he does. If he doesn't want to deal, he probably thinks he's got a strong case. And he's smart enough to know strong from weak. His partner, the trial guy, could sell ice cubes to penguins. So, if I were you, I'd look into Mohammed."

Lucas patted his pocket looking for his cell phone, and realized why he'd felt uneasy walking across the street to the courthouse: he'd left the phone in the car, on the car charger. He borrowed a phone, called Del, and said, "Meet me at Galtier Plaza in fifteen minutes. Bring the Turicek file. We need to talk to a guy."

Lucas talked to Morgan for a few more minutes, then hurried off to Galtier, which was an office and apartment complex on the edge of an area called Lowertown. He'd once seen a woman get murdered in a park across the street, and never walked through the area without thinking about that day.

Flowers had been with him. . . .

Flowers, he thought. "Goddamnit." He should have stopped and gotten the phone. He'd never owned a cell phone until three years earlier, and now he felt naked without it.

Del was waiting outside Ficocello's barbershop on the Skyway level. The Ficocello brothers were both cutting hair, and both took the time to raise a hand as Lucas went by. Del said, "He's on nine."

They went up in the elevator, found a blond-wood door with a sign that said IBRIZ PROPERTY MANAGEMENT, and went in.

478

There were two offices: the outer office, with a secretary staring at a computer, and an inner office, where a tall thin man was reading the *Pioneer Press.* He took down the paper to watch them as they showed their IDs to the secretary, then stood up and came to the door and asked, "Is there a trouble?"

"We're from the Bureau of Criminal Apprehension," Lucas said. "We're looking for a Mohammed Ibriz."

The man said, "That is I. How can I help?"

"Do you know a man named Ivan Turicek?" Lucas asked.

Ibriz cocked his head and said, "No. I believe not."

Lucas opened the file and took out an enlarged copy of Turicek's passport photo and said, "This man?"

Ibriz looked at it for a moment, then said, "What has he done?"

"Do you know him?" Lucas asked.

"Not as this Ivan," he said. Ibriz turned and went back to his desk and pulled out a long card file, looked down a list, then pulled out a card. "I rented an office near I-35E to a man named Carl Schmitz, a German, who is this man. This Turicek. This is the only time I see him."

479

"When was this?" Lucas asked.

Ibriz looked back at the card. "July seventh. A one-year lease."

"Do you have a key?" Lucas asked.

"Maybe I should have a warrant," Ibriz said.

Lucas shook his head. "Turicek is dead. Murdered. His office may be a crime scene, so we don't need a warrant."

Ibriz nodded. "Okay. So I have a key. I'll come with you."

They took Del's car, and followed Ibriz in his Mercedes north out of downtown on I-35E for five minutes. The office was in a long, low white-painted concrete block building with fake-stone accents, and perhaps ten offices. Each office had a big window covered with a white blind, all fronting on a narrow parking lot. There were a half dozen angled parking spaces for each office, but no more than a dozen cars in the entire lot: a start-up office complex, for start-up businesses.

Turicek paid nine hundred dollars a month in rent, Ibriz said, and had paid first and last, as well as a one-thousand-dollar deposit.

Ibriz unlocked the door and stood back: inside, they found a desk, an office chair, a computer that went back to the nineties, a big TV older than the computer, and some other miscellaneous junk. Everything looked spotless, and smelled of Windex.

"It's been wiped," Del said.

There was a door to the back: they looked into a back room, which was empty. There were two more doors, a bathroom and a coat closet, Ibriz said. Lucas looked in the bathroom, and then Del, who looked in the closet, said, "Here's something . . . boxes."

Inside the closet, dozens of small boxes were stacked nearly waist high. Lucas reached out with one hand to pull a box forward, but fumbled it because of the weight: it hit the floor with a solid *thunk.*

"What?" Del asked.

Lucas picked up another box, held it against his stomach, and asked, "You got a knife?"

Del had a switchblade and flicked it open and cut the packaging tape. Lucas reached inside and pulled out a translucent soft-plastic tube stuffed with yellow coins the size of poker chips.

"It's the gold," he said. "It's the fucking gold."

21

Lucas backed away from the pile of boxes and said, "Okay, this could be big trouble. We need to get some guys here, we need Shaffer, we need an accountant. We need the DEA."

"Gold," Del said, with a gleam in his eye.

Ibriz said, "To find this, this is a gift from Allah." He looked at Lucas and Del with anticipation.

"We need a lot of guys," Lucas said. "We need witnesses."

Ibriz groaned, but Lucas said, "Forget about it."

The problem was, Lucas thought, that if you found twenty-two million dollars' worth of gold in a closet, and you were a cop, there were going to be questions about whether all of it made it back to headquarters. He wasn't exactly sure what the price of gold was, but it was something around sixteen hundred dollars an ounce. Each plastic sleeve, of twenty coins, would be worth something like thirty-two thousand dollars. There appeared to be hundreds of sleeves.

Del made the call, while Ibriz went into mourning. They were ten minutes, normal driving, from the BCA building, and Lucas, without timing it, suspected that Shaffer and his team made it in six minutes. Shaffer burst into the office and cried, "You got it?"

Lucas pointed at the boxes, and handed the open one to Shaffer. Shaffer fumbled out a couple of the plastic tubes, and one popped open, and gold coins tumbled to the carpet. "My God, look at this. It's gold," Shaffer said. He started to laugh, uncontrollably, and everybody stood back and looked at him.

The DEA guys were next in. O'Brien looked at the boxes and shook his head. "You guys want to be careful," he said. "You know what the assholes are going to say. That some of it stuck to your fingers."

"That's why we've got everybody here," Lucas said. He nodded at the other two DEA agents. "They're accountants. Let's get them to count it."

They were talking about that when Shaffer said to Lucas, "Hey: Cheryl's been trying to get in touch with you. She said it's urgent."

Lucas borrowed Del's phone, called his secretary, and she said, "Call Virgil an hour ago."

Lucas called Flowers. Flowers shouted at him: "Hey."

"Where are you?"

"I'm lying in a goddamn ditch. Look at that! Look at that!" Flowers was screaming now, but apparently not at Lucas.

"Look at what?" Lucas asked, raising his voice. In the background, he could hear a stuttering sound, which might have been some kind of strange Verizon static, but he was afraid it wasn't.

"One of those sonsofbitches has a machine gun," Flowers shouted. "Holy shit, he took that Chevy out. Hey! Hey! Get out of there! Get out of there!"

"What?" Lucas shouted into the phone. Everybody stopped messing with the gold and looked at him.

"They're shooting at the TV chopper," Flowers yelled. Lucas stepped across the room, bent and turned on the television. The over-the-air picture was a little hazy, showing some kind of reality show rerun, and he clicked around to Channel Three.

The aerial shot popped right up, a circling

tracking of a big red barn, with a bunch of crumbling outbuildings behind it, and a white farmhouse to one side. Sheriff's cars were stacked up in the driveway, and Lucas could see what looked like bodies along the driveway. Then one of the bodies moved, fast, across the driveway, and he realized that they were sheriff's deputies, on the ground.

A runner burst out of the back of the barn, headed toward a woodlot that was embedded in a blue-green grain field — the oat field that Flowers had mentioned. The onboard reporter was shouting, "They're shooting at us, Jim. Get out of here, they're shooting at us, you dumb shit!"

Lucas yelled into the phone, "What the fuck is going on there?"

"We raided the place and ran into a hornet's nest," Flowers shouted back. There was a background explosion that sounded like a howitzer, and Lucas asked, "What was that? What the hell was that?" and Flowers, laughing, said, "Richie's got himself a 50-cal. He's blowing holes in the — Whoa, look at them, they're like ants. . . . They don't like that 50-cal."

On the TV, Lucas could see a half dozen men break from the barn, running toward the back of the farm lot.

On the phone, he heard another howitzer blast, and an instant later, on TV, in full color, the red barn blew to bits in an enormous gaseous fireball that rose into a mushroom cloud.

Flowers: "Holy mother of God . . ."

Lucas shouted into the phone, "I'm coming."

Del took him back to the Victory garage where Lucas recovered the Porsche and his cell phone. He got Flowers on his phone and said, "Keep calling me. What's going on now?"

"We're chasing them. They've stopped shooting, and we've got the farm, and now we're chasing them down. Gonna take a while."

"I'll be there."

"Computer says you're an hour and fifteen minutes away, if the traffic's not too bad," Flowers said.

"Does the computer say how long it takes if you're driving a Porsche with flashers?"

"Don't kill anybody," Flowers said. "See you in fifteen minutes."

He actually took fifty minutes to get to the farm, following the nav system the whole way, busting a lot of stop signs, topping out at 115 miles an hour on clear blacktop; the barn wasn't out in the sticks, he thought. He actually *passed* the sticks fifteen miles before he got there.

The place was a jumble of sheriff's squads, highway patrol cars, ambulances, fire trucks, civilian vehicles, four-wheelers, and three circling helicopters and one light airplane. Lucas was still running with lights when a skeptical highway patrolman pointed him to the shoulder of the county road. Lucas hung his ID out the window, the patrolman said, "Slick ride," and let him through.

He saw Flowers's 4Runner parked on the freshly mown shoulder of the road and pulled up alongside it, all four wheels on the road, hoping that the SUV would cover the Porsche from any fresh outbreak of gunfire. Insurance companies don't want to hear about bullet holes.

Flowers was up the driveway, talking to a sheriff's deputy. He saw Lucas coming, said something to the deputy, and walked down to Lucas. Flowers was a tall man, as tall as Lucas, but slender, with long blond hair. He was wearing a cowboy hat, a pair of aviator sunglasses, a vintage Radiohead T-shirt, jeans, and cowboy boots. He did not, as far as Lucas could see, have a gun.

He walked up and said, "We're still missing about three of them."

Lucas was looking past him at the farm. What had been the barn was now mostly a concrete slab, with what looked like the half-eaten stump of an enormous silver Oscar Mayer wiener sitting on the slab. The ground was littered with splintered barn siding and shingles, two of the outbuildings had collapsed, and the house was covered with fire foam. "It's a fuckin' war zone," he said.

"Got pretty busy, there," Flowers said. "See, what happened was, Richie has this 50-cal, and they were shooting at us with some small machine pistols. He let off a few shots to clear out their nostrils, and then, well, we didn't know it, but there was an industrial-sized propane tank in there. That's what the silver thing is. We think the second-to-last shot knocked a hole through it — that's when everybody ran — and the propane came spewing out under heavy pressure, and then the next shot through probably hit the tank again, or some other metal, kicked out some sparks . . ."

"How many dead?" Lucas asked.

"Nobody, so far. Three shot, none critical, all dopers."

"Meth?"

"No, no, that's where the horse shit comes

in," Flowers said. "They were growing magic mushrooms. Industrial-scale magic mushrooms, on a substrate of horse shit and straw. They'd heat in the winter, cool in the summer, perfect growing temperatures all year long. There's a big plastic tube stuck in the ground in back, an old sewer pipe they got somewhere. There's probably a half-ton of mushrooms in there."

"You're sure they're magic?" Lucas asked.

"Positive." Flowers chuckled. "We'd really be up shit creek if they turned out to be, you know, button mushrooms. Or shiitakes."

"How about my robbers?" Lucas asked.

"They weren't here," Flowers said. "But I was talking to one of the dopers, not a bad guy, for a doper, and he told me where they live, and where they were going this afternoon. They were supposed to bring a load of horse shit back this evening."

"So . . ."

"I was waiting for you," Flowers said. "Let's go get them. Leave the Porsche here. We've got to come back this way anyway, we can drop them off with the sheriff."

"Good. That way, the Porsche won't smell like horse shit," Lucas said.

As they walked down to Flowers's truck,

Lucas asked, "Where're we going?"

" 'Bout five or six miles down the road, to a gravel road called Jenks Trail. Half mile north, there's a trailer sitting on the side with a dirt yard and a pit bull on a chain. That's them. I pulled some stuff off the computer. There's a file on the backseat."

They got in the truck and Lucas reached over the seat and got the file, a stapled printout from the NCIC. He paged through it as Flowers pulled off the shoulder, and they loafed down the county road, over hill and dale, past the tall corn and rolling woods, the soybeans and alfalfa, kids looking over their shoulders as they pedaled along on their bikes.

Duane Bird and Bernice Waters were the kind of minor dirt-bags that made life a little tougher for everybody. They'd steal anything that wasn't nailed down, burglarize any house or business they thought might be empty, get drunk and fight and drive, and choke down any drug they could get their hands on. They weren't killers, not even much in the way of robbers, although what they'd done with Lucas counted as armed robbery.

Bird had once been convicted of stealing a hundred manhole covers from Rochester, a theft carried out in a single night. He sold the covers to a junkyard, for processing as scrap. The owner of the junkyard expressed amazement when he found out that the manhole covers had been stolen and immediately rolled over on Bird.

Waters was believed to be behind the theft of one hundred cartons of Tums from a semitrailer broken down in Park, Minnesota. Each carton contained 144 bottles of Tums tablets, each bottle containing 150 tablets, for a grand total of 2,160,000 assorted fruit Tums. Nobody knew what she'd done with them.

They'd both been convicted of shoplifting, with Target their favored retailer.

When he finished thumbing through it, Lucas tossed the file on the backseat, leaned back, and said, "Nice day."

"When did you lose the cast?" Flowers asked.

"This morning. You know what the goddamned so-called doctor did? . . ."

When they got to Jenks Trail, they decided to make a slow pass on the trailer, to check out the dog situation and see if anybody was around. Flowers cut his speed back to thirty-five or so, kicking up a long trail of gravel dust behind the 4Runner. They came up to the trailer, a twenty-year-old aluminum capsule painted turquoise and desert tan, set up on concrete blocks, in a bare lot carved out of a perfectly good cornfield. The dog was lying in the dirt yard, a white beast with jaws like a bear trap. The dog stood up to bark as they went by.

A pickup sat in front of the trailer, with its hood propped up. It looked as though it'd been propped up for a while.

"Do not want to fuck with that dog," Lucas said, looking over his shoulder.

"Doesn't look like the chain would reach the door," Flowers said. "We could come up from the back, through the cornfield."

"Wouldn't be a surprise . . . and we know they've got that piece-of-shit pistol."

"They never shot anybody," Flowers said.

"Maybe come up behind the trailer, watch it for a while," Lucas suggested.

They parked Flowers's truck on a gravel road on the opposite side of the field, where it would be out of sight for most cars going down to the trailer. Lucas took off his suit coat, and Flowers pulled on a long-sleeved shirt so he wouldn't get scratched by the corn leaves. At the last minute, Flowers went back to the truck, got a pistol out from under the front seat, already in a carry holster. He stuck it in his back beltline and said, "I'm good."

They climbed a barbed-wire fence and submerged in the tall corn. Lucas would have been lost in a minute or two, but Flowers pulled out his cell phone, called up a compass app, and they followed the arrow across the field.

When they got close, they found they were a bit too far to the west, and so went back in, walked east two hundred feet, then climbed another fence and jogged up to the back of the trailer, a single-wide.

"Smell it?" Flowers asked, in a whisper.

Lucas nodded: a faint odor, like a mix of alcohol and ammonia, hung about the trailer. They'd been cooking meth inside. Lucas pressed his ear to the metal siding on the trailer and listened. Not a sound. Not a creak. "Nothing moving," he said.

"That smell — we've got probable cause," Flowers said.

"Let's go. Let's kick the door," Lucas said.

They walked around the side and then the front, and the dog went nuts. His chain would have covered the rut up to the front door, but fell short of the concrete-block stoop. Lucas took his pistol out as Flowers, with cowboy boots, walked up to the door and simply kicked it open.

Lucas went through, with Flowers a

couple steps behind: nobody home, but the place was saturated with the odor of the chemicals.

"Jesus, what a shithole," Lucas said. Dirty clothes were stacked around the built-in couches, papers — bills and advertisements — were scattered over the tiny dinner table.

The dog was still going nuts.

"If we find them, we gotta do something about the mutt," Lucas said.

"There's a pit bull rescue place in the Cities. They'll come down and get him." Flowers shook his head. "A dog like that, you had to abuse it to make it that crazy. Once pits go nuts, sometimes you can't get them back."

They made a wide circle around the dog and hiked back to the truck, Lucas bitching about what the gravel was doing to his Italian shoes.

Flowers had addresses for two horse stables where Bird and Waters might be. He had Google maps for the locations, marked by the county agent. Bird and Waters were driving a rust-red 1994 Ford F-350.

They found them at the first farm, shoveling shit, no clue about the shoot-out they'd missed. The farmer walked Lucas and Flowers down to the main barn, explaining,

"Most of the manure is taken out mechanically, but we've got to clean the last bit by hand."

"That's good information," Lucas said. He stepped in something too soft, looked down at his shoes, winced.

The barn was empty, all the horses being out in a pasture. Flowers pointed them out, and said they were called Appaloosas, identifiable by their dappled asses.

"Then how come they're not called Assaloosas?" Lucas asked. The farmer looked at him oddly, and they went around the barn.

The two robbers were working with coal shovels and brooms, dragging shovelfuls of horse shit off a manure pile and throwing it on the truck. They were dressed in overalls, a tall, tough woman and the skinny man; when the man looked at them, and tried to smile, Lucas realized he'd lost all his teeth.

Lucas recognized them instantly, and said to them, "Yup. You're them."

The woman said, "Who?"

"The two who took five hundred dollars off me up in St. Paul this spring and broke my wrist," Lucas said. He held up his ID. "I'm a cop. You're under arrest."

The couple looked at each other for a moment, and the man's shoulders slumped. The woman had a push broom in her hands and said, "Thank God," and tossed the broom on a pile of lumpy manure.

The man said, "Fuck me. What's gonna happen to my truck?"

"Probably sold for restitution," Lucas said. "Okay. You have the right . . ."

After they read them their rights, Lucas asked Waters, "Why'd you say, 'Thank God'?"

"Because I'm still on parole," she said. "They'll send me back to Shakopee. That's the best place I ever been. Warm dorms, nice beds, good food. I'd live there the rest of my life, if I could. I had a job in the cafeteria."

Bird said, "Got good medical, too. Maybe I can get my teeth fixed."

Lucas looked at them and said, "Well, shit."

Flowers started laughing, clapped him on the back and said, "Revenge is sweet, huh?"

The stable owner wanted the Ford out of his yard, and finally Flowers suggested that they let Bird drive the truck back to the farm, and from there, the sheriff's deputies would take over. Bird agreed to do it, and Flowers tapped him on the chest and said, "If you go anywhere but the farm, we'll bust your ass and pile some more time on you. You're not running anywhere with that truck."

Bird said, "Be lucky if we don't run out of gas."

They made it back to the farm, and the two were turned over to sheriff's deputies. The sheriff came over and said, gleefully, "Boy oh boy, this is the biggest bust since old Marilyn Snow went off the rails and shot up the Hot Spot. I'm smelling like . . ." He sniffed and asked, "What smells like horse shit?"

Bird raised a hand.

They were at the farm when Letty called. She was screaming at him: "Dad, Dad, we've got a problem, Dad . . ."

Lucas listened for one moment and said, "I'm coming, honey, I'm coming, hold on. . . ."

Lucas left Flowers and the sheriff without a word, sprinting in his ruined shoes across the farm lawn, down the driveway. A moment later the Porsche fishtailed past the driveway and they could hear it accelerate off into the distance, ripping through the gears.

"That don't sound good," said Richie, the sheriff.

"No. It doesn't," Flowers said.

22

Letty turned the corner and walked down toward the house, when her hot-chick spider-sense kicked up: the feeling that somebody was watching her. She'd mentioned the spider-sense to Lucas one time, and he'd said, "Yep. It's there. Ask anyone who's done surveillance."

It came, he said, because when people are watching someone, they tend to lock their heads in place; instead of wobbling here and there, making subtle changes each and every second, their head goes still. Even when the watcher points his head in another direction, and watches from the corner of his eye, the head freezes. That's picked up by the human social sense, which can find even the most subtle of cues.

People doing surveillance learn not really to watch the target at all, in a specific sense. They look past the target at something else, or at nothing at all . . . and keep the head moving.

"When somebody's watching you from a car, they almost always slow the car down, to keep you in sight for a longer time. Once the target picks up on that, you're cooked," Lucas said.

That's what she picked up on: the car was moving too slowly, as though keeping her in sight. Could be a couple of guys from school, she thought. A girlfriend had passed along the results of a dirty, rotten sexist jock-o poll in which Letty's ass had ranked among the top five at the school.

She was insulted to be the subject of something so low. Sort of.

So she picked up on the car . . .

As she turned up the sidewalk, she used her key to go through the front door. Heard Weather in the kitchen and called, "Hi, Mom," and Weather called back, "Sam's playing with his Leapster, and he probably needs a diaper change. Could you get him? Could you get him?"

Letty said, "Sure," but before she did that, she stopped and peeked through the palm-sized door window.

The car was in the driveway, and Martínez and a short Mexican man were getting out. Letty recognized them instantly: she'd been working at Channel Three, and Martínez's picture was everywhere. Martínez had a gun in her hand, and the short man was carrying what might have been a log. They were coming, she thought, for Dad, but they wouldn't leave anybody alive.

Letty turned to the kitchen and screamed, "Mom: run upstairs. The Mexicans are here and they've got guns. Mom, run upstairs!"

Weather, sounding confused, called, "What?"

Letty screamed, "Run! Run! Get up in the apartment, block the door, block the door, the Mexicans, the Mexicans . . ."

And she turned and ran up the stairs to the second floor, screaming, "Run, run. . . ."

Martínez had cracked at five o'clock, or thereabouts, an hour after a call with the Big Voice.

The Big Voice didn't believe her. "We have seen this video. They say you have the gold, Ana."

"I have no gold."

"So they are lying on TV, these police."

"Yes, they are lying. It's this Davenport, he's the one. He does this to split us apart."

The Big Voice sighed and said, "I understand. So, tonight, if you will run to Des

Moines, we will have a van for you, and a driver. He can hide you in the van, and you will be back tomorrow night."

To Martínez, it had been quite clear. They were fifty-fifty on whether she was telling the truth. In her shoes, they would have taken the gold. They understood that Davenport might be lying, but then again, he might not be. Once the Criminales had their hands on her, they *would* get the truth.

Martínez might not survive the process, but then, she just wasn't that important at the moment. Whatever importance she had once had, had diminished when Rivera went down, and wouldn't come back until she knew her new assignment with the Federales. If she was shuffled off to a clerical job, the LCN would no longer be interested. If she was attached to another inspector, or even a higher rank, then she might be important again.

But for now . . .

And if the Federales got her, they would get their own truth, and that would not help the Criminales either: she had far too much personal information on them.

The fact of the matter was, Martínez realized as she took a turn around the living-room carpet, she might now be considered a liability to the LCN. They would kill her, perhaps with a twinge of regret, but not too much. Any American police agency would drop her in jail, forever; and the Federales . . .

She shuddered when she thought what the Federales might do.

She went round and round with it, grew angrier and angrier.

No way out. There was no way out.

At five o'clock, she cracked, and growled at Tres: "Get your gun."

Tres had been watching the television: *"¿Qué?"*

"We go to kill this cop," she said. "This cop who lies about us, who has done this."

Tres made a moue, then said, "Okay." He was going to die anyway, pretty soon. The saints had told him so, and one day was as good as the next.

As they came up to Davenport's house, she saw his Lexus truck in the driveway and said, "He's there."

"We will do it?"

"We will do it right now."

The door was a stout one, a cop's door, but gave way before the battering ram, a four-by-four that Tres scavenged from a parking lot.

As the door splintered, Letty screamed a

last time, "Mom, Mom, run in the apartment, run in the apartment, block the door . . ."

Then she turned and ran toward her parents' bedroom.

Tres came through the door first, the four-by-four discarded on the stoop, a Mac-10 in his hand. Martínez was a step behind him with a nine-millimeter handgun. Tres scanned to his left, toward the main part of the house, which may have saved Letty's life, because he did not instantly pick up on her as she fled along the open hallway above the living room. As it was, he got off one burst, which peppered the wall behind her — almost missing.

But not quite. One nine-millimeter slug hit her left forearm, broke the bone, and blew bloody tissue onto the wall behind it; the pain was intense, but she'd been hurt before and didn't slow down. Sam's room was halfway down the hall, on the right, and as she passed his door, she could see him staring at his video game, oblivious to the screaming. She reached out with her good hand and yanked the door shut and went on down to the master bedroom.

Weather was in the kitchen with the baby.

Martínez and Tres couldn't see her, but they heard her when she knocked over a chair as she ran toward the back stairs, up to the housekeeper's apartment over the garage.

Martínez snapped at Tres, "Take the girl," and Tres ran that way, toward the stairs, as Martínez ran toward the kitchen. She expected Davenport to appear, and ran awkwardly, with the pistol extended in front of her, toward the kitchen.

In the bedroom, Letty pulled open the bottom drawer of Lucas's bedside stand, forced herself to calmly go through the quick two-finger-three-finger-two-finger sequence of Lucas's pistol safe's combination lock.

Had to get it right the first time and she did it deliberately, even as she heard the footsteps on the stairs, the man with the machine gun . . .

Tres ran up the stairs and saw the bloody splotch on the wall, and heard the girl in the far bedroom. He smiled and slowed his step: it was over.

Letty looked and mostly behaved like a young upper-middleclass girl, but she'd grown up so desperately poor, in the far-northern Minnesota backcountry, her father long gone, her mother a helpless and hopeless alcoholic.

She had, as a child, learned to fend for herself trapping muskrats off the local swamps, for grocery money. Pushed to the wall, she'd had no problem with killing, either muskrats or people. Davenport met her on a murder investigation, during which her mother had been murdered. He and Weather had later adopted her.

The early desperation had marked her, indelibly. She did all the things that young girls now did, texted and Tweeted and Facebooked, fretted over lip glosses and uncurling her hair, and a few other things as well. When Lucas went to the range to work with his pistols, she went along as often as she could.

And she had an ability.

With her left arm dangling at her side, she used her right hand to do the two-three-two-finger sequence, meant for rapid access to the pistol, and there was the Gold Cup Colt .45. She picked it up and slapped the butt against her thigh, to make sure the magazine was well seated, then, holding the stock between her knees, used her good hand to jack a shell into the chamber. There was a second magazine in the safe, and she

506

stuffed it in her back jeans pocket, gripped the pistol, and turned back toward the door.

All of it, from the time she'd shouted at Weather to the time she turned toward the door, had taken no more than eight or ten seconds; perhaps not that. But she could hear the gunman pounding up the stairs, and she ran toward him, heard him coming down the hallway, lifted the pistol eye-high, stepped sideways, and saw him.

Right there.

Eight feet and coming fast, but his gun pointed sideways toward the bloody wall. He wouldn't have done it that way if he'd believed Lucas was upstairs. He would have moved more slowly with the pistol up.

As it was, he had just tensed his diaphragm for what would have been a grunt of surprise, but he never got it out. Tres never had a chance to talk to his saints, to see that their prediction of his early death would be correct. Before he could begin any of that, Letty, shooting for the white spot in his left eye, pulled the shot a bit and sent the .45 slug through the bridge of his nose. As she stepped over his dead, falling body, she shot him a second and third time in the heart.

Letty spent no time worrying about the

Mexican boy: he was dead. She heard a burst of shots, one at a time but fast, from the stairs to the housekeeper's apartment above the garage, and she went that way, running lightly, quietly, down the stairs, turning the corner, through the living room and kitchen, to the bottom of the stairs, and then up.

Martínez had gone into the kitchen expecting a close-up shoot-out with Davenport, but the kitchen was empty. At the same time, she heard somebody running in the back, and she followed the noise, pushing the pistol out ahead of her, as she'd been trained, found a door going into the garage and a carpeted stairway going up.

She heard a door slam at the top of the stairs, but took just a second to pop the garage door and look inside the garage. There were two cars, but no sign of life. She ran up the stairs, heard a heavy *thump* behind the door, and fired five shots through it, fast as she could, *bam-bam-bam-bam-bam.*

She heard Weather scream something, and she kicked at the door, but it didn't budge, and she fired five shots at the doorknob and lock, and then kicked it, but unlike the usual Hollywood-movie sequence, the door remained closed.

Frustrated, she emptied the gun at the door, ejected the magazine, and fumbled another magazine from her jacket pocket.

A woman's voice, on the stairs, said, "Hey."

Letty was halfway up the stairs when she saw Martínez empty the gun at the door and jack out the magazine. She said, "Hey."

Martínez turned, jerking her head around, saw Letty there, with the big .45 in her hand. Tres, she barely had time to think, must have failed. She blurted, "I have no gun. I am empty."

She dropped the pistol and the magazine.

Letty said, "Bullshit. You tried to kill my mom and my little sister."

She shot Martínez in the heart. Martínez didn't go down, but staggered backward, a shocked look on her face. She lifted her hand, and Letty shot her again, in the heart, and Martínez sagged but still brought the hand up, as if to fend off the bullets. They were now only six feet apart, and Letty shot her a third time, in the face, and then Martínez slid down the wall, leaving behind a smear of blood. Letty screamed, "Mom, are you all right?"

"We're all right," Weather shouted back. "We're all right."

"Stay there," Letty shouted. "Call nine-one-one, call nine-one-one." The house-keeper had a hardwired phone in her room.

The pistol was empty. She ejected the magazine and slapped in the second one, and followed the muzzle down the stairs. Were there more of them, out in a car? She crawled into the kitchen, took Weather's cell phone off the kitchen counter, crawled back to the stairway where she could make a stand, if necessary, and, with her good thumb, punched Lucas's call icon.

He came up five seconds later, and she shouted, "Dad, Dad, we've got a problem, Dad. . . ."

Lucas said he'd be there, and she believed him. Nobody else came through the door. She crawled up to the kitchen doorway, sat with the gun, not at all in shock, feeling not bad, but feeling ready.

Two dead, and she felt not bad at all, except for the ache in her arm. She looked down at it, vaguely surprised by the damage: she knew she'd been hit, but blood was draining out of the wound, so she pressed it against her shirt and looked back toward the door.

From not too far away, a siren started.

23

The house that Lucas and Weather had designed and built, and where they intended to live until they died, was sealed with police tape for two days.

Lucas was profoundly shocked by the shoot-out, and feared in his soul that the house had been ruined for Weather, spoiled by the blood. But Weather was defiant: "Nobody will run me out of my house. Nobody."

Lucas loved the place, and hoped that she could hold to that.

The St. Paul crime-scene people, following Letty's narration of the shooting, confirmed her story and said that it really wasn't all that complex, compared to some scenes. But there'd been a lot of damage, a lot of bullet holes, and a lot of blood, and it would take time to clean up.

While crime-scene specialists did their work, and the DEA and BCA tried to determine whether there was any further danger, Lucas moved the family to a condo in downtown Minneapolis. The apartment was owned by Polaris Bank and normally used to house visiting board members. Jim Bone said they could stay for as long as they wanted.

Three days after the shoot-out, Lucas walked through the house with a carpenter named Ignacio Jimenez, who was a Mexican illegal, though he'd come to the U.S. when he was a year old, and who didn't even speak Spanish. Lucas said, "I want everything with blood on it gone — ripped out, not cleaned up. How long will it take?"

"The biggest problem is the maple walls. I'll do my best to match it, but it could be tough."

"How about if you rip it out?" Lucas asked. "All of it?"

"I've got some gorgeous American cherry planks I've been saving up. They're pricey, and it's a little redder, but it'd look great."

"Do it," Lucas said. "What about the rest of the damage?"

"I'll have the carpeting out of here this evening. I can get a good solid door upstairs, that's not a problem, and a temporary door for the front entrance. It'll take a month or so to get a new custom door in there. But the house'll look okay by the end of the week, except for the paneling. I'll have to have some of that milled. . . ."

And so on.

The house, Weather and Lucas agreed, was the least of it.

Weather had run into the housekeeper's apartment with the baby and dragged a couch in front of the door. Since the door was set down a short entry hall, the couch effectively blocked it, and she lay off to one side, bracing it with her feet.

When Martínez emptied the gun through the door, the slugs came through well above Weather's supine body, and the couch, and buried themselves in the opposite wall.

Then the shooting stopped, and Letty shouted at her, and she'd crawled to the housekeeper's hardwired phone and called 911. That done, she dragged the couch away, picked up the baby, stepped over Martínez's body without a second look, and ran downstairs to find the bleeding Letty still pointed at the door.

Weather took it from there. . . .

The ambulance arrived three minutes after the cops, and Letty was taken to Regions

Hospital in St. Paul. The bullet had shattered the middle of her left arm's radius bone before exiting. She was in surgery by the time Lucas arrived. He waited with Weather outside the OR.

"It's not terrible," Weather told him. "She'll need some pins and braces. She'll be in a cast. . . . Aw, my God, Lucas," and she broke down, weeping, and Lucas put his arm around her and squeezed her tight.

The operation went well, done by the best general surgeon Weather knew. He came out and said, "She'll sleep for a while. There'll be some pain, but she'll be okay eventually."

"Will she have any problems with the arm?" Lucas asked.

"It's too early to tell. She might have some loss of feeling, but I don't think she'll have any loss of function," the surgeon said. He was a short blond man with green eyes.

"But you're not sure."

"The break itself is small, but she lost some bone," the surgeon said. "On the other hand, she's young, and the young come back from this kind of thing. Look, I'll go out on a limb: she's gonna be fine."

Eventually, late that night, with Letty still asleep, Lucas took Weather and the other

514

two kids to the Polaris condo. "They'll keep Letty sedated overnight, so there's no point in our being there," Weather said. "We need to get some sleep, because tomorrow's going to be hell."

He tried to sleep, but woke up at four in the morning to an empty bed, and found Weather sitting in the kitchen. "I'm going over to the hospital," he said. "Could you stay with the kids?"

"No. I'm going with you." She'd already called the housekeeper, who'd been shopping during the shoot-out, and who'd temporarily moved in with a sister; she was on her way over.

Letty's eyes cracked open at six o'clock, about the time the hospital woke up. She was disoriented for a moment, sleepy, then saw Weather and Lucas staring at her face.

"Is everybody okay?" she asked.

Lucas opened his mouth to say, "Yes," but nothing came out, and then, for the first time since his mother died, he put his face in his hands and began choking, which was the only way he knew how to cry.

The DEA debriefing was irritating. Lucas was fine with talking to O'Brien, but then he had to repeat everything to a DEA deputy director in Washington, D.C. The director, Lucas thought, was on a speaker-phone, and shouting.

The most important thing he said was that the Mexican Federales heard things from the Criminales, and they'd heard that the Criminales were done with Minnesota. The gang wasn't completely out of control, and now that one of their members had killed a well-known Federale, and then had attempted to kill an American cop's family . . .

"The bottom line is, they don't want a war. Or, more of a war," the DEA boss shouted. "They're done with you guys. For one thing, we've got the gold, and there's no way they're going to get it back."

"How sure are you about that?" Lucas asked. "That they're done?"

"Pretty sure," the DEA man shouted back down the line. "That's about as good as we can get. I'd even say, 'Very sure.' "

"What about Kline or Sanderson? Do they need protection?"

"I've been reading the reports about the whole thing," the director shouted back. "I think they're probably okay. Did they even have anything to do with it? From what I've read, it seems like they might be innocent."

"They're not — they were in it, up to their

necks," Lucas said. "But we can't prove it."

"So . . . seventy-five percent? That they were involved?"

"More like ninety-five," Lucas said. "The problem is, I'm told, that if we go to court, they can blame it all on Turicek. Especially since we got the gold back, and we know Turicek rented the place where the gold was stashed. Kline's attorney makes the point that if his client was involved, he and Sanderson had to know where the gold was, and they could have picked it up anytime. So if they knew . . . why did they let eighteen million in gold get away? The other thing is, Kline's attorney says that if Kline was involved, he could have stolen the money anytime after he left Polaris, but he didn't, even though he was unemployed and needed money. Our county attorney, our prosecutor, and your U.S. attorney agree they were probably involved, but say it's only ten percent that they can be convicted. And they don't like to lose."

"So we're dead in the water," the director shouted.

"Things still worked out for us," O'Brien said. "Not only did we grab that eighteen mil, but we know how the Criminales are moving and investing a lot of their money. We're gonna be a big pain in their ass for a long time — I'm thinking we can claw back another hundred million."

"A hundred million. I like the sound of that," the director said. "That's a nice round number."

After the call, O'Brien sighed, looked at Lucas, and said, "Well, that's it then."

"I'd really like to get Kline and Sanderson," Lucas said. "And Albitis, for that matter, if she ever comes back."

"We at the DEA have a little . . . mmm . . . aphorism . . . to cover such yearnings," O'Brien said.

"What's that?"

"Tough shit, pal."

The day after the debriefing, the Brooks family was buried. Lucas did not go to the funeral, and was told by Shaffer that for such a well-publicized mass murder, the funeral attendance was remarkably subdued. The Brookses did not belong to a church, and so the funeral was attended mostly by family members, Sunnie employees, and reporters. "Hard way to go, all at once, like that," Shaffer said. "Nobody left behind."

That same day, Albitis opened one eye and looked around, then opened the other.

Hospital room. She felt terrible: her head, neck, spine, arms, and hips hurt. Her mouth was dry, and something stank. She suspected it was her. Her feet seemed okay. She tried to turn her head but couldn't. She managed to raise one arm into her field of view and found it punctured by a number of needles that led to plastic drip lines.

A moment after she woke up, a nurse, apparently alerted by the monitoring equipment, stuck her head in the room and said, "There you are."

Albitis tried to speak, but her tongue was like sandpaper.

"You need something to wet your mouth," the nurse said. "I'll be right back."

She was back a minute later with a bottle of water and a straw. Albitis took a sip, then two more. Her voice didn't seem to work quite right, so she whispered, "Was I in an accident?"

The nurse said, "We don't know exactly what happened to you. We were hoping you could tell us."

Albitis thought for a moment, then said, "I don't know." Then, "You're speaking English. Where am I?"

"You're in a hospital in Minneapolis," the nurse said.

"Minneapolis? In the U.S. What am I doing here?"

"We don't know exactly," the nurse said.

Albitis's eyes wandered away, then came back. "Minneapolis? I live in Tel Aviv."

The nurse said, "Oh, boy."

A week after the shooting, the Davenports moved back into the house. Jimenez had been working his ass off — there were no bullet holes or blood to be seen. He'd replaced the carpet in the hallway where Tres had died, with carpet indistinguishable from the original. He hadn't yet put in the new upstairs hallway wall, but the maple was gone, and the hall showed bare studs and electric wiring down its length.

The hallway where Martínez had died had a varnished hardwood floor. Jimenez had stripped the varnish and redone it. He'd found a good door to replace the one Martínez had shot through, and had already fitted and painted it. The far wall had been peppered with pieces of nine-millimeter hollow-points, and he'd patched the drywall and repainted.

The temporary front door and the bare studs in the upper hallway were the only remaining signs of the fight.

Letty walked through, checked it all out, and pronounced herself satisfied. "If I didn't have this cast . . . I hate this cast."

"Better than the alternative," Lucas said.

She thought about that for three seconds, then said, "But he didn't hit me in the head. He hit me in the arm, and I hate this cast."

"I got this little . . . aphorism . . . from the DEA," Lucas said.

Weather was watching Letty like a hawk, and the third day after they'd gotten back in the house, she said to Lucas, "I hope there's nothing wrong with her."

"Like what?" Lucas asked.

"She's not showing any signs of the psychological trauma that she should be. I've been reading everything I can find on it. The shock —"

"She's okay," Lucas said.

"But —"

"I know exactly what you're saying," Lucas said. "You're worried that she might be a psychopath, or a sociopath, or one of those path things. She's not. Or at least, that's not all she is."

"You know I love her," Weather said.

"Of course you do, but that doesn't have anything to do with what you're worried about," Lucas said. "But stop worrying."

"I'm not sure I can. I want her to be . . . happy. I want her to be well."

"A lot of people think surgeons must have a little psychological thing, you know?" Lucas said. "They take perfectly good people and slice them to pieces so they can have a shorter nose. You'd have to be a little crazy to do that, or to get it done, for that matter. We're all a little crazy, sweetheart."

Weather got puffed up. "Comparing what I do —"

"I know, there's no direct comparison."

They had a little five-minute exchange about the psychological stability of surgeons, punctuated with examples of crazy surgeons that Weather had talked about in the past, and she finally said, "Look, whatever — I'm not talking about all of that. I'm talking about our daughter."

"I know you are," Lucas said. "And like I said, we're all a little crazy, but basically, and overall, Letty's okay."

"How do you know?"

"Because she's just like me," Lucas said. "And I'm okay, mostly."

Lucas and Letty stopped at a coffee shop, and Letty got a grande latte and Lucas got a no-fat hot chocolate, and Letty asked, "Is Mom okay?"

"She's holding up. She'll be working again tomorrow," Lucas said.

"Okay, that's good," she said.

"How are *you* holding up?" Lucas asked.

"I . . ." she said, then stopped. "I don't know." Her voice was distracted, Lucas thought, like she was taking effort just to talk. Usually she was chatty. She didn't sound depressed, though. Just distracted.

"Do you feel bad about it?"

"I don't," she said. "I shot that one guy before, but I didn't kill him. But this . . . nope. Nothing. Just . . . I had to do it, and I did it, and it was done. I'm not worried about it, I don't feel bad. Is that normal?"

"It depends," Lucas said. "Sometimes, if —"

"How many people have you killed?" Letty asked abruptly.

Lucas considered. They'd never talked about it. Not directly. It was known, but it was a topic they'd always avoided. He did a quick tally in his head.

"Ten," he said. "That I know of."

"That you *know* of?"

"There are a few more people dead, that I was responsible for, directly or indirectly," Lucas said. "I'd get in a situation where pretty much it's going to end with a death. That sort of thing."

"Is *that* normal?"

"No. Not for most cops. But I was always

pushed into the rough stuff. All of my professional life," he said. "And sometimes, you'll get something — a hostage situation, say — and you'll find out that there's no way to do it without someone dying. When that happens, if it's your only option . . . I just don't have time to feel too bad about it."

"Do you regret any of them?"

"Some of them," Lucas said. "Sometimes they were just . . . crazy. You get into a situation like that, and what can you do? Like, you remember Alyssa? She was simply insane. Killing people. When we figured that out, we wound up in a confrontation. What happened was her call. She called it, and the whole situation went a certain way. I had no way to . . . to *disarm* her or anything. Either she died, or I did. I regret it because she was insane — she was ill. She might have been treatable. . . . I don't know. It would have been nice to find out."

"Were any *not* like that? Where you had a choice and went for . . . the death?"

"Did I set anything up, you mean?"

"Yeah."

Lucas was silent for a moment, then said, "Twice."

"Tell me . . ."

"One guy — I never talk about this, by

the way, so if you open your trap . . ."

"I don't talk," she said.

"One guy was a lawyer, and a serial killer, and he would have gotten away with everything. Then, sooner or later, because he enjoyed it, because it was the main thing in his life, he would have started killing again. That was more than a decade ago. Now I look back on it and think maybe, maybe there was something else I could have done. But back then . . . no."

"Judge, jury, executioner. Like that?"

"Back then, yeah," he said. "Now I wonder if I wasn't too hasty, if I couldn't have done something more complicated. Couldn't have figured another way to get him. But . . . it's done."

"What about the other one?"

"That was different. That was a hostage thing. You know about that one — the one where Weather was the hostage. I gave the orders to our sniper to take him. Shoot to kill, the instant he had an opening. As it happened, your mom had pretty much convinced him to give up, and he was about to do that, when we killed him. Maybe I could have done something different, but your mom's life was on the line. Or seemed to be."

"I talked to Mom a little about that one,"

Letty said. "It tore her up, you know."

"I know."

There was a silence, and then Letty looked up at Lucas, her eyes clear, and said, "I'm okay."

"At least as okay as I am," Lucas said.

"Yep. Anyway, I'm not worried about me," Letty said. "I'm worried about *Mom*."

"She'll deal with it," Lucas said.

"Then we're good," Letty said. "If she really can."

"We *are* good," Lucas agreed. "She really can."

Lucas and Shaffer interviewed Albitis, but Albitis couldn't remember anything after sometime in May, in Tel Aviv. The very last thing she remembered was being on the beach, and the feeling of hot sand between her toes, and the smell of the hot oil from a beach falafel stand.

"You don't remember anything about the gold?" Shaffer asked. They'd gotten a lot of gold back, but the accountants thought it might be a little short.

"Gold?" she said. "Turicek? What's a Turicek?"

They were persistent, they returned three times, and then they gave it up.

By that time, Albitis was hobbling around

the physical therapy ward, a hemispherical plaster cast, punctured by a metal rack screwed into her skull, covering most of the top of her head. Everyone was encouraged by the speed of her recovery. The extent of her brain damage, however, might not be known for years, the doctors told the cops.

Lucas took away one thing from their interviews: that English speakers called falafel "feel-awful," because that's the way you felt when you ate them from a beach stand.

Del came into Lucas's office one morning, three weeks after the shoot-out, and asked, "Have you ever heard of an artist named Callahan Pitt?"

Lucas did not frequent the art world. "No. Who is he?"

"British guy. Painting, photography, sculpture, installations," Del said. "Everything. He's got a big show over at the Walker, goes on for three months. Anyway, he bought the *Naiads of the North* sculpture."

"What?"

"The bronze one, that got all cut up," Del said. "The one we got back from Anderson. He bought it from the insurance company."

"Oh, yeah? He bought the scrap?"

"For a million bucks, is what I'm told,"

Del said. "The thing is, Anderson cut the sculpture up in big chunks, you know, hands, heads, tits, feet, butts . . . so this guy has already started welding them back together. He's putting the pieces back in a kind of random order, you know, tits welded to butts, hands to the tops of the heads. Like, modern art. He welds them around the rims of the cuts, so you can see both the inside and outside. He's calling it *Rim Job,* and this chick over at the Walker says he's already priced it at six mil."

"What?"

Terrill Anderson, who'd stolen the sculpture and cut it up, would eventually get a year in prison; his two accomplices agreed to testify against him, and walked.

Duane Bird and Bernice Waters, the two tweekers who'd robbed Lucas, pled guilty to armed robbery. Waters was sent back to the women's prison immediately, on the parole violation, and was returned to her job in the cafeteria. She did well with it, and was content. Bird was held in the Ramsey County jail pending sentencing, with a recommended sentence of six years. Waters would get a similar amount of time tacked onto her original sentence.

■ ■ ■ ■

Sanderson and Kline met at a Caribou Coffee in downtown Minneapolis.

"The attorney says we're good. They're not going to prosecute," Kline said, as they huddled over their table. "He thinks we ought to sue the cops for putting those Mexicans on me. If it wasn't for the cops, I never would have gotten shot."

Sanderson said, "Are you crazy? You get into court, you'd have to perjure yourself, you'd have to —"

"I told him I wasn't interested. I just want to get away from everything," Kline said. "I told him I want to travel, maybe get a job on the West Coast."

"Good," Sanderson said. "You think we're safe?"

"The cops say the Mexicans aren't interested anymore. The government's got the gold."

Sanderson thought about it for a moment, then said, "We'll have to go to the farm sooner or later. When the cops are *sure* that we don't have anything."

"That'll be weeks. Maybe months," Kline said.

"Nobody's touched the place for years.

We should be fine."

"What about Edie?" Kline asked.

"If she really has no memory, then I guess we split her share," Sanderson said. "But if she gets her memory back, we cut it three ways, and she gets a million and a third."

"I hated giving back all that gold," Kline said. "Maybe we should have kept *three* million each."

"They wouldn't have bought that," Sanderson said. "I was worried they wouldn't buy eighteen million," Sanderson said. "And giving it back killed any motive they had to keep looking for it."

"Yeah. Still. We were almost *really* rich."

Albitis's father bought a plane ticket that would take his daughter back to Tel Aviv. She got out of the hospital, spent three days in a downtown hotel, making sure she was well enough to fly.

On the last day, as she was crossing the hotel lobby, she saw Sanderson watching from a side hall. She went that way, and Sanderson backed up, into a phone niche.

Albitis took a last look around, stepped into the niche, and grabbed Sanderson by the blouse. Sanderson smiled and said, "How're you feeling, Edie?"

Albitis leaned into her face: "Where's my money, bitch?"

ABOUT THE AUTHOR

John Sandford is the author of twenty-one previous Prey novels and twelve other novels, including six in the Virgil Flowers series and four in the Kidd series. He lives in Minnesota and California. Visit the author's website at: www.johnsandford.org.

CPSIA information can be obtained
at www.ICGtesting.com
Printed in the USA
FFOW051459110413